WITHDRAWN

Rebellious Feminism

Rebellious Feminism: Camus's Ethic of Rebellion and Feminist Thought

Elizabeth Ann Bartlett

REBELLIOUS FEMINISM

© Elizabeth Ann Bartlett 2004

All rights reserved. No part of this book may be used or reproduced in any manner whatsoever without written permission except in the case of brief quotations embodied in critical articles or reviews.

First published 2004 by
PALGRAVE MACMILLAN™
175 Fifth Avenue, New York, N.Y. 10010 and
Houndmills, Basingstoke, Hampshire, England RG21 6XS.
Companies and representatives throughout the world.

PALGRAVE MACMILLAN is the global academic imprint of the Palgrave Macmillan division of St. Martin's Press, LLC and of Palgrave Macmillan Ltd. Macmillan® is a registered trademark in the United States, United Kingdom and other countries. Palgrave is a registered trademark in the European Union and other countries.

ISBN 1–4039–6364–9 hardback

Library of Congress Cataloging-in-Publication Data
Bartlett, Elizabeth Ann.
    Rebellious feminism : Canmus's ethic of rebellion and feminist thought / by Elizabeth Ann Bartlett.
        p. cm.
    Includes bibliographical references and index.
    ISBN 1–4039–6364–9 (cloth)
        1. Camus, Albert, 1913–1960. Homme râvoltâ. 2. Revolutions.
    I. Title.

HM876.B3653 2004
305.42′01—dc21   2003054993

A catalogue record for this book is available from the British Library.

Design by Newgen Imaging Systems (P) Ltd., Chennai, India.

First edition: January, 2004
10 9 8 7 6 5 4 3 2 1

Printed in the United States of America.

To my students

TABLE OF CONTENTS

Acknowledgments

The seed of this project was planted over thirty years ago, when Ron Hustwit at the College of Wooster first suggested I read Camus's *The Rebel* for an independent study project. Without that initial introduction, this book would never have been written and my life would undoubtedly have taken a different course. I will always be grateful to him for this source of inspiration in my life, and for his continued interest in my work over the years.

I cannot begin to name all those who have contributed to the nurture and growth of those ideas planted so long ago. So many have contributed to bringing them to fruition. Richard Taylor and Gordon Keller guided me through my first extensive examination of Camus's work in my Master's thesis, and Trudy Stueurnagel helped me recognize the intersection of Camus's thought with that of a number of other thinkers and first encouraged me to bring my work into a public forum. My dear friend and mentor, Mulford Sibley, encouraged my investigation of feminist thought at a time when feminist scholarship was practically unknown. His wisdom and gentle spirit continue to inspire me.

My thanks to my colleagues and friends, for their conversation and support. Thanks to the many who have listened to and commented on papers and presentations over the years, especially Marge Grevatt, who has for over twenty years regularly supported me in these public endeavors, encouraged my interest in the connections between Camus's thought and feminism, stimulated my thinking in so many ways, and been a wise and generous friend. Susan Coultrap-McQuin was also an early and enthusiastic supporter of my work on Camus and feminism, and has been a friend and mentor in so many endeavors. I am especially grateful to Greta Gaard, who first encouraged me to develop what was a long paper into this book, who read and commented on several chapters, gave me invaluable feedback, and has constantly believed in this project even in my own periods of doubt. Linda Miller-Cleary and Njoki Kamau also read and commented on drafts of sections of this work, walked and talked, and were constant sources of support and wisdom. My thanks as well to Steve Chilton who encouraged me to let the poetry speak. To Joan Mork and Mary Martin, who regularly listened, understood, affirmed my enthusiasm, provided insight, and celebrated with me, I am deeply grateful.

My appreciation goes to the University of Minnesota Duluth for the sabbatical leave that afforded me the time to finish this project. My thanks as well to Barb Lowe for helping to work out the word processing glitches and for helping to see me through this. I am also so grateful to my editor at Palgrave, Amanda Johnson, who has been so enthusiastic from the very beginning; to Matthew Ashford at Palgarve who has patiently answered all my questions; and to my copyeditor, Mukesh, who worked so fastidiously on this manuscript.

My special thanks to my family—especially my sister, Jeannie, my biggest supporter in life, who has thought whatever I did was wonderful from the moment I was born and gave her a sister; my husband, David, for living graciously with the demands this project took on my time and attention; my son, Paul, for keeping me focused on what is really important in life; and, of course, Lucie, for daily dragging me away from my work and getting me outside. Those walks in the woods were always refreshing and enlightening.

But those to whom I owe the deepest gratitude are my students. Several generations of political science students have shared my enthusiasm and passion for Camus, as have my Women's Studies students shared my love of feminist thought. My discussions with all of them have deepened my knowledge and insights, led to new areas of questioning, and have been invaluable in enabling me to see the links between rebellion and feminism. This book is an outgrowth of many discussions, in and out of class. I simply could not have thought it all or written it without all of them. They have challenged and inspired me, made me a deeper thinker and a more compassionate person. This book is theirs as well.

And finally, I am deeply grateful to Albert Camus, Adrienne Rich, Audre Lorde, Susan Griffin, bell hooks, and the many, many others whose words and wisdom have inspired my thoughts and fueled my passion, and to so many in the feminist community whose courageous acts, solidarity, persistence, and compassion have shown me the true meaning of rebellious feminism.

A NOTE ON LANGUAGE USAGE

At the time Camus wrote *The Rebel*, the standard practice was to use *he* and *man* to refer to both sexes. I have, at times that seemed particularly important and possible to do so without changing the flow of the text, inserted more generic language. However, I have for the most part preserved the original language and translation, though I do believe Camus intended both women and men in his reference to the rebel as "he," as I explain in the text.

PREFACE

A well-worn copy of Albert Camus's *The Rebel* sits on my desk. Tattered corners, yellowing pages, barely held together by several applications of Scotch tape, underlined and starred in various shades of pen—blue, black, green, red—with notes scribbled in the margins, sometimes simply the jubilant "Yes!"—in many ways this book holds the chronicle of the development of my own thought. It has been the source of inspiration as well as occasional consternation. I've often thought it would be one of those things I would grab in the event of a fire. It holds within it memories of students with whom I have spent wonderful hours working through passages; of conversations where I would dash off to find just the quote I needed; and of the first time I read *The Rebel* in the spring of 1972. One of my college philosophy professors had suggested I read it for an independent study project. Little did he know what a life-changing event that would be. I spent long afternoons soaking in *The Rebel* as I soaked in the sun. By the time I reached the end, my life made sense in a way that it hadn't before.

The Rebel provided the lens through which I viewed the world, and in many ways continues to do so now, thirty years later. Living in a time of political and social upheaval, I found within it a workable ethic, a political philosophy that made sense. Here was a guide, a way to act, that fit with me; it revealed not a statement of absolute rights and wrongs, but rather a way to live decently in the world.

In the fall of 1972, I was struck with a life-threatening illness and confined to a hospital bed for months. Faced with my mortality and with hours with nothing to do but ponder it, I continually thought over the meaning of life, as well as what I could possibly do with my life that was not ultimately utterly futile. When finally allowed the exertion of reading, it was Camus to whom I turned for solace and connection. Due to an attack of tuberculosis at the age of seventeen, he, too, had spent long stretches of time in his youth in hospitals. I poured over his journals, finding words given to my own fears, frustrations, wonderings, and hopes. From then on, I read everything I could find of Camus's work, and eventually wrote my Master's thesis on Camus's political thought. But Camus's thought held more than an academic interest for me. Something in it resonated with my inner being. It was only later that I realized that it was appealing to the incipient feminist in me.

In the summer of 1979, I started dabbling my toes in the waters of feminism. Feeling lost and adrift in the midst of a massive dissertation project that was going nowhere, I found myself instead reading about the lives of women. In Judith Nies's *Seven Women: Portraits from the American Radical Tradition* I met, among others, Sarah Grimké. She, and two others—Frances Wright and Margaret Fuller—would become the subject of a new doctoral dissertation, an exploration of the intellectual origins of American feminist thought. Also at this time, Gloria Steinem spoke in the small Minnesota farm community where I was living and galvanized my thinking into action. Not long after, I moved to Duluth, Minnesota, became involved in the very active feminist community there, helped to develop a new Women's Studies program at the University of Minnesota-Duluth, marched in Chicago for the ERA, and led consciousness-raising groups for NOW. A new passion had emerged.

In feminism I caught glimpses of Camus's rebellion. Refusing the oppression of women, claiming our dignity, finding solidarity in sisterhood—this was the stuff of Camus's rebellion. But even more than the movement, it was the deep and powerful thoughts of Adrienne Rich, Audre Lorde, and Susan Griffin that caught my soul on fire and challenged my perspectives, just as Camus's had years before. Their words were new, and yet familiar to me:

> That is why the effort to speak honestly is so important . . . because it breaks down human self-delusion and isolation. (Rich, *On Lies* 187–188)

> *The mutual understanding and communication discovered by rebellion can survive only in the free exchange of conversation. . . . falsehood is therefore proscribed* . . . . (Camus, *Rebel* 283)

> Once we move from fear, terror accompanies every outward motion, and we are diminished. (Griffin, *Rape* 62)

> *Irrational terror transforms men into objects.* (Camus, *Rebel* 183)

> *Eros*, the personification of love in all its aspects . . . . When I speak of the erotic, then, I speak of it as an assertion of the lifeforce of women; of that creative energy empowered, ... (Lorde 55)

> *Rebellion proves in this way that it is the very movement of life and that it cannot be denied without renouncing life. Its purest outburst, on each occasion, gives birth to existence. Thus it is love and fecundity or it is nothing at all.* (Camus, *Rebel* 304)

That deep and irreplaceable knowledge of my capacity for joy comes to demand from all of my life that it be lived within the knowledge that such satisfaction is possible . . . . For once we begin to feel deeply all the aspects of our lives, we begin to demand from ourselves and from our life-pursuits that they feel in accordance with that joy which we know ourselves to be capable of. (Lorde 57)

I discovered one must keep a freshness and a source of joy intact within (Camus, *Lyrical* 168). *Now is born that strange joy which helps one live and die, . . . with this joy, through long struggle, we will remake the soul of our time . . . .* (Camus, *Rebel* 306)

Feminism resonated not only with me, but with my Camusian worldview.

I have seen the parallels deepen as feminism has matured and become self-reflective, and extended its scope into ethics, politics, religion, and spirituality. Teaching in all these areas, I have found myself using examples from feminism to help explain Camus to my students, and I have used Camus's thoughts to help elucidate feminism. I have found their combined exploration to be mutually enlightening—some might say "auspicious."

"Auspicious coincidence"—the coming together of phenomena that may at first glance appear to be random, but are not random at all, but rather an occasion for insight and enlightenment.* It is my purpose in this book to make of this auspicious coincidence of feminism and Camus's *rebellion* in my life, an occasion for the insight and enlightenment of others, just as it has been for me. I intend to explore the points of intersection between the two bodies of thought, and as each is illuminated by shedding light on the other, show how the two bodies of ideas inform each other, and how together they can inform us all.

Shortly after I began writing this book, the world, at least as we in the United States knew it, changed. On September 11, 2001, terrorists crashed jumbo jets into the World Trade Center in New York City and into the Pentagon in Washington, D.C. Thousands were killed, and we learned fear and horror in a new way. Yet, as I read and reread the opening pages of *The Rebel*, I was struck by how his words describing the terrors of the era in which he lived—of Nazism and death camps and the Soviet gulag—fit so well the circumstances of our time. *The Rebel* begins with these words:

There are crimes of passion and crimes of logic. The boundary between them is not clearly defined. . . . We are living in the era of premeditation

---

* My thanks to Rita Gross for first introducing me to this concept in talking about the auspicious coincidence of feminism and Buddhism in her life.

and the perfect crime. Our criminals are no longer helpless children who could plead love as their excuse. On the contrary, they are adults and they have a perfect alibi: philosophy, which can be used for any purpose—even for transforming murderers into judges. . . .

The purpose of this essay is once again to face the reality of the present, which is logical crime, and to examine meticulously the arguments by which it is justified; it is an attempt to understand the times in which we live (3).

As I continued in my research and writing, I was struck as well by this passage from the introduction to Susan Griffin's *Made from This Earth*, which though written twenty years ago, could just as easily have been written today:

This is a difficult year. Prospects for women and the world look bleak. The old economies decline, and poverty always falls hardest on the forgotten, other self, the darker, older one, the woman, the child. An American president speaks of the possibility of a "limited" nuclear war. It becomes a part of sanity to fear that soon there will be no human life on earth (20).

At the end of his novel, *The Plague*, Camus warned that "the plague bacillus never dies or disappears for good; . . . it can lie dormant for years and years in furniture and linen-chests; . . . it bides its time in bedrooms, cellars, trunks, and bookshelves" and that the day may come when "it would rouse up its rats again and send them forth to die in a happy city" (278). It would seem that the plague of terrorism, injustice, oppression, and the threat of nuclear war that "roused up its rats" in the 1940s and again in the 1980s, has become active again. Though the manifestations of terror, injustice, and war may take on different faces at different times, the forces at work are the same.

Camus wrote *The Rebel* to try to understand the times in which he lived. The lessons revealed therein can also help us to understand ours. In light of recent events and all of their implications for our political condition and our human condition, my purpose in writing this book has gone beyond the scope of showing how feminism and rebellion enlighten and inform each other. It is also my hope that this exercise will help shed light on the time in which live; that it will help us to understand the forces that have led us to such destruction, terror, and war, and reveal how we might embark upon a different path—a path of healing.

Griffin continues her passage, "As fearful as I am, there is joy in me" (*Made* 20). Given her fears, this may seem an odd statement. However, she is joyful because though she sees destruction, she also sees the beauty of our interconnection with each other and the earth. In this she finds hope. Though rebellion and feminism are difficult, due to their honest revelations of oppression, domination, and deceit in the world, they are nevertheless voices of clear-sightedness, healing, and hope that sustain and inspire. As Camus wrote, they offer "not formulas for optimism, . . . but words of courage and intelligence" (*Rebel* 303).

Lev Braun has written of Camus's ethic of rebellion:

> Here was an ethics offered to a bewildered generation. . . . [it] offered them beauty, friendship, freedom, justice, commitment, and meaning, an ethics based on revolt, not on acquiescence; a hard ethics, without transcendental illusions, and yet embued with all the tenderness and mystery of poetry, and profering the hope of a humanitarian revival. (133)

I offer a new appreciation of this life-affirming ethic, especially as it has been developed and enhanced by feminist thought and practice, in hopes that this bewildered generation might see its way through the terror and destruction of our times to a hopeful path of healing and meaning, of justice and beauty, of solidarity and tenderness.

CHAPTER 1
REBELLION AND FEMINISM

. . . rebellion must respect the limit it discovers in itself—a limit where minds meet and, in meeting, begin to exist. Rebellious thought . . . is a perpetual state of tension. In studying its actions and its results, we shall have to say, each time, whether it remains faithful to its first noble promise or if, through indolence or folly, it forgets its original purpose and plunges into a mire of tyranny or servitude.

Camus, *The Rebel* 22

Colloquially, we tend to associate the term "rebellion" with spontaneous political uprisings—movements that protest against; blind no-saying; negative activity that usually begins in hostility and ends in destruction. Because of this, feminists might reject the notion of feminism being a rebellious movement.[1] But this is not the way in which Camus used the term "rebellion." For him, while "rebellion" does involve a negative activity of resisting oppression, it also acts in a positive way to affirm human dignity, solidarity, friendship, justice, liberation, and beauty. Camus's sense of rebellion is not so simply defined because for him it represented a complex of ideas that delineate an ethic, a rule of action.[2]

Camus came to his ethic of rebellion from a philosophical position of the absurd. In his early works, Camus dealt with themes of the absurdity of existence in the human quest for meaning when encountering only a silent universe,[3] but recognizing the emotional, philosophical, and spiritual dead-endedness of the absurd, as well as the deadly consequences of its political expression, Camus could not rest long in it. Instead, as he explained in *The Rebel*, ". . . the real nature of the absurd, . . . is that it is an experience to be lived through, a point of departure" (9). But departure into what? The absurd left Camus searching for meaning and for a way to live in the world. Traditionally, it has been the role of religion to serve that purpose, the sacred answering all the questions posed by the absurd. But, the rebel, Camus contended, is a person "who is on the point of accepting or rejecting the sacred and determined on laying claim to a human situation in which all the answers are human" (*Rebel* 21). Camus lived, as he said, in unsacrosanct times, where "whole societies have wanted to discard the sacred," and instead sought human answers to the situation of absurdity. However, just as he could find no answers in religious faith and dogmas, neither could he put any faith in their secular substitutes—abstract principles, (e.g., Reason, "the General Will," "Führerprinzip," "Justice") that evolved into absolutist and totalitarian ideologies. He witnessed the destruction these fostered all around him. Profoundly influenced by the times in which he lived—World War II, the Holocaust, and the Nazi occupation of Europe[4]—Camus sought in his examination of rebellion to make sense of how such things could have happened: " 'I wrote *L'Homme révolté* (*The Rebel*) because in the 1940s, I saw men whose system I couldn't explain and whose actions I couldn't understand. In brief, I could not understand how men could torture others while continuing to look at them . . .' " (qtd. in Todd 313). He needed to find a way to account for evil in the world. As he said, he lived in an age in which universal principles, political ideologies, governmental policies and societal practices wove everyone into a web of complicity, so that every action, directly or indrectly, might lead to the suffering and death, the murder, of others (*Rebel* 4–5). For example, in Camus's day, to resist the Nazis could lead to killing and death, but failure to resist amounted to complicity with murder. In ours, paying taxes, tacit support of government policies, simply the choice of what we eat and wear may contribute indirectly to death of others. If we buy articles made in sweatshops we contribute to the misery and death of many, and if we boycott stores that deal in goods from sweatshops we deprive those who work in them of a livelihood, potentially resulting in their starvation and death. Everything we do, and don't do, carries the potential for harm, even unto future generations. But, Camus argued, the very choice to live entails the recognition that life is good, and once recognized as good, it is then recognized as good for all. Thus, murder—by which he meant any action that leads to the death of others, either directly or indirectly—cannot be accepted or legitimated in any way. And so, Camus needed to find a way to act in a world where any action might lead to murder and where universal principles become the justification for putting others to death. Unable to rely on faith or principles, Camus had only the truth of his own experience, which was one of revolt. As stated in *The Rebel*, "I proclaim that I believe in nothing and that everything is absurd, but I cannot doubt the validity of my proclamation and I must at least believe in my protest. The first and only evidence that is supplied me, within the terms of the absurdist experience, is rebellion" (10).[5] Thus, a rule of action could only be determined by an examination of the phenomenon of rebellion itself.

As was his custom, Camus explored the idea of rebellion in several genres: two plays, *The Just Assassins* and *State of Siege*; a novel, *The Plague*; and a philosophical essay, *The Rebel*; as well as essays and articles written during that time; but *The Rebel* was the centerpiece.[6] In it, Camus undertook the task of examining a variety of rebellious actions in order to glean from them a rule of action. The sweep of his investigation included the metaphysical rebellions of Epicurus, gnosticism, Sade, Ivan Karamazov, Nietzsche, surrealism, and others; the historical rebellions of the French Revolution, Russian terrorists, Nazism, Marxism, and others; and the artistic rebellions of the novel and creation itself. Camus found that in nearly every instance these acts of rebellion failed to sustain their rebellious impulse, and instead degenerated into something else, something destructive of their original ends—revolution, totalitarianism, terror, murder.[7] In so doing, each lost "its right to call itself rebellion." Thus, the bulk of *The Rebel* ends up being an examination of rebellions gone awry.[8] Repeatedly, Camus's condemnation of these failed rebellions was that they had not stayed "true to the origins of rebellion." However, *The Rebel* is more of a moral treatise than a philosophical argument, and at no point in it did Camus provide a systematic outline of its philosophical tenets or enumerate specifically just what these origins of rebellion are.[9]

We are left to discern them, first of all, from the few instances he gave in which acts of rebellion did stay faithful to their origins, but primarily from Camus's determination of how these failed acts of rebellion abandoned their original principles. In nearly every case, this happened when the movement became absolutist, oppressive, murderous, and losing solidarity with the people on whose behalf it began, became forgetful of "the love that gave it birth." Camus also "outlined" the defining elements of rebellion through his distinction between rebellion and revolution. Table 1.1 outlines the major distinctions between the two.[10]

It is from this distinction between rebellion and revolution that Camus's own sense of "true" rebellion emerges. As he put it, " . . . when revolution in the name of power and of history becomes a murderous and immoderate mechanism, a *new* rebellion is consecrated in the name of moderation and of life" (*Rebel* 305, emphasis mine). Camus recognized that revolutions began with rebellious impulses, but they were rebellions that became forgetful of their origins. Disregarding of limits, grounded more in ideology than reality, concerned more with life in some golden future than life in the present, revolutions are willing to

Table 1.1 The major distinctions between rebellion and revolution

Revolution	Rebellion
All or nothing	Limits
Totality	Unity
Absolute malleability of humanity	Refuse treatment as object; human nature
Absolute negation; nihilist	Negation supported by affirmation
Sacrifices present to future	Gives all to present
Time of essence; efficiency	Leisured; focus on present
Prefers abstract concept of humanity	Flesh and blood people
Resentment	Love
Monologue	Dialogue
Built on absolutes; ideological doctrine	Relies on reality—struggle for truth
Top to bottom	Bottom to top
History	Nature
Deification of human	Refusal to be a god
Tyranny	Freedom
Kill and die to produce beings we are	Live and let live to create what we are not

sacrifice the lives of individuals living here and now for an idea. In so doing, they try to shape existing humans to their will, and in the name of an abstract humanity, become movements of death and destruction. Rebellion on the other hand, mindful of the limited aspect of its movements and grounded in concrete reality, concerns itself with those living here and now. Refusing oppression, it also refuses to oppress, and in the name of a common humanity, it is a movement of life and creation.

Rebellion: The Framework

In order to set up a theoretical framework of rebellion, and given the void left by Camus, I have taken it upon myself to make such an enumeration of what I call the "core components" of rebellion—that is those things which must be preserved if rebellion is not to self-destruct. Some might regard this to be an impossible task. Doubrovsky, who argued that Camus has no framework, found it impossible to draw a systematic ethic, a morality, or rules for living from Camus's lived, intuitive ethic (153, 156). Camus, himself, repudiated systems of thought, and might find my attempts to systematize his thoughts on rebellion to be inappropriate. I do so in the full realization that devising such a schema may at times distort, oversimplify, or rigidify Camus's thought, but my intent in this is rather to clarify it.

Settling on these core components was no easy task. So many themes recur—the refusal of injustice, the affirmation of dignity, liberation, solidarity, compassion, dialogue, authenticity, nature, happiness, limits—and so many overlap and interweave, one making another possible or being an aspect of another. Ultimately I settled on four core ideas that I find to be fundamental to the origins of rebellion: (1) rejection of oppression and affirmation of dignity; (2) solidarity; (3) friendship and the primacy of concrete relationships; and (4) the valuing of immanence. Any rebellious act that ignores or destroys any of these loses the right to be called rebellion. The list is not definitive. It might be delineated further or made more succinct—at times I even fancied reducing them simply to two: "love" and "justice." But after repeated scrutiny, these four consistently have emerged as those conditions to which every rebellious action must stay true in order not to lose the right to call itself rebellion. In what follows, I will briefly define each and explain why it is necessary to rebellion.

Rejection of Oppression and Affirmation of Human Dignity

As previously stated, rebellion is not so much a philosophical principle as an ethic that emerges from the process of the experience of revolt. The defining moment in this process comes when the victim of oppression refuses that oppression, in affirmation of her or his dignity as a human being. The rebel "says yes and no simultaneously" (*Rebel* 251)—*no* to oppression and injustice, and *yes* to that which the oppressed recognize as valuable within themselves. Rebellion is that moment when the slave refuses enslavement, the battered woman refuses abuse, the colonized refuses colonization—because a limit has been crossed that causes them to recognize their fundamental worth. Rebellion is a refusal to be treated with anything less than the full measure of dignity and decency that one's humanity demands. It is significant that this defining moment of rebellion requires *both* negation and affirmation. Negation not countered by affirmation, that is, absolute negation, implies negation of others. Absolute affirmation, on the other hand, implies the divinity of humanity, for if nothing is forbidden, then everything, including the death of others, is permitted. In either case, the end result is murder, which rebellion condemns. Thus, in order to stay faithful to the origins of rebellion, negation and affirmation must act as limits to each other, for pursuing one without the other denies the rebellious impulse. Both are necessary to rebellion. And, if both are simultaneously denied, then rebellion reverts to silence, submission, and despair.

Implicit in this component are several others. Perhaps the most important is the notion of "limits." As stated earlier, the moment of rebellion reveals a limit within the individual, which is itself suggestive of our inherent value and worth. Also, negation and affirmation act as limits to each other, which disallows either being pursued to its logical and murderous conclusion. It is in this balancing of opposing forces that rebellion refuses absolutes, and seeks, in order to remain true to the origins of rebellion, only proximate solutions.

Also implicit in this component is the refusal of injustice and the affirmation of liberty. In rebellion, liberty and justice find their limits in each other. The liberty of rebellion is not license, but rather a liberty bounded by its extension equally to all. The justice of rebellion is not absolute, but rather a justice bounded by respect for the freedom of each.

Finally, this component implies a refusal of silence and a finding of one's voice. Silence is born of despair; rebellion gives birth to voice. The act of rebellion is one of speaking out against injustice and oppression in affirmation of dignity and self-worth. Fundamental to rebellious coming to voice is the recognition that the voices to which it gives birth are multiple and diverse. It is important, in this regard, to understand the distinction Camus drew between "unity"—which is diverse and multivocal, and "totality"—which is singular and monovocal. Because Camus wrote repeatedly of the rebellious desire for "unity," at a quick glance it might seem that the goal of rebellion is ultimately a unity that is all-encompassing and total. But to interpret Camus this way is a distortion of his use of the term "unity." Rather, Camus consistently declared that "unity" is a very different thing from "totality."[11] Totality is a single voice imposed from without onto the voices and souls of a people rendered "one" through coercion and propaganda. It is a movement in opposition to the uniqueness of individuals and their values. Unity, on the other hand, emerges as a harmony of many voices who discover a connectedness in honoring their uniqueness. It is multiple voices, but in community. Totality is hierarchical; unity is radically egalitarian. In totality, difference is regarded as threatening and is arranged so that those not like the totalizing agent are considered inferior. In unity, difference is embraced and all are accepted as equals. To unite requires an honoring of differences, rather than a suffocation of them. Thus, unity for Camus embraces diversity: "Unity and diversity, and never one without the other . . ." (Camus, *Resistance* 243). Rebellion that does not make possible a diversity of voices turns into monologue, and, as Camus put it, "monologue precedes death" (*Rebel* 284). Without the participation of diverse others, each with an equal voice, rebellion devolves into absolutism, monologue, and totality, and once again, legitimates murder.

Solidarity

Like the term "rebellion," solidarity means many things in the context of Camus's ethic of rebellion, and is often used interchangeably with the term "compassion." One could say that solidarity is the impulse to rebellion since it is out of solidarity with oneself and with others that one is moved to rebel. Beyond this, I have identified four distinct ways in which Camus used the term solidarity in the context of rebellion. The first is a metaphysical rebellion. Camus argued that at least on a metaphysical level, every act of rebellion is necessarily an act of solidarity, because the rebel's claim is for something that surpasses him or herself. With it comes the recognition that suffering is collective. It is in this sense that Camus said that rebellion is the *cogito* of everyday trials: "I rebel—therefore we exist" (*Rebel* 22).

The second sense of solidarity is the mutual understanding and responsibility toward relationships that emerge through common work or through extended dialogue with one another. Camus was particularly concerned that rebellious acts promote a free exchange of conversation, and that conversation in turn sustains rebellion through promotion of mutual understanding.

The third meaning of solidarity might be better understood as "compassionate action"—that is, the choice "to suffer with."[12] Compassion becomes solidarity as that "suffering with" that moves beyond an emotional empathy with and comfort for the oppressed to standing and acting—quite literally suffering—with the oppressed. Such solidarity takes various forms—to witness the suffering of another and thus be moved to act; to refuse individual salvation if it comes at the expense of another; to act from the basis that none are free until all are free and that justice must be extended to all—including the oppressor—if it is to be truly just.

This brings us to the fourth and final element of rebellious solidarity—the refusal to oppress. The rebel is against all forms of domination, including his or her own acts of domination, even against those who have been the oppressors. A basic principle of rebelious solidarity is a refusal to humiliate, degrade, or dominate anyone. Rebellion that abandons solidarity becomes partisanship, hierarchy, egoistic individualism, oppression and worse; in other words, it becomes destructive of its own ends. As Camus himself wrote, ". . . any rebellion which claims the right to deny or destroy this solidarity loses simultaneously its right to be called rebellion and becomes in reality an acquiescence in murder" (*Rebel* 22).

Friendship and the Primacy of Concrete Relationship

Camus opposed the "friendship of people. . . . specific solidarity," to "the friendship of objects, friendship in general . . ." (*Rebel* 239). Friendship grounds the first two components in the concrete, that is love, communication, care, concern, loyalty for the people with whom one is in immediate, daily relationship, not just those at a safe distance. The significance of this component is to prevent a kind of solidarity that enables one to advocate against social injustices, and to feel compassion for total strangers—for "the bleeding crowd"—while at the same time acting without care or concern for one's friends and family. This component also establishes the priority of relationships of family and friendship, of putting people before principles. He was quite clear that a rebellion that becomes devotion to the ideal of justice in and of itself, to the exclusion of caring for particular persons, itself becomes oppressive.

Relationship is at the core of rebellion, and any action that destroys or betrays one's concrete relationships is no longer rebellion. The solidarity implied by rebellion does extend to all, but if it neglects the most immediate relationships in one's life, it becomes empty platitudes at best. At worst, it becomes the legitimation of murder. If all are comrades and none are friends, then friends become expendable for the cause, and rebellion is abandoned. Rebellion, devoid of friendship, becomes revolution, which "in preferring an abstract concept of man to a man of flesh and blood, denies existence as many times as is necessary, [and] puts resentment in the place of love" (*Rebel* 304).

Valuing of Immanence

"Immanence" itself means simply "indwelling," and is usually used in reference to the divine dwelling within. Camus never used the term "immanence,"[13] and used the term "divinity" mostly when reproaching those who would assume the "divinity of man." I borrow the term from the literature of feminist spirituality, where it is often used to denote a collection of qualities that recur throughout Camus's work. These include a love of and immersion in the natural world, a sensual appreciation of the body, a love of life in the here and now, and a joy emanating from spiritual communion with creation. Numerous scholars attest to the pervasiveness and significance of this joyous and sensual communion with nature found in Camus's literary works,[14] but it is in *The Rebel* that Camus testified to the significance of these immanental qualities for rebellion. In contrasting rebellion with revolution, Camus consistently placed qualities of immanence—nature, love, reliance on reality, giving all to the present, refusing to be a god—on the side of rebellion. The rebel acts not with thought of the rewards of a life after death, nor for the end of history, but rather rejects transcendence in honor of living life fully in the present.

Rebellion requires grounding in immanence. When acts of rebellion are forgetful of the sense of wonder and connection with nature, then nature becomes simply a resource to be used against itself for its own destruction. A rebellion forgetful of its origins in the immanent "does not value life and [the] living . . . and amounts to justifying whole centuries of oppression" (*Rebel* 305). Thus, rebellion that abandons immanence becomes desiccated, joyless, violent, and destructive.

These four core components—the simultaneous rejection of oppression and affirmation of dignity, solidarity, friendship and the primacy of concrete relationship, and valuing immanence—make up the origins of rebellion to which rebellious action must remain faithful if it is to remain rebellion. However, while central to the framework of rebellion, these four core components of rebellion do not complete it. The epistemological premises upon which rebellion is based, and the implications for political practice that flow from it, form the remainder of the framework of rebellion.[15] Specifically, rebellion rests on an epistemology of "limits" that is based on the assumption that human knowledge is at best partial. None is omniscient. Nor is any one source of knowledge privileged over another. Rational and nonrational sources of knowledge—reason, along with emotions, passions, and intuitions—must inform and balance each other. Reliance on dialogue and experience help keep our knowledge grounded in the concrete, as opposed to the abstract. In addition, like rebellion itself, the epistemology that informs rebellion exists in the constant tension of paradox, and recognizes that importance of "both/and" thinking, as opposed to thought that imposes "either/or" choices.

Rebellious praxis is similarly based in a politics of "limits." This requires first, that political practice be limited in scope. Rebellion insists on the equal and simultaneous positing of all of its core elements. In their balance and tension with each other, each limits the others from being pursued in their extreme. At best, rebellion seeks proximate solutions. Second, the political practice implied by rebellion is concerned with means more than ends, and is thus limited in its methods. Accordingly, it eschews violence, except as an "extreme limit which combats another form of violence" (*Rebel* 292), and relies instead on dialogue for the resolution of conflicts and for the creation of understanding and community. Finally, rebellious political practice is limited in its basis for action by being grounded in concrete realities. Rather than beginning from ideological principles and shaping reality to them, it begins with concrete realities and acts to alleviate suffering and remedy existing injustices.

My Purpose in Writing

It is my contention that these four core components of rebellion, as well as the epistemological premises on which they are based and the political praxis that flows from them, are central to feminism, and a major purpose of this book is to demonstrate these connections and to show their significance. This significance lies first of all in providing a framework through which rebellious aspects of feminist thought can be identified and in which various strands of feminist thought can cohere and be of use, particularly in the development of an ethic of political practice; and second, in helping to develop and elucidate the meanings and implications of key concepts common to both feminism and rebellion.

First, the framework of rebellion provides criteria by which to determine what aspects of feminist thought and praxis stay "true to the origins of rebellion" and what do not. Certainly not all of feminist thought fits the concept of rebellion; some is quite the antithesis. However, certain types of feminisms—cultural, multicultural, socialist, maternalist, ecofeminist—as well as feminist spirituality, epistemology, and ethics, have fairly strong associations with rebellion.[16] While my emphasis is primarily on those aspects of feminism that resonate with Camus's rebellion, I will occasionally use the framework to provide insights into those aspects of feminist thought that are clearly outside of it. At the same time it is my hope that casting feminism in the framework of Camusian rebellion will enable a different, and I would argue, more accurate vision of the nature of feminism. Society at large tends to associate feminism with one of two things: (1) "women's lib"—women striving not just for equal opportunity and equal treatment, but also for power, wealth, status—the equal chance to be at the top of the existing system based on domination and hierarchy; or (2) what is known colloquially as the "feminazis"—man-haters who elevate "political correctness" to the status of totalitarian censorship of free speech and action. Yet, neither of these are accurate depictions of feminism in my sense of the term, nor for most who identify themselves as feminists. For me, feminism is about resistance to oppression, but it is also an insistence on not oppressing others in turn. It is about equal justice, but none "more equal" than any of the rest. And far from being hateful and censoring, feminism is a joyous, life-affirming ethic of love, that compassionately enables each to find an authentic expression of self. It is, in short, a movement of rebellion—the simultaneous refusal of oppression and affirmation of human dignity, in solidarity with concrete, diverse others and the earth. It is this sense of "rebellious feminism" that I would like to communicate to society at large.

I have especially found the framework of rebellion to be enormously helpful in making sense of and seeing the connections among the many and various schools of feminist theory, as well as disparate areas of feminist thought—epistemology, politics, ethics, spirituality. For me, analyzing and synthesizing elements of feminist thought within the framework of Camus's concept of rebellion makes for useful feminist theory, and a significant aspect of my project is to make elements of feminist thought of more use by placing them in the Camusian framework. By "useful" feminist theory I intend that outlined by Lugones and Spelman in their famous piece, "Have I Got a Theory for You." In this, Lugones and Spelman lay out six aspects of "useful" theory. Useful theory: (1) enables one to see how the parts of one's life fit together, to see connections; (2) helps one locate oneself concretely in the world; (3) enables one to think about the extent to which one is responsible or not for being in that location; (4) includes or begins with moral and political judgments about the injustice or justice of women's position, and judgments about what kind of changes constitute better or worse situations for women; (5) provides criteria for change and makes suggestions for modes of resistance that are respectful of those about whom it is a theory; and (6) has some connection to resistance and change.

Camus's ethic of rebellion, by its very definition and purpose, enables each of these. To begin, rebellion at its core, is resistance—to oppression, domination, injustice—and is a transformative politic. It is inclusive, connecting an epistemology with an ethic, a political practice, and spirituality, and is as much about one's relations with family and friends as it is about one's work or political choices. It grounds one's everyday actions in a framework of their contribution to the justice or injustice of the world. Eschewing abstract thought and principles, rebellion begins with one's concrete location in the world—the realities of one's life, one's experiences and emotions. It is in assessing one's responsibility for one's own suffering and exploitation, or that of others, that one is moved to rebel—to be "neither victim nor executioner,"[17] but rather to act in such a way so as to minimize those injustices to oneself and others. And whether or not one is moved to revolt is in itself the ground on which the moral and political judgment regarding the justice or injustice of one's position is founded. Finally, rebellion provides guidelines for a political practice that is consistent with the origins of rebellion. A few years ago, Nancy Hartsock challenged feminist theorists to address the questions: "What is feminist practice? How can feminist theory inform practice?" (Hartmann et al. 945). The framework of rebellion is especially helpful in this regard. All in all, connecting feminist thought to the framework of rebellion enables a useful feminist theory.

Second, the mutual exploration of feminism and rebellion develops and elucidates the meanings and implications of key concepts common to both. I have found my understanding of feminist ideas enhanced by my understanding of Camus, and even more so, I have found my understanding of Camus's thought to be deeply enriched by feminist articulations of the ideas they share in common. Camus's *The Rebel* has been criticized, fairly, for its failure to clearly define terms and to develop critical components of rebellion (Doubrovsky 152), and I have often found that feminist thinkers develop these important themes left undeveloped by Camus. In many ways, it is as if they picked up where he left off, and in so doing, give us depth and insight into the meanings and implications of such ideas and realities as oppression, silence, authenticity, lying, compassion, care, friendship, and embodiment, as well as highlight certain absences, silences, and problems in Camus's thought. Thus does feminist thought give us insight into the problems and possibilities suggested by Camus.

In this regard, one final area of mutual concern lies largely undeveloped in both feminist thought and Camus's ethic of rebellion. That is the notion of a politics of healing. Occasionally, Camus mentioned a way of acting that seemed to encompass and yet move beyond rebellion, and that was the way of the "true healer." Similarly, bell hooks defines feminist theory as "a location for healing" (*Teaching* 59). I intend to use the conjunction of rebellion and feminism to explore further the meanings and possibilities of the politics of healing.

Is Rebellious Feminism Possible?

The auspicious coincidence of Camus's concept of rebellion and feminism render many fruitful possibilities for insight and use. However, I want to be clear at the outset that while I do contend that the core components of Camus's rebellion are also at the core of that which I find most valuable in feminist thought, I do not intend to argue here that Camus himself was a feminist. To my knowledge, he never specifically addressed the oppression of women; nor did he speak to gender injustice.[18] Feminist critics have found depictions of women in his literary works to be patriarchal and misogynist. Perhaps most biting is that of Jeffner Allen who asserts that the only women in Camus's works are absent, robotic, battered, or dead ("An Introduction" 73). Anthony Rizutto portrays the early Camus as a Don Juan, whose female characters, always beautiful and passive, merge into nature and come to represent both earth and silence (14 ff.).[19] Camus's personal reputation was one of being a womanizer and his wife's family attributed her years of suicidal depression to his infidelities (Todd 319). His journal entries often, though not consistently, reflect a patriarchal disregard of women.[20] His one-time friend and contemporary, Simone de Beauvoir, experienced a similar disregard from Camus. She said of Camus (after the demise of their friendship, and thus to be taken with the proverbial grain of salt) that he was "feudal" in his relations with women, never viewing them as quite equal (*Force* 52), and that his reaction to her *The Second Sex* was "Latin and predictably macho" (qtd. in Bair 611).[21]

Given that Camus was not a feminist in his life or his work, the question must be addressed, which if answered negatively would render the rest of this exercise moot—is there space for women in Camus's philosophy of rebellion? Is the very notion of rebellion so masculinist as to preclude feminist action? Does it require the passivity of women? Does it, like Rousseau's theory of participatory democracy, rely on women being in the private spaces of the home, or like Arendt's theory of action, and Aristotle's from which hers is drawn, require a class of laborers, most often women and slaves, to do the "work of necessity" (or as de Beauvoir called it, "the doom of immanence"—i.e., raising the children, doing the cooking and cleaning, finding and carrying water, tending the sick and dying—i.e., the work of women)?

Jeffner Allen argues that given the way that Camus depicts women, they cannot participate in the existentialist endeavor. Women are denied the possibility of action, and thus of rebellion. The "we" of rebellious solidarity is a male-only club: "*The Plague and The Rebel* . . . present a world from which women have been shut out. . . . These works of protest and rebellion never suggest that 'invisible' women, the women who have been shut out, can 'raise rocks' or 'move mountains'" ("An Introduction" 73–74). Jeffrey Isaac echoes Allen's sentiments, arguing that

"revolt . . . seems a distinctly transcendent, courageous, *male* activity . . . This conception of politics seems to reserve little space for the
participation of women and, more important, associates woman with
the distinctively private and unpolitical sphere of the family and love"
(233). Others as well have similarly noted that in Camus's works, female
characters function outside the realm of activity, and that there seems to
be an opposition between "male fraternity" and "feminine values."[22]
Anthony Rizutto argues that in Camus's early works (prior to World
War II and the birth of Camus's children) the model of fraternity found
in rebellion is that of male friendship that "does not grant women any
true measure of political existence" (58). Moreover, Rizutto continues,
if Camus were to accept women as anything other than objects then the
whole notion of fraternity would disintegrate. (However, Rizutto does
suggest that this is true only of Camus's early works, and that "women
in Camus's works will be gradually admitted into the polis," a point to
be explored further in a moment (68).)

Isaac goes farther than to state there is no space for women in Camus's
rebellion to argue that rebellion finds its "reproach" in women. He
contends that Camus's female characters such as Caesonia in *Caligula*,
Victoria in *State of Siege*, and Dora in *The Just Assassins*, "stand for stabil-
ity, nurturance, happiness, the private," for "intimacy and simple love"
(233).[23] I would agree that characters such as these critique a male logic
of rebellion that is forgetful of love, family, intimacy, children; but I
disagree that their role in so doing is to reproach rebellion. Rather, I would
argue, that their role is to secure a rebellion that is faithful to its origins.

Isaac quotes a long passage from the Female Chorus from *State of
Siege* to make his point. I reiterate it here to make mine:

> Our curse on him! *Our curse on all who forsake our bodies!* And pity on us
> [women] . . . *who are forsaken* and must endure year after year this world
> in which *men in their pride are ever aspiring to transform!* Surely, since
> everything may not be saved, *we should learn at least to safeguard the home
> where love is* . . . But no! *Men go whoring after ideas, a man runs away from
> his mother, forsakes his love* and starts rushing upon adventure. (*State of
> Siege* 229, emphasis mine).

This passage encapsulates the problem of rebellious acts that are
forgetful of their origins—acts of arrogance (i.e., forgetful of the limits
of human knowing) that put ideas before life and the living; acts that
forsake the body; acts that forsake love; acts, in other words, that forsake
the origins of rebellion. This is the life of rebellion gone awry—in which
"dialogue and personal relations have been replaced by propaganda or

polemic . . . [and] abstraction . . . has replaced the real passions, which are in the domain of the flesh and the irrational." It is a rebellion that has become "disembodied" (*Rebel* 239–240). It is not, as Isaac argues, "men with integrity who will forsake their bodies and their women in the name of justice," (233) but rather men who have disintegrated— those who have separated their bodies from their minds, their passions from their ideas, love from justice, in other words, rebels who have been forgetful of their origins and allowed their rebellion to become something else. Just before the passage quoted earlier, Diego, the main male protagonist rebel, says to the Chorus of Women, ". . . this world needs you. It needs our women to teach it how to live. We men have never been capable of anything but dying" (228–229). And earlier, the Chorus of Women proclaims: "We are the guardians of the race" (200). Far from *reproaching* rebellion, the Chorus of Women is *reclaiming* rebellion, insisting that it *not forsake* the very love that gave it birth, that it stay faithful to its origins.

Others, as well, have argued that women have an "essential presence" in the polity and in acts of rebellion (Rizutto 69). Sprintzen argues, as I have, that the role of Victoria and the Chorus of Women is to restrain Diego's rush to revenge, and to insist that revolt is a question of human dignity that can only "find its justification in a sustaining human community" (114). He also points to the example of Dora in *The Just Assassins*, who in representing the critical value of the concrete, similarly reminds the other rebels that their rebellion can only be justified only by life and love (115–116). Bronner also argues that Dora "stresses that the genuine revolutionary [i.e., the true rebel] never forgets the empathy with suffering that inspired his or her actions in the first place" (80). Unlike Allen, who regards the absence of women in *The Plague* as another example of Camus's misogyny, Rizutto interprets this absence as representing sterility, at a time when Camus regards rebellion as fertility (68). The fecundity of rebellion requires the presence of women.

Isaac does suggest the possibility of an alternate interpretation of the role of female characters in Camus's works, in which the reproach of the female characters to the male rebel represents the need for the integration of love and justice (234). In my reading of Camus, clearly this alternate interpretation is the correct one. Isaac does recognize that the Chorus's lament of male pride echoes Camus's lament of European pride in *The Rebel* (234). He goes on to explore the character of the wife of Casado, the self-righteous, legalistic judge in *State of Siege*, who exclaims, "I spit on your law! I have on my side the right of lovers not to be parted, the right of the criminal to be forgiven, the right of every penitent to recover his good name . . . for justice—do you hear, Casado?—is on the side of the sufferers, the afflicted, those who live by hope alone" (192). Isaac regards this as the language of justice and compassion combined. Yet he also argues, along with Michael Walzer, that Camus could have said more explicitly that justice without love is unjust, and love without justice would not be love, rather than setting up an antinomy between the two (234).[24] It is true that Camus sometimes seemed to oppose justice and love to each other, as in his famous statement from the discussion following his acceptance of the Nobel prize: "I believe in justice, but I will defend my mother before justice" (qtd. in Todd 378). However, to suggest that Camus sets up an antinomy between the two, to the extent that one must choose between the two, is to take Camus out of context of the rest of his argument. If this statement represents anything, it is the primacy of relationship over abstract principles, one of the core concepts of rebellion. Camus consistently refused the "either/or" typical of Western dichotomous thinking.[25] Rebellion rests on a notion of "limits," and the limit of any value is the point at which it contradicts itself. Love without justice becomes solitary and exclusionary and no longer love. Justice without love becomes totalitarian and no longer just. As I have argued elsewhere,[26] Camus's rebellion suggests an alternative to the "justice vs. care" debate by requiring "both/and," both justice and care. The justice that Camus embraced is not born of abstract principles and reasoned logic. Rather it is born of compassion, for oneself or others. By the same token, love is nurtured and sustained through actions that refuse the oppression and claim the dignity of those one loves. The *whole* of Camus's argument says exactly what Walzer and Isaac suggest Camus should be saying, that justice without love is unjust and love without justice is less than love. Camus used a passage in *The Just Assassins* to push the point. Dora tries to make her fellow revolutionary and lover Kaliayev choose, asking him whether he loves her more than justice, a distinction that Kaliayev refuses to make. She goes on to ask, "Would you love me if I were unjust?" to which Kaliayev responds, "If you were unjust and I could love you, it wouldn't be you I loved" (270). Admittedly, Camus somewhat confused the issue later in the scene when Dora says that their love is limited by the fact that it is so rooted in the cause (271), but the main message still comes across that love and justice are so intertwined that one without the other would be something different.

Far from isolating the sphere of family and love in a nonpolitical realm, Camus demanded that the values represented and nurtured therein are fundamental to rebellion. For Camus, the tasks of caring that are associated in Western thought with the private sphere are among the very core conditions to which rebellion must remain faithful. Justice that abandons compassion and caring relationships self-destructs. If "the long demand for justice exhausts even the love that gave it birth," (Camus, *Lyrical* 168), the plague of oppression and injustice has won. Compassion, care, love, friendship, family, embodiment—those values so often divided off from justice in Western political thought—are no more nor less necessary to rebellion than demands for justice and liberty, to the point that they find their definition in each other.

I would suggest that an inability to recognize this in Camus's thought may be due to the tendency in Western political thought to designate family and love as nonpolitical. However, as feminists have argued, the dichotomy in Western political thought between public and private is arbitrary.[27] Camus's thought is unlike typical Western political theory in that it does not maintain this dichotomy.[28] Anthony Rizutto argues that Camus's point in *The Plague, State of Siege*, and *The Just Assassins* is to demonstrate that love is no more nor less private or public than politics: ". . . His [Camus's] works demonstrate . . . that love and justice, our private passions and public laws, engage and condition each other" (138). I would go further and say that this is Camus's point in the very concept of rebellion.

If Camus is guilty of anything here it is of using predominantly female characters to represent nurturing, compassion, caring, embodiment; while using predominantly male characters to represent action, logic, adherence to abstract principles of justice. It is not clear whether in drawing these dichotomies he is presenting cultural stereotypes, or whether he regards these characteristics as essentially female and male, but regardless, such division does lend itself to dichotomous thinking.[29] However, because no such female/male division exists in Camus's arguments in *The Rebel*, in it it is more readily apparent that justice and love, as Rizutto puts it so well, "engage and condition each other."

Thus, I would disagree with those who argue that there is no space for women's participation in rebellion, that it is a distinctively male activity. (Apparently so would Camus. It is said that he had Simone Weil in mind as his prototype of the rebel portrayed in *The Rebel* (Bell xii).) Central to my project here is the argument that far from being masculinist, Camus's sense of rebellion relies on what are often considered to be gynocentric values—compassion, relationship, the body, and the earth. Rather than isolating these to a "private" sphere, these values and qualities are necessary components of rebellious action, and rebellious acts that ignore or abandon these can no longer claim to be rebellion.

Outline of the Book

Having staked that claim, I can continue with the investigation of the intersection of Camus's rebellion and feminist thought. In the chapters that follow, I discuss each of the core components of rebellion, as well as rebellion's epistemological base and its implications for political practice at much greater length. I elaborate not only on Camus's meaning of these, but also how each is discovered, articulated, and developed in feminist thought, and how the two inform each other.

I begin chapter two with an exploration of the epistemological assumptions upon which Camus's ethic of rebellion and much of feminist thought are based. I focus on four significant areas of overlap between them: (1) critique of reason and an appreciation of nonrational sources of knowledge; (2) use of dialogue in assessing knowledge claims; (3) valuing of concrete experience as a criterion of knowledge; and (4) a rejection of value dualism.[30] I also show how the central theme of epistemological humility—a recognition of the limits of our knowledge and our capacity to understand—runs throughout these.

The next several chapters are devoted to examinations of the four core components of rebellion and their articulation in feminist thought. In chapter three I examine the first core component, the rejection of oppression and the affirmation of human dignity, showing the parallels between rebellion and feminism, as well the corrective that feminist thought offers to Camus's silence on the issue of the oppression of women. I elaborate on various dimensions of feminist refusals of injustice and oppression as they have been expressed over time. However, the dimension of affirmation of self-worth implicit in feminist rebellion has stirred much controversy in feminist thought. Specifically, the concept of "self-worth" and the worth of "womanhood" raises questions regarding just who and what that "self" and "womanhood" is. In the rest of the chapter, I tackle the issues raised by feminists regarding the "essential" nature of "womanhood" and the "self," exploring both second-wave[31] efforts to define "woman" and the "self," and the critiques by women of color, deconstructionists, and others of these efforts. Ultimately I argue that the dignity and worth revealed by rebellion lies beyond construction.

Chapter four is devoted to an exploration of the themes of silence and finding one's voice in rebellion and feminist thought. In feminist thought, these issues are taken up by a diverse array of thinkers—Adrienne Rich, Audre Lorde, Susan Griffin, bell hooks, María Lugones, and others. Camus's discussion of silence in *The Rebel* provides a way of linking these. He contended that the three causes of silence are false-hood, servitude, and terror. I take up each of these in turn, showing how each has factored into women's silence. In this chapter I also examine how much of feminist thought and action in this regard is devoted to refusing these three conditions of women's lives, and the process of women coming to voice. A significant aspect of this for both Camus and feminist thought is the expression of multiple voices, and the discussion of this in feminism is linked to Camus's distinction between unity and totality. I go on to explore the conditions, articulated in feminist theory and practice, that make coming to voice possible. These include nurtur-ing relationships, safe spaces, and communities within which to speak and be heard.

Chapter five provides an examination of the second core component of rebellion—solidarity. I examine each of the four aspects of solidarity discovered in rebellion: (1) metaphysical solidarity; (2) solidarity in rela-tionship; (3) compassionate action; and (4) refusal of injustice, detailing what each means and how feminist thought and practice has grappled with each of these. With regard to the metaphysical solidarity of collec-tive suffering, I explore the questions raised in feminism regarding "sisterhood," which has been a problematic notion for feminism that has often itself been oppressive and exclusionary of the voices, perspectives, and concerns of women of color, as well as poor women and lesbians of all races and ethnicities. In response to critiques of "sisterhood," femi-nists have sought instead a solidarity based on understanding across differ-ences. This leads to the second aspect of solidarity in relationship, which seeks to build that understanding through dialogue. I borrow Jodi Dean's concept of "reflective solidarity" to help elucidate the various dimensions of this aspect of solidarity in both Camus's rebellion and feminist thought and practice. Third, I show how compassionate action is a centerpiece of femi-nist spirituality and theo/theology,[32] as found in the thought of Beverly Wildung Harrison, Carter Heyward, Rita Nakashima Brock, and others. Finally, I examine the challenges faced by feminists in refusing to oppress others. I explore as well the evolution of feminism as it has come to entail the denunciation of oppression in all its forms—not just sexism, but also racism, classism, heterosexism, ableism, and so on. Further, I show the extension of feminist solidarity to children and other dependents, as well as to all sentient beings and the earth. I end with an examination of feminist self-scrutiny in owning our capacity to add to oppression.

In chapter six, I explore the third core component—friendship and the primacy of concrete relationship. I begin this discussion by entering the "justice vs. care" debate in feminist ethics, and argue that Camus's ethic of rebellion offers a "both/and" solution that insists on the equal valuing of both justice and care. I then explore arguments in feminist thought—such as those of Sara Ruddick, Virginia Held, and Marilyn Friedman—that nurturing relationships provide fundamental insights for our conception of political relations, as well as motivations for politic action. The end of the chapter is devoted to an exploration of the nature and requisites of friendship, an area left largely undeveloped in Camus's thought, though he held friendship dear.

In chapter seven I examine the fourth and final component—the valuing of immanence. Beginning with a more thorough articulation of the expression of themes of immanence in Camus's work—relationship with and awe of the natural world, sensual appreciation of the body, valuing of beauty, and a joy stemming from communion with creation—I then go on to explore its manifestations in feminist thought. Particularly intriguing is the contrast in Camus's thinking on this with that of the foremost feminist among Camus's contemporaries, Simone de Beauvoir. De Beauvoir rejected immanence in favor of transcendence, a theme reiterated by many feminists to follow. However, a growing movement of feminist thinkers, among them Audre Lorde, Susan Griffin, Starhawk, Gloria Anzaldúa, and Carol Christ have embraced the immanent. The very distinction between transcendence and immanence is challenged by ecofeminists, whose rejection of body/mind dualism is also reflected in Camus's thought. Further, I examine the destructive consequences of alienation from immanence, especially as these are articulated by Camus, Susan Griffin, and Maria Mies. I conclude with an exploration of the positive consequences of valuing immanence, specifically the equal valuing of all, the repudiation of dominance, and opposition to passivity in the face of injustice. In other words, I show how valuing immanence is necessary to rebellion.

Finally, chapter eight provides a discussion of the implications of rebellion for feminist political practice. Rebellious acts are guided by a "politics of limits," which limits rebellious practice in its scope, means, and basis. In examining the limited scope of rebellious practice, I focus on the balance of liberty and justice in Camus's thought, and explore this balance in issues of feminist ethics and politics that have particularly struggled with it. I also discuss the implications for a feminist democratic politics that lies between liberalism and socialism.

My examination of the means of rebellious practice is premised on the notion found in both rebellion and feminism that the means must justify the ends. Rebellious practice proscribes any action that would contribute to servitude, falsehood, and terror. I pay particular attention to the question of nonviolence as a political strategy. I also explore at length the feminist development of theories and practices of means that are egalitarian and inclusive. Central among these are the feminist development of participatory organizational structures, as well as processes that enable effective and inclusive discourse.

Third, I examine the basis of rebellious practice in concrete realties—in acts of resistance of specific injustices and oppressions and in the affirmative efforts of rebellious politics, especially as found in feminist grassroots efforts, to do what needs to be done to address a need and alleviate suffering.

In the concluding section of the final chapter, I begin a discussion of a germ of an idea articulated both by Camus and by feminist thinkers bell hooks and Susan Griffin, that being a transformative politics of healing. Drawing particularly on the insights of Camus, bell hooks, Susan Griffin, Audre Lorde, and Adrienne Rich, as well as mind/body healer Stephen Levine, I explore what this means, how it might go beyond rebellion to reconciliation and what hooks calls "redemptive love" (*All About Love* ch.12), and how it may, as Susan Griffin suggests, allow the very wounds that divide us to heal us (*Eros* 153).

Conclusion

Reflecting on Camus's posthumously published novel, *The First Man*, Jean Bethke Elshtain wrote:

> A reappreciation of Camus's greatness is long overdue. Perhaps this small gem will trigger renewed gratitude that he lived the life he lived; wrote the works he wrote; fought the good fight and now, at last, may, perhaps, be allowed to rest in honored peace. . . . perhaps Camus's commitment to lucidity and his recognition of our brokenhearted yearning for a kind or bracing word, an open face, the saving presence of our fellow human beings, will be greeted with honor and with tears. (*Real Politics* 375)

I could not agree more, and perhaps this work, as well, will contribute to a renewed appreciation of the wisdom of Camus, as well as the wisdom of feminism. Both have been misinterpreted, misrepresented, and maligned. It is my hope that in their common exploration, the true vision of both will be revealed.

CHAPTER 2
EPISTEMOLOGICAL BASES

One cannot separate a culture's way of ordering reality, its cosmology, its epistemology, from the social structures it contains.
                    Susan Griffin, *The Eros of Everyday Life* 41

The central quest in Camus's study of rebellion is to find a way to act in the world that does not rely on the abstract ideals and absolute truths constructed by "men," (and I use the word deliberately), that have been used to justify the destruction of lives and civilizations in the name of that "Truth." Camus wanted to find a standard of moral action that is grounded in something more real and concrete than the rationalizations of men's minds and their struggles for power. He was distrustful of the way ideologues used reason to justify their prejudices and their acts of arrogance. To this end, while not discarding reason as a source of knowledge, Camus turned as well to other sources of knowledge—to the body, the emotions, the passions, the longings of the spirit. "We insist," he wrote, "that the part of man which cannot be reduced to mere ideas should be taken into consideration—the passionate side of his nature that serves no other purpose than to be part of the act of living" (*Rebel* 19). In his search for truths by which to live, Camus relied on passion, compassion arising out of deep empathy for others, understanding that comes from sharing truths with each other, concrete struggles, friendships, and dialogue.

Camus's rebel is reminiscent of what Belenky and her colleagues have termed the "passionate knower"—one who knows by entering deeply both into self-awareness and into real relationships with others, and who brings both passions and intellect to the process of understanding (141–144). Belenky and her colleagues describe such passionate knowing as typically "women's way of knowing." Perhaps this is why the sense of understanding and truths I find in Camus are so similar to those I find in much of feminism. Nancy Hartsock, in articulating a feminist standpoint, claims that a female epistemology and construction of self leads "toward opposition to dualisms of any sort, valuation of concrete, everyday life, a sense of a variety of connectednessess and continuities both with other persons and with the natural world" ("Feminist" 298). Much the same could be said of Camus's epistemology. Because how we know affects what we know, it is important to our examination of rebellion and feminism to have an understanding of the epistemologies that underlie both. Looking at Camusian and feminist epistemologies systematically, I find four areas of strong overlap between the two: (1) a critique of reason combined with an appreciation of nonrational sources of knowledge; (2) use of dialogue in assessing knowledge claims; (3) a valuing of concrete experience as a criterion of knowledge; and (4) a rejection of value dualism.[1]

Running throughout these is the central theme of humility—a recognition of the limits of our knowledge and capacity to understand, and "the permanent partiality of all points of view" (Welch 137). Feminist epistemology insists that, at best, our knowledge of the truth is partial. Similarly Camus argued that the most "incorrigible vice was the ignorance that fancies it knows everything," (*Plague* 118) and that conversely, the most important knowledge is of the limits of our own knowledge. Also, what Iris Marion Young has called "moral humility" recognizes that we can never totally understand another (*Intersecting* 53). While it is important in recognition of the limits of our own knowledge that we seek out the viewpoints of others, it is also important to recognize that the more we understand about another person's perspective, the more we should also understand that there is much that we do not understand. A foundation of both rebellious and feminist epistemology is an awareness of how much we do not know, and cannot know, and that even with an everpresent openness to learning more, we will never know it all.

Critique of Reason

They said that in order to discover truth, they must find a way to separate feeling from thought (Griffin, *Woman and Nature* 117).

Men have been expected to tell the truth about facts, not about feelings. They have not been expected to talk about feelings at all. (Rich, *On Lies* 186)

The feminist critique of reason is two-fold. The first is the inappropriate separation of "reason" (conflated with "thought") from the body, nature, relatedness, emotion (all conflated with "feeling"); and the accompanying association of thought with men and feeling with women. The second is the granting of superiority, and thereby the right to dominance, to reason (and all that is associated with it) over "feeling" (and all that is associated with it). The feminist critique has focused primarily upon the way in which patriarchal society has used reason to justify the dominance of men and the subordination of women.[2] Typical is Val Plumwood's argument that the "master model" uses reason as the defining characteristic of the "master," thereby justifying the subordination of less rational creatures such as women (*Feminism*). Certainly the privileging of reason over other sources of knowledge runs deep in the Western intellectual tradition. Plato placed reason as the ruler over the will and the body. Aristotle took this further, claiming the rational capacity as the distinguishing characteristic of the "natural" ruler, with those men capable of reason being the masters, and those not, the slaves. Women, presumably except slave women, he asserted, had some rational capacity, though of an undetermined nature, and certainly not of the quality of free males, thus justifying the subordination of women to men. Aquinas, adapting Aristotelian premises to Christianity, similarly argued that because in men "the discretion of reason predominates," "woman is naturally subject to man" (Q. XCVI: A.3). Of course, this subjection is for her own benefit. Rousseau, drawn to and terrified of passion, regarded both women and men as endowed with "boundless passions," but whereas men have reason by which to control them, women have only modesty (Book V). The favorite subject of ecofeminist criticism on this point seems to be Francis Bacon, who more than the others, justified his use of reason and the scientific method in order to dominate a Nature that is sexualized and feminine (Merchant ch. 7).

Using object-relations theory to analyze this tradition in Western thought, Jane Flax argues that this escape to reason in the Western tradition results from the male need to reject and separate from "the mother," which includes female parts of the male self. Fear of sexuality, body, relatedness, and nurturance is reflected in a separated, abstract reason. Flax's assessment of the Western intellectual tradition's privileging of reason summarizes well this feminist critique of reason:

> In conclusion, then, philosophy reflects the fundamental division of the world according to gender and a fear and devaluation of women characteristic of patriarchal attitudes. . . . The female represents all that is either not civilized and/or not rational or moral. . . . [This] becomes a justification for relegating women to the private sphere and devaluing what women are allowed to do and be. . . . Reason is seen as a triumph over the senses, of the male over the female. ("Political Philosophy" 268–269)

Ironically, Karen Warren uses the logical form of the syllogism to present a similar argument, which she has named "the logic of domination." Having first established how this logic establishes the superiority and dominion of the human over other forms of nature, she goes on to show how this logic is used to legitimate the domination of men over women:

(B1) Women are identified with nature and the realm of the physical; men are identified with the "human" and the realm of the mental (i.e., reason).

(B2) Whatever is identified with nature and the realm of the physical is inferior to whatever is identified with the "human" and the realm of the mental; or, conversely, the latter is superior to the former.

(B3) Thus, women are inferior to men; or conversely, men are superior to women.

(B4) For any X and Y, if X is superior to Y, then X is justified in subordinating Y.

(B5) Thus, men are justified in subordinating women.

Or as feminist theologian Joan Chittister puts it so succinctly, reason is regarded as men's province; feeling as women's. Thus women need men to be their "head" (51).

Simone de Beauvoir went beyond the philosophical exploration of the epistemological and ontological assumptions of Western thought to reveal the way the sexual politics of reason play out in everyday life. She, like other Western philosophers before her, categorized women, somewhat derisively, as having no sense of logic and being more attuned to intuition, nature, and "the carnal world and the world of poetry" than men (*Second Sex* 620).[3] However, she also recognized the ways in which men use reason to intimidate and overwhelm women, and how women experience this as an underhanded use of force: "In masculine hands logic is often a form of violence, a sly kind of tyranny. . . . he tirelessly *proves* to her that he is right" (*Second Sex* 463). While women may sense that the premises on which men's deductions depend are often arbitrary, not being schooled in principles of logic, they don't know how to respond in kind, and simply resign themselves to masculine authority (*Second Sex* 599, 612).

Feminist philosopher Sara Ruddick similarly testifies to the sexual and social politics of reason, discovered in her own love affair with reason, and its demise (*Maternal* 7–9). She herself had gloried in the delights of reasoned argument and profited from the social status her use of reason conferred upon her, largely because it aligned her with the world of men. However, eventually her love affair with reason fell apart, for she, like de Beauvoir, saw how reason was used to dismiss or intimidate, and in the policies of segregation and the Vietnam war, she witnessed the ways in which reason was used to create a detachment from immoral policies and to justify violence. Reason, she said, failed her "as lover, mother, and citizen" (*Maternal* 8). And ultimately it failed her as a woman and a feminist, for she also saw how reason, being contrasted with "feminine" emotion, was used to further purposes of misogyny.

The feminist critique of reason thus goes beyond its use in the domination and subjugation of women, to encompass a critique of the ways masculinist logic has been used to enforce domination and destructiveness of all kinds, in science, technology, power politics, and their combination. The most persistent and profound feminist critique of the abuses to which reason has been put is that of Susan Griffin, who in several forms and repeated ways, has demonstrated the ways in which Western society has developed a "split culture" in which mind is split off from the sources of its wisdom—body, nature, emotion. This has so alienated us from ourselves that we have "come to believe that we do not know what we know" ("Split" 7). She argues that this "mind in exile from its own wisdom" (8), has resulted in disastrous scientific, technological, and political solutions—the Inquisition, the slave trade, Stalinist Russia, Auschwitz, the Cold War, nuclear power and nuclear weapons, fascist eugenics, and genetic engineering, to name a few.[4] She explains, "I do not mean to argue against thought or scholarship but rather to question the separation between thought, feeling and experience. Among other things, this separation ultimately leads to authoritarianism, and to the worship of certain theories for their own sake" (*Rape* 26n.).

Camus's critique of reason parallels the feminist critique in its recognition of the isolation and privileging of reason over other sources of knowledge, with the ensuing consequences of the arrogant and destructive uses of power. Though Camus's analysis of reason lacks a gender analysis, he certainly recognized and was critical of the ways those in power shaped reason's dictates to their own purposes and used it to justify and enforce their domination. He cited the reign of terror during the French Revolution, in which Rousseau's *Social Contract* served as the new dogma, justifying the absolute and inviolable reign of the "General Will," as discovered through the "reason" of the reigning power. Reason became the new god, and people were put to death on the scaffold because their beliefs were contrary to the principles derived through reason. No one dared to imagine that it was the principles, rather than the people, that were wrong (*Rebel* 114–115, 122–129).

Similarly, he argued that "scientific" socialism, the new dogma of the Soviets, was used to legitimate the reign of power and its accompanying oppressions under Lenin, and to justify the subjection of thousands of people to the "rational terror" of Stalin's policies of arrest, trial, imprisonment, torture in the gulag (*Rebel* 226–241). Very much like Griffin, Camus argued that such rational terror was made possible because of the abstraction of "thought" from feeling, the body, and the earth (*Rebel* 240). He critiqued as well the way in which recent scientific and technological advances had been used in ways that threatened survival on the planet (*Neither Victims* 27).[5]

Camus's play, *Caligula*, reflects his critique of the ways in which those in power use reason to justify their domination. As the quintessential characterization of what Griffin called "a mind possessed by madness, by a hallucinated idea of its own power" (*Eros* 13), Caligula represents the absurdity of rational logic taken to its extreme. Following to its logical extreme a subject's offhand remark that the Treasury is more important than anything, Caligula sacrifices anyone and everyone to the Treasury. Ruling thus by a dogmatic logic, his reign becomes one of terror and tyranny.

Perhaps even more significant in terms of the feminist critique of reason are the characters in the play whom Caligula dismisses and destroys. In his perceptive analysis of *Caligula*, David Sprintzen identifies the character of Caesonia with the body, Scipio with nature, and Cherea with others—all of whom are rejected in one way or another by Caligula. Thus, Sprintzen concludes, in his murder of Caesonia, Caligula destroys his relation to body; in his rejection of Scipio he cuts himself off from nature; and he alienates himself from others in his rejection of Cherea (74). Thus, what Camus is suggesting in *Caligula* is that the logic represented by Caligula "neglects . . . the competing logics generated by perspectives rooted in nature, the body, and others" (Sprintzen 74), just as the feminist critique is suggesting that a dogmatic reason is reason separated from body, nature, and relatedness.

It is a separation that Camus and certain strains of feminist thought refuse. Camus's thinking is always deeply rooted in feeling.[6] As Hazel Barnes has written of Camus, ". . . with Camus thought and feeling seem to move together"(187).[7] "Camus" she wrote, "is willing to listen unashamedly to the cry of the heart even when reason is most convincing" (371). The central epistemological premise of Camus's rebellion is that it is rooted in an epistemology other than reason. We come to the point of rebellion, he wrote, "deprived of all knowledge. . . . The first and only evidence that is supplied . . . is rebellion [itself]" (*Rebel* 10).

The origin of rebellion, be it Camusian or feminist, is outrage, but also compassion, for it is our compassion that fuels our outrage at the oppression of others and our outrage that fuels our compassionate actions of solidarity at their side. The two go hand-in-hand—each fueling the other.[8] For Camus, empathy and compassion are valid and vital sources of knowledge. Finally, the body and the earth are also significant sources of knowledge for Camus. Tastes, sights, sounds, the pains and pleasures of the flesh, the wisdom of stones and sun and sea all ground his thought in the concrete realities of the body and the earth. Passion, compassion, embodiment, immanence—these are the origins of rebellion, the sources of wisdom to which all rebellious action must stay true.

Many strains of feminism share this same insistence on the validity of the wisdom of the body, nature, emotions, passions. Belenky and her colleagues note the predominantly female phenomenon of "connected knowing," a knowing based in love and care that grounds so much of feminist thought—from Sara Ruddick's "maternal thinking" to Marilyn Frye's and María Lugones's "loving perception" to the ethic of care. In describing the "ethic of caring" that informs Afrocentric feminist epistemology, Patricia Hill Collins acknowledges personal expressiveness, emotions, and empathy as all being important sources of knowledge (215–217). Radical feminists affirm intuition, mystical experiences, poetic revelations, dreams, emotions, and the body as all being valid and important sources of knowledge. "The unconscious," writes Adrienne Rich, "wants truth, as the body does" (*On Lies* 188). Ecofeminist epistemology grounds itself in an embodied mind that recognizes that it is part of nature.

The theme that underlies them all is a deep appreciation of the passionate, the erotic aspects of our beings. Audre Lorde testifies to the power of the erotic to reveal knowledge:

> ... the considered phrase, "It feels right to me," acknowledges the strength of the erotic into a true knowledge, for what that means is the first and most powerful guiding light toward any understanding. And understanding is a handmaiden which can only wait upon, or clarify that knowledge, deeply born. The erotic is the nurturer or nursemaid of all our deepest knowledge. (56)

This is the sense in which Camus and these feminist writers approach the knowledge derived from our passions—our bodies, sensuality, the earth, emotions, and the unconscious—not that it is the only source of knowledge, but that it is the facilitator of our deepest knowledge, acting to clarify, validate, and ground that which we already know, and to open us to that which we have yet to learn.

Some might critique the validity of such passionate knowledge, claiming that it lacks intersubjectivity. Others, especially certain deconstructionist feminists, would contend that even this passionate knowledge is culturally constructed (Jaggar, *Feminist* 380; Butler). To a certain extent, Camus also seems to recognize rebellion as being culturally constructed, arguing that rebellious thought arises only in Western society, where theoretical equality is at odds with great factual inequalities and where the whole society has rejected the sacred (*Rebel* 20). But this, for him, does not undermine the validity of this passionate source of knowledge. It simply puts it into a context in which it can find expression.

It should be said that in their embrace of the nonrational, Camus and feminist thinkers are not seeking to discard reason altogether, but rather to reconceive it as "strengthened by passion rather than opposed to it" (Ruddick, *Maternal* 9). Camus argued that reason and what he labeled the "irrational" (though perhaps better translated as the "nonrational")—emotion, passions, poetry, body, nature, sensuality—must inform and limit each other. As he explained in *The Rebel*, "the real is not entirely rational, nor is the rational entirely real, . . . The irrational imposes limits on the rational, which, in its turn, gives it its moderation" (295–296). It is in the reintegration of body–mind, reason–emotion, thought–feeling that real knowledge, meaning, and value can be found.

Use of Dialogue

How do we know what we know? How do we assess the validity of ours and others' claims to knowledge? For Camus and certain feminists, the very erotic that reveals knowledge to us also testifies to its validity. As Audre Lorde says, "It feels right to me" is a powerful guide in assessing knowledge claims. Yet, the erotic is useful primarily in assessing only the truth of one's own experience. One cannot crawl inside another's skin to know what feels right to them. If passionate knowing is a major source of assessing one's own knowledge, then com-passionate knowing is the primary vehicle for the assessment of these knowledge claims. While a natural empathy that arises simply in the witnessing of others' suffering is an important source of compassionate knowing for Camus, it goes only so far. We need dialogue to clarify and validate the experience of others. Camus thought it was vital that we recognize the limited nature of our knowledge and understanding, and that we always maintain an openness to having our perceptions challenged and corrected by each other (*Rebel* 304).[9] Camus repeatedly said that we could never be sure that we know the absolute truth about anything, and that the best corrective to this was dialogue with many and diverse others. Camusian dialogue consists in each of us presenting our truths as clearly and simply as possible, always in recognition of the partiality of our perspectives and with openness to the perspectives of others, and through this process to reveal the truth that lies between them.

The dialogical process defined by Camus is very similar to one that Patricia Hill Collins regards as arising from Afrocentric culture and a context of domination. In this feminist Afrocentric process of dialogue, each person or group speaks from their own standpoint, and significantly, recognizes that their knowledge is only partial. This realization makes each better able to consider the standpoint of the others, yet without needing to relinquish one's own standpoint or suppress that of others. Everyone has a voice, and everyone must listen, and respond (236–237).

Collins raises the importance of "connectedness" to the process of dialogue within the Black women's community (212). She refers to the study by Belenky and her colleagues, which discovered the significance of such "connected knowing," a type of knowing found more often among women, in which women share their truths with other women, in as structured relationships as formal consciousness-raising groups and classrooms, to the more informal sharing around the kitchen table. It is important to the revelatory capacity of these conversations that those involved begin with a premise of connection, of trust, with a purpose of understanding, rather than judging. Griffin, hooks, Belenky, and others distinguish this "connected knowing" from "separate knowing," which is more likely to occur in adversarial speech, in which people talk at each other, but not with each other.[10] Griffin expresses her hope that such "us versus them" dialogues, separated knowing, can be transformed into what she calls "liberating speech" (*Made* 161–162). Such liberating speech implies, as bell hooks puts it, "talk between two subjects, not the speech of subject and object. It is a humanizing speech, one that challenges and resists domination" (*Talking* 131). Such "speaking with" means that we not only have the opportunity to speak, but also to hear, understand, and be transformed.[11]

Evelyn Fox Keller has noted the way the Western intellectual tradition uses visual metaphors, such as "the mind's eye," as models for truth. And as Belenky and her colleagues have commented, not only does the Western intellectual tradition emphasize vision, but it also values the *impairment* of sight for the discovery of truth, such as the reference to "blind" or "double blind" studies to indicate ones in which the participants' ignorance prevents them from influencing the results (18). I am reminded as well of John Rawls's "veil of ignorance" that enables the discovery of the true principles of justice. Because one can see great distances, but can hear only in relatively close proximity, such emphasis on vision encourages distance, whereas dialogue, speaking and listening, requires closeness (Belenky et al. 18). The point in dialogue is not to stand apart and assert one's claims, but rather to come to a sense of mutual understanding (hooks, *Talking* 131).

Concrete Experience as Criterion of Knowledge

The fundamental premise of *rebellion* is that values are found in the experience of rebellion itself, not in abstract and absolute principles, not in ideology. The main point of *The Rebel* is to find a system of values that are not based in abstract ideas. Concrete thought corrects ideology by grounding it in reality, thus preventing abstraction, and by setting certain limits of what we can in fact know, thus preventing absolutist ideas. Camus here follows up on the ideas put forth in de Beauvoir's *Ethics of Ambiguity*, that our knowledge can at best be ambiguous, and we cannot act assuming that our truth is absolute forever and for everyone. He found that the valuing of abstract principles over concrete reality not only leads to inaccurate knowledge, but ultimately to the practice of fitting people to principles rather than principles to people, a practice that became the justification for killing people in the name of principles. Camus's concern was the way in which ideologues tend to begin with ideas of their own making and then attempt to shape reality to fit them. Rebellious thought, on the other hand, takes the realities of people's lives and experiences as its starting point of knowledge and action. As he wrote:

> Despite its pretensions, it [revolution] begins in the absolute and attempts to mold reality. Rebellion, inversely, relies on reality to assist it in its perpetual struggle for truth. The former tries to realize itself from top to bottom, the latter from bottom to top. . . . it relies primarily on the most concrete realities—on occupation, on the village, ... (*Rebel* 298)

Camus likened the voice of rebellion to that of the child who announces that the king is naked. The child sees past the idea of the invisibility of the fine robes to the real nakedness of the king, just as the rebel sees through the mystifications of abstract thought, and instead honors the reality of his or her existence.

Feminists have also challenged the validity of principles abstracted from a supposedly universal reason, claiming instead the truth of the concrete realities of our lives.[12] These challenges cluster around two main arguments. The first is that what Western philosophy has presented as universal principles in fact masks the beliefs and values of particular people in particular contexts of power. It has been the task of feminist theory to expose the power relations underlying what has been presented as universal truth.[13] The second is that basing ethical and political decisions in particular contexts is both appropriate and valuable. Feminists value concrete, contextual thought for its tendency "... to relish complexity, to tolerate ambiguity, to multiply options ..." (Ruddick, *Maternal* 93), as well as its ability to yield sound moral judgments appropriate to individual situations. For example, feminist ethic of care theorists argue that the morality of an action is best determined in the context of that particular action and the relationships it seeks to preserve.[14]

On the other hand, feminists have criticized the tendency of abstract thought to overgeneralize and to define alternatives too simply. Adrienne Rich has accurately described this as "a longing for certainty even at the cost of honesty" that tends to shape facts to fit theory rather than vice versa (*On Lies* 193). Along these lines, Susan Griffin argues, like Camus, that theory begins in feeling, but once it becomes ideological— abstract and absolutist—it is no longer informed by experience, and rather than changing to encompass new evidence and insights, discards, distorts, and denies truths that do not fit its world view (*Made* 168).

What is most striking in Griffin's piece, however, is that her critique is not of masculinist ideology, but rather of feminist ideology, which she has found to run a course no different from "the way of all ideology." She found feminist ideology, though begun in feeling and a search for truth, instead acting at times in her own mind like a police force, something many of us in the feminist movement have experienced. The call for political correctness began in the feminist movement long before it became popularized and dismissed. Begun as an appeal for respect, it became instead a vehicle for criticism and self-criticism. As Griffin relates, within such ideological confines, one can even acknowledge only certain emotions, while others are regarded as unacceptable. "Suppose," she asks, "one feels a love for the enemy, or a particular member of the enemy class. Suppose one feels anger and hatred toward another of the same oppressed group? Suppose a woman hates a woman? These emotions are defined as 'incorrect.' And they become hidden" (*Made* 170). This leads to an even more dangerous form of ignorance, ignorance of self (*Made* 169). Thus, does feminism fall prey to the same dangers and dilemmas as other forms of rebellion, that forgetful of their origins, become something else.

Other feminists have critiqued much of the contemporary feminist theoretical endeavor for being too abstract. In a collective interview, several of the "founding" feminist theorists of second-wave feminism criticized contemporary feminist theory as being too esoteric, too much into deconstruction, and too detached from the real world (Hartmann et al.). Initially sprung from real social and political problems, early feminist theory was deeply connected to praxis and activism. However, they argued, with the professionalization of Women's Studies in the academy, feminist theory has become more driven by the "professional standards" of academia and has lost its rootedness in activism. As more and more feminist theory comes out of the humanities rather than the social sciences, it lacks its policy focus and no longer deals with or addresses the concrete, real-world problems facing women.

Feminist theory has also suffered from its tendency to abstract theories of the oppression of all women from the limited perspective of only one—largely white middle-class—group of women. Lugones and Spelman aptly point out that though feminist theory has appropriately characterized philosophical and moral theories for being "arrogant, disrespectful, ignorant, ethnocentric, imperialistic . . . feminist theory is no less immune to such characterizations . . ." (578), due to its lack of grounding in the concrete realities of the lives of women of other races, classes, and sexual orientations.[15]

The alternative is to develop theory out of concrete experiences, which is what rebellious feminism requires. The editors of *This Bridge Called My Back* call for such theorizing: "This is how theory develops. We are interested in pursuing a society that uses flesh and blood experiences to concretize a vision that can begin to heal our 'wounded knee'" (23). This means to start with the real problems and pains of women, and work with them to understand, eradicate or transform them; to build theory from the lessons of our daily lives (Hurtado 146; (*Teaching* 61, 70). This is something feminists have for the most part done. As Nancy Hartsock has pointed out, " 'Women have learned that it was important to build their analyses from the ground up, beginning with their own experiences' " (qtd. in Jaggar, *Feminist* 365 emphasis mine).

One of the best examples I know of creating theory from flesh and blood experiences is the rebellious voice of Sojourner Truth in her "Ain't I a Woman" speech: "Look at me! Look at my arm! . . . I have ploughed, and planted, and gathered into barns, and no man could head me! And a'n't I a woman?" (Stanton, Anthony, and Gage 428). Truth cut through all the devised truths about a "woman's" lot in life with the realities of her own experience as a woman.

Patricia Hill Collins writes of how experience as a criterion of meaning has been fundamental in the epistemologies of African American systems of thought, but goes on to say how this valuing of the concrete is as much a part of women's tradition as it is Afrocentric (209–210). Of course such claims again risk overgeneralizing the experience of the few for the many. However, others have made similar claims. De Beauvoir, in a somewhat derisive tone, though in a conclusion not unlike Carol Gilligan's, characterized "women's" moral world as "a confused conglomeration of special cases" (*Second Sex* 616). De Beauvoir claimed that women were only convinced by immediate experiences, not universally valid reasons. She characterized the world of men as full of abstractions, whereas that of women was "contingent and concrete" (*Second Sex* 625), much due to the nature of women's traditional everyday work: "A syllogism is of no help in making successful mayonnaise, nor in quieting a child in tears; masculine reason is quite inadequate to the reality with which she deals" (*Second Sex* 599).

This point would be taken up thirty years later as the basis of a significant epistemological stance in feminist theory, feminist standpoint theory. Like de Beauvoir, Nancy Hartsock focused her theory around the sexual division of labor. She argued that because women's life activities have traditionally been more grounded in the work of necessity—that is, focused on subsistence and on the production and reproduction of men—than have the activities of men, women have a unique epistemological standpoint, but unlike de Beauvoir, she sees this standpoint as potentially liberating in its insights ("Feminist" 292–293, 304).

Feminist standpoint theory has been used to assess the descriptions of truth espoused by Eurocentric masculinist abstract systems of thought. In many ways, it is the rebellious voice of the child declaring the king naked—"not from where I stand"—and then going on to say, "from where I stand, it looks like this." Standpoint theory critiques the abstract and exclusionary nature of masculinist theories, challenging "truths" long held as universal with the concrete realities of women's lives, and showing how these theories reflect the biases and viewpoints of sex, class, race, and so on.[16]

An important aspect of this grounding of knowledge in concrete experience is the recognition that the concrete is not one fixed, never-changing thing, but is always in process. Again, it is de Beauvoir who notes this as a characteristic of women's thought processes. In this case, de Beauvoir seems admiring of women's ability, due to their daily connection to the changing nature of life, to recognize that there is not a fixed truth, but rather an ambiguity in all principles and values (*Second Sex* 612), an idea she herself espoused in her *Ethics of Ambiguity*. Such is a thought process open to new ideas, or in Griffin's words, a willingness to be surprised. In particular, political action must constantly renew its sense of reality, find truths in the process itself. Alison Jaggar argues that, "The standpoint of women is discovered through a collective process of political and scientific struggle. The distinctive social experience of women generates insights that are incompatible with men's interpretations of reality and these insights provide clues to how reality might be interpreted from the standpoint of women. The validity of these insights, however, must be tested in political struggle . . ." (*Feminist* 371). Similarly, Camus emphasized how the rebel finds his or her values in the process of political struggle: "Far from obeying abstract principles, [the rebel] discovers them only in the heat of battle" (*Rebel* 283). Absolute truth is never attained; truth is always in the process of being defined and refined.

Rejection of Dualistic Thinking

Dualistic thinking is the tendency in Western thought to regard the world conceptually in terms of value-dualisms, disjunctive pairs in which the terms are seen as oppositional and exclusive and that place higher value on one over the other. Examples would be mind/body; culture/nature; reason/emotion; freedom/necessity; transcendence/ immanence; public/private; subject/object; self/other; male/female. As we have seen, both Camus and certain strains of feminist thought have been critical of the dualism that separates reason from body, nature, and emotion. Such separation, they contend, leads to distorted thought, as well as a politics of domination. However, feminists have extended this critique of dualism beyond the separation of mind and body to encompass a critique of all forms of dualistic thinking. The main argument put forth is that dualism distorts our concept of reality by fragmenting an organic whole into isolated and oppositional parts in which Self and Other are regarded as necessarily locked into a battle to determine dominance and subordination. This in turn tends to contribute to an instrumentalist ethic, in which the inferior of the pair is treated as a means to the ends of the superior. It is thus creative of a world that is oppositional, divisive, and adversarial. Nondualistic, nonhierarchical thinking, on the other hand, reveals the ways in which everything is connected to everything else and creates the basis of a cooperative society. A nondualistic construction of self as being in continuity and relation with others, typical of females, provides the ontological base for developing social relations that embrace difference without dominance. Thus, in order to make possible a meaningful conception of difference—one that does not imply superiority/inferiority—dualism and its accompanying logic of domination must be abolished.[17]

On first reading Camus's *The Rebel*, it might appear that his thought is steeped in dualisms. In his pursuit of an ethic that refuses absolute values, Camus juxtaposed oppositional pairs that act as limits to each other—rational and irrational, justice and freedom, violence and nonviolence, absurdity of the universe and affirmation of life. Far from rejecting dualism, he seems to embrace it. Indeed, some have read him this way. "Camus's 'either/or' is relentless and unmediated," critic Hanna Charney writes of Camus's thought. But unlike value dualism, Camus's thought does not value one term of the pair over the other. Indeed, such a choice is the very antithesis of his thinking. Central to his concept of "limits" is the notion that any value held absolutely, unbalanced by its complement, ultimately contradicts itself. Absolute justice becomes unjust in its denial of freedom. Absolute freedom becomes the servitude of the oppressed. Camus, at least in this sense, rejects "either/or" thinking and insists that both terms of seeming opposites be held simultaneously, in constant tension. He insists on a "both/and" appreciation of both terms, defined "in terms of their paradox" (*Rebel* 286). Hazel Barnes has argued that Camus's conception of limits is best understood by viewing it in terms of certain absolutes to be maintained than by seeking a mean between systems of opposites; as a kind of dialectical movement in which contradictions are posited without ever being absorbed. Opposites coexist in Camus's thought; the opposing principles are preserved ("Balance" 434–435). Doubrovsky's image of Camus presenting dualistic terms as two ends of a chain that must be held at any cost represents this aspect of Camus's thinking well (163). Charney depicts Camus's thought as a constant tension of "inalienable antinomies and paradoxes" (100). This embrace of paradox links Camus strongly to feminist thinkers such as Griffin, Rich, and Anzaldúa, who also point out the importance of recognizing that seemingly contradictory thoughts can both be true, that truth lies in the affirmation of the paradox, rather than the dishonest exclusion of paradox in order to make things simpler than they really are.

While Camus does not reduce the terms of the paradox, or value one term over the other, he does nevertheless engage in oppositional thinking, and his thought is dualistic in that sense. Radical feminism, ecofeminism, and Chicana feminism alike would have us eliminate dualistic thought altogether. As Anzaldúa has argued, "The answer to the problem that lies between the white race and the colored, between males and females, lies in healing the split that originates in the very foundation of our lives" and calls for "a massive uprooting of dualistic thinking" ("La conciencia" 379). This means moving from "either/or" and "both/and" thinking to "many and multiple" thinking. Yet, dualistic thought is so deeply entrenched in the Western psyche it is almost impossible to conceive its elimination. But that is their point. Dualistic thought significantly limits our ability to envision our possibilities. How might we view reality differently, act differently, structure our societies differently, value differently if we were to eliminate oppositional thinking altogether—if we regarded *non*violence not as the opposite of violence, but rather as an altogether different yet related concept and way of being; if we did not regard freedom and justice as being in conflict, but perhaps even being one and the same thing; if we had no notion of masculine and feminine whatsoever? This is the challenge and possibility that feminism raises to dualistic thought, and it is in suggesting a way beyond dualisms that feminist thought can be a particularly useful development of Camusian thought.

Though not characterizing Camus as embracing dualistic thought, David Sprintzen has argued that Western dualisms limit his thought. While arguing that Camus's profound sense of the body saves him from mind/body dualism (278), Sprintzen does see Camus as being stuck, unable to get beyond certain other dualisms underlying his thought, such as nature/history, individual/society, fact/value, European/barbarian, ends/means. He argues that while Camus sensed the inadequacy of dualisms, he was unable to envision a way beyond their confrontation. They remain in tension and have no creative future (280). Feminist thought, eliminating dualism altogether, is one way beyond that. There is something to be said, as well, for recognizing the keen appreciation of the truth of paradox, that the creativity is in the tension itself, and that the need to move beyond that is a holdover of dialectical thought. Camusian thought honors the truth of the present.

However, I would agree that certain dualisms do limit Camus's thought. While he is able to go beyond mind/body dualism in certain respects, because his thought is rooted in certain oppositional ways of thinking, certain dualisms simply emerge, almost unconsciously, in his thought. His use of predominantly female characters to represent nurture, compassion, care, and embodiment, while using predominantly male characters to represent action, logic, and adherence to abstract principles of justice has already been noted (chapter one), as has its tendency to lend itself to dichotomous thinking. Similarly, Camus has been criticized for his "colonizing consciousness"—that is, the invisibility of Arabs in most of his literary works set in Algeria and his unwillingness to side with the colonized during the Algerian movement for independence, seeking instead a solution typical of his rebellious principles, that would include both the native and the French Algerian populations in a collaborative government (Peyre 25; Erickson). Patricia Barberto argues that Camus's story "The Adulterous Woman" in which Camus attempts to include more of an Arab presence and awareness, ironically becomes instead the ultimate colonization in that it is written in French for a French-speaking audience (38). He simply was unable to rid himself of dualisms so deeply embedded in his consciousness.

This is particularly striking in Camus's contrast of the Mediterranean and German minds, which he regarded as the primary conflict of the twentieth century. Camus presented the two as opposing cultures and worldviews, the German being that of violence, nostalgia, and history, the Mediterranean that of strength, courage, and nature. In them he saw the opposition of excess and moderation (*Rebel* 299). There is no question here of which term of this oppositional pair Camus values more highly, to the point of a certain amount of racism: "Thrown into the unworthy melting-pot of Europe, deprived of beauty and friendship, we Mediterraneans, the proudest of races, live always by the same light. In the depths of European night, solar thought, the civilization facing two ways awaits its dawn. But it already illuminates the paths of real mastery" (*Rebel* 300). This real mastery, Camus ironically goes on to say, "consists in refuting the prejudices of the time" (*Rebel* 300).

Can one ever escape this kind of either/or thinking? Doesn't feminism, in its rejection of dualism do the same? Its rejection of patriarchy and its limited epistemology parallels Camus's rejection of German ideology. It seems the conundrum, the paradox if you will, of those epistemologies that would be more inclusive is that they must necessarily exclude those epistemologies that are exclusive.

One element of rebellious thought offers a striking alternative to oppositional thinking. In Camus's novel, *The Plague*, one of the characters, Tarrou, dichotomizes the world into victims and pestilences, and says that we have the responsibility not to align with the pestilences, but rather to take the victims' side, so as not to contribute to the harm done in the world. But he adds, there is also a third category, "that of the true healers" and that the third category facilitates the possibility of peace (230). That third category, the one who is neither victim nor executioner, is, I believe, the rebel. Rebellion itself is a third way, not one of dominating nor of being dominated, but in its simultaneous refusal of both it is affirming of another alternative, that of healing and peace. This is the kind of creative possibility that is enabled by allowing oneself to move beyond the box of dualistic thought.

It seems that for those of us enculturated in Western dualistic thought, efforts to move beyond the box will be a continual effort. It so deeply structures our sense of reality. But the possibilities of moving beyond the box are exciting, offering new visions of the world. Camus was not completely successful in ridding himself of dualistic thinking, but he was able to move in that direction in significant ways—in his affirmation of the equal valuation of opposing terms and finding truth in paradox; his deep appreciation and affirmation of body, emotion, and the earth; and finally, his positing rebellion as a third way. Feminist thought continues the effort. What follows in the rest of the book is an examination of this third way.

CHAPTER 3
REFUSAL AND AFFIRMATION

In assigning oppression a limit within which begins the dignity common to all . . . rebellion defined a primary value.

Camus, *The Rebel* 281

The rebel is one who refuses, who resists, who says no. A line is crossed, and something arises in the rebel that says "no more," "you've gone too far," "I won't take one more moment of your humiliation or your abuse." At the moment the rebel refuses, the rebel also becomes aware of something within him or herself that is worthwhile and demands respect:

> The rebel simultaneously experiences a feeling of revulsion at the infringement of his rights and a complete and spontaneous loyalty to certain aspects of himself. . . . Awareness . . . develops from every act of rebellion: the sudden, dazzling perception that there is something in man with which he can identify himself, even if only for a moment". (Camus, *Rebel* 14)

Up until this point, the condition of the rebel has been one of despair—submission, passivity, and silence in the face of injustices, cruelties, and humiliations, but at the moment of refusal, awareness is born. The act of rebellion thus reveals to the rebel a value so significant that she is willing to put her life on the line for it. Camus argued that in risking everything to defend this part of one's being that demands respect, one is making a larger claim, necessarily implying by one's risks that this value extends beyond the self. Thus in rebelling one in a sense asserts oneself "for the sake of everyone in the world" (*Rebel* 16) claiming that which has been infringed upon extends to all. That which resists oppression in oneself simultaneously demands that no one will be treated with anything less than deepest respect of the dignity and meanings of their lives. And this is not because it is written in God's law or in man's, or discovered through reason or revelation, but rather because it is experienced in one's very being at the moment of rebellion. At the moment of refusal of oppression the worth and dignity of oneself and of all others is revealed. This is the value born of rebellion. Thus the rebel "says yes and no simultaneously"—*no* to oppression and injustice and *yes* to that which the oppressed recognize as valuable within themselves.

In defining rebellion as the simultaneous rejection of oppression and affirmation of dignity, Camus drew an important distinction between rebellion and resentment[1] (*Rebel* 17–19). While both grow out of situations of oppression, domination, and prolonged powerlessness, they are significantly different responses to those conditions. Resentment is passive. Feeding on an envy of what one does not have, it eats away at one's sense of worth and ultimately is self-poisoning in its toxic jealousy and hate. Those who act from a place of resentment do not hesitate to humiliate and dominate their oppressors in their turn, and in fact delight in the opportunity to do so, becoming that which they despised. Rebellion, on the other hand, is an active movement of liberation and self-affirmation. Rather than being colored by envy of what one does not have, rebellion claims recognition for who one is. Rebellion stakes a claim for the integrity of one's being. And just as the rebel insists on not being humiliated, so does she or he insist on not humiliating anyone else.

Rebellion is simultaneously a movement against injustice and for liberation. By injustice Camus meant anything that humiliates and degrades, that cuts persons off from their full potential and self-expression, that denies dignity—whether it be the exploitation of workers, poverty, violence, the suffering of children, or the death of innocents. We get perhaps the clearest image of Camus's sense of injustice from his novel, *The Plague*. The story of *The Plague* is of a town in Algeria hit by an epidemic of bubonic plague. It tells of the exiles and separations that result, as well as of the inhabitants' efforts against the plague, and the friendships and solidarity that emerge in their common struggle. On one level, the plague that randomly kills, terrorizes, separates, and silences, is symbolic of the plague of totalitarianism that had just swept Europe during World War II, but on another it is symbolic of the plague of injustice that is part of the human condition. Various characters in *The Plague* have rebellious qualities, but it is from the doctor, Rieux, that we most clearly hear the voice of protest against injustice. Witnessing the death of a child from the plague in the company of the priest (who had earlier blamed the plague on the sins of the townspeople), Rieux protests, "That child, anyhow, was innocent." In response to the priest's surprise about his anger, Rieux continues, ". . . there are times when the only feeling I have is one of mad revolt. . . . And until my dying day I shall refuse to love a scheme of things in which children are put to torture" (196–197). In concrete actions against injustices rebellious acts define justice as that which seeks to prevent suffering and harm, as well as to preserve the dignity and meaning of people's lives.

At the end of *The Plague*, a great exuberance fills the town, loved ones separated by the plague are reunited, love and laughter fill the air. People, filled with "the vast joy of liberation" (268), are finally able once again to be themselves. By liberation Camus intended not merely the release from bondage and oppression, but also the permanent possibility of self-expression and spiritual freedom. Freedom, for Camus, was not so much a thing, as a way—a way to justice and truth, a way to come to understand each other, a way to grow as creative and spiritual beings. "Freedom," Camus wrote, "is nothing else but a chance to be better . . ." (*Resistance* 102). Liberation, as it is affirmed in the act of rebellion, is the expression of who one is and the assertion of the possibility of happiness.

Rebellion is not an attempt to establish the perfect reign of justice, for rebellion recognizes that at best, justice will only be proximate, and that even in a perfect world, children will continue to suffer and die unjustly at the hands of the universe (*Rebel* 303). As Rieux says in *The Plague*, he is not working for salvation, but rather simply for health (197). Similarly the freedom claimed by rebellion is not a demand for absolute freedom, which Camus regarded as libertinism and license that ultimately result in the subjection of the majority to the liberty of a few (*Rebel* 42, 123, 175). Rebellion does not demand the right to destroy, but rather honors the freedom of others: "The freedom of each finds its limits in that of others; no one has a right to absolute freedom" (*Resistance* 101). This limit is found in the rebellious insistence on the simultaneous refusal of injustice and affirmation of liberation. Refusal of injustice carries with it the demand for self-expression, and liberation requires the constant effort to extend that capacity to all. The rebel fights not only for the freedom of the slave, but also against the world of the master and slave (*Rebel* 284).

Camus framed rebellion in terms of a willingness to risk one's life in the claiming of dignity. Certainly in the context of the murderous and totalitarian times in which he wrote, an act of resistance, no matter how small, was potentially life-threatening, as it continues to be for all those around the globe living under authoritarian regimes. In the era of hate crimes, this has been and continues to be true for members of certain groups in this society. It continues to be true as well for women in battering relationships, for women threatened by rape and assault, for women living under patriarchal despotism anywhere—whether it be that of the state or their home—in which to speak or disobey is to risk death. It is possible that one does not know the full measure of rebellion unless one's life is literally on the line, but for most of us rebellions come in less dramatic ways, what Gloria Steinem has coined "outrageous acts and everyday rebellions"—calling a friend on their sexist or racist jokes, suing an employer for discrimination, refusing to conform to gender norms, participating in an act of nonviolent resistance, writing a letter to the editor, speaking up. Yet in each instance of rebellion, large or small, a value is revealed, a recognition of the implicit dignity of our beings and the extension of this to all, demanding that we treat anyone and everyone with decency. We may not risk our lives, but rebellion is never without risk—of imprisonment, ostracism, loss of livelihood, pain. For the rebel, this value, this common human decency, is more important than any of these. Rebellion, in whatever form, is a refusal to be treated with anything less than the full measure of dignity and decency that one's humanity demands.

The Feminist Refusal

The parallels of feminism to this aspect of rebellion seem obvious. Feminist movement and thought has so often been about saying "no"— "I've had enough;" "We won't be silenced any longer;" "I refuse to be treated this way anymore." It is the refusal anymore to be excluded, silenced, battered, degraded, told how to look, act, speak, and behave. A limit is reached, whether individually or collectively, in which the oppressed refuses to be treated as an object, or with degradation, humiliation, or violation of her integrity. The theme is reiterated in feminist thought and action, and from age to age—from Sarah Grimké's refusal to be silenced by her pastoral "brethren" and her demand ". . . that they will take their feet from off our necks, and permit us to stand upright on that ground which God designed us to occupy" (35) to second-wave activists refusing to be used and objectified by their "comrades" in the male-dominated peace movement: "No more, brothers. No more well meaning ignorance, no more cooptation, no more assuming that this thing we're all fighting for is the same: one revolution under *man* with liberty and justice for all. No more . . . ." (Morgan 269). It continues into the present day—shortly after the Anita Hill/Clarence Thomas hearings, a woman overhearing a conversation between two men, degrading women in their accounts of sexual exploitation, is approached by one of them, and

> A torrent explodes: "I ain't your sweetheart, I ain't your bitch, I ain't your baby. How dare you have the nerve to sit up here and talk about women that way, and then try to speak to me.". . . I refuse to back down. The words fly.
> . . . I am sick of the way women are negated, violated, devalued, ignored. I am livid, unrelenting in my anger at those who invade my space, who wish to take away my rights, who refuse to hear my voice.
> . . . I write this as a plea to all women . . . Let this dismissal of a woman's (Anita Hill) experience move you to anger. Turn that outrage into political power. (Walker, Rebecca 532–533, emphasis mine)

Joan Chittister's succinct statement sums up these feminist refusals of injustice and degradation: ". . . the feminist simply refuses to become less than fully human" (174). Robin Morgan gives us a vivid description of this moment of refusal in her "Goodbye to All That":

> There is something every woman wears around her neck on a thin chain of fear—an amulet of madness. For each of us, there exists somewhere a moment of insult so intense that she will reach up and rip the amulet off, even if the chain tears at the flesh of her neck. And the last protection from seeing the truth will be gone. (269–275)

That ripping off of the amulet in resistance to that moment of insult is the rebellious refusal of oppression.

Feminist rebellion begins with refusals.[2] Feminists have refused to be marginalized and excluded from full participation in all realms of life-pursuits and from the decision-making processes that affect our lives—from education, occupation, and political office to sports and religious practice.[3] They have refused the exploitation of their labor and their energies, protesting against inequitable pay; women's "second shift" and the disproportionate share of domestic work performed by women worldwide; and the expectation to perform, without reciprocation or reward, the work of nurture, care, comfort that draw on and use up the life energies of women.[4] They have refused as well the exploitation of their bodies as resources for the reproduction of laborers, warriors, and heirs. Some have rejected primary relationships with men, claiming lesbianism as a political choice of refusing male domination.[5]

Feminists have refused the violation, degradation, humiliation, and abuse of women. The experience or witnessing of violence against women—whether in the form of rape, abuse, incest, battering, pornography, prostitution and sexual slavery, murder, sexual harassment, self mutilation and starvation, or hate crimes—is often the impetus to feminist rebellion. Feminists have refused the cultural norms that condone violence against women, as well as the cultural practices that encourage it. Refusing objectification, they have resisted the treatment of women as sex objects in the media, the culture, and in the bedroom. They have acted as witnesses and advocates for victims of violence. They have established safe houses and shelters, as well as legislation and police practices to protect and prevent further violence.

Feminists have refused to be the Other. The singular importance of Simone de Beauvoir's groundbreaking work of second-wave feminism, *The Second Sex*, was in her recognition and naming of women as the Other:

> . . . humanity is male and man defines woman not in herself but as rela-
> tive to him. . . . She is defined and differentiated with reference to man
> and not he with reference to her; she is the incidental, the inessential as
> opposed to the essential. He is the Subject, he is the Absolute—she is the
> Other. (xvi)

Much of feminist movement since *The Second Sex* has been directed against women being regarded as the "Other" and against the cultural imperialism of white Western male patriarchal culture that regards itself as the norm and imposes it as the universal. And feminists have refused the tendency toward "othering"—of regarding the experience of white Anglo feminists as the norm to be imposed on women of color, lesbians, working-class women, and Third World women—among themselves.[6]

Like Camus's rebel, in multiple ways, feminists refuse the injustice of anything that cuts persons off from their full potential and self-expression, from the fullness of their being.

Feminist Affirmation and the Problem of Subjecthood

Feminist rebellion begins by saying "no"—"no" to being excluded and marginalized, silenced, exploited, objectified, violated, humiliated, degraded, the Other; and with each of these refusals simultaneously comes a "yes"—"yes" I am, she is, we are worthy of respect. In the words of Susan Griffin:

> When the Other stands up and acts as if she is essential, this act by itself
> challenges the existing order. . . . I myself have found a new way of being
> in this world. . . . I become more and more myself, less and less alienated
> from that self for whom, more and more, I feel a great love. . . . We assert

our dignity. . . . We have the power of being no force can resist. *We are here.* (Griffin, *Rape* 43, 45, 63, 68)

Our energies and time are valuable. Our voices and our wisdom deserve to be heard. Our bodies and our spirits are sacred. We are. At the moment of refusal, a limit is declared, and the value and worth of each and every woman is revealed. Sarah Grimké wrote of this moment, "Hitherto there have been at the root of her being darkness, inharmony, bondage, and consequently the majesty of her being has been obscured, and the uprising of her nature is but the effort to give to her whole being the opportunity to expand into all its essential nobility" (163). With each refusal emerges a claim of dignity and worth.

In the act of rebellion, the feminist rebel discovers something in herself that demands affirmation, dignity, and respect. Bell hooks argues that oppressed peoples must move beyond a focus on their pain to a focus on resistance and that to do so requires identifying themselves as subjects by defining their own reality, their own identities, their own history (*Talking* 42–43). Quoting Toni Cade Bambara she writes, " 'revolution begins in the self and with the self' " (*Sisters* 5). The act of becoming a subject, or *self*-recovery, relies on the insistence that a wholeness of being is present and possible; on the claim that a whole self existed prior to exploitation and oppression and that that self can be restored and recovered (*Talking* 29–30).

But to speak in terms of the "subject" or the "self" is to open a huge area of debate and controversy within feminist thought. While much of second-wave radical feminist thought was devoted to recovery and discovery of the "womanhood" and of the "self," other strains within feminism challenged the distortions and totalizing effects of feminist concepts of "womanhood," and questioned the very possibility of "the self." In order to understand what the self-affirmation of rebellion and rebellious feminism is, and is not, we must explore the problem of subjecthood within feminist thought.

Simone de Beauvoir on Women's Subjecthood

At the time she wrote *The Second Sex*, Simone de Beauvoir asserted that women had not claimed themselves as subjects. Rather they lived lives of passivity and resentment. Resentment, it will be recalled, is in stark contrast to rebellion. In resentment, one envies what one does not have, whereas in rebellion, one affirms who one is. But women, it seemed, could not affirm themselves because they did not know who they were. Their identities were shaped by patriarchal culture. Women's search for subjecthood can be understood in light of the work of one of Camus's contemporaries, Albert Memmi. In his *The Colonizer and the Colonized*, Memmi describes two types of colonized—"the colonized who accepts" and "the colonized who refuses." The "colonized who accepts" takes on the colonizer's image of him or herself, internalizes it, becomes it. But the "colonized who refuses" rejects this image, and seeks out his or her actual being. In their attempts to claim themselves as subject, the "colonized who refuse" seek to rediscover their roots and true identities by reclaiming their language, culture, religion.

But women, de Beauvoir suggested, even though they are "colonized" in the sense of being the Other to men's Subject, have no similar resources by which to claim themselves as subject. They have no past, no history, no language, no religion of their own, and no solidarity of work and interest. What is more, unlike other colonized peoples, they live dispersed among their oppressors and feel necessary bonds of loyalty to "their" men, (by which she meant not just their male partners, but also the men of their race and class). But perhaps the most daunting obstacle to women claiming their subjecthood is that they are, according to de Beauvoir's assessment, "well pleased to be the Other," in part because of the economic privileges and protections it affords them (and here she was speaking from the perspective of the leisured women of her class), but more than this, because being the Other lets women off the hook, so to speak. In having their actions, their choices, their very beings dictated to them and proscribed by others, they avoid having to be responsible for their own lives. They can avoid "the strain of authentic existence" (*Second Sex* xix–xxi).

Claiming Woman as Subject

Out of second-wave feminist refusals of oppression grew a movement, like that of "the colonized who refuses," to reclaim, recover, discover, and create a woman-centered womanhood that is defined separate and apart from patriarchal definitions of women's lives, beings, and culture, tackling each obstacle that de Beauvoir suggested lay in their path. Feminists sought out and reclaimed women's roots and traditions. They uncovered the history of women's lives, of ancient goddess-worshipping cultures, of women's traditional arts, and even reclaimed ancient meanings of words. They discovered "women's way of knowing," women's "different voice," and "maternal thinking," developing new feminist approaches to epistemology, ethics, politics, and psychology. They developed solidarity of work and interest through the creation of common spaces—feminist workplaces, health collectives, bookstores, coffeehouses, women-only cultural spaces; as well as the creation of women-centered cultural traditions—music, art, theater, spirituality, and language.[7] This was, in a sense, a "female pride" movement, an affirmation of the dignity and worth of womanhood and of each woman because of her woman-hood, but as defined by feminist women, not by patriarchy.

Second-wave feminists also questioned, scrutinized, challenged, and sometimes severed the "necessary bond to 'their' men." Some argued that living among men, especially within the institution of heterosexu-ality, divides women, saps women's energies, and gives women's loyalties and support to men rather than women because heterosexual privileges (such as the respect given to "traditional" mothers, but not single mothers; social acceptance; economic privilege; physical protection) give women a personal and political stake in maintaining the status quo. Lesbian separatist feminists argued that in order to reclaim a women-identified culture, it is necessary to separate from men and male-dominated society and institutions, asserting that: "Only women can give to each other a new sense of self. That identity we have to develop with refer-ence to ourselves, and not in relation to men" (Radicalesbians 197). Marilyn Frye argued that such exclusion of men by women may be seen as blatant insubordination and a threat to male supremacy, and thus may seem to be an entirely negative move, but that it is in fact a posi-tive move of women affirming their power. Severing bonds with men acts to support feminist movement to undertake self-definition in devel-oping a women-identified culture.

Many women, however, either did not want or were not able to disengage from relationships with the males in their lives—be they husbands, lovers, brothers, fathers, sons, friends, employers, colleagues. Barbara Smith's point, that most women "can't go to a harbor of many acres of land, and farm, and invite the goddess . . ." (121) is well taken. Smith also voices the significant issue that for many women, the bonds shared with men of their race are those not of privilege, but rather of common oppression: "And it's not like we like their sexism or even want to sleep with them. You can certainly be concerned as we are living here this summer in Boston when one Black man after another ends up dead" (121–122).[8] Most women coming into feminist consciousness have found ways to discover and claim themselves as subjects while living, as de Beauvoir said, "dispersed among men." They have found ways to withdraw their energies from masculinist and patriarchal institutions and to create women-identified physical and metaphysical spaces around themselves. Adrienne Rich writes of this expanded notion of women-identified culture and women-identified women as including many forms of female bonding: "... woman-identified experience ... [is] not simply ... desired genital sexual experience with another woman ... [but] many more forms of primary intensity between and among women, including the sharing of a rich inner life, the bonding against male tyranny, the giving and receiving of practical and political support" (*Blood* 63, 51). For many women, finding community with other women has been a traditional and continual part of their experience in their churches and in their kitchens (*Feminist* 28). Others, for whom this has not been a part of their experience, have made deliberate efforts to surround themselves with women friends, develop feminist support groups and consciousness-raising groups, read women's literature, listen to women's music, engage in feminist spiritual practices, rediscover their bodies. Though some feminists have trivialized these developments as "cultural feminism" and as being only about "lifestyle" choices rather than political change,[9] such immersion in women-identified culture has been regarded by many feminists to be an integral part of a process within feminist movement, as well as within individuals coming to feminist awareness, that has enabled women to claim themselves as subjects.[10]

Finally, feminists worked to overcome the third obstacle to women's claiming themselves as subject, the refusal of authentic existence. Far from resisting the "strain of authentic existence," feminists have sought the responsibility of authentic existence, asserting that "Together we must find, reinforce, and validate our authentic selves" (Radicalesbians 197). How does one discover this authentic self? For Camus, this authentic self is not anything that one can set out to discover. Awareness of this self does not precede rebellion, but rather arises in the moment of rebellion. However, Camus argued that the spirit of rebellion rarely exists in cultures where inequalities are great and considered appropriate and just, and where there is absolute equality. Nor does the spirit of rebellion flourish in cultures in which a sacred order is accepted. Rather, it is a phenomenon of Western culture, in which theoretical equality conceals great factual inequalities, and in which values, conduct, and the social order are open to question (*Rebel* 20–21). Yet, I would argue that subcultures also exist within Western culture in which a "sacred order" in which men are regarded as the spiritual, moral, and political "heads" of women, the family, the church, and the state is accepted or has only recently come into question, and in which inequalities, though great, may be considered appropriate and just. This describes the situation of many women around the world, both in Western and non-Western cultures.

Many women at least appear to accept their subordinate and silent position in society as sacred and not to be questioned. Gayatri Spivak has written that in many instances the subaltern woman cannot rebel because she lives in a culture in which even the possibility of conceiving of her position as an injustice cannot arise. If one is to believe Rousseau, the possibility of rebellion in any culture will always be confined to men, for "woman is made to submit to man and to endure even injustice at his hands. You will never bring young lads to this; their feelings rise in revolt against injustice . . ." (251). (Of course, though Rousseau makes it sound as if woman is by nature or by God destined never to rebel, this remark of his follows his own detailed description of how women must be trained to submit.) Contemporary feminist Nelle Morton agrees that women find it difficult to rebel. However, she does not agree that this is because of a woman's nature, but rather because "she has been led to believe that rebellion violates her femininity. . . . By her conditioned nature woman finds it hard to rebel—even from a sexist institution of which she is the victim" (69–70).

Thus the process of discovering and claiming women's authentic selves has needed to consist, first of all, in challenging "the sacred," the norm, the traditional ways, in what has been known in feminist movement as "consciousness-raising" or what hooks has called, after Freire, *conscientizacion*—radicalizing consciousness, which enables us "to know who we are as if for the first time" (*Talking* 31). Freire described this process in his *Pedagogy of the Oppressed* as "problem-posing education"— asking questions and listening to what arises. It is dialogue and communication.[11] It involves "a constant unveiling of reality, [and] . . . strives for the *emergence* of consciousness and *critical intervention* in reality" (62).

Self-discovery and radicalizing consciousness rely on truth-telling, to ourselves and others. The feminist method of consciousness-raising groups, in which women speak their own truths and listen to others, relies on women being honest with themselves and with each other.[12] Adrienne Rich's phrase, "When a woman tells the truth she is creating the possibility for more truth around her . . ." (*On Lies* 191), so aptly describes the process that takes place in consciousness-raising, as well as in honest friendships and family relations, feminist classrooms, and other feminist alliances. Self-honesty shared does create the possibility for more truths. Honest self-disclosure and the vulnerability it entails opens the way for others to speak their truths, often for the first time—even to themselves. As the process continues over time it can be very much what Freire described as "unveiling," as each layer reveals new truths.

Often the image of consciousness-raising is one of indoctrination, instilling in people a predetermined line of thought that must be accepted by all. But this has not been the case of the feminist method of consciousness-raising groups, in which women come to discover and own the truths of their own experiences, not to inculcate others with "the truth." The obligation demanded by feminism is not to adhere to a "line" but rather to adhere to one's truths.[13]

Feminist Critique of "Womanhood" and the Possibility of Self

Feminists have sought to overcome the obstacles to selfhood by claiming the necessary resources, developing a women-identified culture separate and apart from patriarchal culture, and discovering their authentic selves. But many feminists have been suspicious and critical of these attempts to discover and valorize womanhood and the self. They have argued that efforts to identify an "essential" womanhood are potentially oppressive since they could be used to confine women to particular gender stereotypes and gender roles. It seemed for a time that all feminist work became scrutinized for hints of "essentialism," and if found, condemned. Moreover, many feminists rather than finding themselves affirmed by these efforts to affirm womanhood, instead felt excluded and marginalized. They have argued that the history, religion, and language that have been "discovered" have been that of white women only. They have taken issue with the notion of "women-identified culture," arguing that it is based in the experiences, perspectives, and cultures of only certain women. Women of color have argued that the woman discovered in "women-identified culture" is a white/Euro middle-class woman, and that in their definition of "womanhood," white women have totalized their experiences onto all women (Lugones and Spelman). Or as Merle Woo put it, "universal is often a euphemism for 'white'" (144). They have argued further that women bonding against men creates an oppositional thinking that prevents women from seeing the multiplicity of women, as well as the ways that women have been against other women. Even consciousness-raising, claimed by women of color as well as white women as a valuable "feminist method," has been criticized for yielding only a "flattened" knowledge of the subject that reduces the experience of all women to gender, and distorts the conception of subjecthood that we are trying to affirm.[14] Norma Alarcón argues that in this flattening "we lose sight of the complex and multiple ways in which the subject and object of possible experience are constituted. The flattening effect is multiplied when one considers that gender is often solely related to white men. There's no inquiry into the knowing subject beyond the fact of being a 'woman'" (361). Judith Butler has argued that the normative character of "woman" is exclusionary in principle, creating both theoretical and political problems. The concept of "woman," problematic theoretically because it fails to recognize intersections of gender with race, class, ethnicity, age, sexuality, and other currents, fails politically because so many women do not recognize themselves as "women" as it is articulated by feminist theory (325).

One strategy that feminists have tried to deal with the problem of the concept of "woman" is to theorize gender as "multiple," that is, always different as it is constructed through race, class, sexuality, and so on. However, as Iris Young has pointed out, this carries its own problems of conceiving of race, class, sexuality as stable categories, as well as the problem of infinite regress that dissolves groups into individuals (*Intersecting* 19–20). A second strategy has been to conceive of "women" as the identity of those women who come together in collective politics, but due to the fluctuation and voluntary nature of the group membership this carries the problem that the identity of "women" becomes arbitrary (21). Though critical of these approaches, Young still believes that feminism needs some conception of women as a group prior to the formation of feminist politics (21). To this purpose, Young applies Jean-Paul Sartre's concept of seriality to gender. Unlike a "group," which is a collection of persons who recognize each other as being in a unified relation with each other, a "series" is a collection of persons "whose members are unified passively by the relation their actions have to material objects and practico-inert histories" (27). That is, the unity of the "series" "women" does not arise from women having a common nature, or from acting in common coalition (indeed, they are anonymous to each other), but rather reflects a common condition in which members of the series find themselves. The "series" unites women in social relations through structural relations, primarily those of heterosexuality and the sexual division of labor, that either enable or constrain their actions, behaviors, and roles (32).[15] That is, even though women may experience the common conditions of female existence differently from each other, they nevertheless understand themselves as "women" through these common structures of oppressions and constraints. I can identify you as being a "woman," like me, because we both are expected to orient our sexuality toward men (and if we don't, it is considered deviant); because we are valued for becoming mothers (within the institution of marriage, and if we don't, it's considered deviant); because we are enabled to be nurturing and caring and discouraged from being assertive and rebellious, and so on.

While this is a valuable way of understanding the concept of "woman," it still is far afield from the positive affirmation of dignity found in rebellion. Young argues that feminism is a reflexive group of women who seek to change or eliminate structures that socialize women as women. We know that what is revealed in their rebellion are the very structures that constrain them, but know nothing of what is revealed in their beings in this process. We know that they rebel against these structures, but we have no sense of what moves them to want to do so. I would argue that which so moves them to rebel is the sense of self-worth affirmed by rebellion, rather than the structures of the concept of "woman" that they seek to eliminate.

Butler would have feminists abandon this search for a common "womanhood," arguing that gender coherence, rather than being a "common point of liberation," is a "regulatory fiction" designed particularly to regulate our sexuality toward reproduction (339). Given this understanding, perhaps it would be more liberatory not to claim subjecthood at all. Indeed, deconstructionist feminists question the very presumption of the ontological integrity of "woman" and of the "self."

Memmi argued that though "the colonized who refuse" may go in search of their own identities, it is a fruitless journey, for they have only the self-identity invented and imposed on them by the colonizer. If the self is only that determined by the colonizer and internalized by the colonized, then the refusal to be colonized cannot be accompanied by an equal and simultaneous affirmation of the self. The same problem as articulated by deconstructionist feminists is that it is impossible for women to claim the self within masculinist, even misogynist, conditions and characterizations of women. Monique Wittig has been critical of the feminism she describes as "woman is wonderful," arguing that underlying it is a false consciousness that consists of selecting among the features of the myth of woman that look good and using them as a definition for woman. Deconstructionist feminists claim that every source of knowledge about women is so contaminated with misogyny and sexism that women indeed have no "self"; rather only a construct shaped by the oppressor (Alcoff 404). Thus is deconstructionist feminism nihilist with regard to the possibility of a female self.[16] "On a deep level," Julia Kristéva writes, ". . . a woman cannot 'be'; it is something which does not even belong in the order of *being*. It follows that a feminist practice can only be negative, at odds with what already exists . . ." (137). The whole idea of self as a unified subject is called into question by French feminists. For Kristéva the subject is not a unity, but rather multiple desires that do not cohere. The "subject" cannot always know what it means or wants, cannot be present to itself, cannot know itself (Young, "The Ideal of Community" 310).

A New Conception of Self—Multiple Selves

Nancy Hartsock raises the important question, "Why is it that just at the moment when so many of us who have been silenced begin to demand the right to name ourselves, to act as subjects rather than objects of history, that just then the concept of subjecthood becomes problematic?" ("Foucault" 163). Whether the "actual being" of a woman is denied selfhood by the oppressor or by deconstructionists in the name of liberation, the selfhood required for action and agency against oppression is still denied, and it is appropriate to ask why now, why this. Hartsock argues that those who would deny the possibility of subjecthood at this moment in time are suffering from a failure of imagination, and are still imprisoned in Enlightenment paradigms and values that can imagine a self only in opposition to a devalued Other, and that what we need is a new conception of the self that breaks out of the bounds of this paradigm ("Foucault" 164).[17]

Many feminists agree that rather than denying the possibility of the self, we need to reconceive the self, and that in doing so, we need to move beyond the oppositional self/other distinction.[18] I would suggest that Camus's dictum that we be "neither victim nor executioner" is helpful in this. Usually conceived as an ethic determining the appropriateness of our actions in the ethical and political sphere, it is useful to think of it as operating as well on an ontological level. In rebellion and rebellious feminism, claiming ourselves as subjects then means being neither victim nor executioner, neither the other nor the autonomous individualist self as traditionally defined by Enlightenment thought. Camus conceived the self as always in relation, but not in opposition.

Several feminists have written of this self that is defined not in opposition but rather in position—posing itself, in and of itself, in relation but not in comparison to any other—as a plurality of selves, "a site of multiple voicings."[19] "The new *mestiza*," Gloria Anzaldúa writes, ". . . has a plural personality . . . nothing is thrust out, the good, the bad and the ugly, nothing rejected, nothing abandoned" ("La conciencia" 379). Nellie Wong, speaking of herself, writes, "You are fueled by the clarity of your own sight, heated by your own energy to assert yourselves as a human being, a writer, a woman, an Asian American, a feminist, a clerical worker, a student, a teacher . . ." (180). This "whole" subject, rather than being found in a process of winnowing, is discovered in opening to its full multiplicity. As Anzaldúa goes on to say of the new *mestiza*: "not only does she sustain contradictions, she turns the ambivalence into something else" (379). Different from a synthesis, it moves her in the direction of a new consciousness. It is developed and continues to develop in relation to other selves who are in the process of developing, "an ongoing process of struggle, effort and tension" (Alarcón 365). Similarly Teresa de Lauretis has defined this subject as "fluid", as being always in process, and constantly renewed based on interactions with the world. To affirm the self then is to affirm it in its wholeness, diversity, multiplicity, and openness to change and discovery.

Self-Discovery

Rita Gross's application of Buddhist thought to feminist thought offers a helpful way of conceiving of this self in process and this process of self-discovery. Gross applies the Buddhist concept of "egolessness" to the feminist question of the subject (*Buddhism* 157–167). She explains that according to Buddhist thought, ego, (not to be confused with Western conceptions of ego), which can be manifested equally as helplessness or arrogance, exists only in opposition. It is based in a duality of "me" versus "the other." The ego develops a sense of being as an isolated entity confined in its own subjectivity, a subjectivity that in its need to be protected and defended, closes us off to direct experience. It can't allow anything to enter its consciousness or being that conflicts with its (and others') conception of its Self. Gender fixation is one part of ego. Thus to adopt either the femaleness constructed by patriarchy, or that conceived in opposition to patriarchy, is an exercise of ego. Egolessness, on the other hand, drops the burden of ego, and meets all experience with openness. But egolessness is not to be confused with nihilism, or a blank slate, or an indifference or spinelessness that allows oneself or others to be victimized. Rather, while not a reified Self, it is a healthy sense of self arising with awareness, much like the sense of self arising in rebellion, though the process of revelation is quite different. It is fluid and open, calm and compassionate, empowered and energized.

This description is reminiscent of Audre Lorde's sense of the erotic as "a measure between the beginnings of our sense of self and the chaos of our strongest feelings" (54). I liken her description of living on external directives to being directed by ego, and living by internal directives to a healthy sense of self:

> When we live outside ourselves . . . on external directives [read *ego*] only rather than from our internal knowledge and needs [read *healthy self*], then our lives are limited by external and alien forms, and we conform to the needs of a structure that is not based on human need, let alone an individual's. But when we begin to live from within outward, in touch with the power of the erotic within ourselves, and allowing that power to

inform and illuminate our actions . . ., then we begin to be responsible to ourselves in the deepest sense. (58, insertions mine)

In this sense, the erotic is a way of knowing and being that illuminates our sense of self. Lorde claimed that as we listen to the erotic within ourselves, we can discern the difference between those aspects of the self that are authentic and those that have been distorted by patriarchal consciousness. She wrote:

> Our erotic knowledge empowers us, becomes a lens through which we scrutinize all aspects of our existence, forcing us to evaluate those aspects honestly in terms of their relative meaning within our lives. . . . The fear that we cannot grow beyond whatever distortions we may find within ourselves keeps us docile and loyal and obedient, externally defined, and leads us to accept many facets of our oppression as women. . . . We have been raised to fear the *yes* within ourselves, our deepest cravings. But, once recognized, those which do not enhance our future lose their power and can be altered. (57–58, emphasis in original)

I suggest that the *yes* of the erotic and the "yes" of affirmation discovered in the act of rebellion are one and the same. The demand of this "yes" of the erotic as well as the "yes" of rebellion is that we honor and affirm the authenticity of the self it reveals. In this sense rebellion is "profoundly positive" (*Rebel* 19). While Camus claims that this discovery of rebellion leads "at least to the suspicion that a human nature does exist" (*Rebel* 16), he does not intend by this that we are essentially good, bad, selfish, altruistic, trusting, fearful, female, or male, but rather that before and beyond construction, lies something in each and every one of us that demands respect. It may be beaten or indoctrinated into submission or suppression, but it is always there, waiting to arise. And the moment of that arising is the moment of rebellion.

This passage from Nellie Wong's "In Search of the Self as Hero" speaks to the heart of the discussion of self-affirmation as it arises in rebellion:

> You believed once in your own passivity, your own powerlessness, your own spiritual malaise. You are now awakening in the beginnings of a new birth. Not born again, but born for the first time, triumphant and resolute, out of experience and struggle, out of a flowing, living memory, out of consciousness and will, facing, confronting, challenging head-on the contradictions of your lives and the lives of people around you. You believe now in the necessity and beauty of struggle: that feminism for you means working for the equality and humanity of women and men, for children, for the love that is possible. (180)

Conclusion

In concluding, I need to address one more important issue. Following up on de Beauvoir's own admission that only intellectual women can ever even conceive of themselves as conscious subjects, Norma Alarcón argues that knowing oneself as a conscious being, as a subject, requires a certain amount of privilege. Perhaps it does not require that all women be intellectual, but it does require, as we have seen, certain resources of knowledge, support, freedom to question, as well as a cultural norm of equality. She asks:

> what of those women who are not so privileged, who neither have the political freedom nor the education? Do they now, then, occupy the place of the Other . . . while some women become subjects? Or do we have to make a subject of the whole world? . . . Each woman of color cited here, even in her positing of a "plurality of self," is already privileged enough to reach the moment of cognition of a situation for herself. This should suggest that to privilege the subject, even if multiple-voiced, is not enough. (366)

I read this as meaning that it is not a sufficient feminist theory and not a sufficient basis for feminist practice, because it does not extend to all, and Camus would agree. Affirmation always comes hand-in-hand with resistance to oppression, saying yes and no simultaneously, and in this it is never just on behalf of oneself, but "for the sake of everyone in the world." In the quote that opened this chapter, Camus states that rebellion assigns oppression a limit "within which begins the dignity common to all." Rebellious refusal and affirmation is never solely for the good of the individual, but rather the good of all of humanity. Rebellion insists that the affirmation of one's own dignity necessarily extends to all.[20] Luisa Teish sums up this spirit of rebellion well:

> I am shooting for a world where everybody eats, where everybody has decent housing, where everybody has their basic necessities and the freedom to be who they are. The freedom to express the spirit that is inside of them. . . . That's all I'm after—is *everybody's right to express the spirit that lives in them.* (Anzaldúa, "OK Momma" 228)

Rebellious refusal and affirmation necessarily entail solidarity.

CHAPTER 4
CLAIMING ONE'S VOICE

O spirit of revolt, glory of the people, and vital protest against death, give these gagged men and women the power of your voice!

Camus, *State of Siege* 209

The rebel is one who *says* "yes" and "no;" the rebel is one who speaks up, talks back, protests, who claims her voice. An important aspect of refusing oppression and injustice and affirming human dignity is the rebel refusing silence and coming to voice. But in speaking of voice, we must first come to understand the condition that precedes it—silence.

Silence

In Camus's play, *State of Siege*, the new totalitarian ruler, the Plague, under the pretense of avoiding contagion, has ordered that all the townspeople be gagged with pads soaked in vinegar. Words, blamed as the carriers of infection, must be silenced. The scene that begins with a chorus of several voices, ends with a single voice, and finally a pantomime, during which the lips of all are firmly closed. Thus is the power of the people to protest the injustices, cruelties, and indiscriminate death sentences of the Plague eliminated.

Camus described the condition of the rebel prior to rebellion as one of silence. Themes of silence recur throughout Camus's works with many meanings, ranging from the inability to protest, to the act of protest itself, to a communion so immediate that words are not necessary.[1] However, the most significant among these for the understanding of the nature of revolt is the silence of despair, defeat, and oppression. We hear this in Camus's description of his mother, who due to the forces of poverty, deafness, and domination by her mother lived a life of oppression and "mute resignation" (*First Man* 80); and in Camus's own silent resignation to being beaten by his grandmother.[2] We hear it in his descriptions of the colonized population of Algiers as being silenced by the French and of the Hungarian writers under Soviet oppression as gagged (*Resistance* 127, 164), and he undoubtedly felt gagged himself during World War II as a journalist whose words were not acceptable for the "legitimate" press, and who was forced to write secretly in the underground press. He described the death, torture, and destruction rampant in the world in which he lived as "a vast conspiracy of silence" (*Neither* 28)—one in which "the plague has silenced every voice" (*The Plague* 155–156).

Just as Camus described the condition of the rebel prior to rebellion as one of silence, so have feminists described the condition of women as that of silence:

> The screams of the women in pornography are silence . . . . The flat expressionless voice of the women in the New Bedford gang rape, testifying, is silence. . . . Women who submit because there is more dignity in it than in losing the fight over and over live in silence. Having to sleep with your publisher or director to get access to what men call speech is silence. Being humiliated on the basis of your appearance . . . is silence. The absence of a woman's voice, everywhere that it cannot be heard, is silence. (MacKinnon 307)

As Susan Griffin writes, "These several centuries of the silencing of women are a palpable presence in our lives—the silence we have inherited has become part of us. . . . At the heart of our condition, what we know is silence" (*Pornography* 201, 236).

The theme of the pervasiveness of silence in women's lives recurs throughout feminist thought. Belenky and her colleagues relate women's accounts of their lives as "being silenced," "not being heard," "having no words," and "feeling deaf and dumb" (18). Gloria Anzaldúa writes of women-of-color being "besieged by a 'silence that hollows us' " (*Making* xxii). Tillie Olsen argues that multiple forces—family commitments, illiteracy, censorship, self-doubt—have combined to silence the voices of women in the literature of the world. Again and again, feminists write and speak about the silencing of women. Feminist social studies bear out what we have known—that in gatherings of women and men, women talk less and are interrupted more often; and when women do speak, that speech tends to be hesitant, qualified, question-posing, and devalued (Belenky et al. 17; Michell 381).

Adrienne Rich gives us this depiction of women in the classroom:

> Look at a classroom: look at the many kinds of women's faces, postures, expressions. Listen to the women's voices. Listen to the silences, the unasked questions, the blanks. Listen to the small, soft voices, often

courageously trying to speak up, voices of women taught early that tones of confidence, challenge, anger, or assertiveness, are strident and unfeminine. . . . Listen to a woman groping for language in which to express what is on her mind, sensing that the terms of academic discourse are not her language, trying to cut down her thought to the dimensions of a discourse not intended for her (*for it is not fitting that a woman speak in public*); or reading her paper aloud at breakneck speed, throwing her words away, deprecating her own work by a reflex prejudgment: *I do not deserve to take up time and space.* (*On Lies* 244)

"It is not fitting that a woman speak in public. . . . I do not deserve to take up time and space." There is perhaps no more vivid symbol of this in recent history than the *burqa* worn by women under the rule of the Taliban in Afghanistan. Under the Taliban, all women are required to wear the *burqa*, a head-to-toe garment, with a small woven mesh covering the face, that permits only the slightest amount of air to enter. Under it, women are neither to be seen nor heard, and the consequences of public speech are the lash, imprisonment, torture, or death.[3] The rule of the Taliban is but an extreme example of the silencing by state, church, cultural norms, husbands, fathers, sons, mothers and mother-in-laws, and self, that is the condition of so many women's lives.

Women living in various manifestations of tyranny—whether of the strict rule of the Taliban, or the prohibitions of their husbands, or their mothers' instructions to be "lady-like"—live in silence. In mute protest, they swallow their words. In response to the pervasive silence of women, Audre Lorde asks, "What are the words you do not yet have? What do you need to say? What are the tyrannies you swallow day by day and attempt to make your own, until you will sicken and die of them, still in silence?" (41–42).

Lorde herself said that what she regretted most in her life was her silences (41). And yet coming to voice can be so difficult, so fraught with fear and often with very real dangers. In that an ethic of rebellion claims the refusal of silence and the coming to voice as a positive good, it is important to understand those factors that contribute to the continuing silence of so many.

Conditions that Silence

Camus never systematically assessed the forces that contribute to the silencing of the oppressed. Certainly he recognized that prohibitions on freedom of speech silence people's protests, and in order to preserve the power to protest, held freedom of speech as the one absolute value.

However, he recognized that the ability to speak freely also rests on a certain amount of material well-being that not only supports one's physical capacity to speak but also guarantees that the consequences of one's speech do not endanger one's livelihood and very survival.[4] Similarly, feminists have considered several factors to contribute to women's silence, from the material conditions of poverty and motherhood with its daily demands and continual interruptions, to legal prohibitions against women speaking at all.[5]

Camus specifically identified three "afflictions" to be the causes of silence, these being servitude, falsehood, and terror (*Rebel* 283–284). Much feminist work on the silencing of women has also focused on these same three themes of servitude, falsehood, and terror, showing how they interweave to create conditions that lead to the silence in women's lives. We hear this vividly in the words of Gloria Anzaldúa and Susan Griffin:

> The dark-skinned woman has been silenced, gagged, caged, bound into servitude with marriage, bludgeoned for 300 years, sterilized and castrated in the twentieth century. For 300 years she has been a source of cheap labor, colonized by the Spaniard, the Anglo, by her own people. . . . For 300 years she remained invisible, she was not heard. Many times she wished to speak, to act, to protest, to challenge. The odds were heavily against her. She hid her feelings; she hid her truths; she concealed her fire; . . . . She remained faceless and voiceless . . . [under] her veil of silence. (Anzaldúa, *Borderlands* 22–23)

> The silence and the silencing of women. The creation of authority in the image of the male. Of god in the image of the male. Rape. The burning of witches. Wife-beating. Laws against women speaking in public places. Against women preaching. The imprisonment of suffragists. Force-feeding. Harassment on the public streets. Scorn for the woman who dares to *act like a man*. A woman's love for another woman, unspoken, hidden . . . . Woman's word pronounced full of guile . . . . (*Pornography* 201)

They give us strong images of the servitude of women to men within cultures of domination, in marriage, and in the service of the colonizers; of the falsehood of women's inferiority, the lie of the evil of her words, and of women hiding their own truths; and the terror of rape, abuse, battery, torture and murder, of having their babies—born and unborn—taken away from them. Servitude, falsehood, terror—these three causes of silence revealed in rebellion also emerge as causes of silence in women's lives. Examining each in turn helps to illuminate conditions that contribute to silence, and to the silencing of women in particular.

Servitude

Camus used the term "servitude" to denote a relationship of dominance and subordination in which human beings are related hierarchically to each other as Subject and Object. He used it, for example, to describe the condition of the victims of the Marquis de Sade's schemes of imprisonment and torture as well as the condition of the citizenry of Germany under Hitler who had been reduced to that of one ruler ruling over silent masses (or masses shouting slogans, which Camus said was the equivalent of silence) (*Rebel* 182). Camus argued that servitude silences because the oppressor and oppressed have nothing in common, not even, or not especially, their language (*Rebel* 283). Being in a one-up, one-down position reduces their conversation to a monologue flowing from the top, with no possibility of communication between them. However, certainly servitude silences for other reasons having to do with the hierarchy of power, which feminists have more thoroughly examined.

In portraying the servitude of women to men, as well as to other women, in both their individual and collective lives, feminists have detailed the servitude of women as slaves and as prostitutes, but also as secretaries, nurses, and domestic workers, mothers, wives, and daughters.[6] Women living and working in conditions of servitude may be silenced out of expectations of deference;[7] out of learned subordination;[8] out of demands for obedience; out of fear of loss of livelihood or loss of children, beatings, imprisonment, or harm to oneself or loved ones. Under conditions of dominance, the very act of speech is a threat (hooks, *Talking* 31), and punishment is considered an appropriate consequence. As Anzaldúa relates, even mothers and mother-in-laws tell sons to beat their wives for not obeying, for talking back, "for being *dociconas* (big mouths)" (*Borderlands* 16). Women, punished for speaking, become silent, or tell lies, which amounts to the same thing, because it is just another way of silencing their true thoughts and feelings.

Under patriarchy, servitude translates into an entire culture of domination that subordinates and suppresses the speech of women as a class. In Western culture, the Aristotelian premise that women are naturally subordinate to (free) men, and are incapable of the same moral reasoning as free men—a legacy handed down through the thought of Aquinas, Rousseau, Kant, and others—has served as the basis to exclude women from the collective moral discussion, and from having a voice in the governing of the societies of which they are a part. Similarly, Paul's admonition that women should not teach nor usurp the authority of men, "but to be in silence" (1 Tim.2:11) has long been used by Christian churches to justify the silencing of women in places of worship and from the exclusion of women from ministry and priest-hood, even to the present day. Other religions as well silence and exclude women. Until recently, Buddhist women have not been allowed to become priests; in Islamic mosques, women are kept separate from the men and keep silence; and the Hindu Law of Manu states that a female must be subject to her father, and then to her husband, and finally to her sons (Gross, *Feminism* 84). Fearing the capacity of the subordinate to express their voices, dominant cultures prevent their access even to a basic tool of the expression of that voice—literacy. Even today, 90 percent of the world's illiterate are women.[9]

However, even with literacy and opportunities to speak and write and be heard, within a culture of dominance, women still face the barrier to speech articulated by Camus, that the oppressor and the oppressed have nothing in common—not even their language, not especially their language.[10] Feminists have shown how the discourse of the oppressor is privileged over that of the oppressed. While the oppressed may understand the predominant language of the oppressor, the oppressor is unlikely to understand the world of the oppressed. The oppressed have to live, work, and function in the world of the oppressor, and in so doing have to learn its culture and language, whereas the oppressor is ignorant of the language and culture of the oppressed, or at best finds it incomprehensi-ble.[11] And this is as true between and among women as it is between women and men. As María Lugones has articulated:

> . . . we (Hispanas) have had to be in your (white/Anglo women) world and learn its ways. We have to participate in it, make a living in it, live in it, be mistreated in it, be ignored in it, and rarely, be appreciated in it. . . . we have had to learn your culture and thus your language and self-conceptions. But there is nothing that necessitates that you understand our world. (Lugones and Spelman 576)

As long as the oppressed and the oppressor speak only in the language of the dominant culture, and have no mutual knowledge of each other's language, or share a common language, the speech of the subordinate will be suppressed. Without common meaning and communication, speech between the two cultures amounts only to the sounds of silence.

Because the oppressor does not understand the language and world of the oppressed, in trying to communicate within the confines of the dominant culture the oppressed cannot speak in their own language. They may find it necessary to "slant" their communication in a way to make it more effectively heard by the dominant culture, but may lose some accuracy in the translation (Michell). Or they may be forced to express themselves in a language that is not their own, and that is inadequate to express their experiences and emotions and conceptualizations (Lugones and Spelman 575, 577), as exemplified in this excerpt of a letter from Cherríe Moraga to Barbara Smith:

> ". . . in my development as a poet, I have, in many ways, denied the voice
> of my brown mother—the brown in me. I have acclimated to the sound of
> a white language which . . . does not speak to the emotions in my poems.
> I turned only to the perceptions of white middle-class women to speak for
> me and all women." . . . I had disowned the language I knew best. (31)

As discussed in chapter three, based on the premise of linguistic theory that asserts that our very selves are constructed by the language in which we express and understand ourselves, postmodern feminists have argued that being forced to interpret and conceptualize their experiences and thoughts in the language of the oppressor may prohibit the oppressed from ever truly finding their liberatory voices. Subaltern women, living in cultures in which their subordination is believed in in a way that is sacred, similarly remain mute because they cannot even begin to conceptualize their subjection as injustice (Spivak 288; Jaggar, "Globalizing" 12).[12]

In sum, servitude and relations of dominance silence through fear, enculturation, legal prohibitions, the denial of a common language, and the usurpation of the very language itself.

Falsehood

Camus wrote about the problems created by falsehood and inauthenticity in many contexts, but in this context, we need to examine particularly the lies and deceptions that create silence by preventing people from discovering and claiming their voices. In this regard, Camus was particularly concerned with the lies of those who claimed to know the "Truth," and used that justification to manipulate others' perceptions of their own truths and to control others for their own purposes. He pointed, for example, to the way that St. Just, during the French Revolution, used Rousseau's notion of the General Will to put forth his own agenda and stifle dissent. Anyone whose truth was at odds with that of the General Will would literally be silenced—their tongues cut out or their heads cut off. He also criticized Stalinist Soviet Union for deliberately creating lies and justifying them as truths, again stifling dissent, for anyone seeking to expose the lies was purged—either executed or exiled to Siberian prison camps (*Rebel* 233, 283; *Neither* 29).

Susan Griffin has written that it is "the way of all ideology" to hide truths and control perceptions of reality (*Made* 162). And so just as totalitarian governments manipulate with lies that masquerade as truth and so silence dissent, so the patriarchal culture of dominance creates lies that keep women silent. Chief among these is the lie of the "good woman." The good woman is subservient. The good woman is passive. The good woman is silent as Sophocles admonished: "A modest silence is a woman's crown" (qtd. in Aristotle 36).

Girls and women have long received early training in how to be "the good woman." The words of Rousseau's manuals shaped the education of Western women for decades to come to parallel those of the lessons handed down from generation to generation, mother to daughter, culture to culture (the voice of Rousseau in italics):

> *. . . Make her a good woman, and be sure it will be better for both her and us . . .*
>
> My mother used to tell me that I should always be a good, obedient woman . . .
>
> *. . . habitual restraint produces a docility which woman requires all her life long, for she will always be in subjection to a man, . . . and she will never be free to set her own opinion above his. What is most wanted in a woman is gentleness; formed to obey a creature so imperfect as man, a creature often vicious and always faulty, she should early learn to submit to injustice and to suffer the wrongs inflicted on her by her husband without complaint . . . .*
>
> . . . I remember hearing my father criticize my mother, even about the smallest things. "The rice doesn't taste good enough! Now the meat is too hard! You are a bad woman, a stupid woman! No good." And all the while, my mother would go about fixing what she did "wrong" without uttering a word, just wearing her usual invisible mask of sadness. . . .
>
> *. . . If woman is made to please and to be in subjection to man, she ought to make herself pleasing in his eyes and not provoke him to anger . . .*
>
> I was trained to avoid conflict. When my brother lectured me, I'd reply "uh" and shake my head in agreement.
>
> *. . . their soft voice was not meant for hard words . . .*
>
> My voice was soft, sweet, and so delicious to the ear of authority . . . .
>
> *. . . teach them above all things self-control . . . .*
>
> I was punished with harsh reprimands and scorching displeasure if I talked back or offered an opinion, so I was silent. . . .
>
> *. . . Make her a good woman.*
>
> Yes, I was a good girl. Wordless. Humble. Obedient. A perfect Hmong woman.
>
> *. . . the life of a good woman is a perpetual struggle against self . . . .*
>
> My silence killed myself . . . (Thao 17; Rousseau 239, 242–246).

The lies are not solely constructed by men and patriarchal culture. Even in their attempts to express their own voices and to define themselves, privileged, usually white/Anglo women have constructed images of womanhood that are false in that they do not describe the experiences of women of color. Moreover, as outsiders, they have given accounts and interpretations of the lives and experiences of women of color in ways that have suppressed and silenced women of color's experiences of themselves (Lugones and Spelman 577).

Adrienne Rich writes of how patriarchal lying manipulates women, withholds facts that are important for women to know (*On Lies* 190), keeping women in submission and in silence. Further, women have also been expected to be complicit in the lie:

> We have been expected to lie with our bodies: to bleach, redden, unkink or curl our hair, pluck eyebrows, shave armpits, wear padding, . . . take little steps . . . .
> We have been required to tell different lies at different times . . . the Victorian wife or the white southern lady . . . expected to "lie still"; the twentieth-century "free" woman . . . expected to fake orgasms . . . .
> The lie of the "happy marriage," of domesticity—we have been complicit. . . . (*On Lies* 189–190)

The pressure to conform to lies about women's character and expected behavior leads women to silence anything in ourselves that does not fit the idealized norm. We learn to hide our feelings and to lead a false existence, molded to fit society's image of what a woman ought to be (Griffin, *Pornography* 205; Rich, *On Lies* 190). And so women put on masks—masks others impose and masks made from fear, to make themselves less vulnerable to oppressors (Anzaldúa, *Making Face* xvxvi). As the poet Mitsuye Yamada* writes:

> This is my daily mask
> daughter, sister
> wife, mother
> poet, teacher
> grandmother.
> My mask is control
> concealment
> endurance
> my mask is escape
> from my
> self . . . . (114)

---

* Yamada, Mitsuye, *Camp Notes and Other Writings*, copyright © 1976, 1980, 1986, 1988, 1992 by Mitsuye Yamada. Reprinted by permission of Rutgers University Press.

In understanding, interpreting, and conveying their own experiences, women succumb to pressures toward self-censorship—accepting entrenched attitudes, falsifying their realities—"telling it slant" (Olsen 44). What is more, the woman who is lying may then begin to believe the lies she is telling about herself. Or, as she feels in herself a being who contradicts the myth of womanhood, she may begin to believe she herself, rather than the myth, is wrong (Griffin, *Pornography* 201). She may doubt her own judgment and begin to feel a split in her consciousness (Lugones and Spelman 576–577). Or she may simply be driven mad. Whether uninformed, misinformed, doubtful, confused, self-deceived, broken in spirit, or simply insane, the woman who is lied to falls silent.

Terror

Finally, terror silences out of fear—fear of torture, of death, of moral annihilation. When speech leads only to torture and death, the world becomes mute (*Rebel* 184). Throughout *The Rebel*, Camus chronicled how terrorism has been used to silence and disintegrate the individual. In the sexual crimes, torture, and imprisonments of the Marquis de Sade; the terrorism of St. Just that sent hundreds of innocent people to the guillotine; in the terrorist assassinations by the Russian Decembrists; the Nazi concentration camps; the Soviet gulag, he found example after example of how the terror of random, indiscriminate torture and violence has been used to silence. Terror, he argued, transforms human beings into objects. Terror silences absolutely because it disintegrates and annihilates the individual through torture, propaganda, systematic degradation, and forced complicity (183–184).

In an essay written after World War II, Camus described the twentieth century as "the century of fear" (*Neither* 27). Having just lived through an era in which "men lie, degrade, kill, deport, torture," (*Neither* 28), people learned not to speak, seeing its futility and fearing its consequences. Perhaps even more compelling for our own century is Camus's argument that we live in terror because those in positions of power refuse to engage in dialogue, refuse to listen to any other truths than their own, refuse to consider any other viewpoints, especially the viewpoint that their own may be flawed. We live in terror because those in positions of power, locked up in their absolute ideas, their messianism, and their fascination with technology, live isolated from the rest of humanity and from nature, and have lost the ability to be moved by their suffering and their beauty. "We suffocate," he wrote, "among people who think they are absolutely right, whether in their machines or in their ideas" (*Neither* 29). Camus argued that in our fear we have come to accept a conspiracy of silence, fostered by those who benefit from this silence. Certain subjects are not raised; certain questions not asked. In fear, he argued, we become ready, eager to divest ourselves of our speech and civil liberties in exchange for security.[13] "And," he continued, "for all who can live only in an atmosphere of human dialogue and sociability, this silence is the end of the world" (*Neither* 29).

Feminists have similarly described the terrorism[14] that shapes and silences many women's lives. Carole Sheffield delineates the multiple ways that women's lives are shaped by terrorism—terrorism played out in the form of rape, partner assault, sexual abuse, sexual harassment, pornography (Sheffield 60–72). Andrea Dworkin echoes Sheffield's sentiments, writing, "Women are a degraded and terrorized people. . . . Rape is terrorism. Wife-beating is terrorism. Medical butchering is terrorism. Sexual abuse in its hundred million forms is terrorism" (200). Such terrorism gives men the power to intimidate, punish, and silence.

Rape terrorizes. Susan Griffin argues that women are never free of the fear of rape. It is a daily part of women's consciousness. Every girl is taught fear, and fear cripples self-expression. Fear of violence reduces us. Simply to deny our presence in the world becomes our best defense (*Rape* 4, 15, 60).

Pornography terrorizes. Dworkin calls pornography "the propaganda of sexual terrorism" (201). As it titillates with images of bound and brutalized women it creates a climate in which women are intimidated, silenced, and harmed (Dworkin 202). In pornography women are raped, battered, wounded, whipped, mutilated, degraded for others' fun and sexual excitement. And, Dworkin argues, such acts pass as normalcy, creating a climate of violence and intimidation toward women in which women's freedom of speech and movement is curtailed (200). Griffin concurs that the specific intent of pornography is to silence women, pointing even to the graphic images of women gagged with penises and other paraphernalia jammed down their throats (*Pornography* 88–93).

Gloria Anzaldúa speaks of "intimate terrorism"—the terror of abuse and battering within one's relationships, in one's home, in one's bedroom that creates silence out of fear and intimidation (*Borderlands* 20). Battered women learn to lie and keep silent to keep from being brutalized or killed. Dworkin and MacKinnon have argued that sexual abuse and battering take away women's freedom of speech. Not only do physical harm and the threat of further harm prevent speech, they also operate to so undermine a woman's psyche that she no longer trusts her experience of reality enough to speak.[15] In the experience of intimate terrorism, a woman does not feel safe even in her own culture or the inner life of her Self. Moreover, as Anzaldúa points out, women's speech is made even more difficult because their very bodies through which they would speak are stolen and brutalized (*Making Face* xviii).

Women lie and keep silent in the face of a terrorism that defines their lives—the terrorism of random, indiscriminate, unpredictable, and ruthless violence and harm. Living in fear—whether of judgment, or beatings, or punishment, or death, women become silent. However, as Audre Lorde has pointed out, "your silence will not protect you" (41). Paralleling Camus's recognition that one is never safe, that suffering and death, unjust as they are, are the conditions of human existence, comes Lorde's recognition that even if she had stayed silent, she still would have suffered and died (43). And with that recognition comes a certain liberation, a freeing up of the ability to speak.

Coming to Voice

Reflecting on the atmosphere of terror that had engulfed the twentieth century in silence, Camus argued that rather than blaming our silence on our fear, we had to face it and try to do something about it. This would involve cooperative efforts to alleviate material deprivation and the suffering and injustice of poverty, as well as the privileged foregoing their advantages. It would involve as well, at an international level, the collective definition of values by which all might live together in peace. It would necessitate new ways of living in the world, requiring that the rebel ". . . consistently oppose to power the force of example; to authority, exhortation; to insult, friendly reasoning; to trickery, simple honor" (*Neither* 50)—in other words, to turn the proverbial cheek, not as a sign of submission, but as an act of nonviolent resistance whereby one claims one's dignity and shows the power of another way.[16] And even before all the conditions of fear that silence are erased, it would require us to raise our voices. "Yes," he wrote, "we must raise our voices" (*Neither* 52).

Similarly, despite, indeed, because of the conditions that silence, feminists call upon each other to break their silence and come to voice—to resist:

> We are forced either to capitulate, to be beaten back by those images of abuse into silent acceptance of female degradation as a fact of life, or to develop strategies of resistance derived from a fully conscious will to resist. If we capitulate—smile, be good, pretend that the woman in chains has nothing to do with us, avert our eyes as we pass her image a hundred times a day—we have lost everything. (Dworkin 201)

Speaking out against domination and degradation is a fundamental act of resistance.

As Diego exclaims in *State of Siege*, the power of revolt is the power of claiming one's voice. The voice claimed in rebellion is the power to protest, to say clearly what is just and unjust (*Rebel* 291). It is the voice of the child uncovering the falsehoods and deceptions, declaring the king is naked (*Rebel* 237). It is the voice of the judge's wife in *State of Siege*, who, throwing off her subordination, says in response to her husband's commands to "Keep silent, woman!": "No, I must have my say. I have kept silence all these years. . . . I shall not hold my peace" (192).

The rebel, as Camus says, is one who turns and faces his or her master and then speaks in protest and refusal, and in affirmation. The rebel is one who says "no" and in that nay-saying also says "yes." In finding and expressing one's voice, one claims self-worth. In claiming the right to speak, even if it is only to say "no," one says "Yes, my words are worthy of being spoken and of being heard. Yes, I am worthy to speak. Yes, I am worthy." Lorde argues, "the transformation of silence into language and action is an act of self-revelation" (42). Thus, in claiming one's voice one discovers a loyalty to certain aspects of oneself—to that part of oneself that demands respect.

Feminists have argued that claiming one's voice is an essential aspect of developing a critical consciousness necessary for one's liberation and that being able to articulate one's own experience is a hallmark of self-determination.[17] Such speech becomes liberating in the movement from object to subject: "Only as subjects can we speak. As objects, we remain voiceless—our beings defined and interpreted by others" (hooks, *Talking* 12).

In many ways, the story of feminist movement is that of the movement from silence to speech, from objects to subjects.[18] Elizabeth Cady Stanton's silencing and banishment to the balcony during the World Anti-Slavery Convention in London (for it was not proper for women to speak) provoked her to organize the first Women's Rights Convention in Seneca Falls, New York in 1848. Yet she still found that again and again, ". . . liberal men counseled us to silence . . .," until finally ". . . we repudiated man's counsels forevermore; and solemnly vowed that there should never be another season of silence until woman had the same rights everywhere on this green earth, as man" (457). Similarly, over a hundred years later, Casey Hayden, after being patted on the head and told to be quiet at a gathering of Students for a Democratic Society, walked out and formed Redstockings. As Susan Griffin has written, "We are a community of those coming to speech from silence" (*Made* 219). How many stories could be told of women moving toward feminist awareness in that first moment of claiming one's words—the victim of sexual assault who first tells her story at a Take Back the Night rally, the battered wife who testifies in court of beatings, the quiet student who is moved to political action or to speaking up to her father by what she is learning in class.

Accompanying the theme of coming to voice is that of "unmasking"— throwing off the masks of deception and revealing one's true self. Feminists have sought liberation in refusing to wear both the literal and figurative masks of compliance to the expectations of female appearance, behavior, and expression demanded by their cultures:

> We women of color strip off the *mascaras* others have imposed on us, see through the disguises we hide behind and drop our *personas* so that we may become subjects in our own discourses. We rip out the stitches, expose the multi-layered "inner faces," attempt to confront and oust the internalized oppression embedded in them, and remake anew both inner and outer faces. (Anzaldúa, *Making Face* xvi)

In this coming to voice, in this unmasking, women refuse any longer to be silenced and hidden, and affirm that they do indeed deserve to take up time and space, to speak, and to be heard. This "transformation of silence into language and action" is the movement of rebellion.

In talking about the theme within feminist thought of "coming to voice" it is important that I am clear that what is meant here is *not* finding and claiming "*the* woman's voice," but rather of each woman coming to her own voice. Just as the notion of "woman" was originally so often conceived as the experience of white women only, so has the conception of "woman's voice" been for the most part that of privileged women who in conflating their own experiences with those of all women, have imposed their own voices and drowned out all others. The demand for "*the* woman's voice," such a central and significant task of feminist theory, has, ironically, been itself the source of silencing the multiple voices of women (Lugones and Spelman, 574).

From the perspective of rebellion, the configuring of "the woman's voice" as a single voice speaking for all women is an example of rebellion that has become forgetful of its origins. It no longer respects the dignity and voice of each person, but rather imposes one voice on all. It will be recalled that Camus consistently contrasted such "totality" with "unity" (*Rebel* 233, 240, 251).[19] Unity embraces diversity. Whereas totality is based in hierarchy in which difference is regarded as threatening, in unity, difference is affirmed and all are accepted as equals. Whereas totality speaks with one voice imposed from on high, unity emerges as multiple voices come together in a harmony that honors the uniqueness of each voice. Totality is a movement in opposition to the uniqueness of individuals and their values, and as such, the concept of "the woman's voice" found in early second-wave feminism is totalizing. Forgetful of its origins, it becomes oppressive. Rebellion requires the expression of multiple voices.

Feminists have struggled, and continue to struggle with issues of difference that have often been a source of deep division and distrust because of this very issue of silencing and exclusion. However, I would argue that, consistent with rebellion, contemporary feminists now widely regard the expression and the serious consideration of a diversity of voices to be a central tenet of feminist theory and practice.

While the initial process of claiming one's voice may establish feminist awareness and critical consciousness, it is only the beginning of feminist rebellion. Liberation is not something that one achieves in a moment and then rides the wave. When the slave turns and faces the master, says "no I won't" and "yes I am," it would be the exception for the master to back off and acknowledge that all are now free. More likely the master takes out the lash—a lash, (or backlash), that feminists know all too well. Despite women's coming to voice, and perhaps because of it, efforts to silence and subordinate women continue, and in some cases have intensified. Andrea Dworkin has remarked that men have met feminist rebellion with an escalation of terrorism, and the backlash against feminism has been duly noted and documented (Dworkin 201; Faludi).

Camus said that rebellion requires constant vigilance. Though Sisyphus, who was condemned by the gods to push the rock up the mountain, only to have it roll back down, was Camus's symbol of absurdity, I believe he also represents rebellion over the absurd. Just at the moment of achieving his goal, Sisyphus must turn and start over again. Yet, said Camus, one must imagine Sisyphus at the moment he turns to be happy, for he is stronger than his fate (*Myth* 91). Similarly, Patricia Hill Collins writes of feminist coming to voice, "persistence is a fundamental requirement of this journey from silence to language to action" (112). She quotes the song "A Change Is Gonna Come," in which Aretha Franklin sings, in a way quite reminiscent of Sisyphus, of how it's been an " 'uphill journey all the way.' " The rock keeps tumbling down; the rebel keeps returning to push the rock back up, even in the attempted silencing of backlash. This persistence, Collins writes, "is fostered by the strong belief that to be Black and female is valuable and worthy of respect" (112). It is the affirmation of rebellion—yes, I am worthy of respect—that enables us to go on.

Conditions that Make Coming to Voice Possible

If servitude, falsehood, and terror are the conditions which silence, then speech is made possible in conditions of equality, honesty, and safety. Undoubtedly some rebels come to voice spontaneously, despite conditions of servitude, falsehood, and terror in that moment described by Camus as having reached a limit when one refuses to take the abuse, humiliation, oppression any longer, and with no thought to the consequences, talks back. It would seem that everyone has the capacity to rebel when pushed to that limit. But Camus confined his consideration of rebellion and oppression to those situations and cultures in which the sacred order has already been challenged. Camus did not address the situation of those many oppressed for whom oppression is considered the norm, even a sacred norm. It seems not to occur to him that the very conditions leading to revolt may need to be challenged.[20]

Many of the oppressed have never found their voices, and creating the conditions in which the oppressed might come to voice has been one of the many tasks of feminist thought and action. Given the framework of rebellion, the appropriateness of this might be challenged as ideological or as the imposition of someone else's experience onto another. So I must be clear that creating conditions for speech is not the same as creating the speech itself. It is not indoctrination in a political ideology; nor is it imposed from without. Rather, it is the enabling of a critical consciousness arising from within.

Spivak suggests that in order to speak, in other words, in order to come to the point of rebellion, the subaltern woman must create her own language. But this is a collective process. She can overcome her silence only by working with other subaltern women to develop a language that expresses their shared experiences (Jaggar, "Globalizing" 12). Being part of a group that recognizes itself as sharing a common condition of oppression enables subaltern women to assume a collective identity with other women in similar situations. This expression of one's recognition of oppression requires a common language. As an example of the development of such a common language, Jaggar points to the distinct vocabulary of Western feminism—"womanism," "sexism," "date rape," "othermother," "double day," "male gaze" ("Globalizing" 13). The expression of the recognition of one's oppression also requires community. A single individual coming to awareness of oppression is likely to be labeled crazy and dismissed, whereas an entire community is not so easily dismissed, and can support each other in their truth-telling. They can help to keep each other sane.

In writing of the centrality of finding one's voice to black feminist thought, Patricia Hill Collins has similarly argued that black women finding their voices has been made possible by the creation of safe spaces in which women can speak their truths and come to self-definition. Specifically she names three safe spaces that have enabled black women to define themselves and claim their voices: (1) black women's relationships with each other; (2) black women's blues; and (3) black women writers (ch. 5). The latter two are particularly intriguing as spaces for the development of a subaltern language. In song and literature, black women have been able to develop a public language of their shared experiences.[21] But with regard to the necessity of community in coming to voice, I am particularly interested here in the first—black women's relationships with each other.

Many black feminists have written about the importance of black women's relations with each other for the development of voice. Collins argues that among friends and family, and within the more formal organizations of church and protest communities, black women provide the context and community to affirm one another's uniqueness and humanity (97). In community, black women listen to and affirm each other.

Bell hooks similarly writes of how her own voice was nurtured in a black community where the voices of black women were not silenced: "It was in this world of woman speech, loud talk, angry words, women with tongues quick and sharp, tender sweet tongues, touching our world with their words, that I made speech my birthright . . ." (*Talking* 6). She also describes the black homeplace as a site of resistance,[22] a safe space in which black women and men could develop the resources necessary for resistance (*Yearning* 41–42).

I am reminded by this of Audre Lorde's description of black women learning to mother themselves and each other. By mothering she intended a process by which black women establish authority over their own definition, and provide attention and concern to their growth, as well as acceptance. It is the affirmation of worth. It is the practice of:

> how to be tender with each other until it becomes a habit because what was native has been stolen from us, the love of Black women for each other. But we can practice being gentle with ourselves by being gentle with each other. We can practice being gentle with each other by being gentle with the piece of ourselves that is hardest to hold. (*Sister* 175)

In the context of that "rigorous loving," women can begin to tell the truth to each other, and "if we speak the truth to each other, it will become unavoidable to ourselves" (*Sister* 175).

These safe spaces have enabled black women to challenge the controlling images, the masks of conformity that black women, all women, have been required to wear. They are places where they could rip off the masks and internalized oppressions; places where they could move from victimization to self-definition; safe places first to say "no," and to become conscious and clear of one's self-worth.

These safe spaces bear strong similarity to more formalized consciousness-raising techniques that have so often been used by feminists to enable women to discover their own truths. A good understanding of this is given by Nelle Morton in her description of the process of consciousness-raising as "hearing into speech." In the consciousness-raising process, each woman is given all the time she needs to speak. She is not interrupted, not questioned, nor comforted—the process is not stopped in any way. The process is one of a hearing so deep that it enables speech that otherwise is blocked to come out. Here is Morton's description of one incidence of this:

> Hesitatingly she began to talk. Then she talked more and more. Her story took on fantastic coherence. When she reached a point of the most excruciating pain, no one moved. No one interrupted her. No one rushed to comfort her. No one cut her experience short. We simply sat. We sat in a powerful silence. The women clustered about the weeping one went with her to the deepest part of her life as if something so sacred was taking place they did not withdraw their presence or mar its visibility. Finally the woman . . . finished speaking. Tears flowed from her eyes in all directions. She spoke again: "You heard me. You heard me all the way." . . . . "You heard me to my own story. *You heard me to my own speech*". (*Journey* 205)

In the process, the other women walk alongside, accompany another woman, give her safe passage to go down to the depths. There is that sense of going down, uncovering layers, getting to the bottom of things, peeling off the layers of masking, of pain and protection, of lies and falsehoods, to reach clearer truths. Rich says we fear the void (*On Lies* 191), but the process of being heard releases the fear of the void in the sense that one at least has companions on the journey. In one example given by Morton, a woman described the "going down" as "nonspeech"—speech in a language that was not her own, and that was shrouded in patriarchal lies, and described the "coming up" (and that is an important aspect—one does not stay down but rather emerges in the finding of self) as having no words, but in needing to speak, finding the same words now had new meaning, that she had a new woman speech (*Journey* 128–129).

Morton calls hearing in this sense, "redemptive." It is redemptive of the person's spirit. It enables the actualization of a new consciousness, a new personhood. It enables the questioning of one's subordinate status and an affirmation of self that lies at the heart of rebellion. And this, according to Morton, enables rebellion: "there may come a time, and soon, when rebellion becomes her only positive response to that great source of life with which she is now in touch. . . . When the chips are down and women have to choose between what heard us to speech and the hierarchical voices that maintain control, we have no choice, for we know we are in touch with the life sources of our humanness" (*Journey* 60).[23]

In addition to hearing and listening, women create the conditions for each other's speaking by their own speech. As discussed in chapter three, the self-disclosure that occurs in feminist discourse often emboldens others to speak, or helps others to see the realities of their lives in a new way that moves them to speak. Also women enable each other's speech by reflecting their experience back to them in ways that are both accurate and affirming. Rita Nakashima Brock relates the Shinto tale of Amaterasu, the Sun Goddess whose brother, unhappy that he is a lesser god, defiles Amaterasu's sacred Weaving Hall and kills several sacred weavers. Amaterasu retreats to her heavenly cave and remains silent. The gods and goddesses place a mirror at the entrance of the cave and then lure Amaterasu out of the cave by raucous noise. When she emerges, she is so fascinated by her reflection in the mirror that they are able to rope off the entrance to the cave. Brock relates this tale to convey the message that we can help each other from retreating into caves of silence by being good mirrors to each other. A good mirror, Brock notes, is one that tells us the truth about ourselves, giving us wisdom and self-awareness (235–236). In this, I am reminded of Adrienne Rich's imperative that we reflect our and others' experiences accurately (*On Lies* 190).

Thus does our speech move us beyond individual liberation struggle to collective struggle:

> We are both speaking of our own volition, out of our commitment to justice, to revolutionary struggle to end domination, and simultaneously called to speak, "invited" to share our words. It is important that we speak. . . . When we end our silence, when we speak in a liberated voice, our words connect us with anyone, anywhere who lives in silence. (hooks, *Talking* 18)

As Camus said, in the rebellious refusal of silence and coming to voice, we surpass ourselves and identify with others (*Rebel* 17). And so we come to solidarity.

CHAPTER 5
SOLIDARITY

> Solidarity is founded upon rebellion and rebellion, in its turn, can only find its justification in this solidarity.
>
> Camus, *The Rebel* 22

Deeply embedded in the rebellious refusal of injustice and affirmation of dignity is the assertion that every act of rebellion extends to all. Rebellion is never just on one's own behalf, but is always an act of solidarity with the world. Solidarity is central to rebellion, yet its relationship with rebellion is complex. It is at once the discovery revealed by rebellion, the value maintained by rebellion, the motivation of rebellion, and the limit of rebellion. We see these various dimensions of rebellion played out in Camus's novel, *The Plague*.

In *The Plague*, the citizens of Oran, having previously led isolated lives caught up in their personal dramas and business dealings, find themselves flung together in a common destiny by the plague. The very circumstances of their lives, unchosen, bring them together in a solidarity of existence. However, among them is a reporter from Paris, Rambert. He does not belong there. Exiled by the plague from his home and the woman he loves, he resists the solidarity of the circumstances he shares with the people of Oran, and spends nearly all of the duration of the plague trying to escape from Oran. Yet, as months go by, even though an outsider, Rambert finds himself linked more and more to the community of solidarity, ultimately joining with the others in the effort to fight the plague. When Rambert finally does manage to obtain all the forged documents he needs to escape the quarantined town, he chooses not to leave. Having worked side by side with the doctor and others in fighting the plague during his enforced stay in Oran, he has developed a sense of responsibility toward his relationships with the people there. But one also finds in him that aspect of solidarity that is the compassionate choice to suffer with. At the moment he chooses to stay, his solidarity transforms from that of merely finding himself in a common condition of being plague-stricken, to that of refusing his chance to save himself and choosing instead to stay and cast his lot with those who are not saved. Rambert recognizes that his individual salvation from the plague would be meaningless in the face of leaving behind what has become his community. He chooses the solidarity of compassionate action.

The story that unfolds around Rambert in *The Plague* reveals various dimensions of solidarity that emerge in Camus's ethic of rebellion. The first, to which Camus referred as the "solidarity . . . born in chains" (*Rebel* 17), is the metaphysical solidarity stemming from the imposition or recognition of a common fate or condition. The second is a sense of responsibility toward sustaining relationships and mutual understanding that often emerge from working together in common cause or in extended dialogue with one another. Third is that dimension of solidarity that refuses individual salvation if it must be paid for by oppression and injustice toward others—the generosity of compassionate solidarity.

A fourth dimension of solidarity is revealed through the character of Tarrou, one of the citizens of Oran who has put his efforts toward combating the plague. Through their common struggles, he and the doctor, Rieux, have become friends, yet they know little of each other. One night, Tarrou takes it upon himself to reveal his life story to Rieux, and in a somewhat confessional way tells Rieux that he had plague before he ever got to Oran, which, as he said, is tantamount to saying he was like everyone else:

> And thus I came to understand that I, anyhow, had had plague through all those long years in which, paradoxically enough, I'd believed with all my soul that I was fighting it. I learned that I had had an indirect hand in the deaths of thousands of people; that I'd even brought about their deaths by approving of acts and principles which could only end that way. . . .
>
> For many years I've been ashamed, mortally ashamed, of having been, even with the best intentions, even at many removes, a murderer in my turn. As time went on I merely learned . . . that we can't stir a finger in this world without the risk of bringing death to somebody. . . . I have realized that we all have plague, and I have lost my peace. . . . I only know that one must do what one can to cease being plague-stricken, and that's the only way in which we can hope for some peace or, failing that, a decent death. This, and only this, can bring relief to men and, if not save them, at least do them the least harm possible and even, sometimes, a little good. . . .
>
> All I maintain is that on this earth there are pestilences and there are victims, and it's up to us, so far as possible, not to join forces with the pestilences. (*Plague* 227–229)

We all have plague, and in that there is again a certain metaphysical solidarity of existence. But more to the point here is the conclusion that Tarrou draws from this fact, which is not to join forces with the pestilences. The fourth dimension of solidarity revealed by rebellion is the refusal to oppress, the refusal to join in any way with the forces of injustice and domination, and yet always with the somber realization that "we can't stir a finger in this world without the risk of bringing death to somebody."

Camus never systematically spelled out what he meant by solidarity, and often used the terms solidarity and compassion interchangeably. In his discussion of rebellion, he intertwined the four elements I have identified: (1) metaphysical solidarity; (2) solidarity in relationship; (3) compassionate action; and (4) refusal to oppress. So it is at risk of distorting his meaning of solidarity, but in hopes of elucidating it that I examine each dimension in turn, and show how each is also developed in feminist thought.

Metaphysical Solidarity

The solidarity of chains is the metaphysical solidarity discovered in the process of rebellion itself. In the act of rebellion, one recognizes that suffering is collective—that the sufferings and injustices experienced by a single individual are in reality a "mass plague" (*Rebel* 22). The rebel recognizes that all of humanity shares a common condition—that we're all in this together. But more significantly, in the act of rebellion, the rebel discovers a dignity common to all. In risking everything to defend the part of one's being that demands respect, the rebel is making a larger claim, necessarily implying by one's risks that this value extends beyond the self. Thus in rebelling one asserts oneself "for the sake of everyone in the world," claiming that which has been infringed upon extends to all. That which resists oppression in oneself simultaneously demands that no one be treated with anything less than the deepest respect of the dignity and meanings of their lives. As Camus said, rebellion plays the same role as the *cogito* does in the realm of thought, "I rebel, therefore we exist" (22). In his *Notebooks*, Camus wrote that his intention in *The Rebel* was to show how rebellion, by its very logic, refuses selfish motives (125), and that is exactly the case of the metaphysical solidarity discovered in rebellion. It follows logically from the act of rebellion itself. The act of rebellion is not egoistic or selfish, but rather, in accepting death (or, I would extrapolate, other self-sacrificing gestures—loss of job, money, power, status) it is an act in the name of a common good that transcends the individual. "Every insubordinate person, when he rises up against oppression, reaffirms thereby the solidarity of all" (*Resistance* 104).

This sense of the metaphysical solidarity of common suffering and dignity has been both an important focus and a significant problem in feminist thought. Though usually spoken of in terms of "sisterhood" rather than "solidarity," feminist rebellion has revealed a sense of the shared oppression of all women—the common conditions of domination and subordination to men; of violence, rape, and exploitation; of being regarded as "the Other" to Man. Sisterhood has been conceived as the common victimization of all women by all men, who are regarded as the oppressor, or more generally, as the common oppression of women under conditions of patriarchy, and women's bonding and collective rising up in solidarity against oppression and in affirmation of women's worth. This sense of sisterhood often emerged from consciousness-raising groups, in which women in the process of self-disclosure discovered the commonality of their experiences with those of other women. The term "sisterhood is powerful" is symbolic of the second-wave feminist urging for all women to use the solidarity found in these discoveries of commonality to join in common cause with all other women against this oppression.

However, this notion of sisterhood has fallen under two critiques: first, that rather than acting in solidarity with other women, women often oppress other women, and second, that white middle-class feminists narrowly conceived the notion of "sisterhood" around their own issues in ways exclusive of other women. I explore each critique in turn. The first critique of feminist sisterhood is that women, especially women privileged by race, class, and sexuality, are often the oppressors of other women, particularly low-income women, lesbians, and women of color. Bell hooks cites three barriers to bonding among women (1) racism; (2) classism; and (3) sexism toward other women in the forms of trashing, disregard, and professional and competitive violence (*Feminist* 43–65). Racism, particularly that of white women toward women of color, has been most frequently targeted as undermining solidarity among women, within and without of feminist movement. Nancie Caraway has argued that the reality of the notion of "sisterhood" is that it is a "segregated sisterhood," which needs to be discarded. Many trace its manifestation among first-wave feminists and their willingness to use racist arguments to gain support for women's suffrage, as well as the complicity of so many white women in the bondage and rape of black women as slaves. The legacy of racism in feminist movements continued in relationships between black and white women in the civil rights and second-wave feminist movements.[1] Bonnie Thornton Dill argues that this history of oppression and exploitation on the part of white feminists serves as a barrier to any possibility of an all-inclusive sisterhood.

Racism and classism among women and in the feminist movement often go hand-in-hand. Hooks is critical of what she calls "self-proclaimed 'white power feminists'" who undermine feminist politics by placing their own goal of enabling individual white women to gain access to ruling-class wealth and power at the center of the movement (*Killing* 100). In addition, in their pursuit of high-paying, powerful jobs in the name of feminism, upper- and middle-class white women have often relied on working-class women, often women of color, to provide domestic services and childcare at low wages, rather than seeking a greater contribution from the men in their lives, or seeking policy changes that would allow for such things as flex-time, day care, and universal health care that might enable a better distribution of income to all. Hooks argues that the racism and supremacist attitudes of such "feminists" suggest that solidarity among women can never be realized. They also lead women and men of color to reject feminism on its face because they associate feminism with white power feminism. Claiming that liberal feminism ignores or slights issues of poverty, race, and injustice, Jean Bethke Elshtain has also questioned the adequacy of liberal feminism. She argues that liberal feminism is not able to give substance to its demands for liberation and equality, because it regards feminist progress primarily as the integration of a few well-educated, privileged, primarily white women into the existing system—hardly a picture of solidarity (*Public Man* 247).

Racism and classism between women also manifests in the oppression of Third World women by First World women. In addition to the general arrogance of First World feminists toward Third World (Mohanty), First World women are complicit in the oppression of Third World women through imperialism, violence and war, and Western patterns of consumption and development.[2] Like Tarrou in *The Plague*, Pamela Brubaker tells us we must recognize the almost inevitable collusion of First World women in the oppression of Third World women because of the webs of oppression in which First World women are entangled.

Sexism toward other women manifests itself in trashing and disregard of other women, as well as professional and competitive violence toward one another. This may simply be a matter of denigrating other women—such as feminists putting down other women who are not feminists, or of critiquing feminists who practice a different form of feminism from themselves. Women who have spent their lives as homemakers and mothers have felt their life's work demeaned and devalued by those feminists who claim that all such work is oppressive and that the only road to liberation is in joining the "higher" sphere of work outside the home, or to use de Beauvoir's term, the realm of transcendence—of creativity and activity. Those who have spent their lives toiling in oppressive and demeaning work outside the home and not found such work to be at all liberating, and who would welcome the haven of the home, have found their experiences ignored and thus devalued by those same feminists (hooks, *Ain't* 191 and *Feminist* ch. 7). And within the workplace, women adopting masculinist strategies to get ahead willingly climb over each other on the way to the "top," rather than "lifting as we climb." Women in relationship with men have found their affiliations and affections demeaned by those feminists who have argued that only those women who cut their ties to hetero/male privilege can be trusted (Bunch 166). Competition for men turns women against each other, and jealousies and backbiting occur within the lesbian community as well. And these are only some of the ways that women oppress other women. As Weisser and Fleischner have pointed out, the oppression of women by other women is multifaceted—public and private, historical and contemporary, theoretical and practical—ranging across not only race and class, but also sexual orientation, nation, ethnicity, religion, political ideologies, researcher and subject, mother and daughter, and sister to sister.

The other major critique of the feminist notion of sisterhood is that sisterhood so conceived has been that of a narrow group of white middle-class women organized around white middle-class concerns. The foundation of metaphysical solidarity, "I rebel, therefore we exist," raises the problem of identifying exactly who that "we" is, and too often the "we" of feminist sisterhood has been based solely on the experiences of white middle-class women. Critics have argued that this notion of sisterhood, as mythologized by white feminists, is based in an organic and affectional bonding that masks pressures of conformity and erasure of difference. Lynet Uttal describes feminist sisterhood as "protecting ourselves from any differences, maintaining at all costs an image of solidarity" (318). Thus we encounter here again, in slightly different terms, the dilemma of balancing the universal and the particular, commonality and differences—of achieving unity in diversity rather than totality. But here, rather than "woman's voice," it is the concept of "sisterhood" itself that has come to be regarded as an oppressive, totalizing concept.

Calling into question the very idea of a "fundamentally common female experience" that has been seen as a prerequisite for political unity (*Talking* 23), bell hooks has criticized what she calls a "false sisterhood" based on a shallow notion of bonding as victims of men's oppression (*Feminist* 43). Audre Lorde has similarly written of how the term "sisterhood" is a pretense of homogeneity of experience that is actually white women's experience (116). Bonnie Thornton Dill, while acknowledging sisterhood as an important unifying force in the women's movement, also recognizes that it has engaged only a few segments, largely white middle-class, of the female population. She also claims that though sisterhood among black women has been a fundamental of black women's relationships in the church and women's organizations, black women have felt alienated from the concept of sisterhood as it has been used in the feminist movement to place concerns regarding sex above those of race. Similarly Norma Alarcón has argued that the pursuit of a "politics of unity"[3] solely based around gender that is found in the notion of sisterhood prevents the true "pursuit of solidarity." Indeed, she has said that rather than being an expression of solidarity, sisterhood is a barrier to it (364).

Many have argued that the concept of sisterhood based on an assumption of women's similarities needs to be abandoned.[4] But while feminists have called for an abandonment of the notion of sisterhood, they have not abandoned the possibility of solidarity. Building on the wisdom of Audre Lorde who wrote, "it is not our differences which separate women but our reluctance to recognize those differences" (122), they have sought a solidarity that builds on the strengths of difference and plurality, rather than denying difference.[5] This strongly parallels Camus's concept of unity based in differences and multiple voices. He argued that "our differences ought to help us instead of dividing [*sic*] us . . . I believe only in differences and not in uniformity. . . . because differences are the roots without which the tree of liberty, the sap of creation and of civilization, dries up" (*Resistance* 136). Karen Baker-Fletcher has referred to this revised notion of "sisterhood" as "sisterist," that is, womanist[6] yet in solidarity with diverse types of women (9). Hooks argues:

> Women do not need to eradicate difference to feel solidarity. We do not need to share common oppression to fight equally to end oppression. We do not need anti-male sentiments to bond us together, so great is the wealth of experience, culture, and ideas we have to share with one another. We can be sisters united by shared interests and beliefs, united in our appreciation for diversity, united in our struggle to end sexist oppression, united in political solidarity. (*Feminist Theory* 65)

This statement by hooks suggesting that we can be united in our struggle to end sexist oppression comes closest to Camus's meaning of metaphysical solidarity, for it is a solidarity that is revealed in a common struggle against oppression that also reveals a common dignity. This is not the same as a common nature. Metaphysical solidarity has been problematic for feminism because for a long time feminism confused the notions of common struggle and dignity with common nature. If there are common conditions of "womanhood," though experienced differently, as Young has suggested (*Intersecting* ch. 1),[7] then they are ones imposed by political and societal norms and structures, not by a common ontology. A more fruitful avenue of solidarity for feminism is to be found in persistent efforts to understand each other across our differences—the element of solidarity in relationship.

Solidarity in Relationship

A second aspect of rebellious solidarity is the work of sustaining relationships across differences, of coming to understand one another, particularly through efforts at sustaining dialogue. For Camus, solidarity is built from mutual understanding, which comes from continual and persistent efforts of diverse peoples to know and be known, in the hopes of revealing the truths that lie between us. Dialogue is central to rebellious solidarity, especially solidarity across differences. Camus argued that "the mutual understanding and communication discovered by rebellion can survive only in the free exchange of conversation" (*Rebel* 283). For Camus, while solidarity may be discovered ontologically, it must be sustained dialogically.

Toward this end, several feminists have built upon the "communicative" or "discourse" ethics of Jürgen Habermas, which seeks to discern a moral consensus through the use of procedures of discourse. But rather than using discourse ethics to form a moral consensus, feminists such as Sharon Welch, Jane Braaten, Nancy Fraser, and Jodi Dean have argued that a more inclusive and transformative goal for discourse ethics is that of solidarity. Solidarity in this sense is regarded as granting each group or individual sufficient respect to listen to and be challenged by each other (Welch 132–133). I have found Jodi Dean's concept of "reflective solidarity" to be especially helpful in elucidating the potential of discourse ethics for achieving solidarity. She defines "reflective solidarity" as "the mutual expectation of responsible orientation to relationship" (29). She distinguishes her notion of "reflective solidarity" from three other forms of solidarity: (1) "affectional solidarity"—the bonds of mutual care and concern growing out of relations of love and friendship; (2) "conventional solidarity"—the bonds of common interests and concerns, of common struggle and expectations to conform to group norms; and (3) "tactical solidarity"—the temporary bonds formed by coming together in coalition politics. She conceptualizes "reflective solidarity," on the other hand, as engaged discourse among strangers who disagree with one another, yet are committed to working toward relationship with one another. Dean's concept of reflective solidarity resembles Camus's concept of solidarity in several ways. In its rejection of conceiving solidarity as a politics of "us versus them," the concept closely parallels the rebellious refusal to degrade or humiliate anyone, and its affirmation instead of the common ground that lies between us all.[8] Also, like Camus's solidarity of unity in diversity, Dean's reflective solidarity attempts to bridge the universal and the particular. Because her work so closely resembles Camus's, it is helpful to use her reflective solidarity as a framework within which to explore this aspect of rebellious solidarity as relationship. Four key points emerge from Dean's conceptualization of reflective solidarity, these being: (1) basis in disagreement; (2) accountability for exclusion of others; (3) responsibility for relationship; and (4) universality. I examine each of these in terms of both Camusian and feminist notions of solidarity.

Basis in Disagreement

So often, solidarity is built around "us versus them" politics, in which "likes" rally in solidarity around "likes" against those who are "other." Reflective solidarity, on the other hand, is built on the mutual recognition of diverse others, rather than the exclusion of someone else. Thus, unlike conventional solidarity that presumes shared experience, reflective solidarity assumes difference and disagreement, and seeks to create solidarity across those differences through discussion. Similarly, rebellious solidarity refuses the totalitarian impulse to solidify as "one" against a totalized enemy, and embraces instead a unity built on diversity. Dean argues that the "we" of solidarity, rather than being imposed as a totality from without, instead is "discursively achieved," meaning that rather than being constituted as a group solidified against a common enemy, the "we" is constituted "through the communicative efforts of different 'I's'" (29).

Dean's development of this point is informed by Lynet Uttal's account of her experiences of "dialogue," as a woman of color, within Anglo feminist groups. Uttal found these groups to be "supportive," in the sense that no one challenged what anyone had to say—no one disagreed, argued, or even asked questions. When anyone spoke, everyone simply nodded their heads in supportive agreement. However, rather than facilitating her speech and openness, she found that in this atmosphere she rehearsed her words over and over, and still regretted that she had spoken. The polite nods silenced her. Uttal argues that true solidarity can only be built out of dialogue that is willing to "get messy" (319)—meaning that we ask questions, disagree, discuss our similarities and our differences. We validate one another, make each other part of the conversation, only by raising questions and disagreements. Her thoughts are reminiscent of Audre Lorde's injunction that despite our fears of anger, we need to be able to express it. To hide our anger trivializes our efforts, whereas its expression moves us toward clarification of our understandings of each other (127, 130). Others as well have argued that discourse that leads to solidarity requires more than dialogue that amounts merely to tolerance of one another, but rather requires genuine confrontation and active engagement of each other (Welch 16–17). Dean has argued as well that criticism, rather than being unsupportive, actually furthers intersubjective recognition. Reflective solidarity relies on the mutual expectation of each that they are willing and able to make claims, and are able to accept or reject claims of others on the basis of good reasons. It requires a willingness to take risks and engage with each other.

This willingness to take a stand is a central aspect of Camusian dialogue. For example, in his essay, "The Unbeliever and Christians", even though he does not share their beliefs, he calls on Christians to end their passivity and silence toward the political events of the day, and to speak out clearly on their beliefs: ". . . The world of today needs Christians who remain Christians. . . . What the world expects of Christians is that Christians should speak out, loud and clear . . . in such a way that never a doubt . . . could rise . . ." (*Resistance* 70–71). For Camus, dialogue does not mean convincing everyone of the same point of view, or of persuading others to one's own point of view, but rather it is a process of a mutual discovery of agreement that requires that people remain true to themselves (*Resistance* 70–71).

In addition to taking a stand, dialogue requires that each remain open to each other. Sprintzen describes Camusian dialogue as that in which both parties, committed to a world of partial truths and multiple perspectives, remain open to learning and growing, and modifying their position (247). Patricia Hill Collins has similarly described the feminist Afrocentric process of dialogue as one in which, though speaking from their own standpoint, each person or group recognizes that their knowledge is partial, making them better able to consider others' perspectives (236–237). Such openness to learning requires a willingness to ask questions, and to listen to and hear what the other person is saying.

In this respect, Dean emphasizes the importance of "the query" highlighted by Uttal. As Uttal writes, ". . . a question or response lets me know that someone is listening to me and working with me to understand. Instead of a patronizing nod, I prefer the query which makes my comments a building block in the discussion" (319). Others have similarly emphasized the importance of raising questions to feminist discourse practices and building feminist solidarity (Jaggar, "Toward"; Young, *Intersecting*). Young argues that in asking questions we show respect for others because we acknowledge that the questioner does not know what the issue looks like for them. The other aspect of the query, as noted by Uttal, is that it signifies that someone is listening. Other feminists as well have emphasized the importance of listening as an active process.[9] As an example, I have found active listening to be a fundamental aspect of feminist pedagogy, not only in my listening to the queries of students, but also in their coming to understand each other. At times in my classroom when the divisions and antipathies have become so strong that no one is capable of listening and people have felt silenced, the only way through those divides has been to engage the students in specific exercises designed to enable them to listen to each other, especially those whom they discount and feel discounted by.[10] Listening requires moving past walls of anger and hatred, and this takes deliberate effort and process. Camus wrote of the Algerian–French conflict, "Locked up in his rancor and hatred, neither one can listen to the other. Any proposal, which ever side it comes from, is received with distrust, distorted at once and made unserviceable" (*Resistance* 137). And so old wounds can pile up for generations. So just as openness to learning, or what Young has called, after Irigaray (72–82), an attitude of wonder, requires listening, so does genuine listening require an attitude of wonder. With this attitude we are open to the newness and mystery of the other person, even those we know well, recognizing the other as a person always in process (Jaggar "Toward"; Young, *Intersecting* 56).

In sum, a reflective solidarity with a basis in disagreement assumes difference rather than sameness, yet tries to build solidarity across difference by being willing to "get messy"—that is to struggle with each other, to confront, to disagree, to raise questions and to listen—recognizing that these are all ways we engage with each other and validate each other's perspectives.

Accountability for Exclusion

A second key point in Dean's reflective solidarity is the recognition that in our discourse we have a responsibility toward excluded others. This means that we need as much as possible to incorporate the standpoints of others, as well as to recognize the limits of our abilities to do so. Dean suggests that in order to do so we should keep in mind the perspective of what she calls "the situated hypothetical third." The "third" represents an outside perspective, one that is embodied and concrete, from which to evaluate the norms and experiences of the group. The role of the hypothetical third is to keep us accountable for our exclusions, to expose our omissions and blind spots (33–34).

Others have made similar arguments.[11] Because many of these draw, at least in part, on Hannah Arendt's conception of "enlarged mentality," (what others have called "enlarged thought,")[12] it is important to articulate that here. Arendt argued that the development of conscience is a "thinking together," and that "this enlarged way of thinking cannot function in strict isolation and solitude; it *needs the presence of others* 'in whose place' it must think, whose perspectives it must take into consideration . . ." (*Between* 220, emphasis mine). In other words, my own thoughts in isolation and the development of my conscience on my own, lack the wider perspective required in moral and political judgment because my actions affect and include others. The opinions of all who will be affected need to be heard, or at least anticipated, in my coming to judgment. Moral judgment, that is, the development of conscience, is not an enterprise of isolation, but rather one of a coming together of the many voices of those affected.

As Seyla Benhabib has pointed out, Arendt's suggestion that we "think from the standpoint of everyone else" requires both a consideration of every unique standpoint (what Benhabib means by "the concrete other"), and a universal respect for all standpoints (what Benhabib means by "the generalized other"),[13] a respect that is different from agreement or considering all arguments as equally valid. The consideration of every standpoint of course may be an impossibility. How can we possibly gather together all affected persons? It implies as much of an attitude as a reality, an attitude that abhors the arrogance of solipsism. It is a recognition of the value of each person. This is different, Benhabib argues, from empathy because it requires making the other standpoints present—in reality or simulation. It requires a moral dialogue with all concerned (*Situating* 136–140).

On this point, Camus's thought strongly parallels that of Arendt, Benhabib, Dean, and others.[14] As Jeffrey Isaac has argued, "this searching incorporation of the standpoint of others, even when these others are opponents, is the hallmark of Camus's political thinking"

(170). This aspect of Camus's thought is particularly highlighted in his factual and fictional accounts of "the fastidious assassins," (the members of the Russian terrorist organization, the Organization for Combat of the Socialist Revolutionary Party, who in 1905, assassinated the Grand Duke Sergei) (*Rebel* 165–173; *The Just Assassins*). Camus singled them out, because they were both dedicated to their cause and "they never ceased to be torn asunder by it." They "suffered from scruples; were always prey to doubts. . . . The greatest homage we can pay to them," Camus remarked, "is to say that we would not be able, in 1950, to ask them one question that they had not already asked . . ." (*Rebel* 167).

In Camus's play based on the incident, *The Just Assassins*, much of the dialogue centers around this questioning and doubting process. The centerpiece of the play is Kaliayev's moment of doubt, in which he refuses to throw the bomb as originally planned because there were children in the carriage. The discussion that ensues between the hard-hearted and ideological Stepan and all of the others is a testimony to the centrality of continual questioning to the rebellious enterprise. In Camus's testimony, they asked themselves every question. They were scrupulous, fastidious in seeking out other possible standpoints, at least among themselves and in their internal dialogue.

However, as mentioned in chapter two, in the play, Camus also raised a problem in their dialogical process. The problem of course is that though the assassins engaged in dialogue with each other and in their dialogue tried to examine their actions from a variety of the standpoints of those who would be affected by their decision, this dialogue was largely internal to the group. Internal dialogue is problematic in that it still does not fully nor accurately incorporate the standpoint of others outside the group. In the play, Camus used the vehicle of the perspective of the Grand Duchess, the wife of the assassinated man, to make the point. After her husband is killed, the Grand Duchess approaches his assassin, Kaliayev, who is now imprisoned, with her standpoint of her loss and her love for a man she knew as kind and caring—a standpoint that the assassins have perhaps not brought up and here discount of little relevance in the larger political picture. She also informs them that their assumptions about the Grand Duke are wrong. Whereas Kaliayev has projected the Duke's niece and nephew as innocent, and the Grand Duke as hard-hearted and oppressive, the Grand Duchess lets him know that he has got it wrong. When Kaliayev says that he spared the children, saying that they were not guilty, she responds:

> How can you be so sure? My niece is a heartless little girl. When she's told to give something to poor people, she refuses. She won't go near them. Is not she unjust? Of course she is. But my poor husband was very fond of

the peasants. He used to drink with them. And now you've killed him! Surely you, too, are unjust. (287–288)

How can he be so sure? That is the point here. Camus used this vehicle to remind us of the standpoints that may be missed—to point out that perhaps the assassins did not take every perspective into account, or represent them accurately. They only assumed they knew the perspective of the Grand Duke, but in reality, they did not know it. Each carries only a partial perspective, and needs the perspectives of others to correct and fill in the whole picture.

The point raised here by Camus has also been picked up on by feminists grappling with the issue of enlarged thought—the problem of how we attain knowledge of perspectives other than our own, how we know the voice of the concrete other. Specifically, feminists have raised questions about the possibilities of imaginative knowing.[15] Elizabeth Spelman has argued that imagination is inadequate in truly knowing someone else. She argues that one might in fact use imagination to prevent knowledge of another: "If I only rely on my imagination to think about you and your world, I'll never come to know you and it. And because imagining who you are is really a much easier thing for me to do than find out who you are, . . . I may persist in making you an object simply of my imagination, even though you are sitting right next to me" (179–180).

Similarly, Young has suggested that moral respect, rather than entailing being able to adopt the standpoint of others, requires the assumption that one cannot see things from the other person's perspective. To assume that we can is to discount and disrespect their uniqueness in time and place, their unique story. No matter how noble my intentions, in imagining the perspective of another rather than actually seeking it out, I am more likely projecting my own interpretations of experience, and perhaps my fears and prejudices, and presenting it as theirs. In the case of a person of privilege imagining the perspective of the oppressed, I am more likely to legitimate my privilege and continue the oppression (*Intersecting* 44–49).[16]

Accountability for exclusion thus entails respectfully recognizing that, even with the best of intentions, we cannot assume we can imagine the perspective of another. We must actively seek out and incorporate the standpoints of others. When we cannot, solidarity requires at the very least recognizing that all are not included and that our knowledge is at best limited.

Responsibility for Relationship: Respect and Understanding

A third key point is that while reflection, that is, disagreement and recognition of difference and exclusion, is essential to the process of constructing solidarity, solidarity is ultimately about connection. Reflective solidarity entails as well that we take responsibility for sustaining the relationships with those with whom we engage. In part we do this by respecting the shared norms of the group, though these norms are always open to interpretation, discussion, and revision.[17]

Camus similarly recognized that solidarity requires a certain assumption of responsibility to the collective. As he wrote:

> I have need of others who have need of me and of each other. Every collective action, every form of society, supposes a discipline, and the individual, without this discipline, is only a stranger, bowed down under the weight of an inimical collectivity. But society and discipline lose their direction if they deny the "We are." (*Rebel* 297)

Let us return for a moment to *The Plague*. Throughout much of the book, the character of Rambert, the exiled reporter, and Rieux, the noble doctor, have engaged in disagreements over Rambert's leaving or staying, belonging or not, placing love and happiness above the law and society's needs. Rambert consistently declares that he "doesn't belong," and that he chooses love above all else. Yet, when he finally has the opportunity to leave, he discovers that he would feel ashamed to leave. He has adopted the norms of the group, and would feel guilt and shame in not abiding by them. He also realizes that his honoring these norms sustains his relationship with his fiancé as well. He states, "Until now I always felt a stranger in this town, and that I'd no concern with you people. But now that I've seen what I've seen, I know that I belong here whether I want it or not. This business is everybody's business" (188)—and he has made it his business. He feels responsibility toward his relationship.

But Camus also would not lend support to a solidarity to any collective that required one to violate one's solidarity with the greater collective of humanity against oppression and injustice and in favor of human dignity. He takes up this issue in his short story, "The Guest" (*Exile*). Set in an Arab country during a time of growing French–Arab tensions, the story tackles the problems and paradoxes of multiple allegiances. By court order, a French gendarme has delivered an Arab prisoner convicted of murder to a French schoolteacher, who is then under orders to deliver the prisoner to the French prison some distance away. Because he is French, it is expected that the schoolteacher will comply, but he refuses, presumably recognizing the oppressive nature of the French regime and not wishing to be an accomplice to that oppression. He refuses to take on the norms of the "generalized other" of French society in the name of a greater solidarity to humanity. He shows the prisoner both the way to the prison and the way to safety, and leaves it to the prisoner to decide which way to go. (The prisoner, ironically, perhaps as a testimony to the degree of his internalized oppression, chooses to comply with the court order (the "generalized other" of the colonizer), and turns himself in.)

Dean expands on this aspect of reflective solidarity by returning to her insights from Uttal, who in her traveling back and forth between the norms of the supportive nods of the white women's group and the norms of active disagreement of the groups of women of color, testifies to the recognition that there are in fact several "generalized others." Dean likens this as well to Anzaldúa's multiple subjectivities, the fact that those living on the borderlands between cultures travel back and forth repeatedly. In light of these realities of multiple general others, adopting the norm of one group does not mean abandoning one's responsibilities for relationships in other groups. Rather, it enables one to bring the perspectives of various groups to one's travels (36).[18]

Abiding by group norms is only part of sustaining relationship. Responsibility toward relationship also entails a willingness to engage and persist in the relationship, "a commitment to work through the confusion" (Uttal 319) with openness and respect, and approaching it with the fundamental intent not to dominate nor to "win," but to understand. In this respect, we come to the importance of dialogue for Camus in breaking down human isolation. For Camus, genuine speaking and listening enable mutual understanding. This, "small part of existence that can be realized on this earth through . . . mutual understanding" (*Rebel* 283) is after all, the hope of rebellion. However, for Camus, just as mutual understanding makes existence possible, every misunderstanding leads to death.

Camus's play, *The Misunderstanding*, is a striking example of the potentially disastrous consequences of a lack of self-disclosing speech, and of acting on what one only assumes to be true. In this play a long-lost son returns to his mother's home, but wanting to surprise her, pretends simply to be a traveler looking for lodging at her inn. In the many years of his absence, his mother and sister have turned to the murder and theft of their patrons to supplement their meager income. Not recognizing their son and brother, and seeing only a wealthy lone traveler, they plot to make him their next, and supposedly final victim.

In the middle of the night they kill him and steal his money. It is only when they find his passport the next morning that they realize their mistake, and the mother kills herself out of guilt and grief.

The message of the play is that failure to be clear and to disclose one's authentic self can lead to misunderstandings with deadly and tragic consequences. The French title of the play, *Le Malentendu*, far better conveys the gravity of misunderstanding than the English, "misunderstanding," which we so often trivialize with such phrases as a "simple misunderstanding" or "just a misunderstanding"—something that can be cleared up with no profound consequences. The French *malentendu*, however, in its inclusion of the root word *mal*—meaning "evil," "harm," "hurt," "trouble," "wrong"—and its accompanying *malade*—meaning "sickness," expresses the more profound potential of misunderstanding to harm. *Le malentendu* is the malady underlying violence, injustice, hate, and oppression.[19]

Camus argued repeatedly that dialogue was essential for the vital task of coming to understand one another. Similarly, feminists writing on solidarity underscore the importance of approaching relationships with the intent to understand.[20] In her model of "Feminist Practical Dialogue," (FPD) Alison Jaggar emphasizes the intent to understand prominent in the model of moral reasoning practiced by several North American feminists. Feminist Practical Dialogue is the norms of discourse that evolve from this specifically feminist intent to understand. These include: conscious cooperation; responsibility to assure others' right to speak and be heard; responsiveness to the voice of others, meaning to facilitate their speech; and the use of questions to keep the conversation going. FPD does not preclude disagreement, nor does it privilege one discursive style over another. However it does require sensitivity to cultural practices. FPD is critical dialogue, but its process is nurturant rather than adversarial (Jaggar, "Toward").

Understanding can be furthered as well by working together. Dill suggests this as a potential for coalition work. Though some, Dean included, have expressed concern that solidarity built through coalition work would not build lasting relationship,[21] Dill raises the point that though the intended purpose of coalitions may be to achieve a specific political goal, the unintended outcome, and the real potential of coalition work, lies in its capacity to promote understanding. Working together enables participants better to understand each others' needs and perceptions, which also leads to building trust (146). She writes: "for it is through first seeking to understand struggles that are not particularly shaped by our own immediate personal priorities that we will begin to experience and understand the needs and priorities of our sisters—be they black, brown, white, poor, or rich" (148). Working together, as much as talking together, has the potential to "deepen and sustain" relationships. Indeed, Welch has argued that working together—and by work, she means the basic work of physical sustenance—preparing food, building houses, sewing—is necessary to develop truly emancipatory conversations. In such work we reveal our shared humanness, moving us to deeper conversation (135–136).

Rules of discourse, working together, and good intentions all work together to build respect and understanding, but these will go only so far without the willing cooperation of all involved. Relationship also requires "that those we wish to know themselves wish to be known . . ." (Spelman 185). And as Caraway has noted, some people may not want to be known (199).

We can understand only in the revelations of others. Without their self-disclosing speech and action we cannot know them. We cannot understand that which we cannot see, hear, feel, know. Camus was so opposed to lies and falsehood because in lying we close ourselves off from others, preventing understanding (*Rebel* 283). Such dialogue of honest sharing and honest listening invokes the challenge raised by Adrienne Rich to develop "honorable relationships"—"a process, delicate, violent, often terrifying to both persons involved, a process of refining the truths they can tell each other" (*On Lies* 188).[22] Such honorable relationships enable the kind of trust that allows for connected knowing and liberatory dialogue that reveal the complexities of our lives (*On Lies* 187). Rich regards such honesty as an obligation of feminist solidarity:

> We therefore have a primary obligation to each other: not to undermine each others' sense of reality for the sake of expedience; not to gaslight each other. Women have often felt insane when cleaving to the truth of our experience. Our future depends on the sanity of each of us and we have a profound stake, beyond the personal, in the project of describing our reality as candidly and fully as we can to each other. (190)

Lugones and Spelman, however, have raised questions regarding the possibility, as well as the desirability, of genuine dialogue between "outsiders" and "insiders," between white/Anglo women and women of color in particular. The possibility of such dialogue is put in question by the very context of domination in which such dialogue would take place. And the desirability of such dialogue is a matter of the motivations that underlie it. One possible motive is that of self-interest—either to learn more about the subordinates in order to better dominate them or to enable self-growth in the Anglo woman. Another is that of obligation, to right the wrongs that Anglos have done to people of color. Neither of these motivations is desirable. The only appropriate motive for white/Anglo women to engage in the process of dialogue and the task of mutual understanding with women of color is that of friendship.[23] I would argue that it is the only appropriate motive for any genuine dialogue. It is only with the motivation of friendship, that is, with "reciprocity of care for your and our wellbeing as whole beings" (581), that one can truly engage each other subject to subject.

In this regard Lugones suggests that the only way we can fully know each other as subjects, to know each other in friendship, is through "playfulness," that is, to travel to the other's world in loving perception, to know each other in those environments in which we are most free to be fully our own subject (401).[24] Young has likened Lugones's concept of "playfulness" to the attitude of wonder (*Intersecting*, 170, fn. 23).[25] With this attitude of wonder, and in an atmosphere of equality and respect, we can develop the receptivity that is necessary to fully engage each other in dialogue. Responsibility to relationship thus requires our willingness to know and be known, to reveal and to seek, always with an intent to understand. Karen Baker-Fletcher's notion of "sistering" sums up this responsibility to relationship well: "Sistering [allows for] open-ended but committed relationships, in which there is plenty of room for learning, growth, and the love that develops from ongoing talk, listening, work, and play with one another"(9).

Universalism

Finally, the concept of reflective solidarity entails the notion of the universal—or as Dean says, the "we" that is "we all" (45). In her notion of discursive universalism, Dean refuses to construct universality in opposition to particularity, but rather, like Camus, seeks to found universalism (Camus's "unity") on plurality and difference (173). This is similar as well to Uttal's vision of feminist sisterhood as: "*creating* a sense of unity that comes from us all working together, building on our diverse experiences" (319). The point of Dean's "reflective solidarity," Uttal's "sisterhood," and Camus's "unity" is the recognition that we are different, *and* yet we are united. It is the simultaneous affirmation of our uniqueness and of our connection and common condition. It is the recognition that I too could be in your place, and this recognition is fundamental to solidarity.

One example of this aspect of solidarity that has remained with me for many years comes from an Equal Rights Amendment (ERA) rally in

Chicago, Illinois in the spring of 1980. In addition to being one of the few states that had failed to ratify the ERA to the Constitution, Illinois was also the home state of Phyllis Schlafley, one of the main opponents of the ERA. At one point, the crowd of several thousand that had gathered for the march and rally began booing at the mention of Schlafley's name. Gloria Steinem got up and addressed the crowd, and called on us not to demonize Ms. Schlafley, reminding us that any one of us, under different circumstances, could be, and perhaps at one time had been, in her place. That recognition transformed a divisive moment into one of solidarity.

Audre Lorde expressed this aspect of solidarity as follows:

> I am a lesbian woman of Color whose children eat regularly because I work in a university. If their full bellies make me fail to recognize my commonality with a woman of Color whose children do not eat because she cannot find work, or who has no children because her insides are rotted from home abortions and sterilization; if I fail to recognize the lesbian who chooses not to have children, the woman who remains closeted because her homophobic community is her only life support, the woman who chooses silence instead of another death, the woman who is terrified lest my anger trigger the explosion of hers; if I fail to recognize them as other faces of myself, then I am contributing not only to each of their oppressions but also to my own, ... I am not free while any woman is unfree, even when her shackles are very different from my own. (132–133)

In her book, *A Chorus of Stones*, Susan Griffin sought out these connections in order to understand how the consequences of one act bear upon another, which then bear upon another, and another. In this examination of the private life of war she reveals the weave of atom, cell, radiation, cancer, incest, art, Himmler, Gandhi, masculinity, her own father, secrets, the atomic bomb. She shows how every life bears in some way on every other and all consequences are embedded in our experience. She writes: "What we call the self is part of a larger matrix of relationship and society. Had we been born to a different family, in a different time, to a different world, we would not be the same. All the lives that surround us are in us" (168). She would continue this thought in her later work, emphasizing that despite our differences, we are all interrelated:

> That we are all one is true. And yet differences among us are so crucial, determining fate, experience, perception, consciousness. Discerning, discernible being is at the heart of knowledge. Without difference and separation, there would be no meeting . . . .

No one acts alone. No one thinks alone. The threads of connection run everywhere and to unexpected places . . . .

Can we arise to ourselves and see what is in the nature of the soul to see—that we exist on this common ground together? (Griffin, *Eros* 149–154)

In solidarity, we seek the "common ground where all—even the (one) who insults and oppresses—have a natural community" (*Rebel* 16). The solidarity of sustaining relationship across differences through dialogue is a path toward finding that common ground.

To summarize, the aspect of solidarity that affirms our responsibility to sustaining relationship with others begins with an assumption of difference, yet through respectful dialogue seeks to attain a mutual understanding that will lead to a recognition of a fundamental common ground that sustains us all.

Solidarity as Compassionate Action

The third aspect of solidarity that emerges in rebellion is not logical, nor ontological, nor dialogical, but rather is "an insane generosity . . . which unhesitatingly gives the strength of its love and without a moment's delay refuses injustice" (Camus, *Rebel* 304)—insane because it takes risks that make no sense to the "rational actor." In acts of compassionate solidarity, the rebel defies cost/benefit analyses by taking on risks and sacrifices for the benefit of others. Solidarity in this sense is about action, and it is in this sense that true solidarity, in Paulo Freire's words, "risks an act of love" (32). Freire continues, "Solidarity requires that one enter into the situation of those with whom one is identifying; it is a radical posture. . . . True solidarity with the oppressed means fighting at their side . . ." (31). Camus gave us an image of this in *The Plague* with the reporter, Rambert, who chose to stay and fight at the side of the plague-stricken citizens of Oran, even though he had the chance to escape, just as Camus, exiled in Paris during World War II, could have chosen to live out the war quietly in relative isolation and obscurity, but instead chose to join the French Resistance movement, Combat.

Rebellion, in this sense, is compassionate action. Rebellion, Camus wrote, arises not just in refusal of one's own oppression, but in response to "the mere spectacle of oppression of which someone else is a victim" (*Rebel* 16). Rebellion, by its very movement carries an inherent obligation to speak out for those whose dignity is debased (*Resistance* 267).[26] Camus wrote in his *Notebooks* that the meaning of his work was "to do what Christianity never did—be concerned with the damned" (99).[27]

This theme—that he never wishes to be unfaithful to the humiliated (*Lyrical* 170)—is reiterated throughout his works: "Then we understand that rebellion cannot exist without a strange form of love. Those who find no rest in God or in history are condemned to live for those who, like themselves, cannot live: in fact, for the humiliated" (*Rebel* 304).

In *The Rebel*, Camus pointed to Meister Eckhart, a Catholic priest and mystic, as an example of the essence of the love of rebellion, because "in a fit of heresy" he said that he "preferred hell with Jesus to heaven without him" (*Rebel* 19). The love of the rebel (and here Eckhart would include Jesus as a rebel) is the rejection of an individual salvation that is exclusive. The solidarity that arises in rebellion is the choice of compassion—the choice to suffer with. In such acts of rebellion one literally chooses to suffer with another. This particular aspect of compassion entails the refusal of individual salvation until all are saved. Camus called this aspect of compassion "a strange form of love" because it refuses individual justice that comes at the price of the continued injustice and oppression of others. The depth of that compassion is such that individual salvation would be hell. The compassionate solidarity of rebellion consistently refuses salvation and privileges paid for by injustice and oppression (*Rebel* 304, 57).

Camus makes the important distinction, significant for feminism as well, between meaningful sacrifice and self-immolation (Braun 207), a distinction paralleled by Eleanora Patterson's differentiation between meaningful and meaningless suffering. Patterson sees two main differences between meaningless and meaningful suffering. First, meaningless suffering is suffering that is involuntary—thrust upon one by an external source, whether that be illness, natural disaster, or violence and oppression. Meaningful suffering, on the other hand, is suffering that is chosen—deliberately placing ourselves in situations that we know will create stress and potentially serious consequences (the suffering chosen by Rambert in *The Plague*). Second, in meaningless suffering, one acts out of a sense of worthlessness, taking on the suffering as one might take on a punishment for one's sins or simply one's worthlessness;[28] whereas in meaningful suffering, one acts out of a sense of self-worth—the positive affirmation at the heart of rebellion. The positive affirmation that comes in this choice of suffering is saying that this is the only thing a self-respecting person could do. It is similar to Rambert's remark that he could not face his fiancé if he left the citizens of Oran, nor could he respect himself. Rieux tells him there is nothing shameful in preferring happiness, to which Rambert responds, "But it may be shameful to be happy by oneself" (188).[29] One refuses privileges and comforts for oneself out of respect for one's own worth and dignity. The suffering of the rebel who refuses salvation is meaningful. It is a chosen action in affirmation of one's self-worth. Patterson writes, "Sometimes we risk suffering whether or not we act. . . . whether or not to suffer is not the issue. *How* to suffer and what choices we have are issues" (169).

The rebellious refusal of individual salvation is a centerpiece of feminist ethics and spirituality and feminist movement.[30] It is what China Galland calls "fierce compassion," bell hooks describes as feminism's "challenge to love," and Beverly Wildung Harrison calls the "power to act each other into well-being."[31] It entails a core value of not merely empathizing but acting, committing oneself to the work of resisting oppression and injustice that may not directly affect us as individuals (hooks, *Feminist* ch. 4; Dillon, 76). To quote Pamela Brubaker's summary of Harrison's teachings, "genuine solidarity requires concrete answerability to oppressed people, not just subjective identification with them" (53). We find such solidarity in feminist rejection of privileges of race or class or sexual identity—in the refusal to use economic or political or institutional power for self-promotion or the dominance of others. We find it in the committed tireless acts of feminists in solidarity with abused and battered women. We find it in those risking torture, imprisonment, and death—those willing to put themselves on the line—the Chipko women, who were willing to put their bodies in front of bulldozers, axes, and chainsaws in order to save their sacred trees; the Mothers of the Disappeared who, risking their own disappearance, return to La Plaza de Mayo every Thursday to protest their children's disappearance; the women of Greenham Common who left their homes and families for peace rather than war; the weekly vigils of the Women in Black, standing silently for peace on street corners in Jerusalem, Belgrade, and San Francisco despite being cursed, spat upon, and physically threatened; the Revolutionary Association of the Women of Afghanistan protesting their oppression under the Taliban at risk of being stoned to death. Such is the solidarity of feminists who "unhesitatingly give the strength of [their] love and without a moment's delay refuse injustice" (*Rebel* 304).

I believe such generous acts of rebellious solidarity, of love, originate and are sustained by an impulse that is at base spiritual, and by that I do not mean grounded in a religious tradition (though it may be) or hope of a transcendent reward, but grounded deeply in something larger than oneself, in connection with concrete others and the earth. It is primarily in works of feminist spirituality and theology that I see such commitments to love articulated—in Beverly Wildung Harrison's affirmation that living deeply in our bodies and contributing to the basic work of love and care opens us to radical acts of love; in Rita Nakashima Brock's recognition that our capacity to suffer with others leads us to a sense of community and commitment; in Carter Heyward's assertion that it is our passion as lovers that fuels our rage at injustice and our compassionate acts; in Carol Christ's assertion that a deeply felt connection to all beings is what brings us to stop nuclear madness and environmental destruction; in Starhawk's affirmation that valuing immanence shakes us out of our passivity and moves us to act on behalf of all living creatures.

Rita Gross and China Galland have both likened the feminist ethic of compassionate action to the Buddhist path of the Bodhisattva. The parallel could easily be extended to the generous impulse to love found in rebellion. In the experience of "bodhicitta" one senses a spontaneous compassion in the core of one's being. It is uncompelled by fear or need or duty, arising genuinely with no hope of reward or return. Galland has called this "fierce compassion," discovered through the goddess Tara, the Bodhisattva of compassion, who, even though she can enter a state of bliss chooses instead to stay in the world to relieve the suffering of others. Such compassion motivates one to pursue enlightenment for all beings. Experiencing one's enlightened self affirms our fundamental relatedness (Gross, *Buddhism* 180).

Some feminists may protest that this is just more calling upon women to be self-sacrificing. The feminist critique of compassionate action is that because it has been women's expected role to sacrifice their own salvation for others, the expectation that women should sacrifice themselves for others in rebellion is just an extension of women's oppression (Daly, *Gyn/Ecology*; Costello). Some feminists have argued that any concept of sacrifice for social change is unacceptable (Shivers 188; Costello 178). This is an important critique, and the line between acts that are martyring and self-sacrificing and those that are self-empowering acts of resistance must be scrupulously examined.

However, a theme repeated often among feminist writers urging compassionate action is that this should not be confused with actions that are self-sacrificing in the sense of meaningless suffering.[32] Rita Nakashima Brock argues that in order to stand in solidarity with others who are suffering, we do need to acknowledge our own pain and suffering. From this recognition of our own pain, we encounter our connection with others, which enables us to be compassionate. She emphasizes that this is not martyrdom nor masochism that takes on meaningless suffering to improve the soul, nor is it paternalistic rescue work. Rather, it is an acknowledgment that we can change our own lives so as not to contribute more to the suffering of the world and offer what we can for others' healing and liberation.

Rita Gross refutes the feminist critique that women need to stop caring for others and start caring for themselves in two ways (*Buddhism* 182). First, she argues that patriarchal culture needs to be feminized. Thus, the solution is not to call on women to be less nurturing but to call on men to be more so: "Women should not give up what is sane and healthy about their modes of being and knowing, simply because it is not rewarded and affirmed by the general culture" (*Buddhism* 182). Second, she admits that it is important to recognize that women also do care in "unwise and unhealthy ways." But she argues further that compassion is not the first step in spiritual development. The first is non-harming, which includes overcoming self-destructive habits such as loving too much. Compassion is not just about caring and self-sacrifice, but about caring with an all-encompassing compassion of the bodhisattva. To care in wise and healthy ways requires self-development.

Sharon Welch also makes the argument that the willingness to take risks in solidarity, far from being sacrifice, is founded in love of oneself. She argues that the concept of "self-sacrifice" is faulty in two ways. First, it reflects how outside observers perceive the action, rather than the ones acting, who experience their actions not as diminishment, but rather as integrity. Second, it fails to recognize that what is lost in compassionate action is not the self. Rather, though one may lose externalities of the "successful self" such as money and prestige, one gains a "larger self," discovered and maintained in acts of resistance (161–165). Further, she argues that "when we begin from a self created by love for nature and for other people, choosing *not* to resist injustice would be the ultimate loss of self" (165 emphasis in original).

Welch's sentiments are echoed by Carter Heyward and Beverly Wildung Harrison, who both affirm that the passion of love fuels our rage at injustice and our compassion, even toward those who harm us and that those touched by the power of such love refuse to accept anything less than mutuality, self-respect, and human dignity (Harrison 223). If I love you, Heyward argues, I will struggle for you, for us. And like Camus, Harrison asserts that the power of radical love entails a willingness to take risks, even unto death. Like Welch, however, both Harrison and Heyward argue that such acts are not masochism nor self-sacrifice, but rather simply a need to do what is just and to stand in solidarity and right relationship with those who are oppressed, so that none might be excluded. Both argue that the compassionate one, the lover, is one who stands in solidarity. This is the essence of rebellious solidarity.

The compassionate action fundamental to feminist solidarity is perhaps one of the most fundamentally misunderstood, or non-understood, aspects of feminism. Feminism is so often portrayed as either self-seeking, or as angry and vengeful, and indeed both aspects have been pursued in the name of feminism. But the prime spirit among feminists I know and the feminism that I embrace is this feminism that is the work of love. It may be fueled by anger and rage, or by deep suffering, but anger moves us to love, rage moves us to act against injustice, and sorrow waters the connection of compassion. These are merely evidence of the deep connection affirmed by feminist acts of solidarity. It may be said of feminism as much as Camus said of rebellion, that "it is love and fecundity, or it is nothing at all" (*Rebel* 304).

Solidarity as Refusal to Oppress

The fourth and final element of rebellious solidarity is the refusal to oppress. The rebel is against all forms of domination, including his or her own acts of domination. The basic principle that emerges from this is that the rebel limits himself or herself "to refusing to be humiliated without asking that others should be" (*Rebel* 18). The rebel refuses to humiliate, degrade, or destroy anyone, including, and this may be the most difficult part, the oppressor.

We see this attitude in Camus's "Fourth Letter to a German Friend," written during the Occupation of France in World War II. In it, Camus condemned the actions of the Nazis, while affirming their solidarity of a shared human fate. He wrote of how he deplored their actions while refusing to humiliate and degrade them, and of how he still desired to treat their souls with respect: "In order to keep faith with ourselves, we are obliged to respect in you what you do not respect in others. . . . we want to destroy you in your power without mutilating you in your soul" (*Resistance* 30–31). "In order to keep faith with ourselves," in other words, in order to stay true to the origins of rebellion, and to the recognition of that solidarity that reveals itself in the act of rebellion, rebels must continue to treat everyone, even those with the most despicable behavior, with the respect they demand for themselves.

Feminism has faced many challenges with regard to this rebellious refusal to be a party to domination and oppression. I have already taken due notice of the realities of women's oppression of other women, including some feminist agendas that contribute to the oppression of others. But certainly feminists have consistently made efforts toward reducing and refusing the oppression of other women.

A stickier issue may be that of feminist solidarity toward men. Much of feminist solidarity has been sought *against* men. Though a very limited element within feminist movement, both in terms of numbers and in terms of duration, for those involved in the movement, as well as for onlookers, the resentment and hostility, the wishing of ill-will toward men has been a very real part of the movement (and continues to be for a small minority). The epitome of this was SCUM (Society for Cutting Up Men), which advocated eliminating men and denounced those women who sought men's approval (Solanis 516). Whether intended seriously or tongue-in-cheek, the message of the SCUM manifesto is one of degradation, humiliation, and violation of "the enemy."

But most feminists reject this demonization of men as the enemy. Many feminists have found efforts to cast men as the enemy to be denigrating not only of men, but also of solidarity toward women, especially those women of color and working-class women who are engaged in collective struggle with men. A rebellious feminism would do well to heed the words of Jean Bethke Elshtain that "a feminist politics that does not allow for the possibility of transformation of men as well as women is deeply nihilistic; it does not truly believe in transformative possibilities nor the ideal of genuine mutuality" (*Public Man* 349).

Camus's distinction between resentment and rebellion is useful here.[33] Resentment delights in envisioning the pain and degradation of the one envied; rebellion refuses to pass the humiliation on. In this regard, I would argue that those elements within feminism that would seek to oppress and humiliate men in turn are acts of resentment rather than rebellion,[34] and in denying and destroying solidarity lose thereby the right to call themselves rebellion. Rebellion reminds us that feminist affirmation that goes beyond a valuing of one's own worth in and of itself, to a valuing of oneself over against another has lost faith with its rebellious origins, and becomes destructive of its own ends. As Susan Griffin has warned, "When a movement for liberation inspires itself chiefly by a hatred for the enemy . . . it begins to defeat itself. Its very motions cease to be healing" (*Made* 180). Thus, does rebellion's insistence on the refusal to humiliate sustain feminist movement.

As feminist movement has become more inclusive and matured in its rebellious manifestations it has come more and more to recognize the role of feminism in denouncing oppression in all forms—racism, classism, heterosexism, ableism, and others. Bell hooks, for one, has argued that because feminism is "a struggle to end sexist oppression. . . . it is necessarily a struggle to eradicate the ideology of domination that permeates Western culture . . ." (*Feminist* 24). Feminism continues to learn from its mistakes, to open up areas of dialogue and conversation and understanding, and to be vigilant in its refusal to be either victim or executioner, either oppressed or oppressor. In this, it has extended solidarity not only to women and men, but to children and other dependents. Feminists have pointed to situations of dependency as ones in which the power relationship between dependents and caregivers and authorities is necessarily unequal. Because of this, those in power have a particular responsibility not to abuse that power. Any domination in these situations is illegitimate and unjust.[35] Further, ecofeminism has extended feminist solidarity to relationships with the earth. Because in Western culture women are identified with nature, and the subordination of nature and the subordination of women go hand-in-hand, to resist women's oppression necessarily requires resisting the oppression of all beings.[36] But more than seeking to eradicate the practice of domination, in its challenge to value dualism, ecofeminism seeks to eradicate the very concept of domination.

The feminism I regard as rebellious refuses all forms of oppression and affirms the inherent worth of all beings. The challenge of rebellion and rebellious feminism is to end all forms of domination, or the very concept of domination itself. This is what makes feminism a truly "transformational politic" (hooks, *Talking* 19–27).

The solidarity that refuses to oppress and humiliate requires self-honesty and self-recognition regarding our own capacity to oppress. The rebel, in order not to add to injustice in the world must, ironically, recognize the limits of her ability to act justly. The rebel must recognize her own humanity, her flaws.[37] The rebel, said Camus, "knows what is good, and despite himself, does evil" (*Rebel* 285). Despite our triumphs over evil, the Sisyphean rock rolls back down, and we must continually turn and begin again. We may not always be successful at not harming, either directly or indirectly. The best we can do is to diminish the chances of oppression around us (*Rebel* 286).

The honesty and humility of this self-scrutiny are deeply embedded in feminist thought, as reflected in these challenging words from Audre Lorde: "What woman here is so enamoured of her own oppression that she cannot see her heelprint upon another woman's face?" (132). Many feminists argue that solidarity begins with our recognition that we all have the capacity for oppression and domination, that we each play our own part in injustice, from which we will never fully disentangle ourselves; and that we have a responsibility for recognizing our limits and for rectifying damages caused by the violation of those limits.[38] Like Tarrou, feminist theologian Carter Heyward has argued that "regardless of our good intentions, our feet will always be placed squarely on someone's neck—perhaps when we least realize it," and calls on us "to realize our own participation in fear and denial, in injustice and lovelessness; and to do what we can each day "to go and sin no more" (296–297). However, as Pamela Brubaker states, First World women especially may simply have to face the pain of recognizing that we *cannot* "go and sin no more" because of the webs of oppression toward Third World women in which we are entangled. Nevertheless, we can heed the advice of bell hooks to make the effort to reduce our participation in all systems of domination—parent/child, racism, sexism, classism, heterosexism (*Talking* Ch. 4).

One vehicle for the required self-scrutiny and self-reflection is what philosopher Sam Keen has called *metanoia*—turning around and reowning the shadow:

> When I know my shadow, I know that "they" are like me. We share a common human nature. The 50 percent of the human race I cast into the category of aliens are fellow humans who, like myself, are faulted, filled with contradictory impulses of love and hate, generosity, and the blind will to survive. . . . Metanoia brings the enemy within the circle of co-promising, conversation, and compassion . . . . (150)

The notion of *metanoia* is brought to life in Starhawk's utopian novel, *The Fifth Sacred Thing*. *The Fifth Sacred Thing* is the story of two societies—one utopian, the other dystopian. The utopian society, combining ecofeminist principles and Wiccan beliefs, honors all living things, values racial, religious, and sexual diversity; has a cooperative economy; and governs itself according to democratic and nonviolent principles. The dystopian society to the South is its negative image—a repressive regime based on moral, sexual, family, and racial purity. In this scene, the repressive regime has invaded the utopian society. The utopian community has decided to meet the invading army with nonviolent resistance, but the invading army has killed and imprisoned several people. One of the soldiers shoots an entire family in cold blood, but then suffers a catatonic breakdown. He is brought to the healer, Madrone, who simply cannot bring herself to heal him:

"Is there truly no part of you that can understand?"

"No. . . . Lily, you are asking me to heal my mother's murderer."

"What do you mean?"

"My mother was murdered by a death squad in Guadalupe. By men just like him. . . ."

"Then you have a link with him."

"I have no link with him! I'm not a candidate for sainthood; I'm not fixated on forgiveness. . . . They're not like us, Lily. . . . It's a different breed of human being. . . ."

"Is it? Are you telling me that you could not kill? . . . Can't you find some compassion for him in your heart? . . ."

Madrone goes on to say that she cannot find compassion when her heart is so filled with hate, and yet it is through this very hate that she comes to recognize her link with this man:

Rage churned in her, lit a fire in her belly, burst into flame on her breath. Oh, I am tired of being the Healer! I want to be the Destroyer, to rend and tear with my nails, to eat human flesh, to say no! no! no! until it all stops and starts over again, soft and new. I have not killed and I will not kill, not with Lily in the next room, but *Diosa*, I do want to kill, to cleanse, to exact some payment for all the suffering, some justice, some revenge . . . .

Her hands felt hot. . . . If I touch him now, I'll scorch him. I'll change him, it will serve him right. She reached out and took the soldier's hand. An aura, red as flame, enveloped their clasped hands.

His flesh was cold, but it felt familiar, like touching a part of herself, like remembering something she had always known. We are alike, she thought, in some way, flesh of one flesh.

. . . His hand warmed under her touch. She began to heal, which was only to reach and offer, without judgment, to let this power flow. (444–446)

That moment of recognition unlocks her compassion, releasing her capacity to love and to heal.

This message comes out in a slightly different way in Camus's play *Caligula*. In a brief scene, Caesonia tries to get Scipio to feel compassion for Caligula by taking him into the place of grief and rage and loathing that Caligula has felt since his sister's death:

CAESONIA: . . . Try to call up a picture of your father's death, of the agony on his face as they were tearing out his tongue. Think of the blood streaming from his mouth, and recall his screams, like a tortured animal's.

SCIPIO: Yes.

CAESONIA: And now think of Caligula.

SCIPIO [*his voice rough with hatred*]: Yes.
CAESONIA: Now listen. *Try to understand him.* (34, emphasis in original)

Try to understand him. Understanding, Camus says through the voice of Caesonia, is "something that would bring about the one real revolution in this world, if people would only take it in" (*Caligula* 33). I have been quite struck by this line in the play, *Caligula.* Camus condemned all other revolutions as perpetuating the very injustice and domination they seek to eradicate. But he considered *understanding* to be the *one real revolution*—in other words, the one that would in fact bring real change to the world.

I find the potential of such understanding to be revealed in Susan Griffin's attempts to understand one of the most horrific figures of the twentieth century, the mastermind of the Holocaust, Heinrich Himmler. To do so, she enters his world, travels to places he lived and where he carried out his acts of horror, reads his diaries. She takes us back into his childhood, into the German childrearing practices of Dr. Daniel Schreiber, adopted by Himmler's father, which were designed to establish dominance, crush the will, and suppress everything in the child through such devices as tying the child to the bed, enemas before bed, and immersion in ice-cold water. She takes us into Himmler's fetish for listening to the secrets of others, and then repeating them to his father. She takes us into the social constructions of masculinity and the consequences for a man like Himmler who did not measure up to these in so many ways. She takes us into the German history of drowning homosexuals and castigating Russians as vermin. In the process she enables the reader to feel deep compassion for this man who was responsible for such atrocious acts. She shows how indeed understanding can be revolutionary. If we all sought to understand rather than to demonize those whose actions we condemn and repudiate, if we sought their underpinnings in our individual and collective stories, we might indeed find our way to a true compassion that would in fact bring about real change in the world.

Compassion, to quote Starhawk, is "our ability to feel with another, to value other lives as we value our own, to see ourselves as answerable and accountable to those different from me" ("Feminist" 180). Compassion in this sense is solidarity. Indeed, Camus wrote that the recognition of this solidarity in our capacity for error and injustice demands that justice never divorce itself from compassion (*Resistance* 217).

The rebellious requisite of solidarity demands that we "support the common dignity that I cannot allow either myself or others to debase"

(*Rebel* 297). While this struggle is demanding, it is also joyous when it knows the fullness of compassion:

> When women and men understand that working to eradicate patriarchal domination is a struggle rooted in the longing to make a world where everyone can live fully and freely, then we know our work to be a gesture of love. Let us draw upon that love to heighten our awareness, deepen our compassion, intensify our courage, and strengthen our commitment. (hooks, *Talking* 27)

CHAPTER 6

FRIENDSHIP

*Now it occurred to me that a revolutionary ought to have a deep commitment,
not only to abstract humanity, but to actual flesh and blood beings . . .*
Susan Griffin, *Made from this Earth* 8–9

KALIAYEV: . . . we love our fellow men.

DORA: Yes, we love them—in our fashion. With a vast love that has
nothing to shore it up; that brings only sadness. The masses? We live
so far away from them, shut up in our thoughts. And do they love us?
Do they even guess we love them? . . .

KALIAYEV: But surely that's precisely what love means—sacrificing
everything without expecting anything in return?

DORA: Perhaps. Yes, I know that love, an absolute, ideal love, a pure and
solitary joy—and I feel it burning in my heart. Yet there are times
when I wonder if love isn't something else; something more than a
lonely voice, a monologue, and if there isn't sometimes a response . . .
Can you see what I mean?

KALIAYEV: Yes, Dora, I can; it's what is called love—in the simple,
human sense.

DORA: . . . but does that kind of love mean anything to you, really? Do
you love justice with that kind of love? Do you love our Russian people
with that love—all tenderness and gentleness and self-forgetting? . . .
wouldn't it be better to love—like an ordinary person? (*Just Assassins*
269–270)

In the scene presented here from *The Just Assassins*, Camus challenges
a solidarity that knows nothing of real relationship—of love and friendship. As important as solidarity is to Camus's concept of rebellion,
Camus held that unless it is grounded in concrete relationship, solidarity too can become destructive of rebellion. Solidarity and compassion
may too easily become regarded as an empathy for the "bleeding
crowd," and for humanity in the abstract. Camus feared such abstract
love that would sacrifice one's friends living in the present in the name

of a far-distant era of universal friendship. Throughout his works, Camus reiterated the importance of specific, concrete friendship—a friendship that is about love and loyalty to people with whom one shares this existence now:

> The friendship of people—and there is no other definition of it—is specific solidarity, to the point of death, against everything that is not part of the kingdom of friendship. The friendship of objects is friendship in general, friendship with everything, which supposes—when it is a question of self-preservation—mutual denunciation. He who loves his friend loves him in the present, and the revolution wants to love only a man who has not yet appeared. (*Rebel* 239)

Justice Versus Care

Camus repudiated the way that totalitarian politics killed off all possibility of friendship, by abandoning people of today for a far-off justice and requiring friend to denounce friend. He refused dogmatic adherence to a "justice" to which anything and everything, including friendship, must be sacrificed, and claimed the primacy of particular people to an abstract justice. "If anyone," he wrote regarding the Algerian revolts, ". . . still thinks heroically that one's brother must die rather than one's principles, I shall go no farther than to admire him from a distance. I am not of his stamp" (*Resistance* 113).[1]

Feminist Ethic of Care

Camus's concern with the priority of particular people to abstract principles foreshadows the development of the feminist ethic of care that grew out of Carol Gilligan's research on female moral development.[2] Gilligan found that while men were more likely to base moral decisions on abstract principles of rights and universal principles of justice, women were more likely to base moral decisions on context and particularities, and to regard as moral that which tends toward sustaining relationship. Based on her findings, she distinguished an ethic of justice based on abstract principles, rights, and formal reasoning, from an ethic of care based on context, relationship, and responsibility. According to the care ethic, moral decisions are appropriately based on care and compassion toward particular people, rather than on rules. The central effort of the ethic of care is toward sustaining relationship. The ethical self, Nel Noddings argues, is born of a fundamental recognition of relatedness, that connects me to others and through others to myself

(49). Real care requires actual encounters with real people and is manifested in qualities of receptivity, relatedness, responsiveness to and with these real others. The primacy of relationship and the preference to preserve relationship over and above principles are central aspects of the ethic of care (Noddings 44, 57).

Care and compassion and nurturance have traditionally been regarded as gender traits associated with women. Feminists have provided several different explanations as to why women more than men would develop such traits. Some ground this female capacity to connect in female psychological development. Nancy Chodorow has suggested that in a culture of heterosexual nuclear families in which women are the primary caregivers, the primary developmental task of males is to separate and individuate, whereas the primary developmental task of females is to connect and develop the capacity for relationship. This, as Gilligan has argued, results in women's different path of moral development, emphasizing the capacity to care and sustain relationship.

Others emphasize the role of motherhood and caregiving in women's lives as the source of women's heightened awareness of interrelationship. While some emphasize the bodily wisdom of interrelatedness gained in the experiences of pregnancy and nursing (Whitbeck), most have emphasized the unique standpoint gained by women as the primary caregivers in our society.[3] Caregiving in this society, whether of children, the elderly, the sick, the dying, the disabled and other dependents, has largely been the task of women.[4] From this work of caregiving, mothers and other caregivers develop particular capacities and perspectives, prime among these being the capacity for relationship. Eva Kittay has shown how through caring for those dependent on us—that is, unequals, we learn not to abuse relationships of power and to relate in these situations with respect and nondomination. We learn the importance of responding to others in need, and the primacy of human relations for happiness and well-being (113). Others have emphasized women's development of the capacities for trust, cooperation, and caring through their experience as mothers in non-patriarchal households (Held, "Non-Contractual"). As Annette Baier has remarked, unlike the "great male theorists" who relegated trust to the background, women simply cannot ignore trust that is so important to the fabric of our everyday lives ("Trust" 249). Care, cooperation, responsibility, trust, attentive love are all a part of the caregiving that is so much a part of the daily lives and tasks of most of the women of the world.

However, grounding care in biological, psychosexual, or materialist explanations has its problems. Both the biological and psychosexual explanations hint of biology being destiny, with little or no chance of change or of caring being generalizable to men. Materialist explanations raise the specter of the care perspective diminishing as women more and more leave the home, (though certainly someone is still caring for children, but perhaps in such different conditions as to become more and more rule-bound and less and less focused on care of specific individuals) (Tong 5–6). Also, the home is not always a place of nurturance; too often it is a place of abuse. We can learn dominance and distrust in the home just as easily as respect, care, and trust, and far too often.

Citing these and other problems, not all feminists have embraced "care" as "the feminist ethic," or even a feminist ethic. Gilligan's study and the emerging juxtaposition of the ethics of care and justice stirred an ongoing debate (the "justice versus care" debate) in feminist ethics regarding the gendered nature of the two systems of morality, the adequacy of each, and ultimately, the superiority of one to the other. Some feminists embraced the ethic of care as a distinctly female ethic, and argued not only for its difference from the justice perspective, but for its superiority as an ethical system (Noddings). Others, while denying an essential female connection to an ethic of care, nevertheless espoused it as a feminist ethic to be preferred to the masculinist ethic of justice.[5] Others labeled care a "feminine" ethic, but due to its inattention to power relations and oppression, did not regard it as a specifically "feminist" ethic (Tong).[6] Still others found the care ethic not only to be inadequate for political practice due to its inattention to oppression, but also inappropriate. They argued that due to its basis in personal relationship it is inherently parochial and partial. They advocated instead for a feminist ethic grounded in citizenship and its accompanying justice and rights claims.[7]

Love and Justice in Tension

Though Camus recognized a tension between love and justice, and often juxtaposed the two, his ethic of rebellion does not fit easily on either side of the debate. One might be tempted to argue that Camus would come out strongly on the side of the ethic of care. As we have already seen in chapter two, Camus eschewed the basic premises of a morality of "justice." His intent in exploring the phenomenon of rebellion was precisely to find an ethic based on something other than abstract principles. He found rationality to be an insufficient basis of either knowledge or morality, and specifically rejected utilitarian and social contract theories as bases of ethical systems (*Rebel* 18). The morality that emerges from rebellion is one that insists on collectivity and places personal relationship above principle.

On the other hand, as discussed earlier in chapter one, some have found in Camus's juxtapositions of love and justice a repudiation of the "female world" of love, home, and family, and regard him instead as positing rebellion as a "male world" of principled courage and action. They point to such examples as the scene in *The Just Assassins* where Dora puts Kaliayev through an inquisition about his priorities—which does he love more, justice or her? Her or the organization? Would he love her if she were unjust? He answers equivocally that if she were unjust, it would not be her that he loved and she is left unsatisfied. He ultimately puts the cause before their love, and she sadly concedes that theirs is "a love that's half frozen, because it's rooted in justice and reared in prison cells" (270–271).[8] A similar conflict arises between the two lovers, Diego and Victoria, in *State of Siege*. Victoria, siding with love, pleads with Diego not to abandon love and happiness. Nevertheless, he takes the side of justice, and sacrificing his life and their love, goes off to fight the plague. The men, Kaliayev and Diego, are said to represent the rebel, and the women, Dora and Victoria, to represent the repudiation of rebellion. But, as I argued in chapter one, I believe this is a misinterpretation. Rather than seeing Kaliayev and Dora, Diego and Victoria as the juxtaposition of rebellion to its antithesis, I regard them as representing different facets of rebellion. Neither is the solitary rebel figure. Rebellion requires the voices and considerations of both. Camus never intended to dichotomize these and isolate love from rebellion. The rebel does not want to give in to injustice, but neither does the rebel renounce love and friendship. Rather, the claims of love and concrete relation serve to keep rebellious acts toward justice faithful to their origins.

Camus found justice to exist not in opposition to care, but rather to grow from it. We see this, for example, in a scene from *The Plague*, previously described in chapter three, that care is what moves us to act against injustice. Having just witnessed the agonizing death of a child, the doctor, Rieux, in a feeling of "mad revolt" says that he will forever refuse such injustices (196–197). He feels revolt and is moved to act because he cares, because he feels compassion for this child. "Justice . . .," Camus tells us, "cannot by its very essence, divorce itself from compassion" (*Resistance* 217).

Just as some feminists are now coming to the conclusion that an adequate morality and politics requires both justice and care,[9] so did Camus refuse to choose one over the other. Camus did not reject all notions of justice, only a conception of justice that necessarily detaches itself from relationship. He did not frame the debate as one of justice versus care, but rather saw justice arising from care, and care manifesting itself in justice.[10] However, Camus recognized that even though justice is based on interconnection and the solidarity that flows from this, it can, and often does, conflict with loyalties to family and friends. As to which takes priority, there is no easy answer for Camus. In rebellion they coexist in a constant tension.

This places Camus's philosophy of rebellion right in the middle of the "partiality/impartiality debates." Ethics of impartiality require that one make moral judgments detached from loyalties to loved ones; everyone, including oneself, is to be treated with the same consideration. Partialists, on the other hand, argue that partiality toward loved ones is appropriate, perhaps even unavoidable. Close relationships require loyalty, interest, and responsiveness to the unique needs of loved ones. Though Camus emphasized friendship and the primacy of relationship in the concept of rebellion, it should be remembered that this is just one element of rebellion that always stays in tension and balance with the other elements of refusal of oppression and injustice, affirmation of human dignity, and solidarity. As Marilyn Friedman has pointed out, the dilemma that many feminists face in this debate is that while they dispute the demands of moral impartiality, they also insist on the importance of global concerns and cross-cultural solidarity ("Social Self"). Friedman's solution is basically the same as Camus's both/and approach. She argues that rather than choosing one over the other, the direction of one's attentions are more a matter of degree. Feminist partialists, while attentive and loyal to the needs of their loved ones, also devote more than a typical attention, both theoretical and practical, to developing concern for those outside one's immediate circle of care. Friedman explains: " 'global moral concern' does not mean the practice of exactly equal consideration of the interests of all individuals; but it does mean substantially more concern for distant or different peoples than is common in our culture and our time" ("Social Self" 175).

Camus used the tension between these conflicting loyalties to set up one of the main recurring conflicts in *The Plague*. The conflict lies between the reporter, Rambert, whose major efforts are devoted to reuniting with the woman he loves, and the doctor, Rieux, whose efforts are devoted to fighting the plague (even though he too is separated from his wife by the quarantine). Their confrontation emerges not as a straightforward conflict between love and justice, but rather shows the complexities arising from the equally compelling demands of both. In a conversation among Rambert, Rieux, and Tarrou, Rambert declares,

"Man is an idea, and a precious small idea, once he turns his back on love. And that's my point; we—mankind—have lost the capacity for love . . ." to which Rieux responds that Rambert is right, and he won't try to dissuade him from trying to leave. But Rieux does defend his own actions, saying his choice to stay and fight the plague is simply a matter of "common decency." With this Rambert becomes thoughtful, and replies " 'Maybe I'm all wrong in putting love first,' " to which Rieux responds vehemently, "No, . . . you are not wrong" (149–150). Later, when Rambert decides not to escape the city and to cast his lot with those fighting the plague, Rieux tries to talk him out of it, saying if he chose to take a share in other people's unhappiness, he'd have no time left for his own. Rambert retorts by asking the doctor if he has chosen to turn down happiness. After much silence, the doctor replies, "For nothing in the world is it worth turning one's back on what one loves. Yet that is what I'm doing, though why I do not know" (188–189).

Primacy of Relationship

In rebellion, one tries to honor the claims of both justice and the solidarity it requires and the claims of one's loved ones. However, Camus cautioned that if justice becomes a devotion to the ideal of justice in and of itself, rather than a caring for particular persons, it itself becomes oppressive.[11] Contrary to those who have argued that justice is a prerequisite to any caring relationship,[12] Camus would have us remember that it is love, love that grows out of particular, bodily, affectional, attentive relationships of care and concern, family and friendship, that gives birth to sufficient concern for ourselves and others that one seeks justice in the first place, and that it is the possibility of these same affectional relationships that makes the struggle for justice worthwhile. Camus reminds us that "A loveless world is a dead world, and always there comes an hour when one is weary of prisons, of one's work, and of devotion to duty, and all one craves for is a loved face, the warmth and wonder of a loving heart" (*Plague* 237). Love is primary.

A scene in *The Plague* illustrates this point. After months of being locked in the town battling the plague, the doctor, Rieux, and his friend Tarrou decide to break quarantine and go for a swim, " 'for friendship's sake. . . . Go for a swim. It's one of those harmless pleasures. . . . Really, it's too damn silly living only in and for the plague. Of course a man should fight for the victims, but if he ceases caring for anything outside that, what's the use of his fight' " (231). To become so engaged in acts of fierce compassion that one abandons one's loved ones is to have lost the point of the compassion in the first place. Relationship is fundamental to rebellion.

Just as relationship is fundamental to rebellion, so it is to much of feminist thought. Despite the controversy surrounding care, many feminists have reclaimed the capacities to care and to connect as positive goods in our lives and sources for our values and our politics. In feminist epistemology, ontology, ethics, spirituality, politics the recurring themes are ones of care, connection, compassion, empathy, nurturance, interdependence—the primacy of relationship to each other and the earth. In the words of Beverly Wildung Harrison: "relationality is at the heart of all things," which is "to insist on the deep, total sociality of all things. All things cohere in each other. Nothing living is self-contained . . ." (15–16). She goes on to argue that:

> . . . our world is on the verge of self-destruction and death because the society as a whole has so deeply neglected that which is most human and most valuable and the most basic of all the works of love—the work of human communication, of caring and nurturance, of tending the personal bonds of community. This activity has been seen as women's work and discounted as too mundane and undramatic, too distracting from the serious business of world rule. . . . love's work is the deepening and extension of human relations. . . . Through acts of love directed to us, we become self-respecting and other-regarding persons, and we cannot be one without the other. (12)

The importance of Harrison's argument cannot be overstated. The tending of relationship is fundamental to the work of building community, and leaders of cities, nations, and a world in crises of environmental destruction, devastating poverty, and war would do well to learn from the daily invaluable of work of those who foster communication and extend care. There is no more serious business. This is the basic premise of those feminists who emphasize the significance of the primacy of relationship for our society and its political practices.

Effect of Primacy of Relationship on Political Action
Care as Motivation for Political Action

Like Camus, many have commented on the power of caring relationships to move people to political action. Sara Ruddick, for example, whose maternal practice has been criticized for its fostering of a parochialism that would deny our association and care for a larger political community (Dietz), claims that far from fostering parochialism, maternal practice leads one to extend "mothering" to the protection of all people whose lives are threatened by violence and oppression (*Maternal* 232). She points, for instance, to the Mothers of the Disappeared,[13] whose concern for their particular children fostered political protest on behalf of all those who had disappeared. Patricia Hill Collins has similarly written of how the black female community of mothers and othermothers, those who support bloodmothers in the raising of their children—grandmothers, sisters, aunts, friends—stimulates an ethic of caring that leads to an accountability that emerges often as political activism (119–120). Because we are concrete knowers, in order to act in solidarity with others, we need the concrete knowledge of love of specific, particular people (Welch 137). But this does not mean our actions will be limited to the benefit of those particular people. Rather, knowing the needs and sufferings of those in our circle of care serves to inform and extend our compassionate action to the larger community. In her study of the relationships of Buddhism and feminism, Rita Gross came to see how interlinked the primacy of relationship is to the development of the practice of compassion, and from that to the emergence of a compassionate prophetic politics of social justice (*Buddhism* 182–183). Thus care does engender rebellion.

Relationship as Sustenance for Struggle

Others, like Camus, have emphasized the importance of home, friendship, and community to provide inspiration and sustenance for the struggle.[14] These are, as bell hooks has said, "sites of resistance" in which those struggling for liberation can be restored in their dignity and nurtured in their spirits:

> . . . In our young minds houses belonged to women, were their special domain, not as property, but as places where all that truly mattered in life took place—the warmth and comfort of shelter, the feeding of our bodies, the nurturing of our souls. There we learned dignity, integrity of being; there we learned to have faith . . .
>
> Despite the brutal reality of racial apartheid, of domination, one's homeplace was the one site where one could freely confront the issue of humanization, where one could resist. Black women resisted by making homes where all black people could strive to be subjects, not objects, where we could be affirmed in our minds and hearts despite poverty, hardship, and deprivation, where we could restore to ourselves the dignity denied us on the outside in the public world. . . . a safe place where black people could affirm one another . . . . (*Yearning* 41–42)

People so empowered by the love and affirmation they receive and give gain strength to continue day after day to work for justice.[15]

Caring Relationship as Model and Insight for Politics
In addition, several feminists have sought to use the insights and values gained from relationship to change radically the quality of our political relations. Many of those who embrace the values of care have argued that a care ethic should inform our political theory and practice precisely because of the priority it gives to concrete loving relationships, arguing that such a priority would result in a more life-affirming and creative politics.[16] Some have been particularly critical of a politics based in contractarian relationships, arguing that such a contractual society of self-interested individuals, ignorant of trust and care, is always in danger of breaking down (Held, "Non-contractual" 124–125; Baier). They seek instead a conception of politics grown from the lessons of trust, cooperation, and caring that we learn from experiences in the non-patriarchal relationships (Held, "Non-contractual" 122, 136). Lorraine Code suggests that conceptualizing society as concentric circles of caring—of individuals encircled by home encircled by friends and community and on until all are encircled in the global community—rather than in a sharp and artificial division between public and private would lead us to more ecological thinking (371 ff.). Similarly, friendship helps us to extend our circle of care by opening us to standpoints other than our own. Through the understandings and perspectives of our friends, and in seeing how our friends are affected by events, we come to grasp experiences in a new light (Friedman, *What Are Friends For?* 369–370). As bell hooks has noted, for many of us, friendship gives us our "first glimpse of redemptive love and caring community" (*All About Love* 134).

Both rebellion and feminism emphasize that it is in relationship that we learn to care and connect, and that these qualities nurture our spirits and inspire us to act to transform our society and our politics. However, some feminists have questioned the appropriateness of the mother–child paradigm as the basis of an ethic of relationship or a political practice, citing in particular the fact that it is unequal, nonreciprocal, and nonvoluntary (Code). They regard friendship as a more appropriate model (Code; Friedman, "Feminism"), and certainly it is the relationship of friendship that Camus emphasized in his attention to particular relationships. Unlike the mother–child relationship, friendship is a voluntary relationship, with greater possibilities for reciprocity of care and balance between separateness and interdependency.[17] Simone Weil, who regarded friendship above all other human relations, characterized it as a relationship in which both parties allow each other autonomy, with no desire to dominate or wish to please, each respecting the distinctness of each other (369–370). "Friendship," writes Marilyn Friedman, "may emerge, in our culture, as the least contested, most enduring, and most satisfying of all close personal affiliations" (*What Are Friends For?* 187).

In an argument very similar to Camus's, Janice Raymond has cited the importance of specific friendship to feminist politics. She argues that the feminist emphasis on sisterhood, solidarity, and oppression is not sufficient to hold feminists together beyond isolated and temporary communities of resistance. Feminism thus needs to mean something more, a positive bonding defined by female friendship. "Women must be for each other" (29), not just against the forces of oppression. Female friendship, she argues, invests feminism with deeper meaning. She writes: "female friendship gives depth and spirit to a political vision of feminism and is itself a profoundly political act. Without Gyn/affection, our politics and political struggles remain superficial and more easily short circuited" (29). Though Raymond's vision is of a specifically female friendship, the fact that friendship imbues solidarity and political action with depth, spirit, and meaning is at the heart of Camus's argument for the necessity of grounding rebellion in friendship. Friendship gives rebellion its specificity and its meaning, anchoring it in the real world and the real lives of people.

As mentioned in chapter five, others as well have stressed the importance of approaching the task of solidarity, particularly the dialogical process, with a motivation of care and friendship (Jaggar, "Towards"; Lugones and Spelman). This honoring of friendship is one of the central tasks that feminists need to develop in relation to each other. Bell hooks raises the difficult question of where the love is between women of different races, and is candid in saying that there is little friendship between black and white women (though she does not go beyond this to discuss relations among women of other races) (*Killing Rage* 217). Lugones and Spelman speak most directly and eloquently to this aspect of feminist friendship, insisting that the task of mutual understanding across differences of race and culture is only appropriately served through the motivation of friendship (581). So, it is important that we turn our attention specifically to the relationship of friendship.

The Requirements of Friendship

Though Camus valorized friendship, he told us little about it. He gave us two main images of friendship. One is of an affectionate companionship of equals, a seamless and deep communion, as exemplified in this scene from *The Plague*:

> Rieux turned and swam level with his friend, timing his stroke to Tarrou's. . . . For some minutes they swam side by side, with the same zest, in the same rhythm, isolated from the world, at last free of the town and of the plague. . . .
> Neither said a word, but they were conscious of being perfectly at one, and the memory of this night would be cherished by them both. (233)

The other is of a friendship strained by years of living in an atmosphere of hatred and tyranny, but a friendship Camus sought to sustain. He said in a speech to L'Amitié Française (French Friendship) shortly after the end of World War II, "not giving in to hatred, not making any concessions to violence, not allowing our passions to become blind— these are the things we can still do for friendship . . ." (*Resistance* 63–64).

The former is the friendship that inspires, comforts, and sustains, but Camus knew that it is achieved only through the work of the latter. Camus did not seek an easy friendship, what he called "an effusion of feeling among people who get along together" (*Resistance* 61), but rather a friendship that requires effort. The rewards of friendship Camus sought—communion, understanding, affection, respect, attention, regard, warmth, love, and trust—are born of the effort to speak honestly, not to give in to hatred, and no matter what, to treat the other with respect and decency (*Resistance* 61, 30).[18]

Though I have found in rebellion the affirmation of the priority and valuing of friendship and loving relationship, it has been primarily in feminist thought that I have encountered and grappled with what this entails. Many images of communal friendship in feminist thought, poetry, song, and literature have inspired me—from Margie Adam's "Sweet Friend of Mine" and Chris Williamson's "Sister" to Toni Morrison's portrayal of the friendship of Sula and Nel in her *Sula* and Adrienne Rich's poetic portrayal of the friendship of Paula Becker and Clara Westhoff (*Dream* 42–44). But more than this, feminism has taught me about the task of friendship, and the responsibilities it entails. As they continue in their discussion of the motive of friendship, Lugones and Spelman relate some of the responsibilities of friendship:

> If you enter the task out of friendship with us, then you will be moved to attain the appropriate reciprocity of care for your and our well-being as whole beings, you will have a stake in us and in our world, you will be

moved to satisfy the need for reciprocity of understanding that will enable you to follow us in our experiences as we are able to follow you in yours. (581)

Reciprocity of care, reciprocity of understanding, having a stake in our friends' worlds—these and their components of attentive love, honor and trust, loyalty and commitment, and reconciliation and forgiveness are some of the requirements of friendship. I will examine each in turn.

Reciprocity

"Reciprocity of care for your and our well-being as whole beings" involves two different elements, care and reciprocity. Let us first turn to reciprocity. What does reciprocity require? In her book on caring, Nel Noddings describes the caring relation as one between the "one-caring" and the "cared-for." In this relationship, the "one-caring" provides the actual care and the "cared-for" reciprocates by responding to being cared-for with a smile or an expression of gratitude, but not by becoming the "one-caring" in turn. Noddings's model of care has been criticized for the unidirectional nature of the caring, in other words, for its lack of real or adequate reciprocity (Hoagland).[19] Such a caring relationship may be appropriate for a parent and a young child, or for some other "cared-for" who is otherwise unable to return the care—someone who is dying, or disabled, or mentally ill. However, for most friendships, and even for most parent–child relationships, such a relationship lacks sufficient reciprocity. In cases where one friend is always on the giving end, and the other on the receiving end, the friendship tends to break down. It might eventually fail due to feelings of resentment or being taken advantage of on the part of the "one-caring," or of feelings of being patronized on the part of the "cared-for" if she is never allowed to reciprocate. Friendships between equals demand a certain reciprocity. For example, I have a friend whose dog I tend often, and though I tell her it is a pleasure for me (sufficient reciprocity in Noddings's terms), she still feels the need to reciprocate with little gifts—a plant, a loaf of bread. It is part of the give and take of friendship.

Because our needs and gifts are unique, the reciprocity will never be exact. For example, because I have spent so much of my life dealing with illness, much of the care I have received has revolved around that—meals for myself and my family, housecleaning, gardening, massage, childcare, transportation, hospital visits, middle-of-the-night emergency room runs. Though there may come a time when I'll be called upon to provide the same for my friends, it's not fitting that I provide the same now. Instead, my reciprocity comes in the form of being there to listen, comfort and console when one's mother is dying; sharing a meal; giving the gift of a special bow for a violin.[20] These are the reciprocities of friendship—not exact, not measured—indeed if we began to assign values to our gifts of care and to keep an accounting of what was given and what was received, then the friendship would have dissolved into a market exchange. Nor is it a matter of taking care of someone now with the expectation of being cared for by them should the need arise later, for in that case the friendship would be nothing other than a utilitarian calculus. Reciprocity is not the motive of friendship, but rather the mode—a recognition of mutuality and of being equally invested in the friendship.[21]

Care and Attentive Love

Care entails many things—tending to physical, emotional, and spiritual needs; attention; warmth and affection; regard and respect. As friends we nourish and sustain each other. We share activities and experiences, listen attentively, provide emotional and financial support in times of need, give comfort, enjoy each other's company, share tears and laughter, pray and send *metta*, celebrate.

Noddings describes care as "affection and regard" (24), but in describing this aspect of care, I prefer Audre Lorde's use of the word "tenderness." In calling on black women to befriend each other, she describes a process of learning to mother oneself and each other. In so doing, not only do we provide attention and affirmation, we also "learn how to be tender" with each other: "We can practice being gentle with ourselves by being gentle with each other (and) we can practice being gentle with each other by being gentle with the piece of ourselves that is hardest to hold" (175). In the confrontational and hostile places of our lives, and at times even with our friends, we often "steel" or "armor" ourselves. But the caring of friendship requires that we treat each other with genuine tenderness—a softening of the heart.

Many feminists speak of care as "attention," "attentive love," or "loving perception." Sara Ruddick describes the giving of "attentive love" as one of the main tasks of maternal care (*Maternal* 119–123), but it also is a task of friendship. Ruddick takes her concept of attentive love from Iris Murdoch (as do others), who drew her inspiration from Simone Weil. For Weil, love is "intense, pure, disinterested, gratuitous, generous attention" (333). Weil regarded such attention as a moral stance toward others—a recognition of the other as a human being and being able to put oneself in another's place. In practice, it simply means being able to ask "What are you going through?" and then emptying oneself in order to receive the other (Bell 47–50; Weil 49–51). Attentive love is akin to a capacity for empathy in that it provides an ability to suffer and celebrate with another, but that attentive love is not the same as trying to find oneself in another. Rather, in attentive love one tries accurately to perceive the other (Ruddick, *Maternal* 121). In hospice training, we were told that before we entered the presence of the dying person, we needed to "leave ourselves at the door"—to put aside our own agendas, judgments, and needs in order to be fully present to the dying person, or as Weil said, "above all our thought should be empty, waiting, not seeking anything, but ready to receive . . ." (49). In leaving ourselves at the door, we can offer our full attention. Ruddick describes such attention as "knowing that takes truthfulness as its aim and makes truth lovingly serve the person known" (*Maternal* 120). Care then, requires knowledge, but knowledge of a particular kind. It is in friend-ship that we learn I–Thou knowledge, in which we receive and are received fully as subjects.[22] In the best of our attempts at dialogue and mutual understanding, we relate to each other as subjects. In this sense, friendship provides a basis for a politics of nondomination.

Ruddick's attentive love is akin to what Lugones has called, after Frye, "loving perception." Frye distinguishes "the loving eye" from "the arro-gant eye" (66–76). The arrogant eye perceives the other as a means to an end and as either "for me" or "against me." The arrogant eye's perception of the other is not only inaccurate but coercive and manipulative, defin-ing and judging the other only according to the values and beliefs of the perceiver's world. The loving eye is the contrary of the arrogant eye. It knows that the other is different and independent of the knower, and that to know the other requires paying attention to the other, rather than to one's own interests, fears, imaginings, and projects.[23]

Lugones argues that the kind of knowledge required for loving perception necessitates traveling to the other's world—being able to see through her eyes and experience her sense of herself in her world (394). She gives a loving description of her realization of this in her coming to know her mother, to see her with a loving eye. She had previously judged her mother arrogantly. Seeing her as a victim of "the mainstream Argentinean patriarchal construction of her," Lugones did not want to be what she was. She recounts, "I could not see myself in her, I could not welcome her world. I saw myself as separate from her, a different sort of being, not quite of the same species" (393), and experienced this as a lack of love. Loving her mother required traveling to her mother's world. It was there that she realized that her mother was not so pliable and exhausted, and that "there are 'worlds' in which she shines as a creative being'" (402).

But in order to witness the other in her world, Lugones says, one must travel there playfully, rather than agonistically. The agonistic world traveler wants to conquer, to impose her own image on the other. The playful world traveler, on the contrary, is open to surprise, to seeing oneself and others in new ways. With this attitude of wonder we are open to the newness and mystery of the other person and their world, as well as ourselves (Young, *Intersecting* 56).

Lugones says that it was only when she traveled to her mother's world that she could see her as a subject, and this enabled the possibility of understanding between them. Reciprocity of understanding is made possible by all that enables us to know each other as subjects. All that we have previously discussed about creating mutual understanding in relations of solidarity applies to friendship as well. Traveling to each others' worlds, open and honest dialogue, self-disclosing speech, attentive listening, and an attitude of wonder all contribute to mutual understanding. What is different in friendship is perhaps the expectation of the level of intimacy, the degree and range of openness, the depth of honor.

Honor and Trust
And so we come to honor and trust. Annette Baier defines trust as relying on someone to take care of something entrusted to them. We may think of the thing entrusted as possessions, or perhaps an obligation, or even our children. But in friendship, what we most entrust to each other is our hearts and minds, our health and our sanity, our sense of the world—our very beings. Rich writes that when we have been lied to by a friend, we start to feel a little crazy (*On Lies* 186). We lose our sense of reality, of grounding. We begin to question our judgment: "When we discover that someone we trusted can be trusted no longer, it forces us to reexamine the universe, to question the whole instinct and concept of trust. For awhile, we are thrust back onto some bleak, jutting ledge, . . . in a world before kinship, or naming, or tenderness exist . . ." (*On Lies* 192).

Friendships in the sense of Rich's notion of "honorable relationships,"[24] require honesty and truthfulness, a consistent commitment not to deceive and to share our truths to the best of our ability. Also, we trust our friends to bear reliable "moral witness" to our own experiences—to call us on our inauthenticities, our hypocrisies, our misdeeds toward others and ourselves (*What Are Friends For?* 196–200). The value of such honesty and openness lies in breaking down our self-delusion and our isolation from each other and in doing justice to our complexity (*On Lies* 188). Rich argues that this does not mean that in order to have an honorable relationship we must tell each other everything at once, or even know what we need to tell each other. But it does mean that we tell each other those things it is important for the other to know, and at the very least, say that there are things we are not disclosing:

> It means that most of the time I am eager, longing for the possibility of telling you. That these possibilities may seem frightening, but not destructive, to me. That I feel strong enough to hear your tentative and groping words. That we both know we are trying, all the time, to extend the possibilities of truth between us. (*On Lies* 194)

In Camus's play *Caligula*, Caligula wonders aloud whether such a relationship is possible, and asks Cherea, the rebel character in the play, whether "it's possible for two men of much the same temperament and equal pride to talk to each other with complete frankness—if only once in their lives? Can they strip themselves naked, so to speak, and shed their prejudices, their private interests, the lies by which they live? . . . Can they . . . open their hearts to each other?" In Cherea's answer, "Yes . . . I think it's possible," lies the hope of rebellious friendship (50).

Loyalty and Commitment

Finally, Lugones and Spelman say that a requisite of friendship is to "have a stake in our world." Care, attention, knowledge, and understanding take us only so far in friendship. Having a stake in our friend's world requires us to care not only for our friend, but for their communities. It is not enough to know what one is going through. The loyalty asked by friendship calls on us to speak out and act against those things that bring harm to our friends' worlds, and actively to enjoin those things that bring them health.[25]

In the early 1980s, a human rights ordinance that would include rights for gays and lesbians was vociferously opposed by many in our community. Several members of the gay and lesbian community, especially activists for the ordinance, were receiving death threats. I had only recently begun my "travels" into the lesbian community, which was different from my own, but I remember standing in solidarity as we sang together Holly Near's "Singing for Our Lives." I began to make the connections between the lives and the lyrics. The "gay and lesbian people" were also a threatened people, literally singing for their lives.

A few weeks later, I found myself singing the song again, this time in a large auditorium filled with hundreds of women, joined by Holly Near and Ronnie Gilbert, holding and swaying, singing for our lives, and the sense of solidarity grew strong in me. But I did not yet fully realize what it was to have a stake in this world. This grew only as friendships grew. Several years later, the Reverend Fred Phelps was scheduled to come to our town, preaching his message of hate against gays and lesbians. It is possible that had I never become friends with members of the lesbian and gay community, I might have attended the meetings and the vigil, and displayed the anti-hate pink triangle in the window of my home out of solidarity, but for me, this was more than solidarity. These were acts of love for my friends. It was my love for my friends that gave me such a stake in their world that I needed to do whatever I could to end the hate that threatened them. Had I isolated myself in my "safe" community, I could not have faced my friends, or myself. Having a stake in our friends' worlds calls on us to act in loyalty to their lives and the lives of their communities.

The loyalty of friendship may also ask of us to be disloyal to certain other communities. Feminist friendship, in particular, may require that we be, in Adrienne Rich's terms, "disloyal to civilization."[26] Janice Raymond has written that one of the main obstacles to friendship among women has been that assimilation into the male world causes some women to disassociate from other women (164–181). Assimilation into the male world wins women the privileges of that world—money, power, social legitimacy. However, feminist friendship requires us to be disloyal to those aspects of the male world that are misogynist and patriarchal. It requires us to be disloyal to those aspects of civilization that are racist, classist, heterosexist. And disloyalty usually comes with a price, the loss of privilege—esteem, livelihood, social acceptability, perhaps freedoms and life itself. But it also comes with rewards. María Lugones writes that in her arrogant perception of her mother, she was "loyal to the arrogant perceiver's construction of her and thus disloyal to her" (402). In claiming her loyalty to her mother, and becoming disloyal to the arrogant perceiver, she gained a new understanding of both her mother and herself, and a "new understanding of love" (402).

Finally, loyalty to friends means that at times we need to put our friends before our principles. After an altercation with a friend over a political disagreement, Camus said to Simone de Beauvoir, "'What we have in common, you [Sartre and de Beauvoir] and I, is that for us individuals come first; we prefer the concrete to the abstract, people to doctrines, we place friendship above politics'" (de Beauvoir, *Force* 109).[27] Ideally, this is true in the practice of feminist friendship. However, women have lost friends over political differences, specifically over feminist principles (Raymond 6). I have witnessed this too often—feminists ending friendships because their friend did something they did not consider "feminist" enough, or because their friend remained loyal to someone else who did something they did not consider "feminist" enough. The cycles can seem never-ending and quite vicious. Loyalty to friends does not mean we have always to condone our friend's actions, but it does demand certain efforts on the part of both toward reciprocity of understanding and reconciliation (though in harmful and abusive relationships, leaving the relationship is also called for).

Reconciliation

This brings us finally to the task of reconciliation.[28] "Reconciliation," writes bell hooks, "is one of my favorite words. Evoking our capacity to restore to harmony that which has been broken, severed, and disrupted. The very word serves as a constant reminder in my life that we can come together with those who have hurt us, with those whom we have caused pain, and experience sweet communion" (*Sisters* 163). Reconciliation is also one of my favorite words. It first became embedded in my consciousness when I visited the bombed-out ruins of Coventry Cathedral in Coventry, England. The cathedral had been bombed by the Germans in a retaliatory bombing for the Allied bombing of Dresden. It would seem that it would be the site of revenge, rather than reconciliation. But built next to the charred ruins was a new cathedral, a cathedral dedicated to the reconciliation of relationships that had become charred and ruined, a cathedral built from the pennies of German children. Perhaps children know better than adults how to reconcile. They are upfront with their battles, and then quick to make up. Bearing grudges seems to come later in life, and politics can become more important than particular people. Ironically, it may sometimes be easier to forgive strangers and enemies than our friends. Because our bonds are deeper, so are our hurt and sense of betrayal.

Friends can and do hurt us, as we hurt them. We may disagree about how best to live out our feminist vision. Points of contention can become open wounds. Hooks reminds us that in order to be at peace, we need to release the bitterness and reconcile with those who have hurt us (*Sisters* 163–164). Not all feminists agree. Some argue that there may be a healthy quality to bitterness, at least partial bitterness directed toward a particular harm for which there are no legitimate excuses, preferring it in any event to cynicism, and that there may be instances when forgiveness is inappropriate (McFall).[29] But I would contend that the friendship of rebellion requires that "we not give in to hatred," but rather that we strive to reconcile.

Sara Ruddick describes reconciliation as one of the four ideals of nonviolence learned in maternal practice (the other three being renunciation, resistance, and peacekeeping) (*Maternal* 174–176). Reconciliation requires forgiveness, which does not mean that one condones an evil act, but rather that it is no longer a barrier to the relationship. However, before forgiveness can appropriately take place, one must first name the evil perpetrated, and assign or take responsibility for it, for harm is also done if a deed is forgiven before it is named and owned. Hooks agrees that reconciliation requires forgiveness, but says also that this may first require compassion, a compassion that comes in truly understanding another (*Sisters* 168). Hooks cites the teachings of Buddhist monk Thich Nhat Hanh, who tells the story of a brother who upon waking his sister in the morning, gets a hostile response. Then the brother remembers "that during the night his sister coughed a lot, and he realizes she must be sick. Maybe she behaved so meanly because she has a cold. At that moment, he understands, and he is not angry at all anymore. When you understand, you cannot help but love" (Hanh 79–80). Compassionate understanding of the reasons for our friend's actions enables forgiveness to follow.

Hannah Arendt wrote of forgiveness being an act of freedom. In forgiving, ourselves and others, we *act* rather than *react*. We release ourselves and others from past actions. We do not respond in the expected way. We strike out in a radically new and releasing and freeing direction. We can begin anew. (*Human Condition* 236–243). In the same way forgiveness lets us begin our relationships anew. "Forgiveness" writes hooks, "enables the restoration of our mutual harmony. We can both start over again on an equal footing, no longer separated by whatever wrong occurred" (*Sisters* 173).

These then are the requirements of rebellious feminist friendship: reciprocity of care—meaning love and affection, respectful attention and knowledge; reciprocity of understanding; honor, truthfulness, and trust; loyalty; and forgiveness. Friendship, wrote Simone Weil, "consists of loving a human being as we should like to be able to love each soul in particular of all those who go to make up the human race" (370). This is the hope of rebellion.

Love and relationship are at the core of rebellion, and I would contend, of feminism. Thus, feminism, with rebellion, affirms "that if there is one thing one can always yearn for and sometimes attain, it is human love" (*Plague* 271).

CHAPTER 7

IMMANENCE

How can one consecrate the harmony of love and revolt? The earth!
Camus, *Lyrical and Critical Essays* 104

CHORUS: The sea, the sea! The sea will save us. What cares the sea for wars and pestilences? Governments come and go, but the sea endures; how many governments has it engulfed! And how simple are its gifts! Red mornings and green sunsets, and from dusk to dawn the murmur of innumerable waves under the dome of night fretted with myriads of stars.

O vast sea-spaces, shining solitude, baptism of brine! . . . Who will give back to me the waters of forgetting, the slumbrous smoothness of the open sea, its liquid pathways, long furrows that form and fold upon themselves! To the sea! To the sea, before the gates are shut . . . . (*State of Siege* 167–168)

In Camus's play, *State of Siege*, as the plague is seeping into the town of Cadiz and the gates are closing the townspeople in, it is to the sea that the townspeople turn for salvation. But the gates all close, for the Plague "hates the sea and wants to cut us off from it" (169) because it is the source of our strength, our resilience, our meaning, our connection with the universe—with love.[1]

For Camus, immersion in the sea is a form of spiritual renewal. In the connection of the body with the body of water, we connect with the soul of the universe. We need this connection in order to keep rebellion faithful to its origins in love for each other and for the earth.[2] When the winter of the plague is over, the men return to the women, "clamoring . . . for what they cannot do without: the freedom of the great sea spaces, empty skies of summer, love's undying fragrance" (200). The sea, the sky, the sun—these were the riches that sustained Camus in his poverty and that sustained his soul in the poverty of his times. He said that in his youth he "lived on almost nothing, but also in a kind of rapture. . . . It was not poverty that got in my way; in Africa, the sun and the sea cost nothing. . . . the lovely warmth that reigned over my childhood freed me from resentment" (*Lyrical* 7). And in the difficult days of World War II, the memory of this warmth sustained him: "In the worst years of our madness the memory of this sky had never left me. It was this that in the end had saved me from despair. . . . In the depths of winter, I finally learned that within me lay an invincible summer" (*Lyrical* 168–169).

Camus asserts that rebellion that is forgetful of its origin in love of life denies existence, denies life, and heads toward destruction (*Rebel* 304). But love of life and of the earth—of sea and sky and sun, saves rebellion from the futile negativity of resentment and the excesses of revolution. At the origin of rebellion lies a spirituality of immanence.

Camus's Spirituality of Immanence

Camus's works are deeply spiritual, though not in a traditionally religious sense. He never acknowledged a belief in God and his works are filled with his quarrels with and rejections of Christian beliefs.[3] He was uncomfortable with the concepts of sin, salvation, and eternal life. In a significant passage, he wrote that though he had never really understood the meaning of sin, "if there is there is a sin against life, then it lies perhaps less in despairing of it than in hoping for another life and evading the implacable grandeur of the one we have" (*Lyrical* 91).[4] Rejecting a spirituality of transcendence and eternal life beyond this earth, Camus grounded his spirituality in the grandeur of life on this earth.

Examples fill his works, but perhaps the most symbolic of Camus's spirituality is one of his last works, a short story, "The Growing Stone" (*Exile*).[5] In "The Growing Stone," a Western engineer, d'Arrast, has come to a village deep in the forest of Brazil to help the villagers with the flooding that has threatened the very existence of their village. During his visit, he befriends and is befriended by one of the villagers, a ship's cook. D'Arrast has come at the time of the procession to the church of Iguape, a procession filled with significance for the cook, for it is during the festival that he will fulfill a promise made to Jesus. The cook explained that not long ago his ship had capsized, and when he was adrift in the dark waters he promised Jesus that if he saved him, then he would carry a one hundred pound stone to the church in Iguape during the procession. When the day comes, the cook, true to his promise, picks up the stone and begins to carry it on his head to the church. But partway there, overwhelmed with fatigue, he falls and can move no farther. D'Arrast steps in, picks up the stone and carries it. But significantly, when d'Arrast nears the church, he turns away. Instead, he goes to the cook's home, where he is invited to sit down and join them at their table (*Exile* 213). Here "he joyfully acclaimed his own strength; he acclaimed, once again, a fresh beginning in life. . . . He felt rising within him a surge of obscure and panting joy that he was powerless to name" (*Exile* 212).

There is much in this story of the importance of friendship and solidarity, and the joy that comes therein. There is also a message of finding spiritual strength not in the church, but rather in relationships with others and with the earth. In an essay written much earlier ("The Minotaur, Or Stopping in Oran," 1939) Camus had written, "For the initiate, the world is no heavier to carry than that stone. The burden of Atlas is easy; all one need do is choose his moment" (*Lyrical* 132). This was d'Arrast's moment. In carrying the stone, d'Arrast is claiming his solidarity with humanity and with the earth. Camus said that there are moments, and I suspect these are moments of rebellion, when we must "consent to stone. . . . if stone can do no more for us than can the human heart, it can at least do just as much" (*Lyrical* 131). Camus referred to this moment as, "the strange moment when spirituality rejects ethics, when happiness springs from the absence of hope, when the mind finds its justification in the body. . . . I learned to consent to the earth and be consumed in the dark flame of its celebrations" ("The Desert," 1937, *Lyrical* 104). To consent to stone, to consent to the earth is to attend to a wisdom larger than oneself. It is in stone, and sea, and sun, and relationship that Camus found the sources of his spiritual strength, and the origin of rebellion.

Camus's spirituality has variously been called "pagan," "pantheistic," "panentheistic," an "ethic of being," and an "ethic of joy."[6] I prefer to think of Camus's spirituality as "immanental." "Immanence" itself means simply "indwelling," and is usually used in reference to the divine dwelling within.[7] Specifically, Starhawk defines "immanence" as "the awareness of the world and everything in it as alive, dynamic, interdependent, and interacting, infused with moving energies: a living being, a weaving dance" ("Consciousness" 177). Though Camus never used the term "immanence," I see in his thought a valuing of those qualities I would regard as immanental—relationship with and an awe and wonder of the natural world, a sensual appreciation of the body, a valuing of beauty and a love of life in the here and now, and a joy emanating from spiritual communion with all of creation.

Camus's early works, particularly *Nuptials*,[8] reveal a certain pantheism, though more accurately a panentheism characteristic of immanence.

He expressed a worship of the earth and the sea and the sun and the stones, gathering from them a feeling of harmony, resonance, of being part of a "pre-arranged design" (*Lyrical* 71). They enabled him to discover the wisdom of his true nature, to center and ground himself, to find inner peace. "It is not so easy to become what one is, to rediscover one's deepest measure," he wrote. "But watching the solid backbone of the Chenoua,[9] my heart would grow calm with a strange certainty. I was learning to breathe, I was fitting into things and fulfilling myself" (*Lyrical* 67).

His place of worship is symbolized by Tipasa,[10] a place "inhabited by gods," where "the gods speak in the sun and the scent of absinthe leaves, in the silver armor of the sea, in the raw blue sky, the flower-covered ruins, and the great bubbles of light among the heaps of stone" (65). Sun, sea, sky, flowers, light, stones—these, he says, are his "gospels" (101). In Tipasa, "he surrenders to his god" (102).

Camus's immersion in nature is present in much of his work. As Camus said of himself, "The great free love of nature and the sea absorb me completely" (*Lyrical* 66). They nurtured his spirit, his being, as is evident in this passage from "Nuptials at Tipasa":

> Even here, I know that I shall never come close enough to the world. I must be naked and dive into the sea, still scented with the perfumes of the earth, wash them off in the sea, and consummate with my flesh the embrace for which sun and sea, lips to lips, have so long been sighing. I feel the shock of the water, rise up through a thick, cold glue, then dive back with my ears ringing, my nose streaming, and the taste of salt in my mouth. As I swim, my arms shining with water flash into gold in the sunlight, until I fold them in again with a twist of all my muscles; the water streams along my body as my legs take tumultuous possession of the waves—and the horizon disappears. On the beach, I flop down on the sand, yield to the world, feel the weight of flesh and bones, again dazed with sunlight. . . . In a moment, when I throw myself down among the absinthe plants to bring their scent into my body, I shall know, appearances to the contrary, that I am fulfilling a truth which is the sun's and which will also be my death's. In a sense, it is my life that I am staking here, a life that tastes of warm stone, that is full of the sighs of the sea and the rising song of the crickets . . . . (*Lyrical* 68–69)

Jeffrey Isaac is critical of Camus's "unreflective" treatment of nature, finding his portrayal of nature as a source of comfort and of inspiration to be essentialist (232–233). However, it is so only if one regards nature as dead.[11] Regarded as immanental and alive, Camus's experience of nature represents an awareness of the dynamic interplay of energies in all of creation, rather than an essentialist construction of it.

Camus's expression of his relationship with the earth and the sea and the rocks is very bodily—"I consummate with my flesh"; "I was learning to breathe"; "feel the weight of flesh and bone"; "bring their scent into my body"; "the taste of warm stone." These express his deep appreciation of the body and its knowledge. In his posthumously published autobiographical novel, *The First Man*, he writes of his:

> love of bodies, of their beauty, of their warmth that never stopped attracting him, with nothing particular in mind, like an animal—it was not to possess them, which he did not know how to do, but just to enter into their radiance, to lean his shoulder against his friend's with a great sensation of confidence and letting go, and almost to faint when a woman's hand lingered a moment on his in the crowd of the trolley. . . . He found it with his dog Brilliant when he stretched out alongside him and breathed his strong smell of fur . . . . (282)

Camus also reveled in the harmony of the body and the earth: "Being naked always carries a sense of physical liberty and of the harmony between hand and flowers—the loving understanding between the earth and a man delivered from the human—ah! I would be a convert if this were not already my religion" (*Lyrical* 100). His spirituality is deeply embodied. As he wrote, "The immortality of the soul, it is true, engrosses many noble minds. But this is because they reject the body, the only truth that is given . . ." (*Lyrical* 95). He claims the body and the moment as the "twin truths" (*Lyrical* 98). Camus did not separate body and mind, but rather valued and validated the wisdom of the body.

His body was a site of spiritual lessons not only in its pleasures and ecstasies, but also in its sufferings and limitations. Having contracted tuberculosis at the height of his youth (he was seventeen), he experienced recurring long hospitalizations that separated him from the people, the physical activity, and the sun and sea that he loved. In his journals, he referred to his illness as both a cross and a guardrail (*Notebooks II* 54). It gave him a retreat of sorts, to which he referred as the austerity and silence of a convent (*Notebooks II* 41). More than this, Camus credited his illness with teaching him detachment, and that, he said, saved him from resentment (*Lyrical* 9).[12] Illness can provide deep awareness of the body, both in recognition of its limits, and an appreciation of its vigor in times of health. In the latter, it can also provide an extraordinary wonder of the world and love of life. Camus wrote at a very young age of his horror of death, attributing to it an eagerness to live (*Lyrical* 78). Coming so close to the limits of one's physical existence can also give one a great appreciation of it.

A deep genuine love of life fills Camus's works.[13] He wrote passion-ately of "the longing, yes, to live, to live still more, to immerse himself in the greatest warmth this earth could give him" (*First Man* 282). As he expressed in "Nuptials at Tipasa":

> I love this life with abandon and wish to speak of it boldly: it makes me proud of my human condition. Yet people have told me; there's nothing to be proud of. Yes, there is: this sun, this sea, my heart leaping with youth, the salt taste of my body and this vast landscape in which tenderness and glory merge in blue and yellow. . . . Everything here leaves me intact, I surrender nothing of myself, and don no mask: learning patiently and arduously how to live is enough for me . . . . (*Lyrical* 68–69)

And with this love of life comes a deep joy, a joy that inspired him and that he had to follow (*Lyrical* 99, 190–192). As he described himself in his autobiographical novel, he wanted "only joy, and free spirits, and energy, and all that life has that is good, that is mysterious, that is not and never will be for sale" (*First Man* 277–278).

Relationship with and love of the earth, valuing the body, joy in the beauty and goodness of life, living fully in the present moment—these values of immanence are at the heart of Camus's ethic of rebellion.

Feminism and Immanence

De Beauvoir on Immanence

At first glance, Camus's valuing of immanence may seem at odds with feminism. After all, in her *The Second Sex*, the work that inspired much of contemporary feminist thought,[14] Camus's colleague and friend, Simone de Beauvoir, regarded immanence very unfavorably. Dichotomizing immanence and transcendence, and associating tran-scendence with freedom and creativity, she founded her feminism on a rejection of the life of immanence to which women are "doomed" (*Second Sex* 83).[15] It might be objected that de Beauvoir did not use the term "immanence" exactly as I am using it here, as an indwelling of the spirit. Her use of "immanence" has a specific meaning within the context of existentialist philosophy, where immanence represents the flesh, the body, earthly existence, but unlike Camus's encounter with these as enspir-ited, existentialism regards these as passive, inert, repetitious, the stuff of necessity. This "immanence" is opposed to "transcendence"—the stuff of culture, spirit, mind, freedom, that is, action.[16] What de Beauvoir and other existentialists reject in immanence is the lack of possibility of free-dom or of creation. It is not that de Beauvoir rejected the body. Indeed many consider *The Second Sex* to be a very embodied philosophy and have attributed feminism's embrace of embodiment to her work.[17] Rather, she rejected what she regarded as its incapacity for the valued transcendence. But it is specifically her alienation of consciousness and spirit from the body and the earth that is at issue.

Because de Beauvoir viewed the world through the ontological divide of immanence/transcendence, nature/culture, Other/subject, woman/ man, she saw the association of woman with nature as a way that men used women to cope with their fundamental estrangement from nature.[18] However, de Beauvoir argued that rather than woman having an innate connection with nature, "if woman is earthy, . . . it is because she is compelled to devote her existence to cooking and washing diapers . . ." (*Second Sex* 604). She rejected those aspects of the body that impinge on freedom, that doom life to repetition, futility, to making nothing new. She wrote of women's domestic life:

> It is her duty to assure the monotonous repetition of life in all its mind-less factuality. . . . Her life is not directed toward ends; she is absorbed in producing or caring for things that are never more than means, such as food, clothing, and shelter . . . inessential intermediaries between animal life and free existence. . . . woman [is] condemned to passivity (*Second Sex* 604–605). . . . Few tasks are more like the torture of Sisyphus than housework, with its endless repetition: the clean becomes soiled, the soiled is made clean, over and over, day after day. The housewife wears herself out marking time: she makes nothing, simply perpetuates the present. (*Second Sex* 451–452)[19]

Women are particularly burdened, she argued, because they are doomed to have a body that is constantly occupied with reproduction. She called reproduction a "bondage," "a terrible handicap" (*Second Sex* 65). Woman's "misfortune is to have been biologically destined for the repetition of Life, when even in her own view Life does not carry within itself its reasons for being" (*Second Sex* 64). We hear from her that "in maternity woman remained closely bound to her body, like an animal" (*Second Sex* 65), but that man is "raised above the animal": "For it is not in giving life but in risking life that man is raised above the animal; that is why superiority has been accorded in humanity not to the sex that brings forth but to that which kills" (*Second Sex* 64). Because of maternity, "[woman] submitted passively to her biologic fate. The domestic labors that fell to her lot because they were reconcilable with the cares of maternity imprisoned her in repetition and immanence . . . they produced nothing new" (*Second Sex* 63). This latter is a key phrase.

For de Beauvoir, freedom lies in creating something new. If there is only repetition, there is no creation, no culture. De Beauvoir's hope for the liberation of women is that we transcend our lives of immanence—of housework, childbearing and childrearing, of servicing the unending needs of men and children—to join the world of the more enduring acts of creativity and contribution of men.

Building on de Beauvoir's theory, other feminists have similarly devalued and rejected immanence. Synthesizing de Beauvoir, Freud, and historical materialism, Shulamith Firestone developed a materialist view of history based on sexuality, especially as it is formed in the nuclear family. Rather than focusing on the Hegelian concept of Otherness, as did de Beauvoir, Firestone suggested that the biological fact of procreation itself is at the origin of dualism, and that the biological family is inherently unequal because of different roles in reproduction. Due to women being continually at the mercy of biology—menstruation, pregnancy, childbirth, nursing, and the long dependency of human infants, women spend most of their lives dependent on males, which leads to women's subordination. Thus, the obvious solution to dualism and its oppression, she argued, is to end biological reproduction. Through artificial reproduction, daycare, and cybernation (to handle all other distasteful bodily labor), women can find emancipation.

Similarly Jeffner Allen has argued that motherhood is dangerous to women ("Motherhood"). In motherhood, women are viewed only as bodies, as a resource to reproduce men and the world of men. The marking of the female body as MOTHER denies female subjectivity and inscribes the domination of men into women's bodies. Unlike Firestone, however, she does not seek to alter motherhood through alternative means of sex, pregnancy, childcare, but rather seeks to have females claim their power not to have children and in so doing claim their bodies as source, not resource.

In *The Feminine Mystique*, Betty Friedan echoed de Beauvoir's testimony to the doom of domesticity, arguing that "the problem that has no name"—meaning the malaise of suburban housewives—comes from the fact that these women live a meaningless existence of immanence. The solution to their problem was to join the workforce, where they could lead meaningful and productive lives. Liberal, Marxist, and socialist feminisms have similarly sought solutions to women's liberation primarily in women's employment and engagement in the public world.

Sherry Ortner extended de Beauvoir's division of nature/culture, woman/man to argue first, that Nature is devalued in every culture, as evidenced by the fact of culture itself (defining culture as products of human consciousness by means of which humanity attempts to assert control over nature), and second, that because of their universal association with Nature, women are also devalued in every culture. She argued further that culture's project is to subsume and transcend nature, and by extension, subordinate women. Her solution was to align women with culture, not revalue nature.

But much of contemporary feminist thought has rejected these strains in de Beauvoir's thought, regarding them as "rationalistic, too old-fashioned modernist, and above all male biased" (Vintges 133). Many reject the mind/body dualism reflected in her transcendence/immanence, male/female dichotomy. Others have specifically eschewed de Beauvoir's rejection of immanence, arguing that it merely reinforces an ethic grounded in the culture of male dominance (Keller, Catherine 260). Adrienne Rich is sympathetic to de Beauvoir's intent arguing that women have been perceived as Nature and exploited as Nature for far too long. Thus it makes sense that women would want to be identified with Culture rather than Nature. However, she continues, "it is precisely this culture and its political institution which have split us off from itself. In so doing it has also split itself off from life . . ." (*Of Woman* 285). Rather than aspiring to the existing culture, feminists instead should seek to transform it, not in denying our bodies, but in claiming them. It is our fear and hatred of the body, says Rich, that has "crippled our brains." Rather, we need to "*think through the body* . . . converting our physicality into both knowledge and power. . . . We need to imagine a world in which every woman is the presiding genius of her own body" (*Of Woman* 284–285).

Feminist Embrace of Immanence: Embodiment

Much feminist writing has been addressed precisely to this task, of listening to and conveying the insight and wisdom of women's bodies. Most important for our purposes is the embracing of immanence by much of feminist spirituality, whose main problem is countering the spirit/body dualism inherent in the transcendent spirituality predominant in traditional theological doctrine with an embodied spirituality.[20] As Anzaldúa writes, "We've been taught that the spirit is outside our bodies or above our heads somewhere up in the sky with God. We're supposed to forget that every cell in our bodies, every bone and bird and worm has spirit in it" ("Entering" 84). Judith Plaskow and Carol Christ have stated that several feminists suggest that theo/thealogy as a whole should move in a more immanental direction (95). Both within and without traditional religious frameworks, feminist thea/theologians have imaged the divine as immanental—as dwelling within the earth and every being. They have named the divine as that which brings forth life and cares and nurtures. As Shekinah, Tara, the Great Mother, they have revived the image of the goddess as "she who dwells within" (Gottlieb).[21]

A feminist spirituality of embodiment embraces the belief that we are spiritual beings in and through our bodies—through the work and action, the pleasure and the suffering of our bodies.[22] This includes not only encounters with the natural world external to the body, but also of the body and the labors of the body. Repeatedly, feminists write of finding spiritual wholeness not in a rejection of the body, sexuality, childbirth, and the daily tending of home, garden, children, the sick and the dying, but rather through these.[23]

The Tasks of Domesticity

The focus of much of this writing has centered around the traditional work of women, that is, tending to the maintenance of the body. While not suggesting that women's sphere is only in the home, or that the tasks of childcare and domesticity are solely women's work (as did some nineteenth-century feminists), many counter de Beauvoir's denigration of women's traditional work in the labor of the body and its maintenance with the argument that women's traditional work needs to be revalorized.

According to de Beauvoir, the role of the housewife and mother "was only nourishing, never creative. In no domain whatever did she create; she maintained the life of the tribe by giving it children and bread, nothing more" (*Second Sex* 73). As if in response to de Beauvoir, Beverly Wildung Harrison writes that women's domestic activities have been wrongly perceived as passive and reconceives the activity of women in the home as acts of creativity: "Women have always exemplified the power of activity over passivity, of experimentation over routinization, of creativity and risk-taking over conventionality . . ." (9). She calls on us to develop a realistic sense of women's past, arguing that childbearing and nursing have usually given women responsibility for the very activities that make for human survival and sustenance (9): "Women have been the doers of life-sustaining things, the 'copers,' those who have understood that the reception of the gift of life is no inert thing, that to receive this gift is to be engaged in its tending, constantly" (10). To de Beauvoir's statement that "woman is not called upon to build a better world: her domain is fixed and she has only to keep up the never ending struggle against the evil principles that creep into it" (451–452), Harrison responds, "We dare not minimize the very real historical power of women to be architects of what is most authentically human. We must not lose hold of the fact that we

have been the chief builders of whatever human dignity and community
has come to expression. *We* have the right to speak of *building* human
dignity and community" (11, italics in original).[24]

Adrienne Rich similarly has written about the devaluation of the
traditional work of women as a symptom of gynephobia, and applauds
feminism for valuing what patriarchal culture has devalued—the work
of women's hands, the oral culture, the traditional healing arts and
remedies (*On Lies* 262–263). She writes that it is:

> the million tiny stitches, the friction of the scrubbing brush, the scour-
> ing cloth, the iron across the shirt, the rubbing of cloth against itself to
> exorcise the stain, the renewal of the scorched pot, the rusted knifeblade,
> the invisible weaving of a frayed and threadbare family life, the cleaning
> up of soil and waste left behind by men and children . . . unacknowl-
> edged by the political philosophers . . . [that is the] activity of world-
> protection, world-preservation, world-repair. (*On Lies* 205)

But this world has not remained unacknowledged by feminist philosophers. Bell hooks has challenged the notion that work outside the home is
an avenue for women's liberation, arguing that working-class women and
women of color have been working outside the home all along, often in
conditions of drudgery, enslavement, and oppression. Many of these
women, she argues, would find liberation in being able to stay at home
and care for their own houses and children, rather than someone else's. She
argues that we need to rethink the nature of work altogether, and attribute
value to all the work that women do, whether paid or unpaid. She suggests
that rather than a doom, housework can be an avenue to personal satisfaction, well-being, learning lessons of responsibility and respect for one's
environment, and an appreciation of service (*Feminist* 95–105).

Maria Harris writes of the home as a spiritual dwelling place that holds
lessons of ritual, care, and community (99–102). In the daily making of
meals, the making of beds, the washing of dishes, the bathing of children
we perform rituals imbued with meaning, finding the sacred in the ordinary. Some find spiritual fulfillment in the creation of the home as a space
of beauty, or of spiritual retreat, or of relationship and community.

I have elsewhere written of the importance of doing the "lowly"
work—that is, the necessary work, the tedious work, the daily work of
keeping up with the growth and the decay and the dirt—as soul work,
helping to keep us grounded. I have also written of the value of the work
of the hands as a meditative practice:[25]

> For much of my life I thought of spirituality as being somewhere "out
> there;" transcendent. It is the spirit after all. One can't see it or taste it or

hear it or touch it. But the more I live, the more I see it as being connected with the way I walk and talk and go about my daily tasks. The way I hug my child, wash dishes, and cut carrots, has as much to do with spirituality as time spent in church or time spent in prayer. They embody the spirit. (*Journey* 70–71)

Rita Gross has also written of domestic tasks and childcare as opportunities for Buddhist practice. She notes the importance of a feminist revalorization of these experiences, and how this has led to cooking, cleaning, gardening, and maintenance work to being central to formal mindfulness training (*Buddhism* 274–278). She particularly focuses on childcare as a spiritually significant practice,[26] noting that this is something that caregivers feel intuitively. She quotes one mother:

> I have to admit that the strongest teacher I have ever known is my son, Joshua. When he was just a newborn, he opened my eyes to the meaning of practice. Just going to Joshua when he cried, just cleaning up his messes, moving from one thing to another, I experienced being present each moment. :"This is the beginner's mind," I said to myself . . . .(275)

Motherhood

Motherhood has been the subject of much feminist discussion and thought.[27] Though contemporary feminists largely reject motherhood as institutionalized under patriarchy, with some notable exceptions, they have not rejected motherhood itself. Rather, they have claimed that the need to nurture may be an authentic, positive expression of self, and that what we need is a philosophical appreciation of the values and the autonomy that may be found in mothering (something de Beauvoir's biographer, Margaret Simons has argued de Beauvoir was unable to see or to provide (78)). Many have used the insights and practical wisdom gleaned in the work of mothering to inform our concepts of relationship, power, equality, conflict resolution, and the nature of political society.[28]

Many have regarded the entire experience of motherhood—pregnancy, birth, breast-feeding, childcare—as offering the possibility of authentic self-expression and spiritual fulfillment, of deep communion. In mothering we learn spiritual lessons of love, compassion, holding and letting go, openness to who we are to become, finding and giving nourishment of all kinds, and passing on these lessons of love and trust (Ochs). Giving birth has especially been regarded as an opening to spiritual wisdom. Buddhist feminist Linda Chrisman writes of how she came to know the true meaning of Buddhist teachings in the process of giving birth: "It is through the searing pain of surrender in giving birth that I know of suffering and compassion. It is through the molten anguish of rage while birthing that I know of interdependence. It is through the sweet pause between my contractions that I know of emptiness" (39).

A comment by one of my students, a physician, has forever embedded in me the deep spiritual meaning of the process of giving birth. She related that whenever she is attendant at a birth, the phrase that comes to her mind is one traditionally spoken during the Christian ritual of communion: "This is my body, broken for you. This is my blood, spilled for you."[29] I have ever since thought of giving birth, giving life, as true communion.

Sexuality

Such an embodied spirituality has raised particular issues for women, whose bodies have so often been regarded as obstacles to spiritual enlightenment and as unclean due to menstruation and childbirth, and whose sexuality has been associated with sin and evil by the major religious traditions of the world. More and more, feminists are reclaiming earth-centered and female-centered religious traditions, often of their own indigenous origins, in which the body and women are revered, menstruation and childbirth are held in awe and respect, and the womb and vagina are considered sacred.[30] Celebrations of the beginning of a young woman's menses are becoming more common. Pregnancy has begun to be seen as a time of spiritual attunement, and menopause as a time of women coming into their true wisdom and power. And, in contrast to de Beauvoir, feminists have reclaimed women's life-giving capacity as valuable and valued.

Much of the work in feminist spirituality has been directed toward overcoming the deeply held belief in sexuality as sin, and reconceiving loving sexuality, in all its expressions, as an expression of our spirituality. Sexuality that is celebrative and mutually respectful is a central tenet of Wiccan beliefs, as it is for many newly revived feminist goddess-centered spiritualities that celebrate, among others, goddesses of unrestrained sexual love—Astarte, Ishtar, Coatelupeh.[31] Lesbian feminist Episcopalian priest Carter Heyward argues that we need to reclaim the term "lover" to conceive of our sexuality as our desire to participate in making love and justice in the world and a lover as "a person of passion, a lover of humanity" (295–296).

The character Shug, in Alice Walker's *The Color Purple*, conveys this sense of sensuality, sexuality, the body, and the earth as God's gifts and positive goods:

> Here's the thing, say Shug. The thing I believe. God is inside you and inside everybody else. You come into the world with God. But only them that search for it inside find it. . . . I believe God is everything, say Shug. Everything that is or ever was or ever will be. And when you can feel that, and be happy to feel that, you've found It . . . .
>
> . . . My first step from the old white man was trees. Then air. Then birds. Then other people. But one day when I was sitting quiet and feeling like a motherless child, which I was, it come to me: that feeling of being part of everything, not separate at all. I knew that if I cut a tree, my arm would bleed. And I laughed and I cried and I run all around the house. I knew just what it was. In fact, when it happen, you can't miss it. It sort of like you know what, she say, grinning and rubbing high up on my thigh.
>
> *Shug!* I say.
>
> Oh, she say. God love all them feelings. That's some of the best stuff God did. . . .
>
> God don't think it dirty? I ast.
>
> Naw, she say. God made it. Listen, God love everything you love—and a mess of stuff you don't. . . .
>
> Man corrupt everything, say Shug. . . . He try to make you think he everywhere. Soon as you think he everywhere, you think he God. But he ain't. Whenever you trying to pray, and man plop himself on the other end of it, tell him to git lost, say Shug. Conjure up flowers, wind, water, a big rock. (177–179)

Earth

Flowers, wind, water, rock. We find in feminism, especially in ecofeminism and feminist spirituality, a profound relationship with the earth akin to that of Camus's. We find it implicated in an ethico-political stance that includes the earth and other creatures in a liberating justice of nondomination. We find it articulated as well in the type of I–Thou relation we find in Camus's writings. For example, Karen Warren, in writing of her developing ecofeminism, describes a rock-climbing experience in which she perceived being in relationship with the rock:

> I began to talk to the rock in an almost inaudible, child-like way, as if the rock were my friend. I felt an overwhelming sense of gratitude for what it offered me—a chance to know myself and the rock differently, to appreciate unforeseen miracles like the tiny flowers growing in the even tinier cracks in the rock's surface, and to come to know a sense of *being in relationship* with the natural environment. It felt as if the rock and I were silent conversational partners in a longstanding friendship. (134)

Likewise, in Susan Griffin's *Woman and Nature*, it is difficult to tell where woman ends and earth begins, so deep is her connection with it:

> As I go into her, she pierces my heart. As I penetrate further, she unveils me. When I have reached her center, I am weeping only. I have known her all my life, yet she reveals stories to me, and these stories are revelations and I am transformed. . . . I love her daily grace, her silent daring and how loved I am *how we admire this strength in each other, all that we have lost, all that we have suffered, all that we know: we are stunned by this beauty,* and I do not forget: what she is to me what I am to her. (219)[32]

One also finds in feminist spirituality a panentheism akin to Camus's. Gloria Anzaldúa notes this tendency in feminist spirituality: "Stones 'speak' to Luisah Teish, a Santera: trees whisper their secrets to Chrystos, a Native American. I remember listening to the voices of the wind as a child and understanding its messages . . ." ("Entering" 84). In Wicca, the earth, the air, the fire, and the water are all considered sacred. Feminist spiritualities affirm all of creation as being alive with spirit.

Carol Christ's earth-centered theology challenges the value dualism inherent in the transcendent theologies of the major monotheistic religions. "Let us imagine," she writes, "that the life force does not care more about human creativity and choice than it cares about the ability of bermuda grass to spread or moss to form on the side of a tree" (323). In dualistic systems that value human creativity as the quintessential transcendent activity, and thus the most highly valued, Christ's theology would be unthinkable. She invites a value system of radical equality.

Joy

Feminism is rooted in a deep and abiding joy in the wonder of life.[33] We hear this nowhere more clearly than in Audre Lorde's "Uses of the Erotic." Lorde reclaims the word *eros* as "the personification of love in all its aspects. . . . creative power and harmony, . . . an assertion of the lifeforce of women; of that creative energy empowered" (55). In embracing eros we embrace the immanent, feeling deeply in every aspect of our lives, empowering all that we do. The erotic honors the *yes* within ourselves. And it calls us to joy:

> . . . the way my body stretches to music and opens into response, hearkening to its deepest rhythms, so every level upon which I sense also opens to the erotically satisfying experience, whether it is dancing, building a bookcase, writing a poem, examining an idea. That self-connection

shared is a measure of the joy which I know myself to be capable of feel-ing, . . . And that deep and irreplaceable knowledge of my capacity for joy comes to demand from all of my life that it be lived within that knowledge that such satisfaction is possible . . . Once we begin to feel deeply all the aspects of our lives, we begin to demand from ourselves and from our life-pursuits that they feel in accordance with that joy which we know ourselves to be capable of. (56–57)

This demand—that all we do enliven us with joy—is deeply radicaliz-ing. Acted upon, it could empower people to make of their relation-ships, their work, their worship and their political actions, experiences that are life-affirming in all respects.

In spiritualities of embodiment, connection with and appreciation of the earth, and love of life and joyous embrace of eros, feminism joins Camusian rebellion in claiming the value of immanence.

Alienation from Immanence

In *State of Siege*, as Diego lies dying, the Chorus of Women cries out:

Our curse on all who forsake our bodies! And pity on us . . . who are forsaken and must endure year after year this world in which men in their pride are ever aspiring to transform! . . . Men go whoring after ideas, a man runs away from his mother, forsakes his love, and starts rushing upon adventure . . . a hunter of shadows or a lonely singer who invokes some impossible reunion under a silent sky, and makes his way from solitude to solitude, toward the final isolation, a death in the desert . . . . (229)

The curse on those who forsake their bodies, who value ideas and action *on* the world above nature and communion *with* the world is terror and destruction.[34] Rebellion that becomes forgetful of its origins in love of life becomes violent and destructive of its purposes. Camus found such forgetfulness all around him, in Nazi death camps, totalitar-ian ideologies, terror, militarism, and war. "The secret of Europe," he argued, "is that it no longer loves life. . . . they wanted to efface joy from the world" (*Rebel* 305). They had committed the one thing that Camus regarded as a sin (*Lyrical* 91). They had, in his mind, denied the real grandeur of life—the earth, the sky, the sea, joy—and their destructive-ness followed as a result.

Camus argued that the force of ideologies driven by a belief in history rather than a love of the earth have resulted in suffering and sterility. Camus wrote in a metaphorical essay ("Prometheus in the Underworld,"

1946), "History is a sterile earth where heather does not grow. Yet men today have chosen history . . . ." He argues this does not serve the needs of the whole person. We also need beauty and the spiritual resources it provides. What is needed to keep us true to rebellion is ". . . to keep the memory of heather alive" (*Lyrical* 140–142). Many years later, Camus would continue this argument in *The Rebel*:

> His most instinctive act of rebellion, while it affirms the value and the dignity common to all men, obstinately claims, so as to satisfy its hunger for unity, an integral part of the reality whose name is beauty. One can reject all history and yet accept the world of the sea and the stars. The rebels who wish to ignore nature and beauty are condemned to banish from history everything with which they want to construct the dignity of existence and of labor. Beauty, no doubt, does not make revolutions. But a day will come when revolutions will have need of beauty. The procedure of beauty, which is to contest reality while endowing it with unity, is also the procedure of rebellion. Is it possible eternally to reject injustice without ceasing to acclaim the nature of man and the beauty of the world? Our answer is yes. . . . In upholding beauty, we prepare the way for the day of regeneration. (*Rebel* 276–277)

Camus came to identify the forces of history with "German" values and beauty with "Mediterranean" values, and in a rare "us" versus "them" mentality, pitted the two against each other. Camus argued that German ideology consummated two thousand years of struggle against nature, and that its focus on adolescent violence, nostalgia for ideas, and history over strength, courage, and nature was the source of the horrific consequences that German ideology had brought to bear upon Europe in that century. He argued, "When nature ceases to be an object of contemplation and admiration, it can then be nothing more than material for an action that aims at transforming it," and he argued that this action is nothing but "pure conquest" and "an expression of tyranny" (299–300).

He had made a very similar argument, distinguishing the Mediterranean from the Latin (by which he meant Roman) culture, in a lecture predating *The Rebel* by nearly twenty years. Given at the beginning of the build-up of fascism in Germany and Italy (1937), in "The New Mediterranean Culture" Camus looked to Mediterranean values to redeem Europe from the excesses and destructiveness of Latin culture, especially because of its being informed by both Western and Eastern values (due to its physical location). To Mediterranean culture he ascribed a "triumphant taste of life" (*Lyrical* 194). Wanting nothing to do with abstractions and reasoning, the Mediterranean embraces physical life, harmony with the land, love of the trees and hills, sea and sunlight, smiles and humanity, games and joy (*Lyrical* 190). On the other hand, he characterized Roman culture as one that glorifies war and Caesarism, and sacrifices truth and greatness to a violence that has no soul (*Lyrical* 193).[35]

He insisted in both instances that his distinguishing of the two cultures was not meant to cast one as superior to another, stating that there are no higher or lower cultures, only cultures that are more or less true (*Lyrical* 191). But he went on in the earlier essay to argue that there is in fact only one culture—a culture that is necessarily linked to life— to the hills and trees, the sea and sun, and humanity itself (*Lyrical* 197). And in the later essay, *The Rebel*, he said that he raised the importance of the Mediterranean appreciation of mediation, beauty, and nature in recognition of the fact "that it is a thought which the world today cannot do without for very much longer" (*Rebel* 300). Valuing transcendent ideologies over immanent nature would result, he feared, in total domination and destruction. He later argued that we live in terror because we have lost our ability to tap into that part of our beings that is moved by the beauty of nature and by human faces, and thus can more easily destroy these (*Neither* 28–29).

One finds these same sentiments echoed in the works of Susan Griffin. As she says, "Underneath almost every identifiable social problem we share, a powerful way of ordering the world can be detected, one we have inherited from European culture[36] and that alienates consciousness from nature and from being" (*Eros* 10). Like Camus, she argues that for two thousand years Europeans have lived with the prevailing "habit of mind" that places human consciousness and spirit separate from and above nature (*Eros* 29). And Griffin argues like Camus that it is this alienation from nature and being that cuts us off from a world of meaning, and that without meaning, we will cling instead to ideologies (*Eros* 92)—ideologies that take precedence over the lives and loves of real people, ideologies in service of which political movements become totalitarian and terroristic. Rather, she says, "if one would create an egalitarian society, nature must be restored as the common ground of experience" (*Eros* 46).

An Ecofeminist Understanding of the Consequences of Alienation
from Immanence: Susan Griffin and Maria Mies
Susan Griffin and other feminists share Camus's perception that the dominant culture in our society is alienated from the body and nature, but with particular attention to the fact that it is predominantly the white,

upper class, Euro, urban man who suffers this alienation. Maria Mies observes that the average man in industrialized society has hardly any direct body-contact with plants, animals, the earth, or the elements.[37] Rather, his relation to nature is mediated through machines. Similarly, Griffin argues that because of the division of labor, some men, particularly those engaged in white-collar jobs, can live with the illusion that they don't have bodies.[38] Other men and women do the manual labor of production, manufacturing, harvesting, construction, and women do the work of tending the body and taking care of men's messes (*Made* 15).

These feminist theorists also share Camus's understanding of the relation of the alienation of nature and eros with the rise of violence, terror, oppression, and destruction of the earth and its inhabitants. What they add is an in-depth analysis of this correlation, informed by their understanding of the mind/body dualism that follows the splitting of nature and culture, the association of women and nature, and the oppression of both.

Griffin and Mies build their analyses from a critique of mind/body dualism—the Western tendency to divide mind and body and to place the rule of reason over the body's dictates and needs that sets up an ontological and value dualism that places mind, intellect, spirit, culture, and transcendence on one side and body, emotion, matter, nature and immanence on the other. Distancing from nature, moving from immanence to transcendence, from nature to culture, is thus considered a necessary precondition for emancipation.

Many have recognized the association in Western culture of women with matter and nature, and men with culture and spirit.[39] It is the basic premise of ecofeminism. Summarized briefly, women have been identified with nature for various reasons. First, women's biological role in reproduction—menstruation, pregnancy, birthing, lactation—links them more closely to other animals. Second, in women's social roles of the raising of children and the tending of the body, women are regarded as being closer to nature. Finally, women's psyche, being relatively more concrete and subjective in their knowledge as opposed to men's tendency to abstraction and objectivity, is seen as closer to nature (Ortner). To this Griffin adds that women are also associated with nature because we are the first "other" the infant encounters—and one with the power to feed or not feed, comfort or not (*Made* 19).

Karen Warren argues that combining this association of women with value-hierarchical thinking, value dualisms, and a logic of domination explains the subordination and domination of women and the earth. According to this logic, whatever has the capacity to consciously change its environment is morally superior to whatever lacks this capacity.

Humans, having this capacity, are thus morally superior to all other creatures, and justified in subordinating them. However, because women are associated with nature, men are superior to women, and justified in subordinating them. Warren's logic of domination gives us a logical, rational analysis of the relation of women's association with nature with justifications for their domination, but it takes us only so far. De Beauvoir's insights add another dimension to the analysis. She begins with a fundamental assumption of a human need for relationship, and then she argues, following Hegel, that Man (and by this she means males only) seeks to attain the self through his encounter with the Other. Man first attempts this through his encounter with "nature" (*Second Sex* 139), but he experiences nature as silent, impersonal opposition. (De Beauvoir presents this as an ontological fact, rather than a constructed one.) Because Nature does not provide the relationship he needs, Man either remains a stranger, or Nature submits and Man destroys. In either case—Man is alone.

Man's relationship with nature fails because there can be no presence of an Other unless the Other is also present in and for itself, which Nature cannot be. The desired relationship requires "true alterity," that is, for the Other to be at once separate from and identical to Man.[40] So Man then seeks relationship with another being like himself. (De Beauvoir does not tell us what woman is seeking.) However, when encountering another subject, there is always the tendency to assert one's sovereignty over the other.[41] This conflict can only be overridden if each individual freely recognizes the other, regarding each other as subject and object reciprocally. This is friendship—the mutual recognition of free beings who confirm each other's freedom. However, such authentic relationship is difficult, and demands constant tension.

An easier way for Man to assuage his need for loneliness is to find one who is like himself, and yet is already established as inferior—another consciousness like his own, yet without the demands of reciprocal relation—that is, Woman. Woman, who is considered closer to Nature, thus becomes for Man the intermediary between Nature and the too identical male being (though even here, Man does not establish real relationship, and we have no inkling of women's needs for relationship).

Thus, the mythical origin and purpose of Woman is to make Man whole. Eve, for example, was made to rescue Adam from loneliness. But Woman's role as mediator between Man and Nature also results in Woman's symbolic ambiguity, so that the myth of Woman is polarized between extremes of life and death, good and evil (Ortner 211).

De Beauvoir argues that the myth of Woman is the projection of Man's hopes and fears:

> Delilah and Judith, Aspasia and Lucretia, Pandora and Athena—woman is at once Eve and the Virgin Mary. She is an idol, a servant, the source of life, a power of darkness; she is the elemental silence of truth, she is artifice, gossip, and falsehood; she is healing presence and sorceress; she is man's prey, his downfall, she is everything that he is not and that he longs for, his negation and his *raison d'être*. (*Second Sex* 143)

Thus, Woman is associated with life and death; womb and tomb; Good and Evil; both mediator between Man and Nature and the temptation of unconquered nature itself (*Second Sex* 146–147, 192, 197). We find parallels in Western conceptions of nature. Nature is regarded as the enemy, or used as a resource; and Nature is regarded as friend, as the Good Mother that needs protection, but only in museums (Mies). Similarly, indigenous peoples are regarded as "dirty savages" and as "noble" (Mies; Griffin, *Eros* 140).[42] Either woman, native, and nature are idealized and romanticized, yet in a way that is not valued, enabling men to subordinate them, or they are demonized, enabling men to blame them for the evils of the world, thus justifying their humiliation and brutalization. In either case, the result is subordination, domination, and violence.

Another explanation of the polarization and mythologizing of Woman, one grounded more in cultural construction than ontological assumption, is Griffin's account of the creation of the masculine psyche. She argues that the shaping of the masculine psyche is based on the military model of the making of soldiers, who must go through drill after tedious drill to habituate them to respond to the orders of the commanders rather than the needs of their bodies. In isolation from family and friends, soldiers are humiliated and ridiculed, overworked and deprived of sleep in order to learn to disregard their senses and disassociate from their feelings. These same characteristics, (and I would add, often similar training exercises—whether from parents, Scoutmasters, coaches, or peers) are then demanded of anyone adopting the masculine psyche. This can be found in females as well as males, and to a greater or lesser extent certainly does exist in the psyche of anyone raised in this culture—a culture of denial of self, in which we are required to sacrifice all that is "feminine" in us (*Eros* 121) and the child in us (*Pornography* 254). But, she argues, those parts that are denied do not disappear. Rather, we project those parts we have disowned onto others.

Maria Mies connects Man's destructiveness and violence to his romanticization of Nature, women, and indigenous peoples, as well as to his self-denial. She cites urban Man's yearning for Nature and nostalgia for things both rural and exotic. When the work week is done, men flee the city and head to the country and the woods. She notes a similar nostalgia for woman's body, as well as for the tenderness, warmth, Mother, and home of childhood. Man longs for those parts of himself that he has denied and alienated from himself.[43] He seeks to recapture some sense of wholeness in grabbing pieces of it—playing the hunter for the weekend, traveling to distant and exotic lands, sex obsession. (Mies argues that because of the absence of sensual interaction in people's work and our distance from nature in urban environments, the sexual act is often our only direct contact to nature.) But in grabbing pieces, they use it up. They consume the land and the people who inhabit it.[44] With their roads and hotels and golf courses and pollution, tourists use up the very wilderness they are seeking. Sex tourism, combining sex with the allure of exotic lands with the romanticized exotic native, destroys the lives of the young women and the fabric of the community. The more man projects his desires onto a portion of the whole, the greater his hunger for the original whole, wild free nature and women. But the more he seeks to assuage his hunger, the more he destroys. Thus, she argues, "civilization" is founded on violence.

Susan Griffin adds to this the alternate argument, that man's domination rests on the demonization of women and nature. Women become the scapegoats for the evils of the world, and by association, especially those of nature—for death and loss. Thus, the desire to control nature leads to the desire to dominate and control women. She sees this epitomized in the pornographic hero, who, afraid of his own feelings, ridicules feeling in women;[45] afraid of the vulnerability of his flesh, tortures the flesh of women; afraid to lose control of his body, ties and binds, rapes and kills women. Seeking to avoid the knowledge that comes from the vulnerability of sexual intercourse, he turns it instead into an act of aggression. The pornographer, she argues, humiliates women as an act of revenge against the natural world.

Moreover, she says that the pornographer is like the racist. Both seek revenge against the scapegoat through humiliation and acts of dominance. Women and blacks, indeed all those identified as enemy, as "Other," are defined and victimized by the same habit of mind, a habit cultivated in a culture of delusion and self-denial in which women—the enemy, the Other—symbolize the denied self who experiences what it is to be human, to be in and of nature. She concludes that the political significance of self-denial is that out of denied selves and denied realities, the mind creates an enemy. It can be a nation, a race, a sex. But, she adds, the enemy is only a mask for our own hidden feelings (*Made* 175).

And, as soon as we define someone as the enemy, we lose a part of ourselves:

> I begin to exist in a closed system. When anything goes wrong, I blame my enemy. If I wake troubled, my enemy had led me to this feeling. If I cannot sleep, it is because of my enemy. Slowly all the power in my life begins to be located outside, and my whole being is defined in relation to this outside force, which becomes daily more monstrous, more evil, more laden with all the qualities in myself I no longer wish to own. (*Made* 177)

"All the power in my life begins to be located outside . . . ." Here is a key to the consequences of alienation for domination. Traditional definitions of power associate power with coercion, dominance, and violence. One of the main contributions of feminist thought has been its questioning of this conception of power. Hannah Arendt has argued that far from being identical, power and violence are opposites. Indeed, it is powerlessness that breeds violence (*On Violence* 53–55). Jo Velacott elucidates this in her exploration of the roots of violence in "resourcelessness":

> I am a member of an oppressed minority; I have no way of making you listen to me; I turn to terrorism. I am a dictator, yet I cannot force you to think as I want you to: I fling you in jail, starve your children, torture you. I am a woman in a conventional authoritarian marriage situation; I feel helpless and inferior and powerless against my husband's constant undermining; so I in turn undermine him, manipulate him, make him look foolish in the eyes of his children. Or I am a child unable to prevent her parents' sudden outbursts of rage, I smash something precious and run away, or I take to thieving, or I may even kill myself. Or I am President of the United States; with all the force at my command I know of no way to make sure that the developing countries . . . will dance to my tune; so I turn to the use of food as a political weapon, as well as building ever more armaments. (32)

Thus, if I lose my inner resources of power, and all the power in my life is external to me, then I will be tempted to substitute violence for power and to use terror to maintain domination.

Audre Lorde reminds us that our true power lies in our eros, our life force (53–59). When I define power as external to me, when I live outside myself, I cut myself off from that life force, my eros. And, writes Griffin, this eros is:

> Our own wholeness. Not the sensation of pleasure alone, nor the idea of love alone, but the whole experience of human love. The whole range of human capacity exists in this love. Here is the capacity for speech and meaning, for culture, for memory, for imagination, the capacity for touch and expression, and sensation and joy. (*Pornography* 254)

Thus, in cutting ourselves off from our wholeness, in excluding otherness from ourselves, we end up excluding our own vulnerability, tenderness, tears, anger, joy—our selves (*Made* 20). So the habit of mind of self-denial cuts us off from our eros, our life force, our power, and in fear and isolation and resourcelessness we seek dominance, which is different from power, and totality, which is different from wholeness.

It is a habit of mind that deprives us of meaning. Severed from the meaning that comes when consciousness is infused with nature and being, we cling instead to ideology (*Eros* 92). Griffin points to the rise in fundamentalism as symptomatic of the lack of meaning in our lives (*Eros* 9). Mies and Camus make similar arguments regarding the rise of fascism in Europe. What appears on the surface to fulfill our need for meaning actually plays on our deepest hungers for belonging, communion, and relationship with nature, being, and each other, in order to impose its own totality.

And such a habit of mind that alienates itself from nature and being, from eros, from meaning, ultimately becomes destructive. Griffin concludes, "if we would change a habit of mind that has become destructive we must revise the social architecture of our thought" (*Eros* 154). If the social architecture that has led to destruction is one that separates the immanent from the transcendent, the body from the spirit, the intellect from the emotion, then a more creative habit of mind comes from ending such dualistic thinking, such arbitrary distinctions between body and mind, and rejoining consciousness with that of the earth and the body.

The Significance of Valuing Immanence

In Camus's short story, "The Adulterous Woman," the central character, Janine, slips away in the middle of the night and in making love to the night sky, experiences a spiritual renewal:

> After so many years of mad, aimless fleeing from fear, she had come to a stop at last. At the same time, she seemed to recover her roots and the sap

again rose in her body. . . . The last stars of the constellations dropped their clusters a little lower on the desert horizon and became still. Then, with unbearable gentleness, the water of night began to fill Janine, drowned the cold, rose gradually from the hidden core of her being and overflowed in wave after wave, rising up even to her mouth full of moans. (*Exile* 32–33)

This passage has been interpreted as suggesting the possibility in Camus's thought of a feminist recognition of women's liberation, especially in its suggestion that having found her authentic self, Janine may now go on with her own life (Bronner 128).[46] But this may be interpreting the story too literally. No doubt it represents liberation, but far beyond Janine's. Camus writes that Janine is fleeing from fear. Of what is Janine afraid? Of her wholeness, her self. Of her eros. Of the truths of her body. In Janine's liberation lies the way of the liberation of us all, in the reconnection of consciousness with the earth.

Susan Griffin similarly suggested, "If human consciousness can be rejoined not only with the human body but with the body of the earth, what seems incipient in the reunion is the recovery of meaning within existence that will infuse every kind of meeting between self and the universe, even in the most daily acts, with an eros, a palpable love, that is also sacred" (*Eros* 9). Such thought recognizes that we think with our bodies and that our bodies are inspirited, that spirit lies in sea and stone and cell, that the transcendent lies within the immanent, that matter is energy, and that we all—stone and tree and bird and beast—are made of the stuff of stars.[47]

Such thought is thought that is open, that is willing to be surprised, that conveys an attitude of wonder. In this sense, it is thought that excludes nothing—thought that "meets all that exists" (*Eros* 151), a theme recurring throughout Camus's works. As he wrote in "Return to Tipasa," ". . . if we give up a part of what exists, we must ourselves give up being; we must then give up living or loving except by proxy. There is a will to live without refusing anything life offers: the virtue I honor most in this world . . ." (*Lyrical* 167).

Specifically, it is a social architecture of thought that connects the values of freedom and justice with the values of community and relationship with the earth and with each other. Maria Mies has argued that though leftists and liberals advocate for freedom and justice, because they regard Nature as the enemy and as a resource to be used, their thought leads inevitably to exploitation and destructiveness. Conservatives, on the other hand, have regarded Nature as friend and Good Mother, but in a romanticized way. Fascists have mobilized our feelings and needs for belonging and connection with the earth and with each other, but in a way that subsumes the individual into the totalitarian whole, leading inevitably to violence and domination.[48] She has argued that we need a politic that moves beyond the dualistic framework of good and bad nature, rational versus irrational, and "sterile left-right thinking."

Rebellion and rebellious feminism offer such a politic, that affirms both freedom and immanence, individual dignity and community, justice and beauty. Camus reiterated this often:

> Nothing is true that compels us to make it exclusive. Isolated beauty ends in grimaces, solitary justice in oppression. Anyone who seeks to serve the one to the exclusion of the other serves no one, not even himself, and in the end is doubly the servant of injustice. . . . Yes there is beauty and there are the humiliated. Whatever difficulties the enterprise may present, I would like never to be unfaithful either to the one or to the other. (*Lyrical* 165, 169–170)

We find the meaning that heals our lives and restores our wholeness in affirming the value of immanence, or to borrow Morris Berman's term, in "the re-enchantment of the world." This is not to value immanence over transcendence, but rather to abolish the opposition between immanence and transcendence and restore nature as a ground of our being. Just as Camus argued that the attitude of conquest arose from regarding nature as something to be acted on rather than as something to be revered, so does feminism argue that restoring our relationship with and reverence for nature can bring an end to the destruction of the earth and each other. In this regard, Mies argues, "Only if Nature is again recognized as a living being with whom we must cooperate in a *loving* manner, and not regarded as a source of raw material to be exploited for commodity production; can we hope to end the war against Nature and against ourselves" (156). Similarly, Carol Christ writes that what can stop us from destroying the earth is a "deeply felt connection to all beings in the web of life. What can stop us is that we love this life, this earth, the joy we know in ourselves and other beings enough to find the thought of the end of the earth intolerable" (323). In order not to fuel tyranny, we need to reestablish our relationship with nature as one of contemplation and admiration. We need to encounter nature and being with an attitude of wonder.

Starhawk suggests three consequences of valuing immanence for a feminist understanding of ethical living: (1) the equal valuing of all; (2) the repudiation of domination; and (3) opposition to passivity in the face of injustice ("Feminist" 177–178).[49] First, the immanent challenges our sense of values. When the sacred is immanent, then each being has inherent value and cannot be diminished. Carol Christ provides an exquisite expression of this basic belief:

> There are no hierarchies among beings on earth. We are different from swallows who fly in spring, from the many-faceted stones on the beach, from the redwood tree in the forest. We may have more capacity to shape our lives than other beings, but you and I will never fly with the grace of a swallow, live as long as a redwood tree, nor endure the endless tossing of the sea like a stone. Each being has its own intrinsic beauty and value. . . . we are no more valuable to the life of the universe than a field flowering in the color purple, than rivers flowing, than a crab picking its way across the sand—and no less . . . . (321)

Thus does immanence support rebellion's valuing of the dignity of every being.

Second, valuing immanence shifts our definition of power from "power over" to "power within"—this latter being a power that refuses dominance and enables each of us to become who we are meant to be. When we value all lives, then our actions are also limited by the value of other beings, and in connection we desire to enhance the life possibilities of all (Christ 321–322). It is in connecting with the earth and with our bodies and our feelings that we restore wholeness to our lives, a wholeness that works against domination, that refuses either to be victim or executioner.

Finally, immanence works against passivity. Starhawk argues that if the earth is the living body of the Goddess, then no one is coming to save us. Our spiritual growth lies on this earth: "immanence calls us to live our spirituality here in the world, to take action to preserve the life of the earth, to live with integrity and responsibility" (*Spiral* 10). Camus took similar lessons from immanence: "the message of these gospels of stone, sky, and water is that there are no resurrections"; "the world is beautiful, and outside it there is no salvation" (*Lyrical* 101, 103). Camus found no salvation in an eternal life after death nor in an eternal realm of equality and justice on earth. His statement, "I rebel, therefore we exist. . . . And we are alone" (*Rebel* 104), indicates that we cannot seek salvation elsewhere. Rather, he said, salvation lies in our own hands. Our task in life is to make of this existence in this world as decent and ennobling a life as possible. As he wrote:

> He who dedicates himself to the duration of his life, to the house he builds, to the dignity of mankind, dedicates himself to the earth and reaps from it the harvest that sows its seed and sustains the world again and again. . . . [Rebellion's] merit lies in making no calculations, distributing everything it possesses to life and to [the] living. . . . It is thus that

it is prodigal in its gifts. . . . Real generosity toward the future lies in giving all to the present. (*Rebel* 302–304)

A lesson from Meister Eckhart brings us full circle: "This then is salvation, when we marvel at the beauty of created things and praise the beautiful providence of their Creator" (Fox 423). Salvation lies in awe and wonder, and sin, if we can use that word, in a separation from child-like wonder that allows us to squander, neglect, waste, and destroy. True wonder brings forth a reverence for all things. When all are held sacred, all are honored and held in love and respect.[50] In words that invoke the spirit of Camus, Carol Christ similarly concludes, "the ethic that would follow from this vision is that our task is to love and understand, to live for a time, to contribute as much as we can to the continuation of life, to the enhancement of beauty, joy, and diversity, while recognizing inevitable death, loss, and suffering" (321).

Finally, it is important to recognize that it is the joy of immanental connection with the earth and all of creation, with eros, that sustains our spirits for the struggle. As Camus wrote, "In order to prevent justice from shriveling up, from becoming nothing but a magnificent orange with a dry, bitter pulp, I discovered one must keep a freshness and a source of joy intact within . . . in the worst years of our madness the memory of this sky had never left me. It was this in the end that saved me from despair" (*Lyrical* 168–169).

So often, I believe, feminism is regarded as that dry, bitter pulp; a joyless enterprise of angry and humorless women who spend their lives in miserable complaint. But this is not the feminism I know. The femi-nism I know fights against injustice, certainly, and feels the pain of the oppressed, but is forever revealed and replenished by an ebullient joy, that sustains our hopes and visions:

> As fearful as I am, there is joy in me. While one eye sees disaster and the causes of destruction more clearly, the other eye awakens to beauty. I am beginning to put the shattered being, myself and the world, back together. We are all connected. I know this. Dark and light. Male and female. We are a tribe whose fate on this earth is shared. I do not know the outcome. I have moments of despair. But I have learned that when I see out of my own experience, and chart it as precisely and clearly as I can, I see what I have not seen before: I am surprised. This earth holds a vast wisdom and a capacity to heal that we are only beginning to compre-hend. We are made from this earth. This is my hope. (Griffin, *Made* 20)
>
> . . . the earth remains our first and our last love. . . . with this joy, through long struggle, we shall remake the soul of our time. (*Rebel* 306)

CHAPTER 8

A POLITICS OF LIMITS AND HEALING

Perhaps we cannot prevent this world from being a world in which children are tortured. But we can reduce the number of tortured children. . . . it is those who know how to rebel, at the appropriate moment, against history, who really advance its interest.

Camus, *Resistance, Rebellion and Death* 73 and *The Rebel* 302

We have exiled beauty; the Greeks took arms for it. A basic difference—but one that goes far back. Greek thought was always based on the idea of limits. Nothing was carried to extremes, neither religion nor reason, because Greek thought denied nothing, neither reason nor religion. It gave everything its share, balancing light with shade. But the Europe we know, eager for the conquest of totality, is the daughter of excess. We deny beauty, as we deny everything we do not extol. . . . In our madness, we push back the eternal limits, and at once dark Furies swoop down upon us to destroy. Nemesis, goddess of moderation, not of vengeance, is watching. She chastises, ruthlessly, all those who go beyond the limit. ("Helen's Exile," (1948), *Lyrical* 148–149)

Nemesis, the goddess of moderation, is watching.[1] "The men of Europe . . . ," on the contrary, "have deified themselves and . . . had their eyes put out" (*Rebel* 305). Blinded, they are no longer able to see where they cross the limit, and everywhere the limit is crossed—in concentration camps, totalitarian ideologies, arbitrary divisions of labor, abuses of technology, terrorism, war, the atomic bomb. The Greeks never said the limit could not be crossed, only that those who do would be struck down. This, Camus said, was the nature of the times in which he lived. They deified themselves and their misfortunes began (*Rebel* 305). Adopting the Augustinian notion of the original sin of pride by which we fancy we know better than God, Camus argued that "it's pride, just pride" (*Just Assassins* 259)—pride that fancies it knows better than the goddess—that causes us to cross the limit.

Camus ends *The Rebel* with this proscription, that it is the "original rule of life today, to learn to live and to die, and in order to be [hu]man, to refuse to be a god. . . . A limit, under the sun, will curb them all" (*Rebel* 306). The rebel, claiming humanity with all its limitations, rejects divinity. What is required by rebellious politics is an awareness of the limitations of our knowledge and a faithfulness to acting within those limitations. We must acknowledge our ignorance and refuse fanaticism (*Lyrical* 153). For Camus, "ignorance that fancies it knows everything" (*Plague* 118) is responsible for much of the destructive politics in the world today. And so rebellion must choose to be " . . . a philosophy of limits, of calculated ignorance, and of risk. He who does not know everything cannot kill everything" (*Rebel* 289). Sharon Welch has similarly written that the feminist ethic of risk celebrates limits, contingency, and ambiguity (158). In recognizing the ambiguities of moral and political dilemmas and the limitations of our perspective and understanding, the only justifiable politics is one that seeks proximate solutions.

The goddess is watching; and rebellion, Camus claimed, should seek its inspiration from this goddess (*Rebel* 296). In his concept of rebellion, Camus developed an ethic, a political practice of sorts, that embraces this limit. Camus defined rebellion as moderation, by which he meant pure tension—nothing taken to its extreme; nothing taken as absolute; all elements of rebellion in constant tension. The irrational poses limits on the rational; liberty limits justice and justice moderates liberty. Because the limit is the point at which an idea pursued to an extreme contradicts itself, no value is sought in its absolute. Absolute freedom negates itself in destroying the freedom of others; just as absolute justice negates itself in perpetrating acts of oppression and domination in the name of justice. At best, the rebel seeks proximate justice and relative freedom:

> Rebellion itself only aspires to the relative and can only promise an assured dignity coupled with relative justice. It supposes a limit at which . . . community . . . is established . . . . A revolutionary action which wishes to be coherent in terms of its origins should be embodied in an active consent to the relative. Uncompromising as to its means, it would accept an approximation as far as its ends are concerned. (*Rebel* 290)

The symbol of the goddess Nemesis is the wheel, and I have often imaged rebellion as that wheel, with each of its component parts— refusal of injustice, affirmation of dignity, solidarity, friendship, and immanence—as spokes on that wheel. Each pulling equally in its own direction sustains the structure of the wheel. Should any of them loosen its tension or collapse, so does the wheel. Rebellion, wrote Camus, "in order to remain authentic, must never abandon any of the terms of the contradiction that sustains it" (*Rebel* 285). One of the main lessons of rebellion is that each of these original movements of rebellion is just as important as the others. Rebellion demands that they balance each other. The dignity of the individual is affirmed in solidarity with all, which is a compassion grounded in the knowledge, love, and friendship of concrete others and the earth. The practice of rebellion requires the equal and simultaneous affirmation of all of its terms.

Beyond this, rebellion rests on the recognition that we are not gods, that we are limited ourselves, fallible, and likely to do wrong. Despite knowing what is good, the rebel nevertheless makes mistakes, and does harm (*Rebel* 285). Yet it is this recognition that saves the rebel from excesses. This is not to say that the rebel does not try, all the time, to uphold justice and dignity and friendship and the earth. It is to say, that at best, the rebel can work at diminishing oppression and injustice (*Rebel* 286). As Welch has said, while we can't guarantee an end to oppression and violence, we can refuse our own capitulation to it (48).

The political practice that follows from the ethic of rebellion is grounded both in a constant tension of equally important though potentially contradictory values and a recognition of our own limitations and ignorance. This sets up three guidelines for political practice: first, affirming its values equally but none absolutely, it is limited in its scope; second, concerned more with means than with ends, it is limited in its methods; and finally, grounded in concrete realities, it is limited in its basis for action.

Proximate Politics

Proximate politics is the practice of moderation. That is, in proximate politics, no value is pursued to the extreme extent that it would contradict itself or destroy or deny other equally important values. One example of Camus's proximate politics is in the balance and tension of the simultaneous pursuit of the potentially contradictory ends of liberty and justice.

Liberty and Justice in Tension

In rebellion, freedom and justice find their limits in each other. Rebellion insists on the "both/andness" of freedom and justice, rather than the "either/or": "Absolute freedom mocks at justice. Absolute justice denies freedom. To be fruitful, the two ideas must find their limits in each other" (*Rebel* 291). Camus was leery of those who would, in the name of justice, engage in acts of injustice, repression, and domination; who would sacrifice liberty and justice in the present for a perfect justice at the end of history. Similarly, with one exception, that being the absolute liberty of expression, which Camus argued is necessary to keep open the dialogue that prevents injustice, Camus argued that absolute freedom is not freedom at all. Rather, absolute freedom amounts to libertinism and license that ultimately result in the subjection of the majority to the liberty of a few, making life one of terrorism and despotism (*Rebel* 42, 123, 175). Camus argued repeatedly for a limited freedom and proximate justice that find their limits in each other. Camus wrote of liberty and justice, "we cannot choose one without the other. If someone takes away your bread, he suppresses your freedom at the same time. But if someone takes away your freedom, you may be sure that your bread is threatened, for it depends no longer on you and your struggle but on the whim of a master" (*Resistance* 94). He insisted that justice and freedom must always be demanded simultaneously.

I find this same "both/andness" in Iris Marion Young's reconceptualization of justice from a feminist perspective. She defines justice through a sense of injustice, which she regards to be the conditions of oppression and domination. Justice, in this sense, would be those conditions of society that work against oppression and domination, and that help to support the qualities that oppression and domination preclude—self-expression in all its forms and self-determination of all of one's actions (*Justice* 33–38). In other words, justice, for Young, enables freedom of self-expression and self-determination, and these qualities of freedom amount to the same thing as justice. The two are of each other.

Similarly, Nancy Hirschmann's feminist reconceptualization of freedom simultaneously affirms freedom, justice, and solidarity in its foundation of freedom in relationship rather than rights. Hirschmann drew her reconceptualization of freedom from the writings of Patricia Hill Collins and Audre Lorde, both of whom argued that among oppressed peoples, the task of self-definition is possible only within the context of relationships with those who are similarly oppressed. Hirschmann also drew on the Italian feminist practice of *autocoscienza*, a practice similar to that of consciousness-raising groups in the United States, in which women gather together in small groups to help themselves and each other gain a better understanding of the workings of patriarchy in their lives and in the world. While sustaining the centrality of individual choice, this practice of freedom also recognizes that without a community that enables women to evaluate their choices from a critical perspective, women cannot be free to discern their choices. Thus responsibility to others—solidarity—is central to a feminist notion of freedom.

Maintaining the simultaneous demands of freedom and justice, as well as solidarity, friendship, and immanence, can be difficult, and various political ideologies and regimes have often sought one to the exclusion or diminishment of the other. Camus was critical of both the liberalism and socialism of his day on this account. Though he valued liberalism's defense of the dignity of the individual and of civil liberties, especially freedom of speech, he criticized its abandonment of the poor and disenfranchised. He was critical of bourgeois freedom that, forgetful of justice, sees in freedom only privileges and not duties. He criticized liberalism's failure to recognize the need to extend freedom to all, rather than only to those who "make it"—its promotion of a competitive individualism that is willing to step on others in the name of the freedom of a few. He was especially suspicious of the bourgeois notion of progress, in the name of which the destruction and sacrifice of individuals and whole ways of life was justified. By the same token, though Camus valued the socialist affirmation of solidarity and economic justice, he was critical of communism's totalitarian methods that abandoned civil liberties and justified the sacrifice of those individuals living here and now for a notion of the golden age at the end of history (*Resistance* 87–97). Camus was equally critical of bourgeois intellectuals who were willing that their privileges be paid for by the exploitation of workers; and of leftist intellectuals who were willing to have culture dictated in the name of a future justice. While appreciating their respective concerns for liberty, and justice and community, Camus warned against the potential in both for contributing to pain and suffering and the destruction of meaning in people's lives.[2]

Feminism can be, and has been, similarly critiqued. Many feminists have criticized liberal feminism's abandonment of solidarity and justice concerns in favor of the promotion of individual women within the patriarchal power structure. Carol Ehrlich's views are representative of this critique:

> . . . feminism is *not* about dressing for success, or becoming a corporate executive, or gaining elective office; it is *not* about being able to share a two career marriage and take skiing vacations and spending huge amounts of time with your husband and two lovely children because you have a domestic worker who makes all this possible for you, but who hasn't the time or money to do it for herself; . . . it is most emphatically

not about becoming a police detective or CIA agent or marine corps general. (Qtd. in hooks, *Feminist Theory* 7–8)

Yet, the freedom pursued by liberal feminism has for the most part been exactly this—what Camus called "bourgeois freedom," that seeks the privileges of freedom and not its duties. In the name of "liberty and justice for all," liberal feminism has primarily sought to gain access to the powers and privileges of privileged males. Rather than seeking to change a structure based in hierarchy and domination, it has sought entrance into it.

Similarly the tendency in some forms of feminism to proscribe individual choices as the only ones appropriate for a "true" feminist shows a willingness to suspend liberty for justice. There has been the danger within feminism, as Susan Griffin reminds us, to "go the way of all ideology"—to approve or disapprove one's choice of friends and lovers, one's choice of books and movies, even one's tastes and desires and emotions (*Made* 170). This tendency raises its head among feminists when feminists end friendships with other feminists because they find their actions violate their sense of feminist "right action." One of the areas of greatest concern here is the tendency to "group think." I have from time to time heard students complain of the atmosphere in certain Women's Studies classes, that some students condemn and silence other students who counter their interpretation of the "feminist line." Feminists themselves have indicted Women's Studies for this (Patai and Kortege). I, too, have felt this tendency to "group think" in certain feminist organizations and associations. (To a certain extent the judgment of what is acceptable to say, to think, to write hovers in my consciousness even as I write right now, though it is also the feminist urging toward authenticity that urges me to resist it.)

The balance between liberty and justice is a delicate one that is at the heart of many contested issues within feminist ethical and political practice. Issues such as the imposition of Western human rights onto women in Third World cultures; affirmative action; welfare reform; reproductive autonomy and responsibility; sexuality (including a range of issues such as sadomasochism, prostitution, pornography, and heterosexuality); regulation of hate speech; treatment of animals (with issues ranging from vegetarianism to the honoring of traditional indigenous practices); and the presence of women in the military all raise challenges to both liberty and justice. Regarding these in the light of the rebellious concern to balance liberty and justice helps us to see the true complexities of these issues. Rather than asking whether or not a real feminist eats meat, approves of pornography, is a pacifist, enters the institution of marriage, or advocates against female genital mutilation in a culture other than her own, it helps us to recognize in each of these debates a serious grappling with the edge between liberty and justice; between claiming freedom of choice and expression, and resisting oppression. It also suggests possibilities that honor both liberty and justice.

For example, radical feminists have been deeply divided over issues of sexual practice.[3] Radical libertarian feminists argue that feminists should repudiate any legal restrictions or moral judgments that stigmatize sexual practices and restrict the freedom of sexual minorities. They demand the right of fully consenting equal partners to indulge in any practices— including sadomasochism, prostitution, and pornography—that provide them pleasure and satisfaction. Radical cultural feminists, on the other hand, argue that sexuality as currently constructed supports a culture of male dominance over women. They advocate that any practices that derive from and support masculinist sexuality—such as sadomasochism, prostitution, and pornography, and in some cases, heterosexuality— should be eschewed, and in the case of pornography, prohibited. Yet both radical libertarian and radical cultural feminists are seeking to balance justice and freedom. The former recognizes that the free and unrepressed sexual expression they seek is only possible in situations where the partners are equal, that is, where one is not in a position of power over another. The latter argues that because the current sexual culture is by definition unequal and unjust, freedom not only of sexual expression, but also of speech and movement, is not possible within it and will only be made possible by the elimination of certain dominance modes within it. Examining both, Ann Ferguson has argued that feminists need to develop approaches to sexuality that take into account both the pleasures and the dangers of sex, both the possible freedoms and the potential injustices, and envision sexual practices that would emerge from a truly egalitarian society.

Along the same lines, while some feminists seek to equalize relationships within marriage while not condemning the institution itself, others have critiqued marriage as a patriarchal institution, thus rendering participation in marriage supportive of patriarchy by supporting its institutions. As already noted, some feminists have further argued that through participation in any heterosexual relationship, women abandon feminism. But Iris Marion Young finds a "both/and" solution by taking a broader view of the oppressive nature of the choice to enter the institution of marriage ("Reflections"). Young argues that marriage is an exclusive institution that oppresses others by excluding them from certain rights and privileges, among these—parental rights and relationships; respectability and legitimacy in areas of sexuality and procreation; privileges of property and income such as ownership and inheritance, insurance benefits, credit access, tax privileges, social security benefits, survivors' benefits; as well as immigration privileges, preferential treatment by adoption services; and access to, care of, and consent for partners in institutions—hospitals, treatment centers, prisons. Among those excluded from and oppressed by the institution of marriage are homosexuals, single mothers, unmarried people who wish to set up a household or be thought of as a family, extended families, and non-kin household members who share resources and care. Thus in choosing marriage, a person is choosing to enter a situation of privilege, with all its implications for oppressing others. Young's "both/and" solution is a system in which domestic rights and benefits would be extended to all those who self-declare themselves to be "family" under certain conditions and terms of the law.

As another example, the deep dilemma feminists face regarding the issue of Western feminists' intervention into what they perceive to be violations of women's human rights in non-Western countries also challenges the balance between liberty and justice, as well as that of solidarity, friendship, and immanence. In the name of justice, Western feminists have protested against such practices as the genital mutilation of girls and women in certain African countries and the veiling of women in certain Islamic nations. Yet women in these countries have protested the imposition of Western values onto their cultures and have insisted on their rights of self-determination. Western feminists have sought to act in solidarity with non-Western feminists in the protection of their human rights, yet non-Western women often have not regarded their interventions as ones of solidarity. Reexamining the issue in terms of feminist definitions of freedom based in relationship rather than rights, and justice based in self-expression and self-determination, suggests an approach that would involve enabling subaltern women to dialogue with each other in a context that facilitates their agency and yet is honoring of their culture and spiritual practices, as well as engaging Western and non-Western women in conversation with each other so that they might come to mutual understanding of what actions would indeed be honoring of feminist solidarity and friendship.

Rosemarie Tong has said of dichotomized feminist viewpoints and practices that "either/or" approaches "have turned out to be part of the problem of human oppression rather than a remedy for it," and suggests that feminism would be better served by replacing them with "both/and" approaches (*Feminist Thought* 93). In determining feminist practice, rebellion can act as a framework for the careful working out of the affirmation of liberty without contributing further to oppression and domination; of scrupulous attention to the oppressive implications of one's choices, while affirming autonomy. An ethic of rebellion frames the issues and seeks a solution that is "both/and," not "either/or."

Radical Democracy

The implication of this "both/andedness" for rebellious politics is that it does not fall easily into any existing political ideology or practice. I agree with Jeffrey Isaac's assessment that "the lexicons of liberalism and socialism do not fit a rebellious politics. The former is too complacent, the latter too credulous, to suit the self-limiting radicalism that . . . Camus endorsed" (154). The politic implicit in Camus's ethic of rebellion is neither liberal nor socialist, and yet has elements of both, blended as well with values of social democracy and syndicalism (Isaac 42; Bronner 89). In his politics, Camus refused dualistic thinking, and encouraged creative efforts to find a "third way" (Isaac 182). Rebellion is a politic that does not dichotomize, but rather presses in several directions at the same time, all in constant tension with each other.

Though feminism, like other political movements, has divided into liberal, socialist, and Marxist camps, a significant body of feminist thought and movement has sought a "third way" that emphasizes simultaneously the value of individual liberty, the rejection of domination and injustice in all forms, and the value of community. One example of this is found in the work of Chantal Mouffe, whose theories of radical democracy have informed feminist thought.[4] Mouffe has sought to combine the insights of liberal pluralism and communitarianism, blending the liberal recognition of individual liberties and principles of justice with the participatory citizenship and common concerns of communitarianism. She posits a citizenship based on a "common bond." This is to be distinguished from the "common good" valued by communitarians, which Mouffe, along with liberals, regards as having possible totalitarian implications. The "common bond" rather, is a set of ethico-political values. Specifically, the values Mouffe posits are liberty and equality for all. These are understood in such a way as to take account of different social relations and subjectivities such as race, class, sex, and sexual orientation, and are regarded as extending to the many social relations, including but also beyond the state, where domination exists and must be challenged. Like Camus, she regards the liberty of the individual and equality for all as existing in constant and permanent tension. This tension, while limiting democratic politics to proximate solutions at best, she regards to be the source of its vitality ("Democratic Citizenship" 238). Recognizing the impossibility of achieving perfect democracy and political community, rebellious politics nevertheless aims for deepening democracy in a process that is never-ending.

Also of interest here is the alignment of certain feminist politics with the Green movement.[5] Like Camus, the Green movement blends elements of liberalism and socialism with radical democracy, listing among its Ten Key Values: grassroots democracy, personal and social responsibility to respond to human suffering in ways that promote dignity, nonviolence, decentralization, community-based economics, respect for diversity, and the refusal of dominance.[6] It is another attempt to find a "third way" that brings together in a party politics, many of the values embraced by rebellion and rebellious feminism.

Camus's thought has been criticized for its isolation from radical social movements and its overreliance on individual responsibility. Camus lived during a time when radical social movements were absolutist in their aims and often in their methods, and he did eschew these. Perhaps he would have been more at home in the more limited politics of some of the radical movements of our times—the peace movement, the civil rights movement, the Green movement, and certainly the feminist movement (and undoubtedly his work influenced these movements to develop a more limited approach).

Rebellious politics seeks a "third way" that is a mean between the extremes. It does not pursue one goal to the exclusion of all others, but rather seeks to balance the conflicting demands of each, recognizing that each informs the other. Recognizing that the end may always be elusive, it seeks instead proximate solutions, but though compromising as to its ends, as Camus said, it is "uncompromising as to its means" (*Rebel* 290).

The Means Justify the Ends

In *The Rebel*, Camus pointed to the "fastidious assassins" (the Russian terrorists who assassinated the Grand Duke Sergei) as examples of rebels who tried to carry out an ethic of limits in their political practice. They recognized their own fallibilities and scrutinized their actions, asking themselves every question. Though their action was violent, murderous, they limited their act to the death of the one person they held responsible for the deaths of hundreds, even thousands of innocent people. They refused to harm any innocent bystanders. As previously mentioned,[7] in Camus's *The Just Assassins*, the drama unfolds around Kaliayev's refusal to throw the bomb when children are riding in the carriage with the Grand Duke. In the scene that follows, Stepan has just reproached Kaliayev for failing to throw the bomb simply because there were children in the carriage, but the others reproach Stepan:

> DORA: Open your eyes, Stepan, and try to realize that the group would lose all its driving force, were it to tolerate, even for a moment, the idea of children's being blown to pieces by our bombs.
> STEPAN: Sorry, but I don't suffer from a tender heart; that sort of nonsense cuts no ice with *me* . . . .
> ANNENKOV: Stepan, . . . I can't allow you to say that everything's permissible. Thousands of our brothers have died to make it known that everything is *not* allowed.
> STEPAN: Nothing that can serve our cause should be ruled out . . . .
> DORA: . . . Even in destruction there's a right way and a wrong way—and there are limits. (256–258, emphasis in original)

Rebellion is scrupulous with regard to the means employed to confront injustice and oppression. Specifically, rebellious practice proscribes anything that would contribute to injustice, domination, and a silent hostility among people that diminishes the possibilities of solidarity and friendship. In particular, rebellion repudiates servitude, falsehood, and terror. Any act of rebellion that adopted such methods would lose the right to be called rebellion.

Camus on Violence and Nonviolence

Camus stated clearly, as basic premises of rebellion, that falsehood is proscribed, that the rebel humiliates no one, and that the liberty the rebel seeks is always limited by that of every other person (*Rebel* 284). The rebel refuses to lie and deceive, degrade, subordinate, enslave, or debase. But the question concerning means that most occupied Camus is whether or not the rebel has the right to kill or let others be killed. He began and ended *The Rebel* by stating that the rebel, and anyone else, has no such right. He stated clearly, "the freedom to kill is not compatible with the sense of rebellion" (*Rebel* 284). And yet, Camus was not prepared to argue that the rebel could never kill. Though he denounced killing that leads to more killing, he did not, in *The Rebel*, advocate complete nonviolence, arguing that a refusal to kill that allows tacit agreement to injustice and oppression may in the end condone violence and murder. There may be times when violence is necessary, and inexcusable (*Rebel* 169), and that it is inexcusable can be the only attitude with which the rebel could commit an act of violence. Camus posited violence as "an extreme limit which combats another form of violence" (*Rebel* 292). However, though Camus did not deny that in certain exceptional cases violence might be used, he refused to accept that the use of violence should become a policy. Indeed, he argued that if rebellion is to take up arms it can only be "for institutions that limit violence, not for those which codify it" (*Rebel* 292).

He also held the position that in the event that rebels do commit murder, they must "consecrate" it by their own deaths. This is one of the things that makes the actions of the just assassins, just, in Camus's eyes. Though they committed murder in assassinating the Grand Duke, they also willingly paid the price with their own lives, and did not shirk that even when offered an escape from it.[8]

However, in his later writings, specifically his essays "Preface to Algerian Reports" and *Neither Victims nor Executioners*, Camus seemed to have changed his stance with regard to even this limited use of violence. Faced with the terrorism and violence afflicting his own homeland in its struggles for independence, he invoked Gandhian principles of nonviolence to suggest that it is possible to resist violence without becoming a murderer oneself, arguing that "it is better to suffer certain injustices than to commit them even to win wars," (*Resistance* 114) and that in committing acts of violence we do more harm to ourselves. He pledges himself "never again [to] be one of those, whoever they be, who compromise with murder, and . . . I must take the consequences of such a decision" (*Neither* 53).[9] Camus's ultimate position seems to be that the rebel must do everything possible to resist violence, without adding to it.

In sum, a rebellious practice of limits is scrupulous with regard to the means employed, refusing falsehood, domination, and violence. "Does the end justify the means" Camus asks, to which he responds, "That is possible. But what will justify the end? To that question, . . . rebellion replies: the means. . . . it is the only attitude that is efficacious today" (*Rebel* 292).

Feminist Emphasis on Means

Though not all feminist practice has been scrupulous with regard to its means, many strands of feminism do claim that a means-centered orientation to their political praxis is fundamental. Specifically, in her analysis of the dualism of public and private moralities, Jean Bethke Elshtain argues that part of the feminist project is to restore ethics and compassion to a politics that has been divorced from ethics since the time of Machiavelli (*Public Man* ch. 6). This challenge to moral dualities is echoed in ecofeminism. The separation of ethics and politics stems from the deeper issue of dualism, and ecofeminism, in rejecting such dualism, regards the reconnection of ethics and politics to be a central goal of its politics (Gaard, *Ecological Politics* 144). Many feminists have similarly argued that the division of spirituality and politics is an unnatural split founded on dualistic concepts and needs to be abandoned, and that we need to recognize instead that our spirituality inspires, informs, and energizes our political action.[10]

In making an argument for the importance of feminist commitment to nonviolent means, Dorothy Riddle writes, "we need to live out the fact that we become whatever we do . . . the means that we use shape who we are. We cannot separate the means from the end. The end toward which we are moving is constantly changing and the only thing that we have in the present is the means" (377–378). Her views and the general emphasis on means in feminist politics are vividly portrayed in Starhawk's ecofeminist fictional utopia, *The Fifth Sacred Thing*. The central dilemma in the story is whether or not the community will compromise its means, particularly the means of nonviolence, to achieve its ends of protecting and sustaining their society against the invading army that seeks to destroy them. Ultimately, they decide they must maintain their commitment to the means, even at great expense, so rather than return the violence of the invading soldiers, the members of the community invite the soldiers to join them at their table. In justifying their decision, the character Maya says, "The ends don't justify the means. . . . The means shape the ends. You become what you do" (164).

As previously discussed in chapters three and five, feminism, like rebellion, repudiates the use of domination, falsehood, and violence to achieve its ends. Feminist recognition of the contradiction of taking up means of repression, manipulation, and terror in search of a society free of these is evident in Lorde's famous phrase, "the master's tools will never dismantle the master's house." She goes on to say, "they may allow us temporarily to beat him at his own game, but they will never enable us to bring about genuine change" (*Sister* 112). For genuine change, feminism and rebellion insist on using means consistent with the origins of rebellion—means that refuse injustice and sustain solidarity and friendship with each other and the earth.

While Camus related what means are proscribed, he did not detail what means should be employed. However, we can at least infer that means that honor equality, honesty, and self-disclosure, and that restrict violence, are essential to the practice of rebellion. In her description of feminist political culture, Ynestra King invokes Camus to delineate methods appropriate to a feminist politic: ". . . to participate only in totally egalitarian relationships, to always tell the truth and to be non-violent in all interactions (or, as Albert Camus said, to be "neither victims nor executioners"), to never let the smallest act of cruelty pass— such are the daily aspirations of the women who live in the culture of this movement ("If I Can't Dance" 283). As to the actual working out of the practice of these, feminism has been of more help than Camus. We see this particularly in feminist efforts to develop practices of nonvi-olence; egalitarian and inclusive structures and practices; and methods of dialogue and discourse.

Nonviolence

Feminists have a long history of nonviolent practice, as well as a growing body of thought on the practice of nonviolence.[11] Indeed, Gandhi's practices of nonviolence were inspired by the actions of Indian women in the late nineteenth and early twentieth centuries, campaigning against child marriage and the practice of *sati* (widow burning) (Baumgardner and Richards 285–286). From gaining the vote in the United States to achieving civil rights, to protesting the building of nuclear power plants and the shipment of nuclear waste, to saving sacred trees in India and the redwoods in California, to worldwide efforts against war, feminist activists have used, developed, and refined nonviolent practice.

Feminists influenced a once male-dominated nonviolence movement to adopt more inclusive and nonhierarchical structures and practices, and to involve women equally with men in decision-making processes. They also developed methods and processes of nonviolent direct action that honor the intuitive, and spiritual, and the emotional (Wildflower 138–139). They have used their traditional roles as mothers and caretak-ers of children—surrounding the Greenham military base with photos of family and friends, children's drawings, toys, and balloons; carrying photos of their missing children to the Plaza de Mayo; engaging the image of the *mater dolorosa* by dressing in black and standing in silent witness—to protest oppression and war. They have employed women's traditional arts, such as the baking of "peace pies"—small cakes contain-ing messages of peace, and distributing them outside the Bank of England in London, or the weaving of a giant web around the Pentagon during the Women's Pentagon Action—to spread messages of peace. Gwen Kirk has characterized feminist nonviolent action as "celebratory and life affirming," creative and playful (121).

Many feminists, as well, have informed theories of nonviolence. Sara Ruddick, in particular, has contributed to our ideas of nonviolent practice in her development of principles stemming from the everyday maternal practices of children's conflict-resolution. Every day mothers are called upon to resolve conflicts with and facing their children, as well as to teach children to resolve conflicts with each other, ideally in ways that do not inflict physical or emotional harm. From this daily practice Ruddick has discerned four governing ideals of nonviolent action: renunciation of violence; resistance to authorities and policies that are unjust and harmful; reconciliation of the one harmed and the one harming; and peacekeeping—choosing one's battles wisely, and has developed strategies for their enactment similarly (*Maternal Thinking* 160–182). Ruddick has characterized the processes of peacemaking as "active connectedness" and as persistence in relationship (183–184), and as such they fit well with the rebellious concern with the priority of relationship.

Egalitarian and Inclusive Structures and Practices

Camus recognized a need for egalitarian and inclusive structures and practices of governing. Isaac has argued that Camus can be seen as a radical democrat in this regard, that he "sought to multiply the public spaces through which ordinary citizens might empower themselves" (158). In vague terms, he suggested the necessity for organs of mediation between the people and the leaders (*Rebel* 182) and promoted the idea of a democratic form of world government (*Neither*). However, he never went into specifics as to how these might be implemented. Feminists, on the other hand, have done much to contribute to the development of theories and practices of organizational structures and processes that are egalitarian and inclusive. Because feminists live within a cultural context in which "different" necessarily implies "inferior," they have been just as susceptible to regarding differences as a basis for separation rather than solidarity.[12] Thus, one of the main tasks of feminist movement has become reconfiguring the cultural paradigm in which difference is understood in terms of hierarchy to one in which people relate across differences within a context of equality. In reconfiguring this paradigm, feminist theorists have particularly worked on conceptualizing notions of democratic citizenship that are egalitarian and inclusive.

Certainly feminists have long sought to include women in notions of citizenship, beginning with arguments of first-wave liberal feminists for their inclusion in the political process on the basis of their capacity for reason and autonomous judgment as well as their inherent equality with men. However, later feminists came to see problems with including women in a patriarchal notion of citizenship, which confined the political to a specific "public" realm.[13] Instead, they sought in various ways to privilege the private realm of the family, or to construct women's citizenship on the basis of the capacity for motherhood. These arguments, however, still maintain a dualistic notion of public and private and male and female roles. Iris Young sought to break through this public/private divide by reconceiving public space to be one not of homogeneity and a Rousseauian "general will" where individuals are expected to leave behind the "private" interests and needs of their particular constituent groups, but rather one where constituent groups—not only of sex, but also of race, ethnicity, age—can bring their particular interests (*Justice* ch. 8). Appreciative of Young's efforts, Chantal Mouffe is however critical of what she regards as Young's essentialist notion of "group." Instead, she proposes a citizenship that conceives of the political agent as articulating several subject positions,[14] and that constructs a collective based on a chain of equivalence among their demands, while recognizing certain common concerns in liberty and equality ("Feminism" 380–381; "Democratic" 237). However, Mouffe's conception of citizenship continues to rely on a dualistic notion of "us versus them" politics, for she insists that "there cannot be a 'we' without a 'them'" ("Feminism" 379). It thus seems necessarily to exclude some from the process. More helpful is Jodi Dean's concept of reflective solidarity that refuses "us versus them" politics. However, Mouffe's conception of citizenship is helpful in its recognition that there are multiple spheres of power where domination exists and can be redressed, and that citizenship in this sense is not something confined to the state. Similarly helpful in this regard is Val Plumwood's notion of multiple citizenship: political—being our citizenship in the state, economic—being our citizenship in economic activities and entities, and ecological—being our recognition of others in nature and of the political character of our relationships with nature ("Has Democracy"). Inclusiveness and equality are enabled through multiplying the various avenues and spheres in which power is contested and citizens are empowered to act.

In addition to theory building, in their development of decision-making processes internal to feminist movement itself, feminist activists and organizations have experimented with varieties of organizations and processes designed to create egalitarian structures and inclusive practices, such as antihierarchical organizations, racial parity, small groups, revolving chairs, and consensus-based decision-making.[15] These have not been without difficulties. In attempting to avoid hierarchy, feminist organizations have often succumbed to what has been called the "tyranny of structurelessness"[16] (by which a lack of designated leadership results in the de facto power of media-designated "stars" and charismatic leaders), or the veto power of the one not willing to come to consensus, or the deep embeddedness of racial wounds. Best-intentioned endeavors have fallen apart, but others continue to struggle. The National Women's Studies Association (NWSA) serves as an example of a feminist organization that has struggled to come to terms with the divisiveness of racism, classism, heterosexism and embedded hierarchies while trying to implement strategies for inclusion and equality.

Sprung from the grassroots, the NWSA was originally conceived as a nonhierarchical, consensus-building organization with no stipulated leaders. The process of leadership first used was that of the "revolving chair," in which the person speaking recognizes the next speaker first from among those who have not yet spoken, and if all have, from the one who has spoken least. They used a modified Robert's Rules of Order, referred to as "Roberta's Rules," and invented such devices as "Stop Action" cards, which when raised received immediate attention from all present. They utilized small work groups to discuss and carry out the routine tasks of the organization. Nevertheless, this organization quickly clashed with the demands of the patriarchal world. By not stipulating leaders in an attempt to empower everyone, it empowered no one. Lack of support from home campuses or community programs made travel to meetings financially difficult for many who were then left out of the process. A lack of continuity among delegates led to delegates' lack of knowledge and resulting disempowerment. Gradually the organization moved away from its nonhierarchical governance structure, electing cochairs, a treasurer, and a secretary, and finally hiring a salaried executive director. But personal and professional tensions among the salaried staff, along with charges of racism, infected the entire organization, already struggling with racial tensions, leading to its near collapse in 1990. But it did, as Barbara Gerber has said, "rise from the ashes." Significant changes were again made to the governance structure, which provided for elected, volunteer leadership, representation of underrepresented groups, and involvement of the whole membership in major decision-making. The centrality of volunteer labor retains the grassroots aspect of the original organization, and the inclusion of caucuses, interest groups, and task forces in the structure provides space and voice for under-represented members (Gerber 19). However, the NWSA has continued to struggle throughout its history with rifts and divisions and struggles for inclusion of lesbians, women of color, working-class and poor women. The debate and discussion has been heated, sometimes harmful. While many have left, others continue to work to transform the organization. Tucker Pamella Farley has written that the confrontations that have taken place in the NWSA have made it difficult for some to confront racism, but that for herself and for many others, it was more difficult not to. As she says, this was "largely due to the courage of women of color who spoke to my face, and who wrote. . . . In feminist organization there is at least some talk about it all; and perhaps, over time and with the courage of sisters, we hear, we see, we shift" (45). The NWSA's struggles and self-scrutiny are akin to those Camus admired in the fastidious assassins—that they asked themselves every question, and they continue to ask. As President-elect Maria Gonzalez writes, the NWSA, now celebrating its twenty-fifth anniversary, has evolved into:

> an organization that could create a space in which the intellectual work of the women's movement, the lesbian movement, the transgendered movement, the queer movement, the women of color movement could take place. A space where activists and intellectuals traded knowledge, stories, and good times. A space directors of women's studies programs, departments, and women's centers could meet and develop more opportunities. . . . The strength of the organization is in its endless diversity of viewpoints. This is not a mushy-pluralist liberal organization, but one that has had to constantly reconstruct and redefine itself. (80–81)

It has become such an organization through its persistent commitment to egaliatarianism and inclusivity.

Dialogue

As Farley noted, at least feminist organizations talk about it all. Many feminist struggles to provide equality and inclusion have been about providing space for everyone to talk, to participate, to come to voice and to be heard. Much of the feminist focus on means has been directed toward developing processes to create and sustain meaningful dialogue— one of the few areas also addressed by Camus. Above all other means, Camus emphasized *civilisation du dialogue* (*Neither* 51–55). He continually encouraged individuals, groups, and nations to engage in dialogue and to create institutions and processes through which dialogue, rather than force, could be used to resolve conflicts. Despite his condemnation of absolutism, Camus argued that freedom of speech alone must be held as an absolute because it reserves the right to protest (*Rebel* 290). He was opposed to censorship in any form, with a particular interest to keeping dialogue going. He insisted that the cessation of dialogue leads to violence, and that the possibility of further discussion always exists (*Resistance* 136). He did not give us specifics as to how this dialogue is to take place, under what guidelines or agencies, or who is to participate. He said only that plain language is required, and that society and politics have the responsibility to arrange everyone's affairs so each and every one will have sufficient leisure and freedom to pursue a search for a common ground (*Plague* 230; *Rebel* 285, 302). That he says that *each and every one* will have sufficient leisure is significant because Camus's reference is to the Aristotelian premise that politics requires a certain amount of leisure—time to discuss. But in the Aristotelian model, only free men were to be afforded such leisure, made possible by the labor of women and slaves. Camus's statement tells us at least this much—that everyone is to be included in the conversation, but it doesn't tell us how this will be done. Sprintzen argues that Camus did lay out four requisites to dialogue in his "Appeal to a Civilian Truce" (*Resistance* 131–142; Sprintzen 255). These four are: (1) definition of "common ground"; (2) willingness to reflect on the view of the others; (3) willingness to reflect in terms of the future rather than in terms of past responsibility, guilt, and punishment; and (4) recognition of the possibility of difference. However, as Bronner has pointed out, Camus begs the question—what if the other is not willing to listen (88), and I would add, disclose. As discussed previously in chapter five, feminists have raised these questions, and while not immediately solving the problems, have taken them into consideration in the strategies they have developed to increase and enable dialogue that is participatory and inclusive of all.

Central to feminist discussion of the problems and possibilities of dialogue has been the issue of participants regarding each other as subjects.[17] This requires at least that we reveal ourselves, while remaining receptive and not imposing our voice on others. In developing a practice that is responsive to these issues, several feminists have adopted the model of Jürgen Habermas's discourse ethics.[18] Jean Bethke Elshtain has argued that to enable subjects to become more intelligible to themselves requires "an arena in which human speech of discursive reflection is undominated, uncoerced, unmanipulated" (*Public Man* 311). This, she says, approximates Habermas's "ideal speech situation" that requires repudiation of shaming, guilt-inducing, and an absence of abstracted assessments. Jodi Dean also relies on Habermas's discourse ethics as the basis of her notion of reflective solidarity, arguing that his ideal conditions for speech need to be in place in order to achieve the solidarity that grows from discourse. These conditions are:

(1) Every subject with the competence to speak and act is allowed to take part in a discourse.
(2) a. Everyone is allowed to question any assertion whatsoever;
    b. Everyone is allowed to introduce any assertion whatsoever into the discourse;
    c. Everyone is allowed to express his attitudes, desires and needs.
(3) No speaker may be prevented, by internal or external coercion, from exercising his rights as laid down in (1) and (2).
(Habermas, "Discourse Ethics" 89, quoted in Dean 154)

However, while there is much appreciation among feminists of Habermas's theory and intentions, many have raised questions regarding the possibility of actually implementing domination-free communication. Under conditions of real life, many factors operate to impinge on a truly egalitarian discourse. As Alison Jaggar notes: " . . . we must never forget that empirical discussions are always infused with power, which influences who is able to participate and who is excluded, who speaks and who listens, whose remarks are heard and whose dismissed, which topics are addressed and which are not, what is questioned and what is taken for granted, even whether a discussion takes place at all" ("Globalizing" 11). As our conversations take place among more diverse populations, the choice of language—and by this I mean not just national or ethnic language but also vocabularies of class, education, generation, culture—affects who is included and who has power in such discourse. Because some issues or individuals may mute the voices of others, it may be that excluding certain topics or groups from the conversation temporarily may actually serve to increase inclusion (Jaggar, "Globalizing" 20). And some may not be able to speak because they have not had the opportunity even to conceptualize their oppressions (Jaggar, "Globalizing" 11–14; Spivak).

Because the problems and possibilities of inclusion and exclusion are worked out in the actual practices of discourse, whether they be at the kitchen table or in more formalized settings such as the classroom, these are an important resource for developing our understanding of inclusive and egalitarian practices of dialogue. In developing her concept of Feminist Practical Dialogue,[19] Alison Jaggar refers to several such instances. Perhaps the most formalized is that of the Women's Peace Encampment at the Seneca Army Depot in upstate New York that set out detailed guidelines for collective decision-making. Among these are responsibility, self-discipline, respect, cooperation, and struggle. Participants were to be responsible for their own participation in the discussion, to exercise self-discipline in voicing objections, to respect others, to look for areas of common ground, and to use disagreement to learn from each other, not to put others down ("Toward" 120–121).[20]

Another significant avenue for the development of the feminist practice of discourse has been the feminist classroom. Feminist pedagogical techniques are designed to facilitate dialogue among equal and diverse others, even within the context of a hierarchical organization.[21] Feminist teachers often include students in the choices of course content, course activities and evaluative measures, as well as in the evaluation process itself. Feminist pedagogy is participative, using such techniques as small-group activities and dyads to encourage further discussion, and group projects to encourage cooperation. Students are encouraged to talk with each other rather than at each other. Rules of discourse develop out of the need to facilitate such exchange, especially when students are unaccustomed to participative learning. For example, I use the following rules of discourse in all of my classes:

(1) Treat each other with respect. If you disagree with someone's ideas, tell why you disagree with the *idea*. Personal attacks are unacceptable. This carries outside the classroom too.
(2) Recognize others' desires to speak. Don't hog the floor!
(3) Help each other speak. Don't always rely on me. Feel free to engage other people in the class in the conversation.

Perhaps no method of discourse is so distinctly feminist as that of the consciousness-raising group. Initially springing up spontaneously among groups of women gathering to share their lives and experiences, consciousness-raising groups evolved into deliberate and semi-institutionalized gatherings, with trained facilitators, guidebooks, rules, and thoughtfully designed discussion topics and questions.[22] In these groups, all would sit in a circle, each woman having a turn to speak (or not) about her experiences, feelings, thoughts, and perceptions, without interruption, confrontation, critique, or advice. Honest self-disclosure was valued and encouraged, with a purpose to raise consciousness about one's own and others' lives, to recognize common ground, and to move from that to action against oppression.

What these and other feminist practices of discourse have in common are basically these: (1) the creation of opportunities for participants to talk about their own lives, stressing the importance of first-person narratives and of others listening; (2) the equal importance of the experience of every person; (3) an openness to reevaluating one's perspective in light of the process of collective reflection; (4) the inclusion of people whose lives are very different from our own, especially those whose public silence has been most profound; (5) a nurturant, rather than an antagonistic environment, that while not precluding disagreement avoids intimidation and humiliation; (6) participant qualities of self-discipline, responsibility, sensitivity, respect, and trust; and (7) the motivation of care and friendship (Jaggar, "Toward").

This last is particularly important, because if the intent is not one of care and understanding, then the dialogue becomes manipulative and dominating. This intent also suggests one other fruitful means, developed by Lugones, and Lugones and Spelman, as discussed previously, of traveling to each other's worlds. In coming to know and understand each other as subjects, it is not sufficient to talk with and listen to each other, but requires as well to involve oneself, see the world from the perspective of the other, and come to know it and them in that world.

This focus on process is especially important in a politics grounded in the sustenance of relationship, which so much of feminist politics is. I am reminded of two scenes in Marge Piercy's novel, *Woman on the Edge of Time*. In the novel, a woman from our time, Consuelo, journeys back and forth between the insane asylum in which she is incarcerated and a feminist society in the future. During one of her visits to the future, the people in the future are trying to explain their systems for adjudicating conflict and political decision-making. They talk about the time they spend meeting and discussing, and the care they take to mend relationships broken or bruised by political disagreements:

> "There's no final authority, Connie," Luciente said.
> "There's got to be. Who finally says yes or no?"
> "We argue till we close to agree. We just continue. Oh, it's disgusting sometimes. It bottoms you."
> "After a big political fight, we guest each other," the man said. "The winners have to feed the losers and give presents . . . ." (153–154)

In the second scene, reminiscent of Camus's suggestion that society be arranged so that all have the leisure to pursue common ground, the society for all intents and purposes shuts down while a relationship problem is worked through by the community. Consuelo, the woman from our society, is appalled that so much attention is given to this, asking, "Don't you people have nothing to worry about besides personal stuff? . . . What a big waste . . . " to which Luciente responds, " . . . we believe many actions fail because of inner tensions. . . . The social fabric means a lot to us" (207–208). The possibility of inclusive and egalitarian dialogue rests on a willingness to give priority to relationship over efficiency, and to commit to the investment in the time and energy necessary to reach a solution that incorporates the views of all affected.

A striking example of the effectiveness of dialogue in working through conflictual situations is that of Palestinian and Jewish Israeli women who in ten years of continuous dialogue have been able to establish relationships of mutual understanding and have made a commitment among themselves to keep talking rather than shooting. However, and this is the real sticking point of dialogical politics, they have not been given a place at the negotiation table of the powers that be. In May 2002, they called on the UN Security Council to support their efforts for inclusion, citing Security Council Resolution 1325 that calls for equal participation of women in conflict-resolution efforts.[23] However, they have not been given access and do not have the power to bring their peace plan into being. Were these women able to bring their process and their wisdom to bear on the male-dominated political process, we might have seen an end to the Israeli–Palestinian hostilities by now. While undoubtedly their efforts have helped to prevent an even greater worsening of this situation, in order for dialogical politics to have a chance to effect significant change, those who embrace this method must also have the authority to enact the fruits of the exchange.

Concrete Politics

Camus argued that the impulse to revolt extends beyond its limits when it becomes motivated and directed by ideas and doctrine, and then tries to shape reality to fit that doctrine (*Rebel* 298). To stay within its bounds and faithful to its origins, rebellion must begin with specific issues, problems, and injustices, and seek to do what it can to remedy these. Rieux's statement in *The Plague* exemplifies the rebellious attitude: "For the moment I know this; there are sick people and they need curing. Later on, perhaps, they'll think things over; and so shall I. But what's wanted now is to make them well. I defend them as best I can, that's all" (117). In this way, the rebel's actions are limited to addressing particular incidents of injustice as they arise, rather than changing a whole system. Revolutionaries would find such an approach to be piecemeal, reformist, treating only the symptoms rather than the underlying problem. As the revolutionary, Stepan, says in *The Just Assassins*, such actions that "indulge in charity and cure each petty suffering that meets your eye" get in the way of the revolution, whose task is "to cure all sufferings present and to come" (258). But Camus feared a systemic solution that is potentially as deadly as the disease itself. Speaking through Kaliayev he responds to Stepan's concerns, "behind your words, I see the threat of another despotism which, if ever it comes into power, will make of me a murderer—and what I want to be is a doer of justice, not a man of blood" (259). The despotism comes in transgressing one's limits, in acting as if one knows all the consequences of one's actions. Camus argued that in order to sustain a life-affirming politics, the practice of rebellion must be limited to concrete problems.

Camus has been criticized for offering little in terms of analysis of the state or other institutions, or of collective and institutionalized means to combat oppression (Bronner 92; Isaac 246), and in this respect his ethic of rebellion is not as useful for institutionalized feminist politics. However, this was never Camus's intent. As Germaine Brée has argued, rebellion is a practical ethic, not a political solution (97). Rebellion fights oppression on a day-to-day basis, rather than as a system (Peyre 136). What was important to Camus was that people are dying of hunger and need bread (Brée 97), and that is what needs our immediate attention. Rosemary Ruether has similarly said of feminist politics, ". . . it is useful to start locally, where we can be concrete and where there is [sic] often some possibilities of real change," though such local action is always in awareness of global implications (*Gaia* 271).

The one example Camus gave of such concrete rebellious politics is that of trade unionism. Trade union politics address problems of injustice and oppression by tackling the specific issues of working conditions, health and safety, inadequate pay, long and arbitrary hours, lack of autonomy, lack of opportunities for creative expression. By working on specific injustices such as these, the rebel moves in the direction of justice without imposing more injustice in the name of a sweeping vision of a justice yet to come.

Feminists have not consistently suggested such a limited practice. Marxist feminists have sought liberation through the revolution of the proletariat; feminists such as Shulamith Firestone have sought revolutionary changes in reproduction; and a rare few have advocated a violent and revolutionary overthrow of patriarchy.[24] There is even a revolutionary dimension implied in the desire to eliminate the epistemological and normative structures of mind/body dualism. Certainly any tactics that sought to indoctrinate people in revolutionary epistemologies would cross the limit. However, by its very definition, the elimination of mind/body dualism defies such indoctrination. It is necessarily grounded in the concrete, in listening to our bodies. We attend to our visceral responses to injustices, sufferings, environmental destruction as well as to beauty, eros, and joy. In the scrutinizing lens of erotic knowledge lies a radical proposal, grounded deeply in the concrete.

The impulse toward grounding knowledge in concrete experience found in much of feminist epistemology transfers as well to political practice. As such it calls for a politics grounded in grassroots; that is bottom-up, rather than top-down. This has been the reality of much of feminist praxis. Often women have been called into political action by issues affecting the health and safety of their children, whether it to be put in a stoplight at a dangerous intersection, or to clean up the hazardous waste on which their community is built, or to clean up the river on which their very lives depend. What could be more concrete than a rise in miscarriages and childhood cancer rates, or a drying up of a local well, or the displacement of an entire village due to the damming of a river, or the disappearance, maiming, and death of one's children in war? Addressing these and similar issues has been the stuff and substance of much of feminist politics, and in this sense, it has been more rebellious than revolutionary. Much of feminist politics has been realized in acts of resistance against oppression, injustice, and harm. The Chipko movement of Indian women placing their bodies between the chainsaws and bulldozers and the trees they seek to protect is a well-known example of such feminist politics of resistance, as is the steadfast witness of les Madres de la Plaza de Mayo in Argentina to protest the disappearance of their children. Countless other acts could be relayed: the Women's Pentagon Action; Greenham Common; the Code Pink action against the war in Iraq; Take Back the Night marches; the Revolutionary Association of Women of Afghanistan; the witness of Women in Black; tax resistance; trade unionism; the suffrage movement; protests against nuclear waste, hazardous waste, bgh in cow's milk and pcb's in our breast milk—the list could go on and on.[25]

But much of feminist political practice has also been about simply doing what needs to be done, about correcting an injustice, addressing a need. There was a time, in this country, when if a woman was raped, she had to face it alone, and was often blamed for the crime perpetrated upon her.[26] Through the continued efforts of feminists responding to this injustice, addressing this need, victims of sexual assault have advocates and support, and procedures, policies, and attitudes have changed. Similarly, in response to the need of the thousands of women needing to escape battering relationships, feminists have established shelters for battered and abused women and children across the country.

Feminists responded to the obstetrical practices of the 1950s by reintroducing the practice of midwifery and reclaiming natural birthing techniques and establishing birthing centers. Associated with this, feminists have created women's health centers that have informed and empowered women to take charge of their own bodies. Responding to the dearth of knowledge about women in the university curriculum and academic scholarship, feminists have established Women's Studies programs in colleges and universities around the country, contributing to a burgeoning feminist scholarship, which increasingly addresses issues not only of gender, but also of race, class, sexuality, able-bodiedness. These and countless others are examples of what Gloria Steinem has called "outrageous acts and everyday rebellions." "The great strength of feminism," Steinem writes, "like that of the black movement here, the Gandhian movement in India, and all the organic struggles for self-rule and simple justice—has always been the encouragement for each of us to act, without waiting and theorizing about some future takeover at the top" (384). This is not to denigrate theory building, and the explanation and vision it provides. Rather, it is, like Camus, a recognition of the potential for distortion and destruction that can occur when reifying theory takes precedence over real people, a potential prevented by grassroots, concrete approaches. Steinem continues, "It's no accident that, when some small group does accomplish a momentous top-down revolution, the change seems to benefit only those who made it. Even with the best intentions of giving 'power to the people' the revolution is betrayed" (384–385). A rebellious feminist politics, in order to avoid becoming a politics of domination, limits itself to addressing concrete problems from the ground up.

Feminist resistance and rebellious action springs up where there is an injustice to be confronted, a need to be addressed. Because there is no one source of injustice and domination, feminist movements have been multifocal and decentered. Because power (meaning domination) is decentered and multifocal, so must movements in resistance to dominance be so (Quinby 123–124).[27] When asked, "where is the feminist movement?," feminists must reply—everywhere there is an injustice to be resisted or a need to be addressed.

Such grassroots efforts often begin with one person, or a few, willing to confront an injustice, whether large or small. Sometimes these actions are named and known, but many times rebellious movements are built through the small daily unnamed and unknown efforts to act against injustice, to affirm dignity, in solidarity and friendship with each other and the earth. Camus exemplified such daily efforts in the characters of

Dr. Rieux and Grand, the bureaucrat, in *The Plague*. The doctor saw a need and in his daily efforts toward healing the sick, did what he could to fight the plague. But it is especially Grand, a simple bureaucrat, through his daily efforts overseeing the work of the sanitary squads' removal and burial of dead bodies, who embodies the rebel. There is, as Camus wrote, nothing of the hero about it,[28] but rather simply the "true embodiment of quiet courage. . . . He said yes without a moment's hesitation and with the large-heartedness that was second nature to him" (123).[29] Grand's "small daily effort" (127) is the action of rebellion. Rebellion is not a question of heroism, or of salvation, but of "common decency" (150). It is what Welch has called the "nonheroic goodness" of "lives lived in conection, and from that connection, lives lived for justice, for beauty, for compassion" (33).

In rebellious action, we do what we can; we do what needs to be done. We make the decision to care and take risks for justice even though there are no guarantees of success, or of success in our lifetime (Welch 96). As Nellie Wong writes:

> And you will not stop working and writing because you care, because you refuse to give up, because you won't submit to forces that will silence you, a cheong hay poa, a long steam woman, a talker, a dancer who moves with lightning. And you are propelled by your sense of fair play, by your respect for the dead and the living, by your thlee yip American laughter and language, by your desire to help order the chaotic world that you live in, knowing as the stars sparkle on this New Year's night that you will not survive the work that still needs to be done in the streets of Gold Mountain. (Wong 181)

In the words of Joan Chittister: ". . . we do not do feminism to succeed; we do feminism because we cannot morally do otherwise" (44).

These testimonies of rebellious feminism bring to mind Václav Havel's definition of hope:

> Hope is a state of the mind, not of the world. . . . Hope, in this deep and powerful sense, is not the same as joy that things are going well, or willingness to invest in enterprises that are obviously heading for . . . success, but rather an ability to work for something because it is good, not just because it stands a chance to succeed. (181)

Camus wrote of hope, "I have always thought that if the man who has hope for the human condition is a fool, he who gives up all hope is a coward" (*Actuelles* 179). Despite its recognition of the flaws and limits of humanity, of our capacity to oppress and our inability to eliminate all injustices, rebellion is nevertheless a hopeful politic:

> Some will say that this hope lies in a nation; others, in a man. I believe rather that it is awakened, revived, nourished by millions of solitary individuals whose deeds and work every day negate frontiers and the crudest implications of history. As a result, there shines forth fleetingly the ever threatened truth that each and every [one] on the foundation of [their] own sufferings and joys, builds for all. (*Resistance* 272)

Sam Keen has described Camus's rebellious politics as the politics of the lover—one who has the dedication to take a stand against individual instances of injustice. Citing Camus's recognition that our efforts are at best limited to reducing the number of tortured children in the world, Keen says that though what such politics yields is more modest than a utopia or a five-year plan, it sustains the possibility of eros and healing:

> Those men and women who care inordinately—that is, beyond the requirements of duty—choose some place to take a stand against evil and injustice. It may be a narrow place—on a school board, where the fight must be carried on to educate rather than indoctrinate; in the executive committee of an investment firm that manufactures guidance systems for missiles; in a rally to oppose the contamination of a river or the selling of public lands . . . . But the choice to stand for compassion keeps alive the hope and the quest for erotic rather than neurotic corporations, healthy rather than dis-eased body politic. (222)

In this limited yet hopeful, committed, and compassionate politic lies a path of healing.

The Path of Healing

In *The Plague*, the character Tarrou says that while there are victims and executioners, there is also a third category—that of the "true healers" and that we need to discover how to attain to that (230). The "third way" to which I have referred throughout is the path of healing. Camus gave us few specifics of how to attain to this, only the brief mention by Tarrou that perhaps the path of healing lies in the path of sympathy, which I interpret as "compassion." Beyond this, he did not offer strategies and tactics. But this was not his way. The more profound message of *The Rebel* is that rebellion itself is such a path. Healing lies in staying true to the origins of rebellion—in affirming dignity, fighting injustice, acting with compassion, honoring friendship, and sustaining a spirituality that integrates mind, body, spirit, and the earth.

In concluding this study of Camus's ethic of rebellion and feminism, it is valuable to bring together their common insights on the path of healing our individual and collective wounds with the insights of the literature of mind/body healing, as exemplified in the work of Stephen Levine.[30] Both feminism and Camus speak repeatedly in terms of illness and woundedness of the body, the spirit, and the body politic. Certain themes recur—exile, separation, denial, lies, masks, arrogance, pride. Similarly, both speak often of the need for the healing of our lives and the paths that might enable that—humility, lucidity, communion, community, connection, witness, speech, truth-telling, authenticity, listening, compassion, love, eros, passion, life force, body, earth, beauty, wholeness.[31] My intention here is to make the connections by weaving together the words and wisdom of Camus, Levine, and feminist writers on the processes of healing.

Exile

"The first thing that plague brought to our town," wrote Camus, "was exile . . . that sensation of a void within which never left us" (*Plague* 65). Just as the plague begins with exile and separation, so does the disease of our bodies and souls and that of our body-politic begin with the exile and separation of parts of our very beings. Whether these be literal physical separations from the sources of love and meaning in our lives, or psychic and spiritual ones, they leave their wounds. From our original wholeness, we gradually lose pieces of ourselves deemed unacceptable, wrong, shameful to ourselves or to others. We dis-integrate. The stories repeat themselves in different guises: the Native American child taken from her home and family—stripped of her clothes, her language, her religion—her very words, thoughts, and feelings forbidden and beaten out of her; the African slave, stolen from his homeland, separated by an ocean from his people—again, forbidden to speak his language, practice his religion, stripped and beaten; the Jew forced into the ghetto and the cattle car—stripped, shorn, forced to choose which of her children will be saved and which killed, or condemned to kill his mother; the woman forbidden to practice her healing arts, forced to denounce her self and her friends, her body searched for the third teat, accused as a witch—her breasts sliced off and burned alive; the gay man, committed to an insane asylum, or battered and beaten and left to die, or harassed to the point of suicide. The boy who longs to dance, the girl who wants to wander alone in the woods, the child who listens to the whispering of trees—all must learn that their desires are wrong, dangerous, crazy, forbidden. The baby fed on a schedule learns to listen to the dictates of the clock rather than her own body. The toddler with his hands tied to the crib learns he must not seek succor in his thumb nor feel the pleasures of touching his body. The boy teased for crying learns not to feel. The girl victimized by her own father learns not to trust. They say that words will never hurt us, but they do, and they are hurled as weapons—"wimp," "sissy," "witch," "nigger," "fag." And so we learn "to torture and destroy [ourselves] in order to conform" (Griffin, *Rape* 61). We learn to hide that in us which is unacceptable, a source of shame, or guilt, or pain—to deny it, to lie to others and even ourselves about it. We live with secrets and shame, and cast off the child in us. We become exiled from our bodies, the earth, beauty, and "lose faith even with our own lives" (Rich, *On Lies* 188). And in this we know loss, grief, and woundedness: "for every part of ourselves that we hide in darkness, for every lie that we tell ourselves, we suffer. It is this deceit which causes madness, and often, illness in the body, too. . . . We become weak imitations of who it is we think we should be" (*Made* 248–249). Not only does this separation from ourselves result in illness, weakness, and deadening, it also increases our sense of exile from others. In denying pieces of ourselves, we exile ourselves from love and from each other. We live in isolation because relationship and love are not possible where there is no knowledge: "what is kept hidden, secret, cannot be loved. It exists in a place of exile, outside the realm of response" (*Chorus* 98). We cannot love what we do not know. We long for community, but cut off from true community, we seek it instead in totality and ideology.

Our wounds are not confined to our particular bodies, souls, or lifetimes. Rather, they are passed from one generation to another, from parent to child, from culture to culture. Women who learned the deadly consequences of speech taught their daughters to remain silent. Slaves who learned the consequences of insubordination passed on survival tactics of dissembling, pretense, and lies. Men, expected by law to discipline their wives by beating them, instructed their sons likewise. We learn by example. The Celts deprived of their religions by the Romans stripped the Native Americans of theirs. Germans disciplined with torture used these same techniques in concentration camps, and built crematoriums on the very sites where their great-great-great grandmothers had been burned at the stake. Jews forced repeatedly over centuries to leave their homes, today deny Palestinians their homeland. The abused child grows to abuse his own child, or to choose a partner who will continue to abuse her. The ridiculed child grows to ridicule his own child. The wounded pass on their wounds to future generations.

Stephen Levine, a healer who works with the sick and dying, asks, "where does the healing lie?"—to which rebellion and rebellious feminism answer, in returning to ourselves, our bodies, the earth; in recovering our souls, our selves, our being, our eros. The plague ends in reunion. To regain our wholeness, as individuals and as societies, we must liberate and reclaim those aspects of our beings that we have exiled.

Reunion

"We have exiled beauty," Camus claims. We have cut ourselves off from the beauty of the earth, of bodies, of creation—and it is through reconnecting with this beauty that we restore our wholeness. We heal in reestablishing our relationship with the earth—in immersing ourselves in forest, desert, sea, and stars. As Camus wrote, it is in this "nuptials with the world" that one is able to "become what one is, to rediscover one's deepest measure" (*Lyrical* 67). We discover that the earth is the common ground we seek.

We also restore our relationship with beauty in reclamation of the poetic—what Griffin calls the "voice of rebellion"(*Made* 234). Lorde wrote of poetry that it is "a revelatory distillation of experience . . . not a luxury. It is a vital necessity of our existence" (37). Poetry, in this sense, is what Camus would call the "lucid" thought born of rebellion, that is, thought that illuminates our lives. As Lorde reminds us, "the quality of light by which we scrutinize our lives has direct bearing upon the product which we live, and upon the changes which we hope to bring about through those lives" (36). And, such lucidity has the power to heal and deepen us (Levine 7):

> Healing is what happens when we come to our edge, to the unexplored territory of mind and body, and take a single step beyond into the unknown, the space in which all growth occurs. Healing is discovery. It goes beyond life and death. Healing occurs not in the tiny thoughts of who we think we are and what we know, but in the vast undefinable spaciousness of being—of what we essentially are—not whom we imaged we shall become. (Levine 4)

Though speaking metaphorically, Griffin shares the same insight: ". . . To meet all that exists. It is by such a sacrament that wounds will heal us" (*Eros* 151–153).

When "nothing amazes us anymore, everything is known. . . . it is a time of exile, dry lives, dead souls" (Camus, *Lyrical* 165). And so strangely, lucidity requires what Griffin calls "a necessary feeling of ignorance . . . . This ignorance being a kind of rebellion. A refusal to accept that what one thinks one knows is all there is. So that 'somewhere else' the soul knows more, and finding that inner voice in the silence, out of ignorance, is finally like finding what one, in this other sense, *knew*, all along, so that we say we recognize" (*Made* 226). Thus rebellion and illumination, recovery of our being, lies in wonder-ing, that is, in being open to wonder, in being willing to ask questions, and be willing to be surprised—and to do so with tenderness. Levine writes that he witnessed in those patients in the process of healing their lives, "a deepening capacity to touch with mercy that which they had previously experienced only with fear and dread. They were learning to bring into their heart much of what had been eluded during a lifetime. Their healing seemed to be a process of letting life in" (Levine 14).

Karen Baker-Fletcher has written that we as a people have become disembodied, dis-membered from body, community, God, earth, and that to become whole, we need to re-member (57). In healing bodywork, the body literally releases those memories and hidden aspects of ourselves we have locked away in the very sinews of our being. In healing, Griffin reminds us, we discover our body of origin, and in this, our original wholeness (*Chorus* 297). We discover the essence with which we were born—our soul, our spirit (*Rape* 40, 43). But it is not enough to discover and to remember. We also need to bear witness to those discoveries and remembrances. In *The Plague*, the task of Dr. Rieux is not simply to heal those whose bodies were plagued with illness, but also to "bear witness in favor of those plague-stricken people" (278) in order that all might be healed of our larger societal malady. We heal by bearing witness, by giving testimony to our lives. We heal by telling our stories, individual and collective, for they are deeply intertwined. In speaking and listening, hearing and being heard, we reclaim "the visibility without which we cannot truly live" (Lorde 42). But to speak and to be visible in a world that turns a deaf ear or portrays one's truths as lies may simply perpetuate and deepen the wound. To be healing, our witnessing speech needs to be compassionately heard:[32] "To speak to a receiving ear, to be understood, even if only by one another, or by oneself, heals" (Griffin, *Made* 248). In this, feminism has been particularly healing—in creating an atmosphere that enables us all to bear witness, to testify to our lives, our true feelings; in demanding truth-telling; in bringing our secrets, our shames, our denied selves to light, in an atmosphere of understanding and love. Feminism, writes Susan Griffin, has "interrupted the silence of our lives" (*Made* 190): "All the labour of feminism . . . unwrapping yards of bandages . . . from our eyes. Ears. Hands. Skin" (*Made* 226). Allowing us to see, hear, touch, feel, know.

Camus tells us that where minds meet, we begin to exist (*Rebel* 22). The soul is manifested most fully when we are seen by each other—I and Thou, subject to subject. Such dialogue enables us to become more fully ourselves:

> In those moments a self previously buried in propriety and convention, or in the habits of others, or in the fear born to repression, a self not allowed to breathe, whose questions and feeling never reach consciousness, is suddenly revealed. I know these moments to be profoundly healing. And if there has been any consistent shape to my life, it would be that again and again I seek ways to find this authentic self. (*Made* 245)

As we come to greater knowledge of ourselves, we also come to love and hold those "piece[s] of ourselves that [are] hardest to hold" (Lorde 175). For it is knowledge that makes love possible. Love is both the process of refining the truths we can tell each other and the desire to know deeply all that is and accept these truths. In sharing our stories, in truth-telling, in compassionate listening, a way of loving is made possible. We come to know love from those who truly know us and we love those whom we truly know.

As we become more and more whole, more and more ourselves, more fully human—we recover our eros, our passion, our lifeforce. The more loving of ourselves we become, the more we recover the sources of our power. In our wholeness we no longer accept subordination, submission, being treated as an object—by ourselves or by another. "We refuse to be an it" (*Rape* 66). The more we speak, the more we speak out.

But it is not simply knowledge of ourselves that we seek. It is our common knowledge, discovery of the places of common woundedness that finally brings healing to our collective lives:

> any healing will require us to witness all our histories where they converge, the history of empires and emancipations, of slave ships as well as underground railroads; it requires us to listen back into the muted cries of the beaten, burned, forgotten and also to hear the ring of speech among us . . . ." (*Eros* 153)

Thus it is that in the revealing of our secrets, our selves, in telling our stories to each other, we realize a relationship and common connection that is healing of the collective. We come to understand that the same wounds wound us all: ". . . An injury done a student in Prague strikes down simultaneously a worker in Clichy, . . . blood shed on the banks of a Central European river brings a Texas farmer to spill his own blood in the Ardennes. There is no suffering, no torture anywhere in the world which does not affect our everyday lives" (Camus, *Neither* 42). As Levine wrote of one woman's discovery in her course of healing, "She learned that pain was not simply her own but belonged to all who had ever been born" (15). It is in our recognition that "every life bears in some way on every other" (Griffin, *Chorus* 144), and in our ability to see ourselves in others that we find the sources of compassion that heal our lives. And so it is that Tarrou was right, that the path of healing lies in compassion. Thus also do we find the community we have been seeking.

Closing Thoughts

"We will have kept the moral wager and affirmed our humanity only if, with Camus, we refuse to capitulate to the plague" (Elshtain, *Public Man* 352). Elshtain, writing these words in 1981, suggested that perhaps feminist language and theory was not yet adequate to the task demanded by this refusal—of "uniting the material and the spiritual, the public and the private, by achieving a dialectics of choice, variability, and possibility grounded in a conviction which disallows absolute certitude and the destruction it brings in its wake" (*Public Man* 352–353). Now, more than twenty years later, with much richness in the development of theory, culture, and politics, we know that it is adequate to the task, adding significantly to our understandings of all of the elements of rebellion. Similarly, placing the wisdom of feminism within the framework of rebellion reveals the convergences of its often disparate and isolated elements, and as Griffin has written, "the convergences we notice, the ones that excite us, are transformations . . . " (*Made* 219). The convergence of Camus's rebellion and feminism brings such transformation.

I concur and conclude with the gratitude and hopefulness of bell hooks as she writes:

> I am grateful that I can be a witness, testifying that we can create a feminist theory, a feminist practice, a revolutionary feminist movement, that can speak directly to the pain within folks, and offer them healing words, healing strategies, healing theory. (*Teaching* 75)

Such a healing feminist theory and practice is that revealed by rebellion. Thus rebellion brings us to understand that the work of rebellious feminism is that of those who "while refusing to bow down to pestilences, strive their utmost to be healers" (*Plague* 278).

NOTES

Chapter 1   Rebellion and Feminism

1. For example, Greta Gaard argues that ecofeminism is unlike rebellion in that it offers an alternative, in addition to rebellion's perceived limitations in critique alone (*Ecological* 31).

2. John Cruickshank also argues that the meaning of "rebellion" changes from the beginning of *The Rebel*, in which it is a metaphysical concept and a philosophical attitude, to the end, in which it is a political philosophy of moderation and political reform. I would agree with his further argument that the multiple uses of the word "revolt" causes confusion in Camus's work (118).

3. Camus also explored the question of absurdity in three genres: (1) a play, *Caligula*; (2) a novel, *The Stranger*; and (3) a philosophical essay, *The Myth of Sisyphus*. These early works are the ones with which most people in the United States are familiar, especially since they are often assigned in high school English or French classes, or in college survey courses on existentialism, but being only the first stage in a long series, they are hardly representative of Camus's thought.

4. Though born in Algeria into a poor family of European descent, Camus spent the bulk of World War II in Paris, where Nazism and resistance to it were everpresent realities. A recurrence of tuberculosis had prompted him to travel to the mountains of France in the winter of 1942, during which time the Allies invaded North Africa, preventing his return to Algeria. He and his wife were separated for the remainder of the war. Already a noted author, Camus took up residence in Paris where he was employed as an editor at the Gallimard publishing house, and soon became part of the intellectual circle that included Jean-Paul Sartre and Simone de Beauvoir (though never becoming one of Sartre's disciples or one of "The Family"—which seemed to irritate de Beauvoir), Maurice Merleau-Ponty, Arthur Koestler, and Jean and Michel Gallimard. After the occupation of Paris, Camus became active in the resistance group, Combat, eventually becoming the editor of their underground newspaper by the same name, and was renowned for his rebellious editorials.

5. This was the development of a theme he had actually contemplated nearly twenty years earlier. He wrote in his journal around 1932, " 'Should one accept life as it is? That would be stupid, but how to do otherwise? Should one accept the human condition? On the contrary, I think revolt is part of human nature' " (qtd. in Todd 21).

6. At the time it was published (1951), *L'Homme révolté (The Rebel)* was hugely controversial, particularly within the French intellectual community, who were appalled by Camus's critiques of revolution and communism. *The Rebel* received a scathing review in Sartre's *Les Temps Modernes* (though Sartre himself did not write it), to which Camus responded bitterly, provoking an even more biting response from Sartre himself: " 'And what if your book bore witness merely to your philosophical incompetence? If it were composed of hastily gathered knowledge [It took Camus six years to write *The Rebel*.], acquired secondhand? If, far from obscuring your brilliant arguments, reviewers have been obliged to light lamps in order to make out the contours of your weak, obscure, and confused reasoning?' " Sartre, "Réponse à Albert Camus," *Les Temps modernes*, 82, August 1952, rpt. in *Situations IV* (Paris: Gallimard, 1964, 90–126, qtd. in Judt 100). Camus found himself dismissed by the community of which he had once been a part.

His work, however, was embraced by others. The poet, René Char, wrote to Camus that he thought *L'Homme révolté* was Camus's best book so far. Polish painter and writer Josef Czapski told Camus, " 'Immediately after the attack that was concentrated on you, I wanted to write to tell you why I love you, and why you have more friends than you might think' " (qtd. in Todd 314). Witold Gombrowicz asked Czeslaw Milosz to send Camus a copy of his own works as an act of solidarity with him. Hannah Arendt wrote Camus a letter of admiration and praise for *The Rebel* (Judt 129).

Camus suffered from the controversy, writing to his wife in September 1952, " 'Decidedly, this book has cost me dearly, and today I only have doubts about it, and about myself, who resembles it too much' " (qtd. in Todd 311). Nevertheless, Camus continued to believe that *L'Homme révolté* was his best work, writing, " 'It's a book that has provoked lots of noise, and which has earned me more enemies than friends, . . . but if I had to do it all over again, I would rewrite the book just as it is. It's the book of mine which I value the most' " (qtd. in Todd 315).

Writing thirty years after its publication, Camus-scholar Raymond Gay-Crozier writes: "The significance of *The Rebel* clearly transcends the political and historical circumstances of its gestation and the acrimonious polemics that accompanied it," Gay-Crozier, *La Revues lettres Modernes: Albert Camus, 12: la révolté en question* (Paris: Minad, 1985, 3 (qtd. in Brée 88)).

7. Susan Griffin has made a similar argument that until the rebel comes to understand him or herself, rebellion ultimately imitates what it rebels against (*Pornography* 16). Rebellion that ends in imitating what it rebels against is revolution. Rebellion that stays true to its origins is that in which the rebel understands herself, especially her capacity to engage in the very acts she is fighting against.

8. Eric Bronner makes an important criticism of Camus's tactic in *The Rebel* of embracing the initial source of rebellion, but critiquing it when it goes awry. As he suggests, plenty of Nazis began their efforts with rebellious attempts to eradicate injustices while invoking a value of something they believed worthwhile (91). I do believe, however, this is exactly why Camus needed to investigate rebellions, in order to discover *all* the initial sources of rebellion, not

just the initial impulse to refuse injustice. The enumeration of all of these initial sources is my task in the next few pages.

9. Beginning with the initial critiques of *L'Homme révolté* following its publication (see note 7), Camus has been criticized for the weakness of his philosophical argumentation. As Tony Judt writes, "Sartre was right, at least so far as the structure and arguments of Camus's book were concerned . . . " (100). Likewise, Eric Bronner argues that *The Rebel* "lacks philosophical grounding" (86). Henri Peyre calls *The Rebel*, "a confused and imperfect volume that fails to come up to its philosophical claims," and should instead be read as a collection of maxims (27). Lev Braun states that *The Rebel* is not a systematic philosophy but rather an "unwieldy and rather confused sequence of ideas" (107). Serge Doubrovsky says that Camus "has no system, no general framework, no philosophy" (153). But Camus's French biographer, Olivier Todd has argued that it was in fact Camus's opposition to systematic thinking that has contributed to advances in political philosophy, likening Camus's maxims more to a "clash of cymbals" than to philosophical ideas. "Not being a philosopher did not prevent him from being a stimulating thinker" (418). As for himself, Camus never claimed to be a philosopher, " 'I am not a philosopher, because I don't believe in reason enough to believe in a system. What interests me is knowing how we must behave, . . . " (qtd. in Todd 408). Tony Judt sums it up: "These—philosopher, engaged intellectual, Parisian—are all the things Camus was not. But he was, despite his misgivings at the idea, quite assuredly a moralist. . . . a moralist in France was someone who told the truth" (121–122).

10. I have distilled the elements in this chart distinguishing rebellion from revolution primarily from pages 246–252 of *The Rebel*, though Camus wrote about the distinction throughout.

11. Please refer back to the chart contrasting rebellion and revolution. Unity, a characteristic of rebellion, is distinguished from totality, a characteristic of revolution.

12. My appreciation to Rita Gross and China Galland, whose discussion of the meaning of compassion in the contexts of Buddhism and feminism in their works enabled me to recognize this equivalence of compassion and solidarity.

13. I should point out that despite popular conceptions of Camus as an existentialist, stemming from his friendship with Sartre, he never regarded himself as such. The nonexistence of such key existentialist terms as "immanence," "poursoi," "en soi," and "mitsein" in his works also is evidence of this.

14. For more discussion of this quality in Camus's works, see Judt 97 ff.; Bronner 14–18; Sprintzen; Tisson-Braun; and Amoia.

15. Some have argued that one of the failings of *The Rebel* is that it has no suggestions for political practice (Doubrovsky 153; Sprintzen 280). This will be taken up further in chapter eight.

16. Though I do not know of any particular direct intellectual links between the works of Camus and feminist authors and activists, beyond my own, it is possible that certain elements of feminist thought were directly

influenced by Camus's philosophy of rebellion. A confluence of events—Camus's winning the Nobel Prize for literature in 1957, Camus's untimely death in an automobile accident in 1960, and the rise of various protest movements in the United States in the 1960s—catapulted Camus to a position of a sort of folk hero of the New Left. "He [Camus] was the single most popular writer during the student revolt of the 1960's" (Bronner 143). *The Rebel*, with its emphasis on dialogical politics, was read all over college campuses as providing a basis for participatory democracy, and became one of the key texts of the New Left and student movements of the 1960s (Bronner 89). In that certain branches of feminism grew out of—or away from—the New Left movement, one can surmise that at least some of the leaders of the second wave of feminism, especially those associated with Redstockings, which split off from Students for a Democratic Society, were familiar with Camus's work. At various feminist conferences where I have presented papers on Camus's work, feminists who came of age in that era often express nostalgia for Camus's work, especially *The Rebel* and *The Plague*. But I know of none who explicitly acknowledge or reference Camus, with the sole exception of Jean Bethke Elshtain, who refers to Camus as a "moral guide" (*Public Man* 300). (I did ask Susan Griffin, whose work, especially in *The Eros of Everyday Life* and *Made from this Earth*, so deeply parallels that of Camus's, if she had been influenced by Camus's *The Rebel*. While she did remember being deeply affected by his writing style in *The Stranger*, she had not read *The Rebel*, or any of his other works on the theme of rebellion (e-mail correspondence).) One intriguing possibility linking Camus's thought to feminist thought is that both have been strongly influenced by the work of Simone Weil. So, Camus's work on rebellion may have directly influenced other feminist authors and activists, beyond myself. But while this is intellectually and historically intriguing, the main point here is not to draw the intellectual genealogy of the feminist movement.

17. The phrase, "neither victims nor executioners" is the title of one of Camus's short essays.

18. Jeffrey Isaac has also criticized Camus's failure to raise the important questions not only of gender, but also of race and sexuality (235).

19. Rizutto argues that Camus's female characters become the essential point of contact between man and nature. The idea of women taking on the role of intermediary between man and nature on a mythic level was first explored by Camus's contemporary, Simone de Beauvoir, in *The Second Sex* (ch. 5).

20. Take for example this entry, dated November 11, 1942: "Outside of love, woman is boring. She doesn't know. You must live with one and keep silent. Or else sleep with all and make love. What matters is something else" (*Notebooks* II: 42). He also at times writes of women as objects or possessions. There are moments in his journals that are reminiscent of Rousseau, in his need to "give up the tyranny of female charm" (March 18, 1940; *Notebooks* I: 191). Struggling with his own sexual impulses, Camus, like Rousseau, would project the blame onto women, regarding them as a distraction and as "opium." This statement about Adam and Eve is also

reminiscent of Rousseau's *Émile*: "he formed for contemplation and courage; she for softness and alluring grace. He for God alone; she for God in him" (March 1942; *Notebooks* II: 7). Yet, in all fairness, his later works occasionally show a shift in his regard. In 1947, he wrote notes for a play on a government of women that fails miserably as long as the women are ruling as men did, but then thrives as they decide to rule as women. In 1948, there is a smattering of references to the works of philosopher Simone Weil, whose works Camus was instrumental in getting published.

21. De Beauvoir reported an early admiration of Camus ("I liked the 'hungry ardor' with which he abandoned himself to life and pleasure, I liked his enormous consideration for others." *Force* 53). She noted as well as his encouragement of her work, (He was the one who encouraged her to write *Ethics of Ambiguity*.), and said this of his response to her novel *The Blood of Others*: "One remark of Camus's moved me a great deal. . . . he drew me aside and said enthusiastically, 'It's a fraternal book' " (*Force* 53). He also asked her to let Éditions de Minuet (a paperback version) have *The Blood of Others*, presumably so that it could reach a wider audience (*Force* 67; *Prime* 445–446). Nevertheless, the majority of her remarks regarding Camus, his work, and his attitude toward women are disparaging. She said in an interview in 1982: " 'Camus couldn't stand intelligent women. They made him uncomfortable, so he either mocked them or ignored them, depending on how much they irritated him. . . . His usual tone of voice for me was, to say it politely, ironic mockery. That stops short of what it really was—generally insulting' " (qtd. in Bair 290). " 'Camus,' " she reiterated in another interview, "never lost a chance to belittle me . . . " (qtd. in Bair 394). Of his reaction to *The Second Sex*, she wrote: "Camus, in a few morose sentences, accused me of making the French male look ridiculous. A Mediterranean man, cultivating Spanish pride [Camus's mother was of Spanish heritage.], he would allow woman equality only if she kept to her own, and different, realm. Also, he was of course, . . . the more equal of the two. He had blithely admitted to us once that he disliked the idea of being sized up and judged by a woman: she was the object, *he* was the eye and the consciousness. He laughed about it, but it is true that he did not accept reciprocity. Finally, with sudden warmth, he said: 'There's one argument that you should have emphasized: man himself suffers from not being able to find a real companion in woman; he does aspire to equality.' He too wanted a cry from the heart rather than solid reasoning; and what's more, a cry on behalf of men" (*Force* 190).

However, Simone de Beauvoir's biographer, Deidre Bair quotes Patrick McCarthy as saying that de Beauvoir's memoirs are " 'a dubious source for Camus because by the time she wrote them she cordially detested him' " (*Camus* 183, qtd. in Bair 290). Also, it should be noted, contrary to de Beauvoir's depiction of Camus's attitude toward intellectual women, that though he never knew her, Camus was a great admirer of the work of Simone Weil, and was one of the prime movers in the posthumous publication of her work. It is said that Camus spent an hour in meditation in Weil's room in Paris before boarding the plane to Stockholm to accept the

Nobel Prize (Gray 229). Also, another contemporary, Hannah Arendt, apparently did not feel his condescension and said of him in 1952, "'he is, undoubtedly, the best man now in France. He is head and shoulders above the other intellectuals'" (qtd. in Isaac 17).

22. For further discussion of this point, see Irene Finel-Honigman, "The Orpheus and Euridyce Myth in Camus's *The Plague*," *Classical and Modern Literature* (Spring 1981): 207–218, 211 and Alan J. Clayton, "Camus ou l'impossibilité d'aimer," *Revues des lettres modernes* (1975): 9–34, 21 qtd. in Rizutto 101–102).

23. In *Caligula*, the Roman emperor, Caligula, has seemingly gone mad with grief over the death of his sister. Representing the absurdity of "being logical at all costs," Caligula follows the logic of an off-hand remark that the Treasury is of prime importance, and thus is ready to sacrifice anything and anyone to it, beginning a rein of terror lasting three years, ending only in his own death. Caesonia, Caligula's lover, repeatedly is the voice for "simple love," but in the end Caligula kills her as well.

   In *State of Siege*, a Plague has come to rule the city, randomly killing citizens of Cadiz. Diego and Victoria are lovers, soon to be married, but Diego risks his life and thus their future together by risking infection when he helps others who are infected. Victoria pleads with him to put their love first.

   Finally, *The Just Assassins* is the story of the 1905 assassination of the Grand Duke Sergei by the Organization for Combat of the Socialist Revolutionary Party. In *The Rebel*, Camus exemplified this group as maintaining rebellion that is faithful to it origins. In their first attempt to assassinate the Grand Duke, they refused to throw the bomb because children were riding with him. Thus, they recognized that even murder had its limits, and ultimately had to be paid for with their own lives. In the play, the character Dora (of whom Camus later said of all his characters he was most fond), based on the real-life Dora Brilliant, is again a voice of love, but also of limits, saying, "But the death of the Grand Duke's niece and nephew won't prevent any child from dying of hunger. Even in destruction there's a right way and a wrong way—and there are limits" (258).

24. The full citation for Isaac's reference to Michael Walzer is "Albert Camus's Algerian War," in Walzer's *The Company of Critics: Social Criticism and Political Commitment in the Twentieth Century* (New York: Basic Books, 1988), p. 145.

25. This is not to say that Camus was not dualistic in his thinking, a topic to be taken up in more detail in chapter two. He has been characterized as a "paradoxical" thinker; and some have interpreted this quality as "either/or" (Charney 104). However, Camus was clear that rebellion insists on maintaining seemingly opposed values in tension with each other, finding the truth within the paradox. Rebellion requires "both/and."

26. See my "Beyond Either/Or." This topic will be discussed further in chapter six.

27. Several feminist theorists have challenged the public/private divide in Western political thought. For further discussion of this point see e.g. Ackelsberg and Shanley; Elshtain, *Public Man*; Okin, *Justice*; Pateman.

28. Camus felt he was misunderstood in *The Rebel*, and he was, primarily by the French intellectual Left, which being highly grounded in Western political thought was deeply based in dichotomous thinking. However, those not steeped in that tradition—poets, sculptors—admired and appreciated his work, and undoubtedly understood it at a core level because they were not strapped into dichotomous thinking.

29. Linda Forge Mellon presents an intriguing argument that from a Jungian perspective, the female character in Camus's short story "La Pierre qui pousse" ("The Growing Stone") represents the *anima*, or "the woman within." In this story, a highly masculine protagonist—a rebel character—d'Arrast, comes with Western engineering skills to save a remote Brazilian village from the flooding of the river that flows by it and is caught up in the drama of a man, Coq, who has made a bargain with God that requires him to carry a one hundred pound stone to the church. When he fails, d'Arrast, who once found the bargain absurd, picks up the stone, and carries it not to the church but to Coq's home, or in Mellon's representation, to the home of Coq's daughter. Mellon presents several points that suggest that Coq's daughter represents the positive qualities of the *anima*, and that d'Arrast's encounters with the girl represent his need to include the feminine principle to complement his "excessively masculine activity." The central theme of the story then is that d'Arrast has learned from and finally accepted his own *anima*, thus completing the process of individuation, or becoming whole.

   This suggests the possibility that viewed on the mythic level, Camus's female and male characters are not intended literally to represent women and men, but rather the *anima* and *animus* present in every individual that must each be accepted in order to attain wholeness. (Though this does not move us any further from essentializing the masculine and feminine.)

30. The first three are a variation of a schema developed by Patricia Hill Collins.

31. Feminism is usually referred to as "first-wave"—the feminist movements of the United States and Great Britain beginning in the 1830s and continuing through the attainment of suffrage until the 1950s; "second-wave"—the feminist movements, beginning for the most part in the United States but then expanding globally, from the late 1960s through the end of the twentieth century; and "third-wave"—the latest interpretation of feminism by young women just coming of age politically at the beginning of the twenty-first century.

32. Rita Nakashima Brock coined the term "theaology" to recognize the study of the female divine.

Chapter 2   Epistemological Bases

1. The first three roughly parallel those set forth by Patricia Hill Collins in her exposition of an Afrocentric feminist epistemology. These include: (1) an ethic of caring, which includes personal expressiveness, emotions, and empathy; (2) concrete experience as a criterion of knowledge; and (3) use of dialogue in assessing knowledge claims. Collins includes a fourth, an

ethic of personal accountability in making knowledge claims, which while being present in Camus is not highlighted in the same way as the others. In developing her epistemology, Collins is trying to develop the points of parallel between Afrocentric and feminist apologies. Given his Algerian upbringing, it is possible that Camus's epistemology so closely parallels Collins's because it has Afrocentric roots.

2. For further discussion of this point see Flax, "Political"; Lloyd; Merchant; Harding and Hintikka; Keller, Evelyn; Plumwood, *Feminism*.

3. For those not familiar with de Beauvoir's work in *The Second Sex*, it should be noted that she made generalizations about all men and all women based in large part on her knowledge of the women and men of her own leisured and educated upper-middle class France. Her work has been subjected to much feminist criticism on this account.

4. Griffin addresses these issues in "Split Culture" 13 ff.; *Eros* 135 ff.; *A Chorus of Stones*; and *Woman and Nature*.

5. Camus was the only journalist in France to speak out against the bombing of Hiroshima. In his editorial written on the day after the bomb was dropped he decried not only the fact that technological civilization "had just reached its greatest level of savagery," but also the fact that it was being celebrated as a great discovery. "There is something indecent," he wrote, "in celebrating a discovery whose use has caused the most formidable rage of destruction ever known . . ." (*Between Hell* 110).

6. David Sprintzen also makes this assessment of Camus's thought (124).

7. Barnes contrasts Camus with Sartre and de Beauvoir whom she regards as subjecting emotions to analysis for justification, rejection, or classification (*Literature* 187).

8. David Sprintzen also writes of how rebellion begins with outrage (124), but compassion is also an important piece. Carter Heyward also makes the argument that outrage and compassion, rather than being mutually exclusive, "belong together"(296).

9. This point is particularly highlighted in Camus's play, *The Just Assassins*. This will be examined in detail in chapter five.

10. Many feminists draw this distinction between nurturing speech and adversarial speech. See e.g. Belenky et al. ch. 6; Griffin, *Made* 161; hooks, *Talking* 16; Jaggar, "Towards." Returning for a moment to Camus's *Just Assassins*, the character of Stepan represents the separate knower, being an adversary, talking at the others in a monologue that is not open to new information or perspectives. The others are clearly searching their hearts. But it is again the Grand Duchess who tries to create connection, trying to make Kaliayev understand.

11. The conditions that make genuine discourse possible is a complex topic that will be explored in greater length in chapters four, five, and eight in this book.

12. We find this for exmaple in the works of Chodorow; Gilligan; Jaggar, *Feminist Politics*; Benhabib, "The Generalized"; Plumwood, "Nature, Self, Other"; Moraga and Anzaldúa; and Ruddick, *Maternal*. A notable exception is bell hooks, who is critical of feminists for dismissing work for being

too "abstract." Yet she does acknowledge that abstract theory can emerge from concrete experience, and my sense is that this is what Camus had in mind (*Talking Back* 39).

13. See for example the critiques of major political concepts in Hirschmann and DiStefano.

14. See e.g. Gilligan; Noddings; and Held, *Feminist Morality*.

15. This issue is discussed at length in chapters three, four, and five in this book.

16. For further discussion of standpoint theory see Jaggar, *Feminist Politics* 305; Hartsock, "Feminist Standpoint"; Hirschmann and DiStefano; Ruddick, *Maternal Thinking*; and Young, *Justice*. Feminist standpoint theory has similarly been critiqued for essentializing women's experience (Haraway 200).

17. The basic lines of this argument are present in many aspects of feminist thought—multicultural, radical-cultural, ecofeminist. See e.g. Anzaldúa, "La consciencia"; Hurtado; Hartsock, "Feminist Standpoint"; Plumwood, "Nature" 17–19; and Jaggar, *Feminist* 367.

Chapter 3   Refusal and Affirmation

1. In making the distinction between rebellion and resentment, Camus drew on Freiderich Scheler's work, *Ressentiment*, a book much referred to at the time, certainly one that also influenced Simone de Beauvoir.

2. In arriving upon these examples I have found Iris Marion Young's enumeration of the five faces of oppression to be quite helpful. These are (1) exploitation—being "the transfer of the results of the labor of one social group to benefit another" (49); (2) marginalization—the expelling of whole categories of people "from useful participation in social life" (53) (the old, racial groups, mentally and physically disabled, single mothers, etc.); (3) powerlessness—not participating in the decisions that affect the conditions of one's life and action; (4) cultural imperialism—"the universalization of a dominant group's experience and culture, and its establishment as the norm" (59) in a way that "renders the perspective of one's own group invisible at the same time as they stereotype one's group and mark it out as the Other" (59); and (5) violence—including physical violence and terror, as well as harassment or intimidation simply for the purpose of degrading and humiliating the members of one's group (*Justice* ch. 2).

3. Even having achieved entrance to these, they have still had to resist women's marginalization within these pursuits. Indeed, both the 1840s "Women's Rights Movement" and the 1960s radical feminist movement grew from women within progressive organizations refusing any longer to be marginalized by their male colleagues. And feminists, particularly lesbian feminists, feminists of color, and poor and working-class feminists, have also resisted marginalization by white middle-class heterosexual feminists who have continued the same patterns of exclusion that they experienced from men of their race and class.

4. Ann Ferguson has called this practice "sex-affective production." Marilyn Frye has also argued that taking care of men's needs drains women's life energies (98–102).

5. See e.g., Bunch, "Lesbians in Revolt" and Radicalesbians.
6. This will be discussed in more depth in chapters three, four, and five.
7. What language can women claim? Women are not like indigenous people who in their rebellious acts can reclaim their native language. This problem has been central to the deconstructionist case that "woman" is not possible, and that because we have no language of our own, we can think only in the language of the oppressor. Thus our very thoughts oppress us (Wittig, Kristéva, LeClerc).

   Mary Daly's work is particularly significant in this regard, in her reclaiming of such words as "hag," meaning "wise woman" and "spinster," meaning "a woman who spins," (and for Daly one who spins a new universe of female empowerment); her hyphenation of words for new emphasis, e.g., Be-Friend, Be-Witch, and Be-Wilder; her creation of new meanings of such terms as "gross national product" (being "any lethal or toxic commodity produced by phallotechnological nation. Examples: pesticide-poisoned produce, pornography, nuclear weaponry") (*Websters'* 204); and the creation of new language, such as "wickedary" and "gynocide." A compilation of Daly's new words and new definitions of words can be found in her *Websters' First New Intergalactic Wickedary of the English Language.*
8. While de Beauvoir was undoubtedly correct in unmasking the ways that women, particularly white middle-class women, may give their loyalties to men of their race and class in order to secure privileges, she did not recognize how some women might give their loyalties to men of their race and class out of shared oppression.
9. Bell hooks, for example, has raised concerns that the emphasis of radical feminism on "lifestyle" choices diverts feminist attention from feminist struggle to end sexist oppression (*Feminist* 26–27). Radical feminist Tania Lienert, on the other hand, argues that this characterization is misrepresentative of radical feminism.
10. Even Charlotte Bunch, who was so adamant in her separatism, has since argued that separatism ultimately is not empowering because it is so isolating. Nevertheless, she did find it helpful as a way to be able to learn about her identity (Hartmann et al. 935).

    Through a series of case studies, I discovered that such "metaphysical" separatism is an important stage in the process of women coming to feminist consciousness. See my "A Time Apart" for more information.
11. This raises the large issues of what the role of the rebel is in asking questions, and the problem of outsiders even asking questions. Does asking questions in itself impose a point of view? One of the strengths of the feminist method has been that of asking questions of ourselves, rather than those put to us by others. What then is the role of Western feminists vis-à-vis women in other cultures?
12. The actual process and significance of consciousness-raising groups is discussed in more detail in chapters four and eight.
13. That is not to say that one cannot find such pressures to adhere to a line within feminism. It is only to say that this is not consistent with rebellious feminism.
14. While this may have been true of the exercises in many consciousness-raising (CR) groups, the CR manual we used did discuss class, age, and

sexuality. However, it is strikingly lacking in that it had no discussion of race. However CR groups were supposed to be diverse in race, class, sexual orientation, etc., under the supposition that this would yield diverse insights into the nature of the topics discussed.

15. Young's argument is reminiscent of one made twenty years earlier by Zillah Eisenstein regarding the radical potential of liberal feminism. Eisenstein argued that liberal feminists, seeking individual advancement, would find themselves being identified by and treated according to a group characteristic (perhaps more accurately termed a serial characteristic)—their sex, and that had the potential to radicalize them.

16. In a way quite reflective of Camus's indictment of rebellious movements that had become absolute negation, whether or not these French theorists should even be considered feminists has been the subject of controversy (Bell and Klein section three).

17. Hartsock argues further that this conception need not be totalizing, and that feminists, because of our history, will work against this ("Foucault" 171).

18. See e.g. Hartsock, "Foucault on Power" 171; Yeatman 290; and Alarcón.

19. This idea of "multiple voices" has been developed in the work of many feminist theorists, among them: Lugones, "Playfulness" 398; Anzaldúa, "La conciencia" 378–379; Alarcón 365; and Yeatman.

20. This will be discussed further in chapter five.

Chapter 4   Claiming One's Voice

1. Silence is used to express communion in many of Camus's writings regarding his communion with nature, including the wife's communion with the night sky in "The Adulterous Woman" (*Exile*). In "The Silent Men" (*Exile*), the coopers return to work in a defeated silence after a failed strike, and then use silence toward the owner as a form of protest and ostracism.

2. In his autobiographical novel, *The First Man*, Camus described his patient acceptance of being beaten by his grandmother. But he also described his moment of revolt when he resolved never to be beaten again, and tore the leather whip out of his grandmother's hands. She never did beat him again (275).

3. The Taliban also prohibits women from laughing, riding bicycles and motorcycles, showing their ankles, wearing make-up or shoes that click, leaving home without a male relative, speaking to men who are not close relatives, attending school, and working (Dalal; Lacayo). Long before the U.S. bombing of Afghanistan focused media attention on the Taliban, feminists around the world had been protesting the oppressive conditions of women under Taliban rule.

4. The essay in which he spoke to this issue most directly is "Of Bread and Freedom" in *Resistance, Rebellion, and Death*.

5. As this goes to press, a bill is before the Minnesota legislature that would prohibit public funds to go to any organization that "maintains a policy in writing or through oral public statements that abortion is considered part of a continuum of family planning, reproductive health services, or both"

(Minnesota H.F. 436/S.F. 431). The bill is in essence a gag rule. No other such requirement dictating what a medical provider can or cannot say exists within the profession. Indeed, the code of ethics requires physicians to inform patients about all legal options, risks, and benefits.

6. Feminists often critique the fact that women have been expected to serve men, and other women. However, it is important to make the distinction between *servitude* and *service*. Servitude is coerced in some respect—physically, psychologically, culturally. It is a condition of domination and it is not mutual. Service, on the other hand, is freely chosen, under conditions of equality and mutuality. Service becomes servitude when any of the following three factors occurs: (1) the service is not freely chosen, (2) the service makes demands on one who is already depleted; and (3) the service lacks mutuality and reciprocity.

7. Judith Rollins details the expectations of deference made of domestic workers in her piece, "Deference and Maternalism," in Jaggar and Rothenberg 335–345.

8. Kathy Ferguson demonstrates how subordinates within a bureaucratic system learn to silence themselves in her *The Feminist Case Against Bureaucracy*.

9. I have often thought, during the process of writing this, of Camus's mother, literally deaf and mute, but also illiterate. Though he continued to send her his writings, she could never read them, nor could she hear them being read to her. Tillie Olsen has remarked that had it not been for her class status, and I would add, except for her sex-class status, Camus's mother might have been one of the voices of literature (184).

10. Camus himself seemed ignorant of his own participation in this. There has been much critical discussion of the fact that he spoke and wrote in the language of the colonizer. Even in his attempts in the last few years of his life to make the Arab characters in his works more visible, he still wrote in French, the language of the colonizer. See e.g. Barberto and Horowitz.

11. For further discussion of this point see Schaef; Spender; Michell; Memmi; and Lugones and Spelman.

12. Please see chapter three in this book for a more detailed discussion of both of these points.

13. We have seen this same phenomenon in the silence growing in the United States since the terrorist attacks of September 11. There is pressure to speak with one voice (only one Congresswoman was brave enough to vote against the bombing of Afghanistan), not to criticize government policy for to do so is deemed unpatriotic. Military tribunals have been set up for the trials of accused terrorists who are not allowed the civil liberties of a court of law.

14. In these times of global terrorism, some may object to the use of the word "terrorism" to describe the conditions of women's lives. But given a definition of terrorism as random acts of violence with the intent to induce fear and compliance, I would agree that the use of the word "terrorism" is appropriate.

15. Dworkin introduced an ordinance in Minneapolis, Minnesota that would have outlawed the sale of pornographic materials. She based her argument in the Equal Protection clause, arguing that because pornography

undermines women's safety and security, it violates their equal protection under the law.

16. Walter Wink has provided an interpretation of the Christian teaching to "turn the other cheek" that suggests that, given the cultural context of Jesus's day, the message is one not of passivity, but rather of nonviolent resistance. He argues that the first blow to the right cheek would have been made with the back of the right hand. (The Biblical passage states "if any one strikes you on the right cheek . . . .") The left hand was only used for unclean tasks, so the right hand would be used, and to hit someone on the right cheek with the right hand would necessitate using the back of the hand. The meaning of hitting someone with the back of the hand was one of humiliation or admonishment of an inferior. To then offer them the other, left cheek, would mean establishing yourself as their equal, a rebellious action that refuses being demeaned. Further, were the person actually then to strike the person on the left cheek, it would be with a fist or open hand, which would establish the opponent's equality. It is interesting, given Camus's reference to the path of the rebel being "a third way," that Wink calls the rebellious elements of Jesus's teachings "Jesus' Third Way" (254–256).

17. See e.g. hooks, *Talking*, and Lugones and Spelman 574.

18. Nineteenth-century radical reformers were disparagingly called "Fanny Wrightists" in reference to Frances Wright, one of the first feminist activists in the United States, who dared to speak in public, and to "mixed" (male and female) audiences.

19. See the discussion of unity and totality in chapter one in this book. Audre Lorde warned that the term "unity" has been a disguise for "homogeneity," and a fear of difference, but I think her understanding of the term "unity" is closer to what Camus described as "totality," and it is important to distinguish the two.

20. Camus's own rebellion was fostered in the tradition of the French Revolution, of philosophical training, and within a culture that despite his poverty, taught him that as a white male colonizer, he had worth. The possible caveat to my statement regarding Camus's failure to address conditions that enable revolt is the fact that he does acknowledge that loving relationships are necessary to inspire revolt, a theme that will be pursued in chapter six.

21. According to Collins, the blues and literature have offered safe vehicles for self-expression. Singing the blues has been a safe place for black women not only to deal with their pain, but also to express their self-definition and develop a black women's standpoint. Particularly in the days when so much of the black population was kept illiterate, the blues served as a significant vehicle of expression. Collins argues that black women blues singers used the blues to challenge the controlling images of black women, to claim a spirit of independence, and, as in Billie Holiday's "Strange Fruit," to overtly protest racism and the lynchings it inspired (99–102). And, Collins argues, with increasing literacy, black women's scholarship and literature have provided safe sites of resistance to domination, to explore taboo subjects, and have provided a community in which black women dialogue with each other, and to articulate a self-defined standpoint (102–103).

22. Though hooks recognizes the importance of home as a safe space in which black women and men could develop the resources necessary for resistance,

she has also said that she does not agree with the trend in feminist practice of providing safe spaces in the classroom but rather hopes to foster women coming to voice in the context of conflict and the need to defend their voices.

23. It is intriguing to me that Morton then goes on to talk about how the process of hearing into speech has brought her to a different understanding of God, and how God's silence has been misperceived. Rather than being indifference and hardness, that silence might be God hearing persons to response (60). So much of Camus's struggle with the absurdity of the universe was with its silence, and the silence of God in the face of injustice and tragedy. How might this interpretation change his sense of meaning? I think we get a glimpse of that in his depictions of encounters with nature, for nature hears Camus into response continually.

Chapter 5   Solidarity

1. For further discussion of this see Caraway; hooks, *Ain't* and *Feminist* 43–65; Davis; Dill; Evans.
2. See Shiva 1989; Mies and Shiva; and Brubaker.
3. The terms "unity" and "totality" can be and often are confused with each other. Given Camus's meanings of these terms, Alarcón's use of the phrase "politics of unity" refers to what Camus meant by "totality," not "unity."
4. See Caraway; hooks, *Feminist* 43–65; Dill; Alarcón; Uttal.
5. Lorde (*Sister* 114–123), hooks (*Feminist* 43–65), Dill, and Uttal all suggest this as a strategy.
6. The term "womanist" was coined by Alice Walker. She defined it as: "1. a black feminist or feminist of color. From the black folk expression of mothers to female children, 'You acting womanish,' i.e., like a woman. Usually referring to outrageous, audacious, courageous or *willful* behavior. . . . 2. *Also*: A woman who loves other women, sexually and/or nonsexually. Appreciates and prefers women's culture, women's emotional flexibility, . . . and women's strength. . . . 3. Loves music. Loves dance. Loves the moon. *Loves the Spirit*. Loves love and food and roundness. Loves struggle. *Loves* the Folk. Loves herself. Regardless. 4. Womanist is to feminist as purple is to lavender" (*In Search of Our Mother's Gardens* xi–xii).
7. For the full discussion of this, please see chapter three in this book.
8. Camus highlighted the endemic nature of "us versus them" solidarity in his short story, "The Guest" (*Exile*). Set in an Arab country during a time of growing French–Arab tensions, the story pits French against Arab, as well as shows the lonely path of one who refused to take sides. By court order, a French gendarme has delivered an Arab prisoner convicted of murder to a schoolteacher, who is then ordered to deliver the prisoner to the French prison some distance away. The solidarity of the French schoolteacher with the French gendarme, as well as the French government is simply assumed, for it is expected that the schoolteacher will comply, siding with the French versus the Arab. However, the schoolteacher defies this expectation, refusing to take sides and refusing to obey the order. The French gendarme takes

this as a personal insult. The schoolteacher also treats the prisoner as a guest in his home, something that seems to confound the prisoner, presumably because he expects to be treated as "the enemy." When the time comes to escort the prisoner, the teacher shows the prisoner the way to the prison, as well as the way to safety, and leaves it to the prisoner to decide. The prisoner, ironically, perhaps as a testimony to the degree of his internalized oppression, chooses to comply with the court order, and turns himself in. But in another twist, when the teacher returns to his home, he finds written on the blackboard, " 'You have handed over our brother. You will pay for this.' " The Arabs as well have taken on "us vs. them" solidarity against the French schoolteacher, who they presume has acted in solidarity with the French. There is no dialogue, only misunderstanding and the continuing cycle of division and revenge. As Camus wrote at the end, the schoolteacher finds himself very much alone.

9. See Young, *Intersecting* 52–53; Lugones; Jaggar, "Toward."

10. One particularly effective exercise I have used is to break the class into dyads specifically on the point of disagreement that has brought the class to a halt. Students must pair up with someone with whom they disagree. Each person in the dyad has the opportunity to explain their point of view to the other without interruption. Afterward, the listener may ask questions of clarification only. The intent is to understand, not to challenge, nor to form a response. The two then switch positions. Each then relays their understanding of the other's position back to the other, and then to the class as a whole.

11. See e.g., Benhabib, "Generalized"; Young, *Intersecting*; and Fraser.

12. Seyla Benhabib, Iris Marion Young, and Jodi Dean all indicate their reliance on Hannah Arendt's concept of "enlarged thought."

13. Benhabib acknowledges that she borrows George Herbert Mead's term "generalized other," though she defines it differently ("Generalized" 37, fn. 8).

14. Arendt criticized Camus's rebellion as being subjective and solitary, arguing that it did not include the perspective of others (*Crises* 58, 98). But this is to take Camus out of context. Camus argued that the impulse to justice begins in our compassion, our community, or association with each other and that the real evil in injustice is that "it perpetuates the silent hostility that separates the oppressor from the oppressed. It kills the small part of existence that can be realized on this earth through . . . mutual understanding . . ." (*Rebel* 283). To destroy community is also to destroy the basis of justice. This is the difference, it seems to me, between totalitarian politics that would establish one voice, theirs, and those civil disobedients who seek to include more voices in the public discussion. Despite Arendt's concerns about Camus, we see that Arendt's position that conscience is something that we discover and discern in community is not far from what Camus argues for.

15. See Caraway, 198; Spelman 178–182; Young, *Intersecting* 41–42. Dean's inclusion of "the third"—the perspectives of the third parties not included in the discussion—is an important aspect of achieving reflective solidarity.

It shows an openness and expansiveness, a desire not to exclude any, not even the oppressor. However, it is not clear how this perspective will be attained, whether through imagination, study, or literal inclusion of all heretofore excluded others. She seems at once to be arguing, like Benhabib, that given the fact that we cannot possibly include everyone affected in the discussion, we must at least arrive at their perspectives imaginatively, and like Spelman and Young, she argues that the images we have of others may be the result of ignorance or bias (171–173).

16. This is the concern raised by Paulo Freire, that others acting in the name of the oppressed without listening to the oppressed themselves, merely continue the oppression.

17. Dean here is adopting George Herbert Mead's concept of the "generalized other," which refers to an organized set of expectations of a social group. Dean says that she seeks to reverse Benhabib's meaning of generalized other (and Benhabib specifically states that her concept is not the same as Mead's).

18. Sharon Welch has similarly argued that we can only see the flaws in the foundations of an ethical system from the perspective of another system, thus pluralism is required for enlarging our moral perspective (126).

19. I wrote this section only a few months after the bombing of the World Trade Center on September 11. It seemed at the time that the most frequent response was simply the longing cry, "Why?" Why?—the search for understanding. Many sought to understand, asked for dialogue and genuine listening—Camusian, feminist, nonviolent solutions. But these appeals were drowned out by those who regarded them as "weak," (i.e., feminine) and the efforts at revenge eroded efforts to understand, piling one misunderstanding on another. I wonder how different our global relations might be if rather than asserting our point of view and seeking solutions in violence we respected the basic human need to understand. Suppose instead of bombs we sent emissaries of understanding—in Fran Peavey's words, "Americans willing to listen." So little has been tried.

20. Dean, Uttal, Young, Jaggar, and Dill all emphasize the importance of the intention of understanding.

21. For some feminists seeking an alternative to sisterhood, building solidarity across differences has necessarily implied coalition politics, in which groups and individuals would engage each other under conditions of equality and mutual respect to pursue a common cause (Bunch, 149–157; Caraway; Young, *Intersecting* 36; Dill). However, some feminists have been skeptical of the possibility of coalitions to build solidarity, arguing that they are temporary, lasting only until the specific goal has been met; arbitrary, in the sense that they include only those women who choose to come together; and consumerist, using others as means to an end rather than as ends in themselves, which is destructive of the solidarity they would hope to achieve (Molina; Young, *Intersecting* 21; Dean 27). Dean's concern here is reflective of Camus's assertion that acts of rebellion are not motivated by any calculus of return or reward, or even success.

22. Rich's concept of honorable relationships is discussed in more detail in chapter six in this book.

23. The importance of this intent of friendship, with which Camus would agree, will be taken up further in chapter six in this book.

24. This is discussed in more detail in the section on Care and Attentive Love in chapter six in this book.

25. Young's adoption of Lugones's view that we need to travel to others' worlds and stand in their place seems a bit at odds with her earlier incorporation of Nancy Love's argument that we cannot stand in another's world (50).

26. In invoking this, it is important to remember the danger of speaking for another, which as Freire has reminded us, can be an action of oppression.

27. To a certain extent, Camus here is working out his problem with the Christian doctrine that only true believers in Christ will be saved from eternal damnation. He brings out example after example of grappling with this doctrine, and rejecting it. He points, e.g., to Ivan Karamazov, who he says, takes up the "essential undertaking of rebellion . . . replacing the reign of grace by the reign of justice" (*Rebel* 55). The reign of grace, of the sacred, requires that we love what we cannot understand, including the injustice, cruelties, sufferings, and oppressions, as being part of God's plan. Faith, in this sense, according to Camus, demands resignation to injustice—to the suffering of children and the death of innocents. Faith, therefore, must be rejected by the rebel.

Camus revisits this problem in *The Plague*, in which the town priest delivers a sermon, which conveys the message that faith requires that we must love what we don't understand. But the doctor responds to the priest that he refuses passively to accept that notion of love and will commit his efforts to working against any scheme in which innocent children suffer and die needlessly (196–197).

He revisits it once again in his play, *The Just Assassins*. The Grand Duchess has come to visit her husband's murderer, Kaliayev, in prison. She comes in a spirit of atonement, hoping to bridge that which separates them in this world with the promise of their meeting in God. Kaliayev responds that he's given up on counting on his agreement with God but that he will keep his agreement with his brothers. She pleads with him that there is no love without the love of God, but he replies that yes, there is. There is love for God's creatures. She responds that God's creatures are abject, either to be forgiven or destroyed, but Kaliayev responds that there is another choice, that being to die with them.

In his "Letters to a German Friend" (*Resistance*), Camus recounted an incident from World War II in which a German priest was faced with the dilemma of whether or not to alert the German soldiers to the fact that a 16-year-old boy awaiting execution with ten other French men, a boy whom he has befriended, has escaped out the side of the truck. The priest ultimately decided to alert the soldiers. Camus argued that in so doing, the priest decided to side with the executioners. He had made his faith serve his country, rather than the humiliated (*Resistance* 15–18).

28. This sense of suffering, ironically, comes up in one of Camus's sources of inspiration, the works of Simone Weil. While her self-sacrificial motives may have inspired Camus, they are not part of the suffering chosen

in rebellion. Weil's self-punishing behaviors are also consistent with the anorexia that plagued her. It is quite common for anorexics to feel a need to sacrifice their bodies in order to prove their worth (Golden).

29. The way Rieux and Rambert have reversed positions on this particular point is reminiscent of Benhabib's notion of reciprocity.

30. See e.g. Brock; Harrison; Heyward; and Welch, 35.

31. Galland; hooks, *Feminist* 26–27; Harrison 217.

32. See e.g. Brock; Heyward; Harrison; Gross, *Buddhism* 182.

33. See chapter three in this book.

34. Elshtain also has remarked how Atkinson's and Brownmiller's visions of feminist futures would oppress men in kind, and thus fall prey to the politics of *ressentiment*—i.e., Camus's notion of resentment (*Public Man* 244–245). These would thus be utterly at odds with Camus's notion of rebellious solidarity.

   This attitude of resentment was more common among feminists moving from a situation of powerlessness to one of empowerment. De Beauvoir wrote in *The Second Sex* about how woman is condemned to passive existence and haunted by the "specter of her own powerlessness" (605). Unable to claim agency for her own life, she lives in a state of "impotent rage," blaming others for everything that happens to her. "She feels she has been swindled. She puts the whole masculine universe under indictment. Resentment is the reverse side of dependence . . ." (605). In this state of resentment, she wishes to have the same transcendence men have, but also, because resentment leads one to find pleasure in the degradation of those envied, wants to confine men in the same way she has been confined. "She can do away with this inferiority only by destroying the male's superiority. She sets about mutilating, dominating man, she contradicts, him, she denies his truth and his values" (717). But, she went on to say that she was beginning to see changes in the uprising of women, that they no longer sought to drag men down, but rather were focusing on their own emergence (717). In this we begin to see a move from resentment to rebellion.

35. See e.g. Kittay; hooks, *Talking* and *All*.

36. Carol Adams has particularly advocated solidarity with animals, arguing that trafficking in animals (eating them, wearing their fur) ontologizes animals as "being for others," specifically going against Freire's definition of solidarity as transforming the objective reality that makes the oppressed "beings for others" ("The Feminist Traffic" 213).

37. That we are all flawed and capable of error was the basis of Camus's rejection of the death penalty. In condemning someone to such an ultimate punishment, we might be wrong. "There is a solidarity of all men in error and aberration. Must that solidarity operate for the tribunal and be denied the accused?" (*Resistance* 217). Camus also rejected the death penalty on the grounds that it violated "the only indisputable human solidarity—our solidarity against death" (*Resistance* 222).

38. See hooks, *Talking* 20; Molina 330; Heyward 206–297; Brubaker; Welch, 139–140.

Chapter 6   Friendship

1. Camus wrote this in response to the significant controversy stirred by a remark he made after receiving the Nobel prize. During a question period following the awarding of the prize, Camus was questioned by a member of the FLN (Algerian independence movement) about his stance on terrorism. For him this was no abstract question, but one that had concrete implications for the people he loved living in Algeria. . . . " 'I believe in justice, but will defend my mother before justice' " (Todd 378). This remark caused a furor in France and around the world. In this subsequent essay, he explained that when one's own family is in danger, one still feels a natural solidarity with them (*Resistance* 113).

2. Gilligan's study of female moral development, published in her *In a Different Voice*, challenged the conclusions of her mentor, Lawrence Kohlberg, who had argued that on the whole, women were less morally developed than men. Kohlberg's and Gilligan's studies were based in part on presenting subjects with a hypothetical moral dilemma that has come to be known as "the Heinz dilemma." The dilemma is that of a man, Heinz, whose wife is dying but cannot afford the overpriced drug that would cure her. The question posed of the subjects then is, should Heinz steal the drug. Based on the very different responses of male and female subjects, Kohlberg had developed a 6-stage theory of moral development, and his studies revealed that most women did not develop morally beyond the Stage Four "law and order orientation," whereas most men achieved the highest level of moral development, Stage Six, the "universal ethical principle orientation." Gilligan, however, concluded from her study that women are not more or less morally developed than men, but rather that their process of moral development and their resulting ethical systems were different from those of men.

3. This argument has been made by many, foremost among them being Sara Ruddick in her arguments regarding "maternal thinking."

4. While I am emphasizing here the role of care of dependents, Ann Ferguson, in her discussion of "sex-affective production," also notes that women take on the role of caregiving in many other capacities as well.

5. See e.g. Held; Friedman, "Beyond Caring;" Ruddick, *Maternal*; Baier.

6. Rosemarie Tong, borrowing from philosopher Barbara Sichel, distinguishes "feminine" approaches to ethics from "feminist" approaches (4–11). By "feminine" approaches she means those that regard traditionally female gender traits of care, compassion, nurturance, relationship, and so on as positive goods. "Feminist" approaches, on the other hand, though they may value such traits as care and compassion, are political in that they regard women as oppressed and seek to eliminate their subordination and oppression. Though she does admit that Gilligan's and Nodding's ethics have certain feminist "twists" (158), she generally places them in the "feminine" category. She categorizes as "feminist" such theorists as Ruddick, Jaggar, Held, and Baier.

7. See e.g. Broughton; Dietz; Card, "Caring and Evil;" Hoagland. There have been numerous criticisms of the ethic of care, many of them specifically

addressing the work of Gilligan and Noddings. Rosemarie Tong provides an excellent summary account of these in her *Feminine and Feminist Ethics*. Stated briefly, criticisms of Gilligan's work are primarily these: (1) Gilligan misunderstands Kohlberg's work; (2) the distinction between justice and care is an old one—she is presenting nothing new here philosophically; (3) justice and care are not different but rather complementary approaches to morality; (4) care is not as good a moral basis as justice; (5) care is not gender correlated; (6) the cultural identification of women with care has negative consequences for women; (7) if justice and care are nothing more than the perspectives of oppressor and oppressed, then valorizing care may worsen the position of the oppressed; and (8) presenting care as "woman's voice" makes care exclusive. Noddings's work has been criticized on similar grounds, as well as on others more specific to her argument. These criticisms include: (1) the nearly exclusive focus on unequal relations; (2) the slighting of our duties to strangers; (3) the confusion of reciprocity with receptivity; and (4) its contribution to women's oppression by valorizing exploitative work.

8. Dora goes on in a very revealing passage to say "Summer, Yanek, can you remember what that's like, a real summer's day? But—no, it's never-ending winter here" (271–272). Camus often used the metaphors of summer and winter to represent the warmth of love, friendship, and joy and the coldness of the unending demand for justice and duty, respectively. But though winter makes its demands, it is summer that sustains us. As he wrote: "In the depths of winter, I finally learned that within me lay an invincible summer" (*Lyrical* 169).

9. For example, Sharon Welch argues that the feminist ethic of risk emphasizes neither rights nor care, but rather responsible accountability to others and openness to critique, in other words, solidarity. Solidarity thus acts as a "check" to the tendency of care to become manipulative and controlling and the tendency of justice to circumscribe one's actions (18). This fits well with the insistence in Camusian rebellion of the simultaneous assertion of all elements of rebellion, which would include justice, care, and solidarity. Thus just as care grounds solidarity in real relationship, so does solidarity extend that care to others.

10. For a more thorough discussion, see my "Beyond Either/Or: Justice and Care in the Ethics of Albert Camus."

11. As is true of most of us, Camus did not necessarily practice what he preached. It is reported that upon showing his wife parts of *The Fall* she said, " 'You're always pleading the causes of all sorts of people, but do you ever hear the screams of people who are trying to reach you?' " (Todd 342).

12. See e.g., Claudia Card who argues that until we have a just society in which all persons are equally well treated, we cannot have a caring society ("Caring and Evil"; Tong 126).

13. The Mothers of the Disappeared is a women's movement of resistance to Argentinean and Chilean dictatorship and their policies of kidnapping, imprisoning, torturing, and murdering citizens who simply disappear. The Mothers have gathered every Thursday at La Plaza de Mayo in the capital

city of Buenos Aires, silently marching, carrying photographs of their children and other loved ones who have "disappeared."

14. For more discussion of this, see e.g. hooks, *Yearning*; Welch 165.

15. Welch makes a similar argument, 165.

16. See e.g. Ruddick, "Remarks"; Elshtain, "Reflections"; Held, "Non-contractual"; Gross, *Buddhism* 182.

17. See e.g., Friedman, "Feminism" 93, *What* 207; Code 370; hooks, *All About Love*; Daly, *Gyn/ecology*; Raymond; Warren.

18. Hazel Barnes has argued that Camus only addressed the issue of "good faith"—that is, honesty and authenticity, in terms of male friendship, not in relationships between men and women, which she says he presents as only sexual (40, 230). However, we know from de Beauvoir that for a time, he had a close, authentic, nonsexual relationship with her.

19. Hoagland continues that she is also not convinced that one who only receives care as the "cared-for" will grow up to be "one-caring." She is particularly skeptical of the ability of a male child to do so (110).

20. Iris Marion Young notes gift-giving as an example of the "assymetrical reci-procity" in relationships. Gifts are inherently not equivalent, and the giving of them is separated by intervals of time, and yet there is a mutuality and reciprocity in gift-giving (*Intersecting Voices* 54).

21. An extended version of this notion of reciprocity is of a larger circle of reci-procal caring. I pass on the gifts I receive to others in my circle of care who are in need of them, who then pass them on to others. Eventually, all comes full circle.

22. This term, "I-Thou," was originally coined by Martin Buber in his famous *I and Thou*. The term is used by many feminists writing about the ethic of care.

23. See chapter five in this book as well.

24. See the earlier discussion of "honorable relationships" in chapter five in this book.

25. Andy Smith has raised the important point that white "New Age" feminists, in their "discovery" and "practice" of Native American spiritualities, have not acted in a way that is supportive of feminist friendship, in large part because they have not had a stake in the Native world.

26. Rich actually borrowed this term from Lillian Smith, "Autobiography as a Dialogue between King and Corpse," *The Winner Names the Age,* Michelle Cliff, ed. (New York: Norton, 1978: 191).

27. De Beauvoir recounts that Camus made this remark to her after an incident in which their mutual friend, Arthur Koestler, got into a literal fist fight with Camus, raving about how it's impossible to be friends if you disagree about politics. Camus at that time disagreed, and undoubtedly wanted it to be so, but a few years later, his own friendship with de Beauvoir and Sartre would end, in part, over political disagreements. But it also ended because of Camus's felt sense of betrayal of their friendship over the scathing review of *The Rebel in* Sartre's *Les Temps Moderne,* a very public breech of loyalty.

28. As a note of interest, Vera Brittain chose the title *The Rebel Passion* for her history of the Fellowship of Reconciliation, an organization formed by a

British Quaker and a German chaplain toward the end of World War I, who vowed that they would refuse to sanction war and would sow seeds of love and peace in the world (Deats, "The Rebel Passion," xv).

29. McFall points, e.g., to the case of the battered wife, for whom forgiveness may be inappropriate and destructive. McFall does believe, however, that it is important that she free herself from vengeful rage and all-consuming bitterness. But if the batterer never owns responsibility for his actions, he may have abandoned his claim for compassion (152). She also references Susan Jacoby, *Wild Justice: The Evolution of Revenge* (New York: Harper and Row, 1983: 351–352).

Chapter 7   Immanence

1. In *The Plague*, the plague-ridden town of Oran has similarly "turned its back on the sea," and Rieux's and Tarrou's swim is renewing of more than their friendship. In an essay about the actual town of Oran, Camus described it as "a city with its back to the sea, built turning in upon itself, like a snail. . . . The people of Oran, it would seem are like that friend of Flaubert's who, from his deathbed, cast a last look on this irreplaceable earth and cried out: 'Close the window, it's too beautiful.' They have closed the window, they have walled themselves in, they have exorcised the landscape" (*Lyrical* 116, 128).

2. To be sure, swimming was filled with meaning for Camus—the scene of some of his favorite moments of life—swimming with friends, swimming with his uncle, or just being alone in the water for hours. He referred to it often in his works of fiction and nonfiction. See, e.g., *The First Man*, 49, 100; "Summer in Algiers," (*Lyrical* 82–83); and the Preface to *Lyrical and Critical Essays* 8.

3. For an in-depth examination of Camus's grappling with issues of Christian belief, see Richard H. Akeroyd's *The Spiritual Quest of Albert Camus*.

4. Twenty years later Camus would reiterate this phrase to explain the totalitarian destruction that had swept across Europe in the intervening years. Writing of the "men of Europe" who "writhe in mortal combat," he says, "Denying the real grandeur of life, they have had to stake all on their own excesses" (305).

5. Eric Bronner has also noted that the message of "The Growing Stone" is one of spiritual solidarity and a hope for the re-enchantment of the world (134).

6. Peyre, Barnes, Sprintzen all called Camus a pagan (28; 187; 6, 18). Hazel Barnes called Camus a pagan but denied that he was pantheistic, saying that he did not deify nor personalize nature (190). Though some of his earlier writings would belie this, his later writings would support her (*Lyrical* 328). Cruickshank labeled his spirituality "pantheistic" (33); Tisson-Braun, "panentheistic" (43); Doubrovsky, an "ethic of being" (56); and Braun, an "ethic of joy" (206).

7. This should not be confused with the existentialist use of the term "immanence." Existentialism uses the term "immanence" to denote flesh and

earthly existence, but not one that is inspirited. A fuller discussion of the existentialist meaning of the term is upcoming in the next section.

8. *Nuptials* is now included in *Lyrical and Critical Essays*. There has been some disagreement as to the relationship of the ideas expressed in *Nuptials* and Camus's philosophy of rebellion. Thomas Hanna has argued that Camus's logic of the absurd is an aberration in an otherwise consistent flow of thought from an early love of nature to a philosophy of revolt. He writes: " ' . . . this tenderness toward the world is extended to a concern for human justice and solidarity' " (quoted in Barnes, 393, fn. 4). While Barnes does not agree with Hanna, it is not clear whether her disagreement is with the connection of Camus's love of nature to his philosophy of revolt, or to his philosophy of the absurd being an aberration. David Sprintzen has also argued that *Nuptials*, though often overlooked, is crucial to an understanding of Camus's thought (xvii).

9. The Chenoua is a mountain range near the Mediterranean village of Tipasa.

10. Tipasa is a village on the Mediterranean coast. Camus went there often in 1936 and 1937. It is the source of inspiration for "Nuptials at Tipasa" and "Return to Tipasa" and is symbolic of his immersion in love and life and the earth.

11. Carolyn Merchant has argued that problems of the destruction of nature and the domination of all those associated with nature became exacerbated when science declared nature to be dead, and humans no longer experienced nature as alive and capable of interrelationship. To argue that Camus's attitude toward the earth is essentialist presumes that he could not experience an exchange of energy or be in relationship with the earth, because it is not alive.

12. I am struck here with the similarity to the Buddhist concept of "nonattachment." Also, it will be recalled that Camus had earlier credited the sun and sea with saving him from resentment. As discussed in chapter 3 in this book, Camus distinguished resentment from rebellion, noting that rebellion runs the risk of falling into resentment. Thus it was both his bodily love of the earth and his bodily limitations that sustained his rebellious attitude.

13. He contrasted this genuine love of life with those who "affect a love of life in order to avoid love itself" (*Lyrical* 91). Genuine love of life is that of the sensualist, who lives out life without intellectualizing about it.

14. Many have credited de Beauvoir's *The Second Sex* as being the foundation for much of contemporary feminist thought. See e.g. Levy 16; Henderson 116; Whitlock 128; and Berry 168. Virginia Berry writes: "Beauvoir's *oeuvre* has provided late twentieth century Western feminism with some of its most fundamental assumptions" (168).

15. Many feminists now question the rigidity of this divide in de Beauvoir's thought, finding it to be ambiguous (Secomb, Heinämaa, Fulbrook, Holwerk, Vintges). Some find in her thought suggestions of immanence leading to transcendence. Secomb regards the plane of immanence to be the background and context out of which de Beauvoir wrote, and argues that de Beauvoir's work is very grounded in Merleau-Ponty's flesh and Husserl's embodied perceptual experience (101). Holwerk finds in de Beauvoir's

The Ethic of Ambiguity, an ethic of action ground in lived concrete experience and the joy of existence, and in *The Blood of Others*, an ethic of care and connection. (It is interesting to note that de Beauvoir wrote *The Ethic of Ambiguity* at Camus's suggestion that she work out an ethic of action. I see strong similarities between de Beauvoir's *Ethic* and Camus's *Rebel*, but also significant differences, the accounting of which goes beyond the scope of this book.) For example, de Beauvoir does suggest the possibility of entering transcendent, pour-soi existence in the immanent condition of pregnancy (Mortimer 191). De Beauvoir claims that: "the pregnant woman feels the immanence of her body at just the time when it is in transcendence," arguing that when the reproductive process begins "it assumes transcendence," but then goes on to say it is an illusion because the woman does not really make the baby, it makes itself within her, and it will have to establish its existence itself (495–496).

One can also find a sensual appreciation of nature and the possibility of transcendence through nature in *The Second Sex*. It is, in part, in this sensuous appreciation of nature that de Beauvoir's conception of immanence becomes ambiguous. Perhaps she does not hold so tightly the sharp line between immanence and transcendence. Perhaps one can find transcendence, the life of the *pour-soi*, in the realm of the flesh and of the earth. De Beauvoir herself suggests this in her earlier writings: "I should like to be the landscape which I am contemplating, I should like this sky, this quiet water to think themselves within me, that it might be I whom they express in flesh and bone, and I remain at a distance. . . . my contemplation is an excruciation only because it is also a joy. I can not appropriate the snow field where I slide. It remains foreign, forbidden, but I take delight in this very effort toward an impossible possession" (*Ethics* 12). But she does, as she says, remain at a distance. And as much as she expresses a *joie d'éxistence*, it is not the same as *joie de vivre*. Existence is somewhat at a remove from life. (Hazel Barnes notes the difference between Camus's attitude toward nature and Sartre's and de Beauvoir's, noting that unlike Sartre and de Beauvoir, Camus made no metaphysical distinction between organic and nonorganic existence, and merged with nature with a great joy of life (370).)

I see elements of these aspects of care and connection and joy in *The Second Sex*, but it seems de Beauvoir ultimately decides that: "the man's [situation], [that is, transcendence] is far preferable; that is to say, he has many more opportunities to exercise his freedom in the world. The inevitable result is that masculine accomplishment is far superior to that of women, who are practically forbidden to *do* anything" (627).

16. For Sartre, immanence is reflected in the life of *en-soi* and transcendence in the life of *pour-soi*. De Beauvoir carries a similar equivalence. I do not know that they use the terms interchangeably so much as to assume that within the confines of immanence, no *pour-soi* existence (freedom, creativity, life for the being in itself) is possible.

Hannah Arendt makes similar distinctions, between labor that is confined to the tasks of "necessity"—the sustenance and maintenance of bodily needs, and "action"—that she associates with freedom and power (*Human Condition*).

17. As many feminists have come to appreciate, de Beauvoir took a disembodied philosophy of existentialism and worked it through women's bodies (Fulbrook, Gothlin, Secomb, Heinämaa, Linsenbard).

18. This is addressed in more detail in the next section.

19. I found myself wondering about Camus's thoughts on maternity, childrearing, and domesticity. He was, in most of his work, silent on this, as is often typical of even the most progressive men. However, his later works show quite an awareness and appreciation of women's domestic labors, as well as men's typical expectation of being served. In his short story, "The Artist and His Time" (*Exile*), a story that is presumably autobiographical, he tells of Louise, the artist's wife, who gave up her own pursuit of literature to further his career, and whose unceasing and unresentful toil showered him with "treasures of self-sacrifice . . . ." In addition to taking care of the house and the children, bringing him meals and doing his laundry, "that angel spared him the purchases of shoes, suits, and shirts. . . . She resolutely took upon herself the thousand inventions of the machine for killing time, from the hermetic brochures of social security to the constantly changing moods of the internal-revenue office. . . . she telephoned and made the appointments, . . . took care of changing the oil in the tiny car, of booking rooms in vacation hotels, of the coal for his stove; she herself bought the gifts Jonas wanted to give (to her)" (*Exile* 116–117). Louise's efforts only increase as she has more children and Jonas, the artist, becomes more involved and successful in his work. Jonas suffered somewhat over Louise's toil and fatigue, but it is not until many years have passed that "it occurred to him that he had never really helped her" (154).

Camus also showed quite an awareness of the domestic tasks of his mother's life, especially in his posthumously published autobiographical novel, *The First Man*. However, he, like de Beauvoir, tends to represent domestic tasks more as toil than a possibility for immanent meaning. He described his own experiences of manual labor as "work so stupid you could weep and so interminably monotonous that it made the days too long and, at the same time, life too short" (*First Man* 270). He was deeply concerned about how most factory workers are deprived of their dignity by such monotonous, repetitive work (and cites Simone Weil in this), and believed that work that is interesting and creative is a fundamental need.

Yet when I read de Beauvoir describing housework as "like the torture of Sisyphus," I also think of Camus's statement that, "One must imagine Sisyphus happy" (*Myth* 91). Sisyphus's happiness lies in the way he responds to the tediousness, the repetitiveness, of his task. The rock does not crush him. He turns, and goes back down the mountain, ready to begin again.

I think it is also significant that in his novel, *The Plague*, Camus chose the immanental task of caring for the sick to symbolize the task of rebellion. It is the day-to-day work of doing what needs to be done, not the work of heroics, that is rebellion. De Beauvoir criticized Camus for writing an ahistorical novel about the plague of totalitarianism in Europe, but it is quite fitting with rebellion that he should choose immanence over history as the background for a novel about rebellion.

20. See e.g. Christ.

21. See also Ruether, "Toward"; McFague; Morton, "The Goddess as Metaphoric Image"; Christ; Gross, *Buddhism*; Welch; and Starhawk, "Feminist," "Toward," and *Spiral Dance*.

22. I can only give a representation of all that has been written about embodied spirituality in feminist literature. Nearly every feminist writing about spirituality conceives it as embodied. I have chosen to focus on issues of domesticity, maternity, and sexuality, since these have been so central in traditional religious and culture definitions of women's lives, but an embodied spirituality touches on so many issues—appearance and body image, physical activity, rape and violence, disability, death, poverty, race, the arts, physical practices such as yoga and body prayer, addiction, and illness. Gerda Lerner has noted that it was often the spiritual power women attained through illness that gave them the self-authority to speak out. Many feminists have written about the impact of illness on their spiritual lives (e.g., Griffin, *Body*; Cohen; Gates; and Bartlett, *Journey*.)

23. See Plaskow and Christ; Anderson and Hopkins; Friedman and Moon; Gross, *Buddhism* 274–278; Harris, *Dance*.

24. De Beauvoir would probably respond that "she values these triumphs of immanence only because immanence is her lot. . . . She wallows in immanence, but she has first been shut up in it" (*Second Sex* 603).

25. For a fuller discussion see the chapter on "Mindfulness" in my *Journey of the Heart*.

26. And she notes that this is one of only two physical activities (the other being sexuality) that has not been revalorized by Buddhist traditions, and that it is only those experiences traditionally central to women's lives that have been left out (277).

27. See e.g., Trebilcot; Rich *Of Woman*; and Ruddick *Maternal*. Eighteenth- and nineteenth-century feminists often pointed to mothers' roles in educating their children, particularly their sons, as a justification for women's education, but I am specifically interested in the contemporary debate regarding the institution and practice of motherhood itself.

28. See e.g. Ruddick, *Maternal*; Kittay; Held, *Feminist Morality*; and Rich, *Of Woman*.

29. My thanks to Dr. Kelly Jewett for this wonderful insight.

30. See e.g. Paula Gunn Allen; Anzaldúa, "Entering"; and Starhawk, *Spiral Dance*.

31. See e.g. Sjöö and Mor; Anzaldúa, "Entering"; and Starhawk, *Spiral Dance*.

32. It should be noted that one can also find a sensual appreciation of nature in *The Second Sex* in her description of the adolescent girl. De Beauvoir describes nature as a refuge from the strictures of home, law, and custom. She describes the adolescent girl's encounter with nature as: "a tangible image of her transcendence . . . among plants and animals she is a human being; she is freed at once from her family and from the males—a subject, a free being . . . . In the rush of water, the shimmer of light, she feels a

presentiment of the joys, the tears, the ecstasies she has not yet known . . . The flesh is no longer a defilement: it means joy and beauty. At one with earth and sky, the young girl is that vague breath which animates and kindles the universe, and she is each sprig of heather. . . . she is at once spirit and life; her being is imperious and triumphant like that of earth itself"(363–364). Her words are reminiscent of Camus's and suggestive of contemporary ecofeminist writing, such as this of Susan Griffin's: "*We remembered*. And the one I found in my memory was a girl. A girl who loved to be alone in the woods, never worried about grass stains, or wet earth, whose spirit was over there to see beyond the phenomenal because, she was along, she *withdrew to the center of herself*" (*Rape* 49).

33. This theme is reiterated often. See e.g. Christ; Ruether *Gaia*; Welch; Griffin, *Eros*.

34. I am reminded by this of Alice Walker's warning, writing about the nuclear threat and its link to the white man's crimes against humanity that "only justice can stop a curse" (*In Search* 338–342).

35. He also contrasted the Christianity of the Roman Church, which he characterized as an inward-looking, tormented religion, with that of Francis of Assisi, a Mediterranean, who "transformed Christianity into a hymn to nature and simple joy" (*Lyrical* 192).

36. And like Camus, she argues that this European culture is more specifically the culture of the Roman Empire. She notes its links to our language of religion and learning, to our nomenclature of law, science, and medicine, of the Roman symbols of military might and of the *E Pluribus Unum* under which we in the United States stand united, and how we associate excellence and superiority with the Roman and inferiority with the non-Roman (*Eros* 109). She notes that it was in being Romanized that Europeans lost a sense of sacredness in their land base as well (*Eros* 110).

37. All of the following argument from Mies is taken from ch. 10, "White Man's Dilemma: His Search for What He Has Destroyed," in Mies and Shiva.

It should also be pointed out that Karen Baker-Fletcher and bell hooks have argued that this spiritual dispossession is not limited to white men, but also particularly afflicts African Americans who have left rural areas in large numbers and live in highly urban, industrialized areas (Baker-Fletcher 55; hooks, *Sisters* 180–182).

38. Camus could not live with this illusion, because of the presence of illness and the limits imposed by the body, nor did he want to. He delighted in the body. In his youth, Camus was poor, not a man of privilege. He and his family survived by bodily labor.

39. See e.g. de Beauvoir, *Second Sex*; Ortner; Griffin, *Made*; Ruether, *Gaia and God*; King, "The Ecology of Feminism"; and Warren.

40. De Beauvoir's concept of alterity is similar to Hannah Arendt's concept of plurality. Arendt argues that true plurality requires that individuals be similar enough to understand each other, and different enough to need to be understood (*Human Condition*).

41. Here again, de Beauvoir follows Hegel. It is this agonistic conception of the self with which many feminists have trouble. Camus would as well.

42. Coming from a slightly different perspective, Griffin writes, in an argument that would apply to all, that the European wants to believe "that the peoples newly encountered are less than human, more like children, uncivilized. A desire, perhaps, to regain a half-remembered state of mind, a past existence not so separated from the earth" (*Eros* 103).

43. Mies's argument is so reminiscent to me of Camus's regarding the curse on men who forsake love and the body in *State of Siege*, quoted earlier. Reading this passage as symbolic of the human psyche, we read that those who alienate themselves from their bodies, from the maternal body, from the earth, living in a world of ideas detached from nature, continually seek reunion with these in the wrong places and wrong ways, resulting in solitary deaths.

44. Living in a tourist town, I see this evidenced on a daily basis, from the steady weekend flow of traffic from the city to the woods, to the ways in which development for the tourists has destroyed the wilderness they seek and we loved. Hotels block the view of the lake, traffic makes access to the beach difficult, and the beach, once a pristine and safe place for women, is now littered and a "hunting ground."

45. Audre Lorde has also written of how the pornographic is "sensation without feeling" (54).

46. However, Bronner argues that this liberation, if there is one, is temporary.

47. For a beautiful account of this from a physicist's point of view, see Brian Swimme's *The Universe Is a Green Dragon*.

48. Michael Lerner has made a similar argument in his *The Politics of Meaning*.

49. As an intriguing aside, Anne Rush has noted the phrase in Samuel I 15:23, "Rebellion is as the sin of witchcraft" (383). Indeed there are significant links between rebellion and witchcraft, as is evident here, but perhaps not the ones Samuel meant.

50. For a fuller discussion of this, see the chapter "Born Again" in my *Journey of the Heart*.

Chapter 8   A Politics of Limits and Healing

1. According to legends, Nemesis, known as the goddess of "due enactment," was the original Nymph-goddess of Death-in-Life and the moral control on Tyche, daughter of Zeus. Zeus gave Tyche the power to decide the fortunes of mortals, and she arbitrarily heaps fortunes on some and deprives others of all their worldly goods. If she would happen to heap fortunes on someone who is already rich, and if he were to boast of this and neither sacrifice part to the gods nor do anything to alleviate the suffering of those living in poverty, then Nemesis would step in to humiliate him. She carries an apple bough and a wheel, usually seen as the wheel of the solar year (Graves 125–126).

2. Camus's views on liberalism and communism are very similar to ones developed later by Peter Berger in his *Pyramids of Sacrifice*. His ethic of "the calculus of meaning" and "the calculus of pain" gives a specific application to Camus's ethic of rebellion.

3. The terms "radical cultural" and "radical libertarian" are Rosemarie Tong's. I am indebted to Tong's excellent synopsis of the sexuality debate between radical cultural feminists and radical libertarian feminists in her *Feminist Thought*, ch. 2.

4. See e.g. Caraway and Gaard *Ecological* 248, 250–252.

5. For an excellent account of the interconnections between the ecofeminist and the Green movements, see Greta Gaard's *Ecological Politics: Ecofeminists and the Greens*.

6. In brief, the original Ten Key Values of the U.S. Greens were: (1) ecological wisdom; (2) grassroots democracy; (3) personal and social accountability; (4) nonviolence; (5) decentralization; (6) community-based economics; (7) postpatriarchal values; (8) respect for diversity; (9) global responsibility; (10) future focus.

7. See chapter five in this book.

8. I have found myself wondering in these times, whether such an argument provides both a justification and a motivation for suicide bombers, for it almost seems to. However, I find a significant difference in the killing being regarded as an act of glory as opposed to one that is inexcusable; and in the sacrifice of one's life as a path to eternal life, rather than as a sacrifice of a life regarded as a gift. The difference in attitude is significant to the ethic and the scope, though for the one killed and their loved ones, it is of little consequence.

9. *Neither Victims nor Executioners* has become a classic of nonviolent theory.

10. See e.g. Heyward and Harrison.

11. See e.g. McAllister, *Reweaving*; Ruddick, *Maternal*; Reardon, *Sexism and the War System* and *Women and Peace*; and Harris and King.

12. This argument was first made by Audre Lorde (118).

13. See e.g. Elshtain, *Public Man* and Pateman.

14. Young's later works reflect Mouffe's concerns, and she too speaks in terms of multiple subjectivities.

15. For several examples of these see Plant and Harris and King.

16. This term was first coined by Jo Freeman.

17. See e.g. Dean; Young, *Intersecting Voices* 38–59; bell hooks, *Talking* 27; and Maria Lugones, "Playfulness."

18. Among these are Jean Bethke Elshtain, Jodi Dean, Iris Marion Young, and Seyla Benhabib.

19. Refer to chapter five in this book.

20. For another account of the Seneca Women's Peace Encampment as an example of feminist and practical discourse, see Simone Chambers, "Feminist Discourse/Practical Discourse."

21. Since feminist teachers began practicing feminist pedagogical techniques, institutions of higher learning have adopted them in strategies called "participative learning."

22. These are some of the guidelines from the C-R handbook used by the National Organization for Women (Harriet Perl and Gay Abarbanell, *Guidelines to Feminist Consciousness Raising*): "(1) Feminist CR is unisex: women's CR and Men's CR, but not mixed CR. (2) A CR series should

meet weekly for ten weeks. (3) The CR group should have a definite membership. (4) Steady attendance is required. (5) The size of a CR group should be limited. (6) CR should begin and end promptly at an agreed-upon hour. (Late starts not only waste time but are an insult to the women who take the trouble to arrive promptly . . . . A vague ending time works real hardships on the woman who is paying a babysitter or who has to get up early. . . .) (7) CR requires absolute confidentiality. (8) Close friends, relatives or attachés should not be in CR together. (9) CR does not allow confrontation. (Women are up against the wall everywhere in their daily lives; CR should be one place where they can be absolutely secure, knowing that here they will not be challenged, argued with, made to explain and justify themselves. What a woman says is her truth, and the women in the group accept her position without argument. There must be no questions designed to put her on the defensive, no psychological probing, no leading and put-down questions. . . . Moreover, there should be no antagonistic body language either; raised eyebrows, a tossed head, turned body, significant glance at someone else—all have the same effect as hostile words. . . . The value of this rule cannot be overestimated . . . .) (10) Every woman owes every other woman her undivided attention. (One person speaks at a time, and everyone listens to her. Knitting, sewing, doodling, and so on are ways of not listening, quite as much as side conversations are . . . .) (11) All women are expected to participate in the CR. (However, no woman should ever be required to speak or be "called on" as in a classroom. A woman may "pass" when her turn comes in a discussion going around the circle, and she is entitled to another chance when the circuit has been made. On the other hand, no woman has the option of being simply a spectator . . . .) (12) CR should meet in a secure, private place. (13) No one should be assumed to be hostess . . . . (14) CR meetings should not provide refreshments. (. . . Women are so conditioned to offering food in their homes that it is almost automatic to expect such service from them, and CR must be able to break away from this form of forced role-playing . . . .) (15) No charge may be made for CR. (16) As much as possible, CR groups should be heterogeneous, composed of a variety of ages, life styles, backgrounds, etc. (17) Each CR session should end with an action period" (12–17). Topics for discussion included: "Masculine/Feminine/Roles/Anger," "Do Women Like Women?"; "Lesbianism and Feminism"; "Sexual Oppression"; "Rape and Violence"; and "Stirrup Table Blues." Questions were also included, such as these for the topic of "Rape and Violence": (1) What kind of experience have you had with rape? Has anyone in this room experienced rape or attempted rape, or does anyone know someone who has? (2) What has been your experience with battering or threats of violence? Were you able to protect yourself then or from recurrence? (3) To whom did you talk about your experience with batter/rape? How did you feel about telling someone else? etc. Obviously, the sessions were often very intense, difficult, and healing.

23. For more information, see "Joint Plea," *Ms.*, Vol: XII (3) (Summer 2002): 17.
24. See e.g., Atkinson and Solanis.

25. For an excellent discussion of feminist politics of resistance see Charlene Hinckley's "Ecofeminism as a Politics of Resistance: Practice in Search of Theory."

26. Though of course it needs to be recognized that there are still cultures in which a woman may even be condemned to death for being raped.

27. For examples of such feminist actions, see e.g. Galland; McAllister, *This River of Courage and You Can't Kill the Spirit*; and Caldecott and Leland.

28. This is a very significant statement. The mythic icon of the Homeric warrior hero acts at a remove from everyday life, and in defiance of the limits of human power seeks to gain public esteem, honor, and immortality through the doing of great deeds and the facing of death. The need for heroism underlies a politic that pursues glory and honor above the real needs and the good of the community, thereby putting all life at risk. It is a politic underlying most of the destructive acts of terrorism, militarism, and war at work in the world today. (Nancy Hartsock was among the first to bring a feminist critique to the Homeric warrior hero myth. For a fuller discussion, see her *Money, Sex, and Power*, esp. 141–145.)

29. The words Camus used to describe rebellion, which "unhesitatingly gives the strength of its love and without a moment's delay refuses injustice" (*Rebel* 304) are almost identical to those he had used earlier to describe Grand.

30. This literature is vast. Some representative examples include: Bernie S. Siegel, *Peace, Love and Healing: Bodymind Communication & the Path to Self-Healing: An Exploration* (New York: Harper & Row, 1989; Deepak Chopra, *Quantum Healing: Exploring the Frontiers of Mind/Body Medicine* (New York: Bantam, 1989); Joan Borysenko, *Minding the Body, Mending the Mind* (New York: Bantam, 1988); Joan Borysenko, *Guilt Is the Teacher, Love Is Lesson: A Book to Heal You, Heart and Soul* (New York: Warner, 1990); Louise L. Hay, *You Can Heal Your Life* (Santa Monica: Hay House, 1984); Caroline Myss, *Anatomy of the Spirit: The Seven Stages of Power and Healing* (New York: Three Rivers Press, 1996); and Jean Shinoda Bolen, *Close to the Bone: Life-Threatening Illness and the Search for Meaning* (New York: Scribner, 1996). I have chosen to use Stephen Levine's *Healing into Life and Death* as exemplary, because it brings together much of the wisdom found in the others, and of all of them, I have found this work to be the most helpful in my own process of healing from life-threatening illness.

31. I have not cited each particular reference. Generally, these thoughts on healing in feminism are drawn primarily from Audre Lorde's *Sister Outsider*, Adrienne Rich's essay "On Women and Honor" in *On Lies, Secrets, and Silence*; bell hooks' *Talking Back, Sisters of the Yam* and *All About Love*; and Susan Griffin's *Made from this Earth, Rape: The Power of Consciousness, The Eros of Everyday Life*, and *A Chorus of Stones: The Private Life of War*.

32. Susan J. Brison has also written of the need of trauma survivors not only to tell their stories, but to be heard and understood. By telling their stories and being understood, they can begin to make sense of the trauma in their lives. The "empathic other" is essential in this process. To have one's story denied or shamed is to deliver another blow. To be listened to begins the process of recovery.

Works Cited

Ackelsberg, Martha A. and Mary Lyndon Shanley. "Privacy, Publicity, and Power: A Feminist Rethinking of the Public-Private Distinction." Hirschmann and DeStefano 213–233.

Adam, Margie. "Sweet Friend of Mine." *Margie Adam Songwriter*. Pleiades, 1976.

Adams, Carol J. "Ecofeminism and the Eating of Animals." *Hypatia* 6.1. (Spring 1991): 125–145.

Adams, Carol J. *Ecofeminism and the Sacred*. New York: Continuum, 1993.

Adams, Carol J. "The Feminist Traffic in Animals." Gaard, *Ecofeminism* 195–218.

Akeroyd, Richard H. *The Spiritual Quest of Albert Camus*. Tuscaloosa, AL: Portals Press, 1976.

Alarcón, Norma. "The Theoretical Subject(s) of *This Bridge Called My Back* and Anglo-American Feminism." Anzaldúa, *Making Face* 356–369.

Alcoff, Linda. "Cultural Feminism Versus Post-Structuralism: The Identity Crisis in Feminist Theory." Kolmar and Bartkowski 398–413.

Allen, Jeffner. "An Introduction to Patriarchal Existentialism." *The Thinking Muse: Feminism and Modern French Philosophy*. Ed. Jeffner Allen and Iris Marion Young. Bloomington, IN: Indiana University Press, 1989. 70–84.

Allen, Jeffner. "Motherhood: The Annihilation of Women." Trebilcot 315–330.

Allen, Paula Gunn. *The Sacred Hoop: Recovering the Feminine in American Indian Traditions*. Boston: Beacon, 1992.

Amoia, Alba. "Sun, Sea and Geraniums: Camus *en voyage*." Knapp 56–72.

Anderson, Sherry Ruth and Patricia Hopkins. *The Feminine Face of God: The Unfolding of the Sacred in Women*. New York: Bantam, 1991.

Anzaldúa, Gloria. *Borderlands/La Frontera: The New Mestiza*. San Francisco: Spinsters/Aunt Lute, 1987.

Anzaldúa, Gloria. "Entering into the Serpent." Plaskow and Christ 77–86.

Anzaldúa, Gloria. "La conciencia de la mestiza: Towards a New Consciousness." Anzaldúa, *Making Face* 377–389.

Anzaldúa, Gloria, ed. *Making Face, Making Soul/Hacienda Caras/Creative and Critical Perspectives by Women of Color*. San Francisco: Aunt Lute, 1990.

Anzaldúa, Gloria. "O.K. Momma, Who the Hell Am I?: An Interview with Luisah Teish." Moraga and Anzaldúa 221–231.

Aquinas, Thomas. "Summa Theologica." Sterba 106–109.

Arendt, Hannah. *Between Past and Future: Six Exercises in Political Thought*. New York: Viking, 1961.

Arendt, Hannah. *Crises of the Republic*. San Diego: Harcourt Brace, 1969.

Arendt, Hannah. *The Human Condition*. Chicago: University of Chicago Press, 1958.

Arendt, Hannah. *On Violence*. San Diego: Harcourt Brace Jovanovich, 1970.

Aristotle. *The Politics of Aristotle*. Ed. and Trans. Ernest Barker. London: Oxford University Press, 1976.

Atkinson, Ti-Grace. "Theories of Radical Feminism." *Notes from the Second Year: Women's Liberation*. Ed. Shulamith Firestone. n.p., 1970.

Baier, Annette. "Trust and Antitrust." *Ethics* 96.2 (January 1986): 231–260.

Bair, Deidre. *Simone de Beauvoir: A Biography*. New York: Summit, 1990.

Baker-Fletcher, Karen. *Sisters of Dust, Sisters of Spirit: Womanist Wordings on God and Creation*. Minneapolis: Fortress Press, 1998.

Barberto, Patricia. "Perception and Ideology: Camus as 'Colonizer' in 'The Adulterous Woman.'" *Celfan Review* 7.3 (1988): 34–38.

Barnes, Hazel E. "Balance and Tension in the Philosophy of Camus." *Personalist* 41 (October 1960): 433–447.

Barnes, Hazel E. *The Literature of Possibility: A Study in Humanistic Existentialism*. Lincoln, NE: University of Nebraska Press, 1959.

Bartlett, Elizabeth Ann. "A Time Apart: Metaphysical Celibacy and the Process of Feminist Self-Definition." Unpublished manuscript delivered at the Annual Meeting of the National Women's Studies Association, 1984.

Bartlett, Elizabeth Ann. "Beyond Either/Or: Justice and Care in the Ethics of Albert Camus." Cole and Coultrap-McQuin 82–88.

Bartlett, Elizabeth Ann. *Journey of the Heart: Spiritual Insights on the Road to a Transplant*. Duluth, MN: Pfeifer-Hamilton, 1997.

Baumgardner, Jennifer and Amy Richards. *Manifesta: Young Women, Feminism, and the Future*. New York: Farrar, Straus, and Giroux, 2000.

Beauvoir, Simone de. *Ethics of Ambiguity*. Trans. Bernard Frechtman. New York: The Citadel Press, 1972.

Beauvoir, Simone de. *Force of Circumstance*. Trans. Richard Howard. New York: G.P. Putnam's Sons, 1964.

Beauvoir, Simone de. *The Prime of Life*. Trans. Peter Green. Cleveland and New York: The World Publishing, 1962.

Beauvoir, Simone de. *The Second Sex*. Ed. and trans. H.M. Parshley. New York: Alfred A. Knopf, 1953.

Belenky, Mary Field et al. *Women's Ways of Knowing: The Development of Self, Voice, and Mind*. New York: Basic Books, 1986.

Bell, Diane and Renate Klein. *Radically Speaking: Feminism Reclaimed*. Melbourne: Spinifex, 1996.

Bell, Richard H. *Simone Weil: The Way of Justice as Compassion*. Lanham: Rowman & Littlefield, 1998.

Benhabib, Seyla. "The Generalized and the Concrete Other: The Kohlberg-Gilligan Controversy and Feminist Theory." *Praxis International* 5.4 (January 1986): 402–424.

Benhabib, Seyla. *Situating the Self: Gender, Community and Postmodernism in Contemporary Ethics*. New York: Routledge, 1992.

Berger, Peter L. *Pyramids of Sacrifice: Political Ethics and Social Change*. Garden City, NY: Doubleday-Anchor, 1976.

Berman, Morris. *The Reenchantment of the World*. Toronto: Bantam, 1984.

Berry, Virginia. "Of Hegelian Bondage." *Hecate* 26.1 (2001): 161–170.

Braaten, Jane. "From Communicative Rationality to Communicative Thinking: A Basis for Feminist Theory and Practice." Meehan 139–161.

Braun, Lev. *Witness of Decline: Albert Camus: Moralist of the Absurd*. Rutherford: Farleigh Dickinson University Press, 1974.

Brée, Germaine. "Climates of the Mind: Albert Camus 1936–40." Knapp 88–99.

Brison, Susan J. "Outliving Oneself: Trauma, Memory, and Personal Identity." *Gender Struggles: Practical Approaches to Contemporary Feminism*. Ed. Constance L. Mui and Julien S. Murphy. Feminist Constructions. Lanham, NJ: Rowman & Littlefield, 2002. 137–165.

Brock, Rita Nakashima."On Mirrors, Mists, and Murmurs." Plaskow and Christ 235–243.

Bronner, Stephen Eric. *Camus: Portrait of a Moralist*. Minneapolis: University of Minnesota Press, 1999.

Broughton, John M. "Women's Rationality and Men's Virtues: A Critique of Gender Dualism in Gilligan's Theory of Moral Development." *Social Research* 50 (1983): 597–642.

Brubaker, Pamela K. "Sisterhood, Solidarity and Feminist Ethics." *Journal of Feminist Studies in Religion*. Special Issue in Honor of Beverly Wildung Harrison. 9.1–2 (Spring/Fall 1993): 53–66.

Bunch, Charlotte. *Passionate Politics: Feminist Theory in Action*. New York: St. Martin's Press, 1987.

Butler, Judith. "Gender Trouble, Feminist Theory, and Psychoanalytic Discourse." Nicholson 324–340.

Caldecott, Leonie and Stephanie Leland, eds. *Reclaim the Earth: Women Speak Out for Life on Earth*. London: Women's Press, 1983.

Camus, Albert. *Actuelles (1944–1948)*. Paris: Gallimard, 1950.

Camus, Albert. *Between Hell and Reason: Essays from the Resistance Newspaper Combat, 1944–1947*. Selected and trans. Alexandre de Gramont. Foreword Elisabeth Young-Bruehl. Hanover: University Press of New England, 1991.

Camus, Albert. *Caligula. Camus, Caligula and Three Other Plays* 1–74.

Camus, Albert. *Caligula and Three Other Plays*. Trans. Stuart Gilbert. New York: Vintage-Knopf, 1958.

Camus, Albert. *The First Man*. Trans. David Hapgood. New York: Alfred A. Knopf, 1995.

Camus, Albert. *Exile and the Kingdom*. Trans. Justin O'Brien. New York: Random House-Vintage, 1991.

Camus, Albert. *The Just Assassins*. Camus, *Caligula and Three Other Plays* 233–302.

Camus, Albert. *Lyrical and Critical Essays*. Ed. and with Notes by Philip Thody. Trans. Ellen Conroy Kennedy. New York: Vintage-Knopf, 1970.

Camus, Albert. *The Misunderstanding*. Camus, *Caligula and Three Other Plays* 75–134.

Camus, Albert. *The Myth of Sisyphus and Other Essays*. Trans. Justin O'Brien. New York: Vintage-Random House, 1955.

Camus, Albert. *Neither Victims nor Executioners*. Introduction by R. Scott Kennedy and Peter Klotz-Chamberlin. Trans. Dwight Macdonald. Philadelphia: New Society, 1986.

Camus, Albert. *Notebooks: 1935–1951*. New York: Marlowe & Company. This was originally published as *Notebooks 1935–1942*. Trans. and with preface and notes by Philip Thody. New York: Hamilton Ltd. and Alfred A. Knopf, 1963. *Notebooks 1942–1951*. Trans. and annotated by Justin O'Brien. New York: Alfred A. Knopf, 1965.

Camus, Albert. *The Plague*. Trans. Stuart Gilbert. New York: The Modern Library—Random House, 1948.

Camus, Albert. *The Rebel: An Essay on Man in Revolt*. Foreword by Sir Herbert Read. Trans. Anthony Bower. New York: Vintage-Knopf, 1956.

Camus, Albert. *Resistance, Rebellion, and Death*. Trans. and with an Introduction by Justin O'Brien. New York: Vintage-Knopf, 1974.

Camus, Albert. *State of Siege*. Camus, *Caligula and Three Other Plays* 135–232.

Caraway, Nancie. *Segregated Sisterhood: Racism and the Politics of American Feminism*. Knoxville: University of Tennessee Press, 1991.

Card, Claudia. "Caring and Evil." *Hypatia* 5.1 (Spring 1990): 101–108.

Card, Claudia, Ed. *Feminist Ethics*. Lawrence, KS: University Press of Kansas, 1991.

Chambers, Simone. "Feminist Discourse/Practical Discourse." Meehan 163–179.

Charney, Hanna. "*Supplementarity* in Camus." Knapp 99–107.

Chittister, Joan. *Heart of Flesh: A Feminist Spirituality for Women and Men*. Grand Rapids, MI: William B. Erdmans and St. Paul University; Ottawa: Novalis, 1998.

Chodorow, Nancy. *The Reproduction of Mothering: Psychoanalysis and the Sociology of Gender*. Berkeley: University of California Press, 1978.

Chrisman, Linda. "Birth." Friedman and Moon 59–64.

Christ, Carol P. "Rethinking Theology and Nature." Plaskow and Christ 314–325.

Code, Lorraine. "Second Persons." Hanen and Nielsen 357–382.

Cohen, Darlene. "The Only Way I Know of To Alleviate Suffering." Friedman and Moon 10–17.

Cole, Eve Browning and Susan Coultrap-McQuin, Eds. *Explorations in Feminist Ethics*. Bloomington, IN: Indiana University Press, 1992.

Collins, Patricia Hill. *Black Feminist Thought: Knowledge, Consciousness, and the Politics of Empowerment*. Perspectives on Gender, Volume 2. New York: Routledge, 1991.

Costello, Judy. "Beyond Gandhi: An American Feminist's Approach to Nonviolence." McAllister, *Reweaving* 175–180.

Cruickshank, John. *Albert Camus and the Literature of Revolt*. London: Oxford University Press, 1959.

Dalal, Anaga. "Afghan Women." *Ms.* Vol XII (1) (December 2001/January 2002): 52–54.

Daly, Mary. *Gyn/ecology: The Metaethics of Radical Feminism*. Boston: Beacon, 1978.

Daly, Mary with Jane Caputi. *Websters' First New Intergalactic Wickedary of the English Language*. Boston: Beacon, 1987.

Davis, Angela. *Women, Race, & Class*. New York: Random House, 1981.

Davis, Judy and Juanita Weaver. "Dimensions of Spirituality." Spretnak, *Politics* 368–372.

Dean, Jodi. *Solidarity of Strangers: Feminism after Identity Politics*. Berkeley: University California Press, 1996.

Deats, Richard. "The Rebel Passion: Eight-five Years of the Fellowship of Reconciliation." *Peace Is the Way: Writings on Nonviolence from the Fellowship of Reconciliation*. Ed. Walter Wink. Maryknoll, NY: Orbis, 2000. xv–xxii.

Diamond, Irene and Gloria Feman Orenstein. *Reweaving the World: The Emergence of Ecofeminism*. San Francisco: Sierra Club Books, 1990.

Dietz, Mary J. "Citizenship with a Feminist Face: The Problem with Maternal Thinking." *Political Theory* 13 (1985): 19–37.

Dill, Bonnie Thornton. "Race, Class, and Gender: Prospects for an All-Inclusive Sisterhood." *Feminist Studies* 9.1 (Spring 1983): 131–150.

Dillon, Robin. "Care and Respect." Cole and Coultrap-McQuin 69–81.

Doubrovsky, Serge. "The Ethics of Albert Camus." Knapp 151–164.

Dworkin, Andrea. *Letters from a War Zone: Writings 1976–1989*. New York: E.P. Dutton, 1988.

Eisenstein, Zillah. *The Radical Future of Liberal Feminism*. New York: Longman, 1981.

Elshtain, Jean Bethke. *Public Man, Private Woman: Women in Social and Political Thought*. Princeton, NJ: Princeton University Press, 1981.

Elshtain, Jean Bethke. *Real Politics: At the Center of Everyday Life*. Baltimore and London: Johns Hopkins University Press, 1997.

Elshtain, Jean Bethke. "Reflections on War and Political Discourse: Realism, Just War, and Feminism in a Nuclear Age." *Political Theory* 13 (1985): 39–57.

Erickson, John. "Albert Camus and North Africa: A Discourse of Exteriority." Knapp 73–88.

Evans, Sara M. *Personal Politics: The Roots of Women's Liberation in the Civil Rights Movement and the New Left*. New York: Random House-Knopf, 1979.

Falk, Marcia. "Notes on Composing New Blessings." Plaskow and Christ 128–138.

Faludi, Susan. *Backlash: The Undeclared War Against American Women*. New York: Anchor-Doubleday, 1991.

Farley, Tucker Pamella. "Speaking, Silence, and Shifting Listening Space: The NWSA Lesbian Caucus in the Early Years." *NWSA Journal* 14.1 (Spring 2002): 29–50.

Ferguson, Ann. "On Conceiving Motherhood and Sexuality: A Feminist Materialist Approach." *Mothering: Essays in Feminist Theory*. Ed. Joyce Trebilcot. Totowa, NJ: Rowman and Allanheld, 1984. 153–182.

Ferguson, Kathy. *The Feminist Case Against Bureaucracy*. Women in the Political Economy. Philadelphia: Temple University Press, 1984.

Firestone, Shulamith. *The Dialectic of Sex: The Case for Feminist Revolution.* New York: Bantam, 1971.

Flax, Jane. "Political Philosophy and the Patriarchal Unconscious: A Psychoanalytic Perspective on Epistemology and Metaphysics." Harding and Hintikka 245–281.

Flax, Jane. "Postmodernism and Gender Relations in Feminist Theory." *Feminism/Postmodernism.* Ed. and with an introduction by Linda J. Nicholson. New York: Routledge, 1990. 39–62.

Fox, Matthew. *Breakthrough: Meister Eckhart's Creation Spirituality in New Translation.* New York: Doubleday-Image Books, 1991.

Fraser, Nancy. "Toward a Discourse Ethic of Solidarity." *Praxis International* 5.1 (January 1986): 425–429.

Freire, Paulo. *Pedagogy of the Oppressed.* Rev. ed. Trans. Myra Berman Ramos. New York: Continuum, 1993.

Friedan, Betty. *The Feminine Mystique.* New York: Norton, 1963.

Friedman, Lenore and Susan Moon, eds. *Being Bodies: Buddhist Women on the Paradox of Embodiment.* Boston: Shambhala, 1997.

Friedman, Marilyn. "Beyond Caring: The De-Moralization of Gender." Hanen and Nielsen 87–137.

Friedman, Marilyn. "Feminism and Modern Friendship: Dislocating the Community." Cole and Coultrap-McQuin 89–97.

Friedman, Marilyn. "The Social Self and the Partiality Debates." Card 161–179.

Friedman, Marilyn. *What Are Friends For? Feminist Perspectives on Personal Relationships and Moral Theory.* Ithaca: Cornell University Press, 1993.

Frye, Marilyn. *The Politics of Reality: Essays in Feminist Theory.* The Crossing Press Feminist Series. Freedom, CA: Crossing, 1983.

Fulbrook, Edward. "*She Came to Stay* and *Being and Nothingness.*" *Hypatia* 14.4 (Fall 1999): 50–69.

Gaard, Greta, ed. *Ecofeminism: Women, Animals, Nature.* Ethics and Action. Philadelphia: Temple University Press, 1993.

Gaard, Greta. *Ecological Politics: Ecofeminists and the Greens.* Philadelphia: Temple University Press, 1998.

Galland, China. *The Bond Between Women: A Journey to Fierce Compassion.* New York: Riverhead, 1998.

Gates, Barbara. "A Mama Raccoon in the Net of Indra." Friedman and Moon 24–34.

Gerber, Barbara W. "NWSA Organizational Development: A View from Within, at 25 Years." *NWSA Journal* 14.1 (Spring 2002): 1–21.

Gilligan, Carol. *In a Different Voice: Psychological Theory and Women's Development.* Cambridge, MA: Harvard University Press, 1982.

Golden, Stephanie. *Slaying the Mermaid: Women and the Culture of Sacrifice.* New York: Harmony, 1998.

Gonzalez, Maria C. "This Bridge Called NWSA." *NWSA Journal* 14.1 (Spring 2002): 71–81.

Gothlin, Eva. "Simone de Beauvoir's Notions of Appeal, Desire, and Ambiguity and their Relation to Jean-Paul Sartre's Notions of Appeal and Desire." *Hypatia* 14.4 (Fall 1999): 83–95.

Gottlieb, Lynn. *She Who Dwells Within: A Feminist Vision of a Renewed Judaism*. San Francisco: HarperCollins-HarperSanFrancisco, 1995.

Graves, Robert. *The Greek Myths*. Complete Edition. London: Penguin, 1992.

Griffin, Susan. *A Chorus of Stones: The Private Life of War*. New York: Anchor-Doubleday, 1992.

Griffin, Susan. E-mail correspondence. September 5, 2001.

Griffin, Susan. *The Eros of Everyday Life: Essays on Ecology, Gender and Society*. New York: Anchor-Doubleday, 1995.

Griffin, Susan. *Made from This Earth: An Anthology of Writings*. New York: Harper & Row, 1982.

Griffin, Susan. *Pornography and Silence: Culture's Revenge Against Nature*. New York: Harper & Row, 1981.

Griffin, Susan. *Rape: The Power of Consciousness*. San Francisco: Harper & Row, 1979.

Griffin, Susan. "Split Culture." Plant 7–17.

Griffin, Susan. *What Her Body Thought: A Journey Into the Shadows*. San Francisco: HarperCollins-HarperSanFrancisco, 1999.

Griffin, Susan. *Woman and Nature: The Roaring Inside Her*. New York: Harper & Row, 1978.

Grimké, Sarah. *Letters on the Equality of the Sexes and Other Essays*. Ed. and with an Introduction by Elizabeth Ann Bartlett. New Haven: Yale University Press, 1988.

Gross, Rita M. *Buddhism After Patriarchy: A Feminist History, Analysis, and Reconstruction of Buddhism*. Albany, NY: State University of New York Press, 1993.

Gross, Rita M. *Feminism and Religion: An Introduction*. Boston: Beacon, 1996.

Gray, Francine du Plessix. *Simone Weil*. Penguin Lives. New York: Penguin-Lipper/Viking, 2001.

Hanen, Marsha and Kai Nielsen, eds. "Science, Morality & Feminist Theory." *Canadian Journal of Philosophy* 13. Calgary: University of Calgaray Press, 1987.

Hanh, Thich Nhat. *Peace Is Every Step: The Path of Mindfulness in Everyday Life*. Ed. Arnold Kotler. New York: Bantam, 1991.

Haraway, Donna. "A Manifesto for Cyborgs: Science, Technology, and Socialist Feminism in the 1980s." Nicholson 190–233.

Harding, Sandra and Merrill B. Hintikka, eds. *Discovering Reality: Feminist Perspectives on Epistemology, Metaphysics, Methodology, and Philosophy of Science*. Studies in Epistemology, Logic, Methodology, and Philosophy of Science. 161. Dordecht, Holland and Boston: D. Reidel, 1983.

Harris, Adrienne and King, Ynestra, eds. *Rocking the Ship of State: Toward a Feminist Peace Politics*. Boulder, CO: Westview, 1989.

Harris, Maria. *Dance of the Spirit: The Seven Steps of Women's Spirituality*. New York: Bantam, 1991.

Harrison, Beverly Wildung. *Making the Connections: Essays in Feminist Social Ethics*. Ed. Carol S. Robb. Boston: Beacon, 1985.

Hartmann, Heidi, et al. "Bringing Together Feminist Theory and Practice: A Collective Interview." *Signs* 21.4 (Summer 1996): 927–951.

Hartsock, Nancy. "The Feminist Standpoint: Developing the Grounds for a Specifically Feminist Historical Materialism." Harding and Hintikka 283–310.

Hartsock, Nancy. "Foucault on Power: A Theory for Women?" Nicholson 157–175.

Hartsock, Nancy. *Money, Sex, and Power: Toward a Feminist Historical Materialism*. The Northeastern Series in Feminist Theory. Boston: Northeastern University Press, 1985.

Havel, Václav. *Disturbing the Peace: A Conversation with Karel Hvizdala*. Trans. Paul Wilson. New York: Alfred A. Knopf, 1990.

Heinämaa, Sara. "Simone de Beauvoir's Phenomenology of Sexual Difference." *Hypatia* 14.1 (Fall 1999): 114–132.

Held, Virginia. *Feminist Morality: Transforming Culture, Society, and Politics*. Women in Culture and Society Series. Ed. Catharine R. Stimpson. Chicago: University of Chicago Press, 1993.

Held, Virginia. "Non-contractual Society: A Feminist View." Hanen and Nielsen 111–137.

Henderson, Margaret. "The Girl Who Met Simone de Beauvoir in Brisbane, or, Must We Burn Beauvoir?" *Hecate* 26.1 (2000): 113–117.

Heyward, Carter. "Sexuality, Love, and Justice." Plaskow and Christ 293–301.

Hinckley, Charlene. "Ecofeminism as a Politics of Resistance: Practice in Search of Theory." Unpublished paper presented at the Annual Meeting of the Midwest Political Science Association. Chicago. Illinois, April 18–20, 1996.

Hirschmann, Nancy J. "Revisioning Freedom: Relationship, Context, and the Politics of Empowerment." Hirschmann and DiStefano 51–74.

Hirschmann, Nancy J. and Christine DiStefano. *Revisioning the Political: Feminist Reconstructions of Traditional Concepts in Western Political Theory*. Boulder, CO: Westview Press, HarperCollins, 1996.

Hoagland, Sarah Lucia. "Some Concerns about Nel Noddings' Caring." *Hypatia* 5.1 (Spring 1990): 109–114.

Holwerk, Eleanne. "*The Blood of Others*: A Novel Approach to *The Ethics of Ambiguity*." *Hypatia* 14(4) (Fall 1999): 3–16.

hooks, bell. *Ain't I a Woman: Black Women and Feminism*. Boston: South End Press, 1981.

hooks, bell. *All About Love: New Visions*. New York: William Morrow, 2000.

hooks, bell. *Feminist Theory: From Margin to Center*. Boston: South End Press, 1984.

hooks, bell. *Killing Rage: Ending Racism*. New York: Henry Holt, 1995.

hooks, bell. *Talking Back: Thinking Feminist, Thinking Black*. Boston: South End Press, 1989.

hooks, bell. *Teaching to Transgress: Education as the Practice of Freedom*. New York: Routledge, 1994.

hooks, bell. *Yearning: race, gender, and cultural politics*. Boston: South End Press, 1990.

Horowitz, Louise K. "Of Women and Arabs: Sexual and Racial Polarization in Camus," *Modern Language Studies* 17 (Summer 1987): 54–61.

Hurtado, Aída. "*Sitios y Lenguas*: Chicanas Theorize Feminisms." *Hypatia* 13.2 (Spring 1998): 134–161.

Irigaray, Luce. *An Ethics of Sexual Difference*. Trans. Carolyn Burke and Gillian C. Gill. Ithaca: Cornell University Press, 1993.

Isaac, Jeffrey C. *Arendt, Camus, and Modern Rebellion*. New Haven: Yale University Press, 1992.

Jaggar, Alison M. *Feminist Politics and Human Nature*. Totowa, NJ: Rowman & Allanheld, 1983.

Jaggar, Alison M. and Paula S. Rothenberg, Eds. *Feminist Frameworks: Alternative Theoretical Accounts of the Relations between Women and Men*. 3rd Ed. New York: McGraw-Hill, 1993.

Jaggar, Alison M. "Globalizing Feminist Ethics." *Hypatia* 13.2 (Spring 1998): 7–31.

Jaggar, Alison M. "Toward a Feminist Conception of Moral Reasoning." James P. Sterba et al. *Morality and Social Justice: Point/Counterpoint*. Studies in Social and Political Philosophy. Lanham, MD: Rowman & Littlefield, 1995. 115–146.

"Joint Plea." *Ms.* (Summer 2002): 17.

Judt, Tony. *The Burden of Responsibility: Blum, Camus, Aron and the French Twentieth Century*. Chicago: The University of Chicago Press, 1998.

Keen, Sam. *The Passionate Life: Stages of Loving*. San Francisco: Harper & Row, 1983.

Keller, Catherine. "Feminism and the Ethic of Inseparability." Plaskow and Christ 256–264.

Keller, Evelyn Fox. "Feminism and Science." Keller and Longino 28–40.

Keller, Evelyn Fox and Helen E. Longino, eds. *Feminism and Science*. Oxford Readings in Feminism. Oxford: Oxford University Press, 1996.

Kesselman, Amy, Lily D. McNair, and Nancy Schniedewind, eds. *Women: Images and Realities: A Multicultural Anthology*. 2nd ed. Mountain View, CA: Mayfield, 1999.

King, Ynestra. "The Ecology of Feminism and the Feminism of Ecology." Plant 18–28.

King, Ynestra. "If I Can't Dance in Your Revolution, I'm Not Coming." Harris and King 281–298.

Kirk, Gwen. "Our Greenham Common: Feminism and Nonviolence." Harris and King 115–130.

Kittay, Eva Feder. *Love's Labor: Essays on Women, Equality, and Dependency*. New York: Routledge, 1999.

Knapp, Bettina L., ed. *Critical Essays on Albert Camus*. Boston: G.K. Hall, 1988.

Kolmar, Wendy and Frances Bartkowski. *Feminist Theory: A Reader*. Mountain View, CA: Mayfield, 2000.

Kourany, Janet A., James P. Sterba, and Rosemarie Tong. *Feminist Philosophies*. 2nd ed. Upper Saddle River, NJ: Prentice-Hall, 1999.

Kristéva, Julia. "Woman Can Never Be Defined." *New French Feminisms: An Anthology*. Ed. and with Introductions by Elaine Marks and Isabelle de Courtivron. New York: Schocken, 1981. 137–141.

Lacayo, Richard. "About Face: An Inside Look at How Women Fare Under Taliban Oppression and What the Future Holds for Them Now." *Time*. (December 3, 2001): 34–49.

Lamont, Rosette. "Two Faces of Terrorism: 'Caligula' and 'The Just Assassins.' " Knapp 128–135.

Lauretis, Teresa de. *Alice Doesn't*. Bloomington: Indiana University Press, 1984.

LeClerc, Annie. "Woman's Words." Kourany, Sterba, and Tong 436–439.

Lienert, Tania. "On Who Is Calling Radical Feminists 'Cultural Feminists' and Other Historical Sleights of Hand." Bell and Klein 155–168.

Lerner, Gerda. *The Creation of Feminist Consciousness: From the Middle Ages to Eighteen-seventy*. Women and History. Vol. 2. New York: Oxford University Press, 1993.

Lerner, Michael. *The Politics of Meaning: Restoring Hope and Possibility in an Age of Cynicism*. Reading, MA: Addison-Wesley, 1996.

Levine, Stephen. *Healing into Life and Death*. New York: Doubleday-Anchor, 1987.

Levy, Bronwen. "Agony and Ecstasy: Feminists Among Feminists." *Hecate* 26.1 (2000): 107–112.

Linsenbard, Gail E. "Beauvoir, Ontology and Women's Human Rights." *Hypatia* 14.4 (Fall 1999): 145–162.

Lorde, Audre. *Sister Outsider: Essays and Speeches by Audre Lorde*. Trumansburg, NY: Crossing, 1984.

Lloyd, Genevieve. "Reason, Science and the Domination of Matter." Keller and Longino 41–53.

Lugones, María C. "Playfulness, 'World'-Travelling and Loving Perception." Anzaldúa *Making Face* 390–402.

Lugones, María C. and Elizabeth V. Spelman. "Have We Got a Theory For You! Feminist Theory, Cultural Imperialism and the Demand for 'The Woman's Voice.' " *Women's Studies International Forum* 6.6 (1983): 573–581.

MacKinnon, Catherine. "Pornography, Civil Rights, and Speech." Kourany, Sterba, and Tong 367–380.

McAllister, Pam, ed. *Reweaving the Web of Life: Feminism and Nonviolence*. Philadelphia: New Society, 1982.

McAllister, Pam. *This River of Courage: Generations of Women's Resistance and Action*. The Barbara Deming Memorial Series. Philadelphia: New Society, 1991.

McAllister, Pam. *You Can't Kill the Spirit*. The Barbara Deming Memorial Series. Philadelphia: New Society, 1988.

McFague, Sallie. "God as Mother." Plaskow and Christ 128–138.

McFall, Lynne. "What's Wrong with Bitterness?" Card *Feminist* 146–160.

Meehan, Johanna. *Feminists Read Habermas*. New York: Routledge, 1995.

Mellon, Linda Forge. "An Archetypal Analysis of Albert Camus's "La Pierre qui pousse: The Quest as a Process of Individuation." *The French Review* 64.6 (May 1991): 934–944.

Memmi, Albert. *The Colonizer and the Colonized*. Expanded Edition. Trans. Howard Greenfield. Introduction by Jean-Paul Sartre. Afterword by Susan Gilson Miller. Boston: Beacon Press, 1965.

Merchant, Carolyn N. *The Death of Nature: Women, Ecology, and the Scientific Revolution*. San Francisco: Harper & Row, 1980.

Michell, Gillian. "Women and Lying: A Pragmatic and Semantic Analysis of 'Telling It Slant.'" *Women's Studies International Forum*. Special Issue featuring *Hypatia* 7.5 (1984): 374–383.

Mies, Maria and Vandana Shiva. *Ecofeminism*. Halifax, Nova Scotia: Fernwood & London: Zed, 1993.

Mohanty, Chandra Talpade. "Under Western Eyes: Feminist Scholarship and Colonial Discourses." *Third World Women and the Politics of Feminism*. Ed. Chandra Mohanty, Ann Russo, and Lourdes Torres. Bloomington: Indiana University Press, 1991. 51–80.

Molina, Papua. "Recognizing, Accepting and Celebrating Our Differences." Anzaldúa, *Making Face* 326–331.

Moraga, Cherríe. "La Guera." Moraga and Anzaldúa 27–34.

Moraga, Cherríe and Gloria Anzaldúa, eds. *This Bridge Called My Back: Writings by Radical Women of Color*. Foreword by Toni Cade Bambara. Watertown, MA: Persephone, 1981.

Morgan, Robin. "Goodbye to All That." *Voices from Women's Liberation*. Ed. Leslie B. Tanner. New York: Signet, 1970. 268–276.

Morrison, Toni. *Sula*. New York: Plume, Penguin, 1973.

Mortimer, Lorraine. "Adventures of the Mind and Living Warmth: A New Encounter with Simone de Beauvoir." *Hecate* 26.1 (2000): 185–196.

Morton, Nelle. "The Goddess as Metaphoric Image." Plaskow and Christ 111–118.

Morton, Nelle. *The Journey Is Home*. Boston: Beacon, 1985.

Mouffe, Chantal. "Democratic Citizenship and the Political Community." *Dimensions of Radical Democracy: Pluralism, Citizenship, Community*. Ed. Chantal Mouffe. London: Verso, 1992.

Mouffe, Chantal. "Feminism, Citizenship, and Radical Democratic Politics." *Feminists Theorize the Political*. Ed. Judith Butler and Joan W. Scott. New York: Routledge, 1992.

Near, Holly. "Singing for Our Lives." Hereford Music, 1979.

Nicholson, Linda J., ed. *Feminism/Postmodernism*. New York: Routledge, 1990.

Noddings, Nel. *Caring: A Feminine Approach to Ethics & Moral Education*. Berkeley: University of California Press, 1984.

Ochs, Carol. *Women and Spirituality*. New Feminist Perspectives Series. Totowa, NJ: Rowman & Allanheld, 1983.

Olsen, Tillie. *Silences*. New York: Delacorte Press/Seymour Lawrence, 1965.

Ortner, Sherry. "Is Female to Male as Nature Is to Culture?" *Women, Culture and Society*. Ed. Michelle Rosaldo and Louise Lamphere. Stanford: Stanford University Press, 1974. 67–87.

Patai, Daphne and Noretta Koertge. *Professing Feminism: Cautionary Tales from the Strange World of Women's Studies*. New York: Basic Books, 1994.

Pateman, Carole. *The Disorder of Women: Democracy, Feminism, and Political Theory*. Stanford, CA: Stanford University Press, 1989.

Patterson, Eleanora. "Suffering." McAllister, *Reweaving* 164–174.

Peavey, Fran, with Myra Levy and Charles Varon. *Heart Politics*. Philadelphia: New Society, 1986.

Perl, Harriet and Gay Abarbanell. *Guidelines to Feminist Consciousness Raising*, 1979.

Peyre, Henri. "Presence of Camus." Knapp 15–36.

Piercy, Marge. *Woman on the Edge of Time*. New York: Fawcett Crest, 1976.

Plant, Judith, Ed. *Healing the Wounds: The Promise of Ecofeminism*. Philadelphia: New Society, 1989.

Plaskow, Judith and Carol P. Christ, Eds. *Weaving the Visions: New Patterns in Feminist Spirituality*. San Francisco: HarperCollins, 1989.

Plumwood, Val. *Feminism and the Mastery of Nature*. New York: Routledge, 1993.

Plumwood, Val. "Has Democracy Failed Ecology? An Ecofeminist Perspective," *Environmental Politics* 4 (Winter 1995): 134–168.

Plumwood, Val. "Nature, Self, and Gender: Feminism, Environmental Philosophy, and the Critique of Rationalism." *Hypatia* 6.1 (Spring 1991): 4–27.

Quinby, Lee. "Ecofeminism and the Politics of Resistance." Diamond and Orenstein 122–127.

Radicalesbians. "The Woman Identified Woman." Kolmar and Bartkowski 195–198.

Raymond, Janice G. *A Passion for Friends: Toward a Philosophy of Female Affection*. Boston: Beacon, 1986.

Reardon, Betty A. *Sexism and the War System*. New York: Teachers College, 1985.

Reardon, Betty A. *Women and Peace: Feminist Visions of Global Security*. SUNY Series, Global Conflict and Peace Education. Albany: SUNY Press, 1993.

"Redstockings Manifesto." *Voices From Women's Liberation*. Ed. Leslie B. Tanner. New York: New American Library, 1970.

Rich, Adrienne. *Blood, Bread, and Poetry: Selected Prose: 1979–1985*. New York: W.W. Norton, 1986.

Rich, Adrienne. *The Dream of a Common Language: Poems 1974–1977*. New York: Norton, 1978.

Rich, Adrienne. *On Lies, Secrets, and Silence: Selected Prose: 1966–1978*. New York: W.W. Norton, 1979.

Rich, Adrienne. *Of Woman Born: Motherhood as Experience and Institution*. New York: W.W. Norton, 1976.

Riddle, Dorothy I. "Politics, Spirituality, and Models of Change." Spretnak 373–381.

Rizutto, Anthony. *Camus: Love and Sexuality*. Gainesville: University of Florida Press, 1998.

Rollins, Judith. "Deference and Maternalism." Jaggar and Rothenberg 335–345.

Rousseau, Jean-Jacques. "Emile." Sterba 238–252.

Ruddick, Sara. *Maternal Thinking: Toward a Politics of Peace*. New York: Ballantine 1989.

Ruddick, Sara. "Remarks on the Sexual Politics of Reason." *Women and Moral Theory*. Ed. Eva Feder Kittay and Diana T. Meyers. Totowa, NJ: Rowman & Littlefield, 1987: 237–260.

Ruether, Rosemary Radford. "Ecofeminism." Adams, *Ecofeminism* 13–23.

Ruether, Rosemary Radford. *Gaia & God: An Ecofeminist Theology of Earth Healing*. San Francisco: HarperCollins-HarperSanFrancisco, 1992.

Ruether, Rosemary Radford. "Toward an Ecological-Feminist Theology of Nature." Plant 145–150.

Rush, Anne Kent. "The Politics of Feminist Spirituality." Spretnak 382–385.

Schaef, Anne Wilson. *Women's Reality: An Emerging Female System in the White Male Society*. Minneapolis: Winston, 1981.

Scheler, Friederich. *Ressentiment*. Ed. with and Introduction by Lewis A. Croser. Trans. William W. Holdheim. New York: Free Press of Glencoe, 1961.

Secomb, Linnell. "Beauvoir's Minoritarian Philosophy." *Hypatia* 14.4 (Fall 1999): 96–113.

Sheffield, Carole J. "Sexual Terrorism." Kourany, Sterba, and Tong 45–59.

Shiva, Vandana. *Staying Alive: Women, Ecology and Development*. London: Zed Books, 1989.

Shivers, Lynne. "An Open Letter to Gandhi." McAllister, *Reweaving* 181–194.

Simons, Margaret A. *Beauvoir and The Second Sex: Feminism, Race, and the Origins of Consciousness*. Lanham: Rowman & Littlefield, 1999.

Sjöö, Monica and Barbara Mor. *The Great Cosmic Mother: Rediscovering the Religion of the Earth*. San Francisco: Harper San Francisco, 1987.

Smith, Andy. "For All Those Who Were Indian in a Former Life." *Ms.* (November–December 1991): 44–45.

Smith, Barbara and Beverly Smith. "Across the Kitchen Table: A Sister-to-Sister Dialogue." Moraga and Anzaldúa 113–127.

Solanis, Valerie. "Excerpts from the SCUM (Society for Cutting Up Men) Manifesto." *Sisterhood Is Powerful: An Anthology of Writings from the Women's Liberation Movement*. Ed. Robin Morgan. New York: Random House, 1970. 514–519.

Spender, Dale. *Man Made Language*. London: Routledge and Kegan Paul, 1980.

Spelman, Elizabeth. *Inessential Woman: Problems of Exclusion in Feminist Thought*. Boston: Beacon, 1988.

Spivak, Gayatri Chakravorty. "Can the Subaltern Speak?" *Marxism and the Interpretation of Culture*. Ed. Cary Nelson and Lawrence Grossberg. Urbana: University of Illinois Press, 1988. 271–313.

Spretnak, Charlene, ed. *The Politics of Women's Spirituality: Essays on the Rise of Spiritual Power Within the Feminist Movement*. Garden City, NY: Anchor-Doubleday, 1982.

Sprintzen, David. *Camus: A Critical Examination*. Philadelphia: Temple University Press, 1998.

Stanton, Elizabeth C., Susan B. Anthony, and Matilda J. Gage, eds. "Selections from the *History of Woman Suffrage*." *The Feminist Papers: From Adams to de Beauvoir*. Ed. and Introductory Essays by Alice S. Rossi. New York: Columbia University Press, 1973. 413–470.

Starhawk. "Consciousness, Politics, and Magic." Spretnak 172–184.

Starhawk. "Feminist Earth-based Spirituality and Ecofeminism." Plant 174–185.

Starhawk. *The Fifth Sacred Thing*. New York: Bantam, 1993.

Starhawk. *The Spiral Dance: A Rebirth of the Ancient Religion of the Great Goddess*. 10th Anniversary Edition. San Francisco: HarperCollins-HarperSanFrancisco, 1989.

Starhawk. "Toward an Ecofeminist Spirituality." Plant 127–132.

Steinem, Gloria. *Outrageous Acts and Everyday Rebellions*. 2nd Ed. New York: Henry Holt, 1995.

Sterba, James P. *Social and Political Philosophy: Classical Western Texts in Feminist and Multicultural Perspectives*. 2nd ed. Belmont, CA: Wadsworth, 1998.

Swimme, Brian. *The Universe Is a Green Dragon: A Cosmic Creation Story*. Santa Fe: Bear & Co., 1985.

Thao, Mai Kao. "Sins of Silence." Kessleman, McNair, and Schneidewind 17–18.

Tisson-Braun, Micheline. "Silence and the Desert: The Flickering Vision." Knapp 42–55.

Todd, Olivier. *Albert Camus: A Life*. Trans. Benjamin Ivry. New York: Carrol & Graf, 1997.

Tong, Rosemarie. *Feminine and Feminist Ethics*. Belmont, CA: Wadsworth, 1993.

Trebilcot, Joyce, ed. *Mothering: Essays in Feminist Theory*. New Feminist Perspectives Series. Totowa, NJ: Rowman & Allanheld, 1984.

Uttal, Lynet. "Nods that Silence." Anzaldúa, *Making Face* 317–320.

Velacott, Jo. "Women, Peace, and Power." McAllister, *Reweaving* 30–41.

Vintges, Karen. "Simone de Beauvoir: A Feminist Thinker for Our Times." *Hypatia* 14.4 (Fall 1999): 133–144.

Walker, Alice. *The Color Purple*. New York: Washington Square Press-Pocket Books, 1982.

Walker, Alice. *In Search of Our Mothers' Gardens: Womanist Prose by Alice Walker*. San Diego: Harcourt Brace Jovanovich–Harvest, 1984.

Walker, Rebecca. "Becoming the Third Wave." Kesselman, McNair, and Schneidewind 532–533.

Warren, Karen J. "The Power and Promise of Ecological Feminism." *Environmental Ethics* 2.2 (Summer 1990): 125–146.

Weil, Simone. *The Simone Weil Reader*. Ed. George A. Panichas. New York: David McKay, 1977.

Weisser, Susan Ostrov and Jennifer Fleischner, ed. *Feminist Nightmares: Women at Odds: Feminism and the Problem of Sisterhood*. New York: New York University Press, 1994.

Welch, Sharon D. *A Feminist Ethic of Risk*. Rev. ed. Minneapolis: Fortress, 2000.

Whitbeck, Caroline. "The Maternal Instinct." Trebilcot 185–192.

Whitlock, Gillian. "My Mother's Mouth." *Hecate* 26.1 (2000): 128–132.

Wildflower, Caroline. "How Feminism Changed the Peace Movement." McAllister, *Reweaving* 135–142.

Williamson, Chris. "Sister." *The Changer and the Changed*. Olivia Records, 1975.

Wink, Walter. "Jesus' Third Way." *The Universe Bends Toward Justice: A Reader on Christian Nonviolence in the U.S.* Ed. Angie O'Gorman. Philadelphia: New Society, 1990, 253–265.

Wittig, Monique. "One Is Not Born a Woman." Jaggar and Rothenberg 178–182.

Wong, Nellie. "In Search of the Self As Hero: Confetti of Voices on New Year's Night: A Letter to Myself." Moraga and Anzaldúa 177–181.

Woo, Merle. "Letter to Ma." Moraga and Anzaldúa 140–147.

Yamada, Mitsuye. "Masks of Woman." Anzaldúa, *Making Face* 114–116.

Yeatman, Anna. "A Feminist Theory of Social Differentiation." Nicholson 281–299.

Young, Iris Marion. "The Ideal of Community and the Politics of Difference." Nicholson, 300–323.

Young, Iris Marion. *Intersecting Voices: Dilemmas of Gender, Political Philosophy, and Policy*. Princeton: Princeton University Press, 1997.

Young, Iris Marion. *Justice and the Politics of Difference*. Princeton: Princeton University Press, 1990.

Young, Iris Marion. "Reflections on Families in the Age of Murphy Brown: On Gender, Justice, and Sexuality." Hirschmann and DiStefano 251–270.

INDEX